Sea to Shining Sea

The Journals of
Corrie Belle Hollister

Sea to Shining Sea

The Journals of Corrie Belle Hollister

BOOK FIVE

MICHAEL PHILLIPS

HENDRICKSON
PUBLISHERS

Sea to Shining Sea

Hendrickson Publishers Marketing, LLC
P. O. Box 3473
Peabody, Massachusetts 01961-3473

ISBN 978-1-59856-962-9

Printed in the United States of America, by Versa Press, East Peoria, Illinois

First Hendrickson Edition Printing — June 2012

Cover Photo Credit: Mike Habermann Photography

12 16

To Judith Pella

the greatest writing partner a fellow author
could wish for, with deep gratitude and
prayers for your best in all the future holds.
Thank you for allowing me
to be part of your life!

A Note to the Reader

The idea for the story of Corrie was born two decades ago in the living room of a Eureka, California, home. Michael Phillips had gotten to know Judith Pella from a Bible study they both attended, and their common interest in writing began the conversations that ultimately resulted in a collaboration and the launch of THE JOURNALS OF CORRIE BELLE HOLLISTER series.

Then these talented and dedicated novelists had the idea for a totally different historical series, THE RUSSIANS, and decided to work on the two projects simultaneously! Their enthusiasm and discipline got them through the first two novels in both series, but reality raised its head—they decided that each would continue on with one series. As it turned out, Michael was captivated by courageous Corrie and the frontier setting not too far from his home, and Judith loved the drama, complexity, and the intensive research required by the Russian story. So this is the reason Michael Phillips' name appears solo after book two of the series.

Judith and Michael went on to collaborate on several other historical series over the years. They love to hear from their readers.

The authors may be contacted at:

Michael Phillips   Judith Pella
P. O. Box 7003   judithpella.com
Eureka, CA 95502
macdonaldphillips.com

Contents

San Francisco Again

CHAPTER ONE

*T*he setting was unbelievable!

When I first walked into the huge ballroom of the Montgomery Hotel at Pa's side, I could not take in all the magnificence of the place. Under the bright lights of chandeliers, the men sauntered around in expensive black suits, and the women in long gowns. Waiters carried food and drinks about on silver trays, and hundreds of important people milled together in that gigantic fancy room.

All I could think was, *What are we doing here?*

But we *were* there. And as we walked in, I think Pa sensed my nervousness.

"Come on, buck up, Corrie," he whispered down to me, placing a reassuring hand on my arm. "They invited us. And you're every bit the lady any of these other women are."

He patted my hand. "So don't you go willowy on me or faint or nothin'," he added. "I'm just as nervous as you are."

When the invitation had come a month earlier for Pa and me to attend the Republican reception in June of 1860 at the Montgomery Hotel in San Francisco, at first I didn't think too much of it. But a few days later Pa said, "We oughta go to that shindig, Corrie. It's not every day a couple of country locals like us get the chance to mix with important folks. What do you think?"

"You really want to, Pa?"

"Sure, just so long as you come too."

"I don't know why they invited me," I said. "You're mayor of a town. But why me?"

"Because you're a prominent young lady writer," said Pa. "Ain't no big mystery in that."

"Maybe it was Jessie Fremont's doing," I suggested. "She and Mr. Fremont probably know every important Republican in California. Maybe they told somebody about me before they left for the East."

"Never hurts to know high-up people," said Pa with a wink. "Anyhow, what do you think—you up for a trip to San Francisco?"

And so there we were. Pa in his new suit, fresh-shaved, looked as handsome and important as ever a man could. And I wore my new dress—yellow, with ruffles and a sash, and my hair fixed up with a matching ribbon in it. We walked into the ballroom of the Montgomery Hotel to join all the men who would play a leading role in the upcoming national election of 1860.

"Hey, Hollister!" called out a voice. We both turned to see Carl Denver hurrying our way. He greeted us and shook our hands. "Come with me," he said. "There's someone I want you to meet."

Before we could say much in reply, Mr. Denver had us in tow, steering us through the crowd. Then all of a sudden we were face-to-face with one of the tallest, most handsome men I had ever seen.

"Cal," said Mr. Denver, "I want you to meet two friends of mine from up in Miracle Springs—this is Corrie Hollister and her father, Drummond Hollister, the mayor of Miracle. Corrie, Hollister . . . meet Cal Burton, an important fellow here in San Francisco these days."

Pa shook the man's hand. I just stood there watching and listening to him laugh at Mr. Denver's words.

"Come on now, Carl," he said, "you shouldn't lie to these good people. I'm no more important than the shoeshine boy on the street outside."

"Don't let his modesty fool you," said Mr. Denver, turning to me and speaking as if it were confidential. "Cal works for Leland Stanford, and from what I hear, he is moving up fast. You keep your eye on him, Corrie. He might get you a story or two that'll make you famous."

"A story—what are you talking about, Carl?" said Burton, turning away from Pa and toward us.

"Corrie here's a writer, Cal—you know, California's woman reporter."

"Why, of course!" he said. "Now I remember you telling me about her." He took my hand, but instead of giving it a manly shake, he just held it softly for a moment.

My heart started beating fast, and I could feel my face reddening all the way up the back of my neck and cheeks. My eyes had been following my hand as it was swallowed up in his. And now I found myself slowly glancing up as he released it. His eyes bored straight into mine.

I'm embarrassed to admit it, but the touch of his hand, the look in his eyes, and his smile made me feel a little lightheaded for the rest of the evening. I'm sure Pa noticed, especially when he caught me staring in Mr. Burton's direction a couple of times. But he was nice enough not to say anything about it.

He was too busy anyway, meeting people and listening to speeches. I met a lot of other people too, but as I think back on the evening, I only remember a few of the names. Cal Burton did take me to meet his boss, the important railroad man and politician, Mr. Stanford. I couldn't say I actually spoke to him, because he was busy talking with some important Republicans about the election and slavery and the need for railroad development in California.

I wish I could recall more of the things I heard everyone talking about, because those were important times for California's future. The election, the railroad, and slavery were the subjects on everyone's minds and the topics of every conversation.

But I don't remember very much, because I couldn't keep my eyes off Cal Burton, and I couldn't keep down the fluttering in my chest. I thought everybody in the huge ballroom must have been able to hear the pounding of my pulse, although nobody seemed to pay much attention.

Cal was tall, with straight light-brown hair, parted in the middle and coming down over his forehead almost to his eyebrows, then falling around the sides just above his ears. He wore a fancy suit, light brown like his hair, and a ruffled shirt and polished boots. What a figure he cut, with those blue eyes that contrasted with the brown of his hair and suit and the tan of his face! He had a friendly smile and a warm tone, yet a thoughtfulness that made his brow crinkle when he was thinking about what to say.

Altogether, Cal Burton had a lively, interesting, intelligent, pleasant face. How could I help giving it a second, or even a third look?

I heard Pa's voice at my side. "He's going to get a headache if you keep looking at him like that!"

"Oh, Pa!" I said, blushing again. "I was just—"

"I know what you was doing, Corrie," Pa added. "And there's nothin' wrong with admitting you like the looks of a good-looking young man." He gave me a smile. "You just might want to not be so obvious about it."

"I didn't know I was."

Pa chuckled. "Everybody in the place is gonna know if you don't pull those eyes of yours back inside your head! Now come on, what do you say you and I go over and hear what some of those men in the fancy suits are saying about the election?"

$\mathscr{A}$s much as I had been interested in the election of 1856 because of my involvement with the Fremonts, the election of 1860 was a far more important one for the future of the whole nation. Mr. Fremont's being halfway a Californian had stirred up California quite a bit. But now even larger issues were at stake. Everything had grown more serious and heated, and even though it mostly had to do with the South and slavery, Californians were mighty interested too.

Slavery had been an issue for a long time. Pa said he remembered them talking about it back in the East when he was in his teen years. There had been preachers and politicians talking out against it and trying to get it abolished for a lot of years. But there was never anything they could do about it. Throughout the 1850s, although the debate had gotten pretty heated, the government in Washington had been almost completely controlled by the South. The southern states had kept the northern states from making any changes. And the border states were usually more sympathetic with the South, since most of them allowed slavery too.

So even though there had been growing opposition to slavery all through the 1850s, there had been nothing any of the northern politicians could do about it. I had just been growing up during those years, and hadn't known or cared much about it. But now it was 1860, and I *was* interested. So I asked people lots of questions to find out all I could. And gradually toward the end of the decade that had just passed, it began to look as if a change might be coming.

For one thing, Abraham Lincoln was becoming more and more well known, especially after the famous debates with Stephen Douglas in 1858 when they'd both been running for Congress in Illinois. Lincoln was known to be antislavery, and his abolitionist views made southern politicians angry.

Meanwhile, the country just kept growing, just like Miracle Springs and Sacramento and San Francisco and all of California had grown.

But the westward expansion meant that most new states were in areas where there was no slavery. Minnesota became a state in 1858, and then Oregon in 1859. Counting California too, there were eighteen northern and western states, while the southern and border regions had only fifteen. The southerners who had been in control for all that time started to get nervous because there weren't any new places for slavery to expand. Westward lay the Nebraska Territory and the Dakota Territory and the Colorado Territory and the Washington Territory and the Utah and Nevada and New Mexico territories. And all of those places, if they ever did become states, weren't very likely to side with the powerful slave men from the South.

All these things combined to make the year of 1860, and the election which would be held in November, one of the most important years in the whole history of our country.

Only a month before Pa and I went to San Francisco, the leaders of the Republican party had nominated Abraham Lincoln of Illinois to be their candidate for president of the United States. Against him would be running the man he already knew so well from his home state—Stephen A. Douglas.

Southerners realized the fate of slavery if Lincoln were elected, especially now that the number of slave states was in a minority. They were determined to defeat him!

That's what some of the men were discussing that evening at the Montgomery. The speeches were all about the future of the Union, they called it, and the reasons why all God-fearing and slavery-hating Californians had to do everything they could to work for Mr. Lincoln's election in California. And it wouldn't be easy—there were many more Democrats in California than Republicans.

Mr. Thomas Starr King made a speech that stirred every-body up about the need to support the northern states, even though we were so far out West. He was the pastor of the Uni-tarian church in San Francisco, but had only recently arrived from Boston where the man introducing him said he had been a famous preacher and lecturer. He had come from the East only a month or two earlier, and he made it sound as if de-bate was heated back East over which direction the nation was going to go. As for the election, however, he said he still wasn't sure how much to involve himself, being a minister.

Other men at the Montgomery were talking about issues not directly having to do with the disputes between North and South, but having to do with the future of California it-self, and what the election would mean out here.

Economics and money and growth were the issues they were talking about—travel and gold and population changes and the expansion of the railroad both up and down the state and toward the East. Communication with the East was a major concern. Even though Oregon up to the north was now a state too, there had still always been the feeling that we were isolated from the rest of the country, and that the states in the West weren't as important as the other states.

Of course, nobody here believed that! To listen to them talk, California was the *most* important state! But they wanted everybody else to know it too.

The Pony Express had just started up two months earlier. At least now mail and news didn't take so long to reach back and forth across the huge continent. News used to take three weeks by the fastest stagecoaches to get across the plains and mountains and prairies from Missouri to California. Now it took only nine or ten days from St. Joseph to Sacramento! Since there were telegraph lines from there to the big cities on the East Coast, the whole country was separated from each other by less than two weeks as far as news was concerned.

Mr. Stanford was talking about this very issue. "Mail is one thing," he said, "but *people* are another. Getting *people* quickly back and forth between California and the East— *that's* what it will take before California can truly stand up and fully take its place alongside the other states of these great United States of America."

"Horses and stagecoaches," Mr. Stanford said, "are the transportation and communication methods of the past. But the future lies with machines and inventions." He went on to make a speech about how the equality and impact of full statehood could be achieved only by a railroad line stretching all the way across the country.

While I was listening to all this, I felt a touch on my arm. "Miss Hollister," a voice said, "I wonder if I might have a word with you."

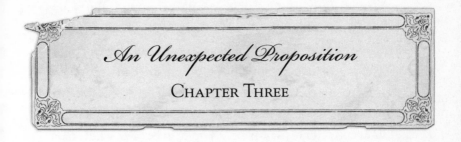

An Unexpected Proposition
CHAPTER THREE

I turned, and my heart took off racing again at the sight of Cal Burton!

I glanced toward Pa, and before I knew it I was walking across the room at Mr. Burton's side. I was afraid to look at him and at the same time unable to keep my eyes off him.

"There's somebody I want you to talk to," he said as he led me through the maze of people. In another minute I was standing in the middle of a small group of four or five men. One of them began talking to me, but I forgot his name as soon as I'd been told, and I remember only about half of what he said, even though it turned out to be a conversation that changed the whole course of my life.

"I heard about you from Cal here," the man was saying, "and of course I'm on close terms with your editor, Ed Kemble. So I'm not altogether unaware of the role you played on behalf of our Republican party four years ago."

"I didn't do anything that did any good," I said, finally finding my voice.

"Perhaps not," the man went on. "You may have considered all that happened a waste of time and energy, but I would disagree with you."

"The story I wrote about Mr. Fremont was killed," I said.

"True enough. Your article was never printed. But what would you say if I told you I had read it?"

"I don't know," I replied. "I'm not sure I would believe you."

The man laughed, and all the others in the small group listening to our conversation followed his lead. It was the first time I had seen Cal Burton laugh, and I enjoyed the sound of it. His even white teeth and broad smile gave me a whole new reason to like his looks. But the man was still talking to me, so I had to do my best to pay attention.

"Well, I have," he said. "I should have known from reading your words that you would be a plain-talking young lady, even if it means calling an important man a liar to his face!"

He chuckled again, but as I started to tell him I hadn't meant anything by it, he held up his hand and spoke again.

"Don't worry, Miss Hollister," he said. "I took no offense at what you said. I admire a woman who's not afraid to speak her mind in front of men. Especially a young pretty one like you."

I blushed immediately. It was an awful embarrassment!

I'm not pretty and you know it, I said to him in my mind. But outwardly I just glanced down at the floor for a minute. My first reaction was that he was probably poking fun at me like Uncle Nick always did. But then I realized he hadn't been doing that at all. Neither he nor any of the other men seemed to make light of his words a bit. I recovered myself and looked up. His face was serious, and I could see that he'd meant what he'd said.

"I'm very earnest, Miss Hollister, in what I say. You see, my friends consider me a pretty straightforward man myself. So I recognize honesty and fearlessness for the virtues they are. A lot of folks who are involved in politics do so much double-talking you can't tell what they're saying. Most of them aren't saying much worth listening to. But I've always been of a mind to speak out what's on my heart, and then people can do what they want with your words. Wouldn't you agree that's the best way of going about it when you have something to say?"

"I reckon so," I answered.

"That's another thing I like about you, Miss Hollister. You don't try to put on airs. You're a country girl and you never try to hide it. You speak honestly, you speak out as the young lady you are, and as far as I can tell, you aren't much afraid of anyone or worried what they'll think." He paused and looked me straight in the eye. "Would you say that is an accurate representation of yourself?" he asked after a moment.

"I . . . I don't know," I said, stumbling a little. The man certainly was straightforward, I'll say that for him! "I wouldn't say I'm not afraid of anything. But I guess you're right about speaking my mind honestly. My minister back home, and my mother—my stepmother, I should say—"

"That would be Almeda Parrish, would it not?" he interrupted.

"Almeda Parrish *Hollister*," I corrected him.

"Yes, of course. I knew of Mrs. Parrish before I had heard of either you or your father. A woman with a fine reputation. But I don't suppose you need me to sing her praises, do you?"

I smiled and shook my head.

"And I read some of your articles about the Miracle Springs election, the whole feud between your family and that skunk of a banker Royce. You see, I do some checking to make sure of myself before I become involved with anyone. I make a habit of going into things with my eyes open."

"I can see that," I said.

"I admire your stepmother, and I have been keeping an eye on your father as well. He strikes me as a man California might hear more from one day."

"He's here," I said eagerly, "if you would like to meet him."

The man chuckled again. "Of course he's here. I'm the one who arranged for both of you to be invited! I have every intention of speaking with your father before the night is done. But right now I'm speaking with you, and we were talking about your work for the Fremont cause four years ago, and the bravery you displayed in uncovering that story. Printed or not, it was a fine piece of work, and a courageous thing to do. But a great many things have changed since 1856. Our party was just in its infancy then, and John Fremont did not have the nationwide strength to stand up against Buchanan. Even had your article made it into the *Alta*, it is doubtful it would have had much of an impact, and it would have been too late even to be picked up in the East. Therefore, what I want to talk with you about, Miss Hollister, is not your work of the past, but what you might do for the Republican party in the future."

He stopped, looking at me intently.

"I'm not sure I understand you," I said. "I don't know much about politics. I haven't paid much attention since then. Except for what my pa does as mayor, that is."

"I'm not concerned how much you know of what used to be. This is a new day, Miss Hollister. This election of 1860 is the one that's going to change the direction of this nation forever. Don't any of the rest of you tell John what I've said," he warned, glancing around at the other men in the small group before turning his eyes back to me. "But John Fremont, as much as I admire the man, represents the Republican party of the past. He was an explorer, after all. That is how he will be remembered. But the future, both of our party and of this country, lies with the man from Illinois who is heading our presidential ticket this year. I'm sure you've heard of Abraham Lincoln, Miss Hollister?"

"Of course," I answered. "There was already talk about him in 1856."

"Well, I am convinced his time has finally come, and that he is the man to take our country forward—into the new decade, into the future, and away from the Democratic control that has dominated Washington for the past thirty years."

He stopped again, still looking at me with an almost inquisitive expression.

"I'm not sure I understand," I said finally. "You're probably right about everything you say. But I don't see what it has to do with me."

"Simple, Miss Hollister. I want to enlist your support in the cause. I want you to help us with the campaign, in even a more active way than you did for John Fremont four years ago."

"Help . . . in what way? How could I possibly help?"

"Writing articles on Mr. Lincoln's behalf. Perhaps even taking to the stump once in a while. Women might not be able to vote, but men sure pay attention when a woman speaks out!"

"The stump . . . what do you mean?"

"Speaking, Miss Hollister. Giving speeches to go along with your writing, helping us raise money and votes for the Republican ticket in November."

"You're talking about speechmaking—me?" I exclaimed.

"That's exactly what I'm talking about," he replied with a broad smile. "I want you on our side."

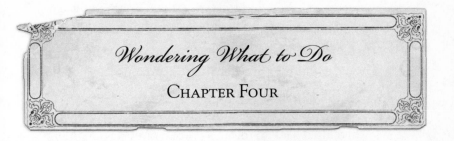

*T*he rest of the evening was lost in a blur.

There was music and more discussions and a few other speeches and refreshments. I stayed close to Pa. There weren't but a handful of other women present, and I'm sure no one as young as I was. But Cal Burton seemed to be keeping an eye on me. He was very polite and not the least bit forward; he treated me as if I was the most important person there.

As Pa and I walked back to Miss Sandy Bean's Boarding-house from the downtown district, the night fog had rolled in and a chill was in the air. But my face felt hot, even more so in the brisk night, and I felt so full and alive that I could hardly keep from skipping up the walk. I tried my best to keep it under control, but I know Pa couldn't help but notice.

He walked along beside me, the sound of his boots clump-ing along the boards of the walkways and thudding dully on the hard-packed dirt of the streets we crossed, talking and smiling and laughing lightly with me. He didn't do a thing to make me feel foolish for being . . . well, just for being the way a young woman sometimes is!

Before we parted for the night, Pa took me in his arms, gave me a tight squeeze, then said, "You're some lady, Corrie

Belle. You do your pa right proud, whether it's ridin' a horse in the woods or at some fancy big-city political gathering."

Then he kissed me good-night and sent me into my room.

The next morning we left Miss Bean's and caught the steamer across the bay and up the river to Sacramento. As we moved out across the water, although it was still early, some of the fog had lifted back to reveal a portion of the city in bright sunlight. It was different than any time I'd left the city before. Instead of being anxious to get home, there was a lump in the pit of my stomach, pulling at me and making me wish I could stay. Pa seemed to know I was full of new and unaccustomed thoughts, and neither of us said much during the quiet boat ride across the bay.

About halfway across, a small cloud of lingering fog drifted by and settled down on top of the boat. With the sun gone, suddenly a chill came over me. I shivered and turned away from the railing, then sat down on a nearby bench with a sigh.

The fog seemed to fit my mood perfectly, although I didn't even know what my mood was. A cloud had settled over my spirits just as the fog had engulfed the boat in its white, quiet chill. Pa stayed at the railing, leaning over, looking down into the water as it splashed rhythmically by. I was so absorbed in my own thoughts that I was hardly aware that he had a lot on his mind, too.

It was still pretty early in the day, and as the river narrowed and we lost sight of the city, we went inside and took some seats next to a window. We floated along awhile in silence. Then all of a sudden, without hardly even thinking what I was saying, I blurted out:

"Well, Pa, do you think I ought to do it?"

"Do what?" he said, glancing over at me. He had no idea what I could be talking about.

"Get involved with the election," I answered. "You know, try to help Mr. Lincoln get elected."

"My daughter, the speechmaker!" said Pa with the first smile I'd seen on his face all day.

"Come on, Pa! You know I'll never be that kind of person. Maybe I'll just write some, like I did about the election before."

"It'd be sure to help the Republican cause," he said. "You ain't just a curiosity no more. You saw the byline Kemble put on your article last winter about the flood of California's rivers—*Corrie Belle Hollister, California's Woman Reporter.*"

"That doesn't mean much."

"Sure it does! You're not just a kid wantin' to write any more. You're just about Kemble's most famous reporter."

"But not the best paid!" I said, trying to laugh.

"You're still a woman, and you can't expect to get close to what a man does. But if Kemble knows what's good for him, he'll keep you happy. That's just what I told him too, last night."

"Pa, you didn't!"

" 'Course I did. It's the truth, too. He's got all kinds of men writin' for his paper. There are hundreds of men writing for the papers in San Francisco and Sacramento. But there's only one woman. And you're it, and he's got you. So I told him he'd better treat you like the important young lady you are or else I'd tell you to take your writing someplace else."

"Pa, that's downright embarrassing."

"It's the truth."

"What did he say?"

"Aw, you know Kemble. He flustered some, but he didn't deny a word of it. That fellow Cal Burton was listening too, and he gave Kemble a few words to back up what I'd said besides."

I glanced away. I didn't want Pa to see the red in my cheeks just from the mention of Cal's name. He kept right on talking, but I'm sure he knew. Pa usually knew most things I was thinking . . . more than he liked to let on.

"I tell you, Corrie, you shouldn't underestimate yourself. You just might have the chance to influence this election. You know that folks pay attention to what you write—men as well as women. You wanted to be a writer, and you've done it. You just might be able to help elect the first Republican president this country's ever had."

"My writing's not that important. You just think so because you're my pa."

"Well, I got a right to be proud! If you ask me, there's not a better person they could get to stand up and tell folks they oughta vote for Mr. Lincoln for president. When folks hear your name, they're all gonna know who you are. *Corrie Belle Hollister.* Why, maybe nobody thought nothing of it back in '55 when you wrote about the blizzard. But now when folks see those words above a piece of writing, they know they'd better pay attention, because *the* woman newspaper writer of California is speaking to them. And they're gonna know your name just as well if you're speaking out to a crowd of people."

"I'm not so sure," I said. "I don't know if I want to do that anyway. It sounds pretty frightening to me, getting up in front of a bunch of men. What if they yell at me or don't listen or say rude things?"

"Then you yell right back at them and tell 'em to shut their mouths and pay attention. Ain't that what Almeda'd do if a group of rowdy men got rude at her?"

I smiled at the thought. That was exactly what Almeda would do.

"Besides, if word got out that you were gonna be someplace, I got no doubt there'd be plenty of women there too, and they'd keep the men quiet."

"I don't know—"

"You got a duty to your country, Corrie. Maybe when me and Nick was fighting the Mexicans back in '47, it wasn't all that patriotic a thing. We were just a couple of men not knowing what to do with ourselves. We didn't know much about all the disputes with President Polk. But you see, now you've got a chance to do something and know it's important at the same time."

"I'd like to hear about the Mexican war, Pa."

"Ask Almeda about it."

"Almeda?" I said. "Why her? *You're* the one who fought in it."

"Nick and I may have fought in it, but we didn't know anything of what it was about. Your pa wasn't much of a literate man back in those days, I'm sorry to say, Corrie. Almeda told me what I was really fighting for."

"What was it, then, you and Uncle Nick were fighting for? Wasn't it just to keep the Mexicans from taking our territory?"

"That's the way Polk and the Democrats would like to tell it. But according to Almeda, that wasn't it at all. It was actually the other way around—we were taking *their* territory in the Southwest, just like we've been doing from the Indians in the North."

"So what *were* you fighting for?"

"You sure you want to know? It ain't too pleasant a notion."

"Of course I want to know."

"We were fighting for slavery, Corrie—nothing less than just that. Even in California like we were, that's what it was about."

"But . . . how could it have been about slavery way back then, Pa?"

"The southerners have been trying to hedge their bets for a long time. Grabbing up all that land in the Southwest, all the way from Texas to California. You see, that was the Democrats' way to get their hands on lots of new territory that would become slave states someday. Polk wasn't no fool. He was a southerner himself, and he saw the handwriting on the wall. They knew clear back then that slavery didn't have much of a chance unless they got lots of new slave states eventually."

"That's what Almeda says?"

"She gets downright hot in her breeches about slavery. Being a northerner herself, and a woman mighty full of strong ideas, she hates the very thought of it. She says that we attacked the Mexicans and forced the war ourselves, even though the government was saying they attacked us and we were only defending the cause of freedom. Hoots, that's just exactly what Nick and I was told when we joined up."

"How does she know all that?"

"She says it comes from reading what she calls between the lines, reading what nobody says but what's there if you know how to look for it."

I was quiet awhile, thinking about all he'd said.

"But you see, Corrie," Pa went on, "that's all the more reason for you maybe to help Mr. Lincoln. Back then, without knowing it, I helped the South and the Democrats. Now you can do something about it on the other side."

"It still doesn't seem as if I'd make much of a difference."

"I'm telling you, Corrie, people aren't just listening to you out of curiosity. You're writing news that's important. You know as well as I do what Kemble said, that folks back East read your articles on the flooding and it was their way of finding out what was happening here. News, Corrie, not just curiosity writing. You're a genuine newspaper reporter whose words are being read from the Pacific all the way to the Atlantic. You're making a way for a lot of women who never figured they could do anything in this man's world. You're doing it, and they're proud of you—just like I am."

"You make it sound so important, Pa," I said.

"Maybe I am your pa, but I still say it *is* important. Your articles are sure more important than anything that weasel O'Flaridy's ever done!"

I laughed at the thought of Robin's condescension toward me the first time we met in Mr. Kemble's office.

"I'm glad to see you can laugh," said Pa. "You were downright furious with him over the Fremont article. Whatever became of him? I haven't heard you mention his name in more than a year."

"Mr. Kemble told me he left the *Alta* and went back East somewhere. St. Louis, I think it was at first. He always did have big ambitions, and I know it stuck in his craw that I was getting more well known than he. He couldn't abide getting outdone by a woman, and I think he wanted to get out of here and make a name for himself."

"Well, he can make his name however he pleases, but I'm proud of my own Corrie's name and what she's done with it. And I think you oughta do what the man asked you to do and help out the Republicans to get Mr. Lincoln elected."

I was quiet for a minute or so, thinking about what Pa'd said.

"But how do I know if it's the right thing?" I asked after a bit.

"You mean whether Lincoln's the right man to be president?" said Pa.

"That too, but mainly whether it's the right thing for *me* to do. I mean, just because something's there to do, and just because somebody *else* thinks I ought to do it, that doesn't necessarily make it right, does it?"

I paused. Pa didn't say anything but just kept looking over at me, and then I continued.

"I knew for a long time that I wanted to write. It was something I wanted to do inside *myself*, whether anybody else cared, or whether anybody else ever read anything I wrote. But then when something like this comes along, from the outside, so to speak, and not from inside myself, it's an altogether different thing. I just can't do something because somebody wants me to. There's got to be a rightness about it."

"I hadn't given a thought myself to the idea of running for mayor until Almeda and Avery and Nick and the rest of you all talked me into it."

"But after a bit, didn't you start thinking it was the right thing for *you* to do too, no matter what we thought?"

"Sure. I wouldn't have done it otherwise."

"That's what I mean, Pa. Even if Mr. Lincoln is the right man, I can't do it because anyone else thinks I should. It's still got to be right for *me*."

"Well, then, do you think Mr. Lincoln's the man who ought to be the country's president?"

"I don't guess there's any doubt about that. Slavery's no good, and, like the man said, it's time the southern states didn't control things as they have for so long."

"So then, there's your place to start thinking about it. At least you're in agreement with the cause they're talking about. You sure couldn't do it if that weren't true. Now all you have to do is decide if it's something *you* want to do, that you feel is *right* for you to do."

"Sometimes that's not an easy thing to know."

We were both silent awhile. Finally Pa reached over and took my hand, then bowed his head and closed his eyes right there on the steamer.

"God," he prayed out loud, "me and Corrie here, we've got some things to decide about our future, and about what we ought to do about some things. And we ain't altogether sure in our own minds what's best. So we ask you right now to help us, and to guide us in what we do. We need your help, God, to keep us walkin' right along the path you want us on. Neither of us want to be anywhere else but right where you'd have us. So show us where that is."

He looked up and opened his eyes. "Amen," I added.

Again we sat in silence for a while as we floated along.

"You just never know where something's going to lead you," I said at length.

Pa nodded.

"Just like starting to write and getting that first article published in the *Alta*, or walking into the Gold Nugget, looking for Uncle Nick that day and having you walk out instead. Things have a way of piling onto each other. Something you do today can change the whole direction of your life."

"Makes you think about being careful before you jump into something new, don't it?" said Pa. "Whether it's writing or mayoring or anything else."

"Yeah, I reckon that's what I'm thinking now. If I say that I'll write and maybe even talk to some folks about voting for Abraham Lincoln and Hannibal Hamlin, who can tell what it might mean in my life a year from now, or even five years from now? It might change things as much as writing that first article did."

"You heard what all them men in San Francisco were saying," said Pa. "This year of 1860 is just about the most important year this country's ever faced. So I reckon you're right. If this election's the most important in a long spell, then it's bound to have some effect on your life too."

"That's what I'm thinking, Pa. But how do you know what to do when you can't see up ahead what that effect might be?"

"You can't see into the future, that's for sure, Corrie."

"I know," I laughed. "Sometimes I'd like to, though."

"Well, look at it this way—if this election is gonna help decide which direction the nation's going from now on, maybe you can't see into the future, but you might have a hand in helping decide it."

"But electing either Lincoln or Douglas could change my life as much as it's sure to change the country one way or the other."

"Yep, I figure it could."

I let out a sigh. "I don't suppose there's much else to do but wait for God to show me something," I said finally.

"I reckon he will," said Pa.

"I hope so."

"If you're looking for it, he won't leave you in doubt for too long a spell about what to do."

The Rock of Changing Circumstances
CHAPTER FIVE

We rode along for fifteen or twenty minutes without saying anything more. Outside, the rolling landscape passed slowly, reminding me of the time I'd first made the leisurely trip down the river with Almeda.

It seemed so long ago now!

The country was shrinking; California was shrinking. Stagecoaches ran daily to most places north from Sacramento. The Pony Express delivered mail in record time; rail lines were being laid down all over the country, and the national election seemed so much closer and important than ever before! I felt I was being stretched, so that the whole country was part of my life, my world.

Just the thought that my writing went all the way from the Pacific to the Atlantic was enough to make me stop and wonder what God was doing with me. Nobody paid any attention to what a woman did, and yet people *were* reading my words all the way back there in the East, as well as at home in Miracle Springs. It was sometimes more than I could imagine!

"You know, Corrie," Pa said after a while, "I've got a future to be thinking about too."

I looked up from the midst of my daydreaming. "You mean whether to keep being mayor?"

"There's that too," answered Pa. "But plenty more besides."

"What, Pa? You sound as if it's something serious."

Pa sighed and looked out the window thoughtfully.

"Is there something wrong?" I asked.

He gave a little laugh, although there wasn't anything comical in the sound of it.

"Wrong, Corrie?" he said wistfully. "No. I was just reflecting on all the changes that come even when you're not looking for them. Life has a way of bringing things to you and plopping them smack in your way so there's no way you can avoid them. You may be thinking you're heading down one road toward somewhere, but then all of a sudden a giant rock falls in the middle of your path. And you figure, that's okay, you'll just walk around it. But in getting past it, without realizing it, you change directions, and then all of a sudden you're going along a different path toward someplace different. You never knew there was someplace different to go, but you're headed there, and you never set foot on the first road you was on again."

"You're going to have to try again, Pa," I said. "I don't suppose I'm used to hearing you philosophize about life quite like that."

Pa burst out laughing so hard he couldn't stop. Several of the other people in the boat turned their heads to see what the joke was.

"I must've been around you and Almeda and Avery too much," he said finally, still half laughing. "Or too long trying to make sense of being mayor to that town of miners, farmers, ranchers, and kids!"

"But I still want to know what you meant by the road with the big rock falling in the middle of it."

"Well, for example, Nick and I coming west, we didn't plan on all that trouble we got into. I always figured on farming my land and raising my family in what you'd call a normal way. Then all of a sudden, the rock of circumstances fell— the robbery, the shooting. Suddenly Nick and I were running from the law and heading west.

"That's what I mean, Corrie. There we were on a new path toward someplace we never figured on going. We never set foot on the first road again. I've been out West ever since, never saw your ma again. It was a long time before I could even think about Aggie without getting pretty stirred up inside. You know that, 'cause I shed my share of tears with you after finding out she was gone. You understand? A change comes out of nowhere—you don't see it coming, you don't expect it, you ain't done nothing to plan for it . . . but your life will never be the same again."

"Now I see, Pa."

"Same thing that day you and the rest of the kids showed up in Miracle. I stumbled out of the Gold Nugget and there the five of you was standing there, with Almeda wagging her tongue at me. And *wham*—my life took off in a new direction!

"I guess we get blindsided by circumstances every now and then. So when one of them big boulders slams down in front of you, it makes pretty good sense to look things over a spell before you start off either moving around it or in a new direction. You never know what tomorrow's gonna bring, and you just might never get back to the same place again."

"Like that man asking me if I'd help with the election?"

"Exactly like that. You see, that's a big rock in your path. It's not anything bad, like me and Nick's getting into trouble.

Why, it's a real opportunity for you—might be the best thing that ever came along. But you just can't ever know ahead of time what might come next on account of it. That's why you gotta stop and take a good look at things and at the decisions you make. If you say yes to the man, it might change everything for you, Corrie. It might not . . . but then it *might*. You just can't know for sure."

As I watched Pa and listened to him, I realized that his being a father and a husband for the second time in his life, the mayor of a growing community, and a man who took his faith in God more seriously than most men did—all that had changed Pa *inside* more than even he realized. Just to hear him talk amazed me when I thought back to those first couple of years after the kids and I came to California. He might talk about the boulder and his and Uncle Nick's coming out West and being mayor, but I could see that the most important new path Drummond Hollister was walking along was deep inside his heart and mind, and maybe didn't have as much to do with all those other things as he might think.

"It's the same with the country, Corrie," Pa went on, "or with a town, a community, a family. Things come up, and then things change. Everything around here for two hundred miles is the way it is because a man named Marshall found a pretty little rock in a mountain stream up in the hills. And Miracle Springs became what it did 'cause our friend Alkali Jones found a piece of the same kind of rock in the creek up behind our place."

"According to him, at least," I said with a smile.

"You're right there, Corrie!" laughed Pa. "But *somebody* found gold there anyhow, including Tad when he was just a little runt. And then all of a sudden everything's changed.

"And this election—all those men back there were saying how important it is for the future of the country. Why, who can tell, we might look back someday and say that the election of 1860, and whoever becomes the new president next year, steered the whole country off in a new direction. You just never know what might be around the corner, and so you oughta be watching and paying attention as best you can."

Again he fell silent and gazed out the window for a while.

"I see what you are saying, Pa," I said. "And I'm sure going to take your advice and try to think carefully through what's best for me to do. If it's going to change the direction of my future, it can't be something I do without thinking and praying. But I don't think you were really talking about my decision, were you, Pa, when you first said it? There's something else on your mind, isn't there?"

He sighed, then and turned his head back and looked at me.

"Can't ever fool you, can I?"

"You said you had your future to be thinking about," I said, "more than just mayoring."

"Yeah, I guess I did say that, didn't I?"

"Yes, you did. So, what is it you've been beating around the bush to try to tell me about?"

Pa took a deep breath. "Do you know who that man was who asked you about helping out with the election?" he asked.

"I got introduced to him," I answered, "but I forgot his name."

"His name's Alexander Dalton."

"That's right, now I remember. But I'd never heard of him, Pa."

"He's not the kind of man people do hear of. Crocker and Hopkins and Stanford and Fremont—they're the public men, the famous, the names folks hear about. Lincoln and Douglas—they're the ones running for president. But back behind men like that there are always other folks making things happen that nobody ever sees. Kingmakers, they're called. They'll never be kings themselves, but they hold power to *make* kings. You see what I mean?"

I nodded. "So, is Mr. Dalton like that—a kingmaker?"

"That's exactly what he is," replied Pa. "He's just about one of the most important men in all the West, even though he's practically unknown except by the people who need to know him. Fremont, Stanford—he's helped make them the important men they are."

"So that's why he was the one talking to me about getting involved."

"He's the top Republican in California, Corrie—the chairman of the Republican party for all of California and Oregon. It's his job to make sure Lincoln carries the state."

"Is that all he does?"

Pa chuckled. "Not by a long shot, Corrie! He's got to see to all kinds of business besides just presidential politics."

"Like what?"

"California politics, the state's future, all the kinds of things politicians think about. He's got to raise money for the party, he's got to see to the state's growth, he's got to make decisions about who does what, who's in charge of what. He's the one more than anyone else who has power to get people elected to committees and even to the Congress in Washington. Leastways, if the Republican party keeps growing like it has, he'll be doing all those things. The way I hear it, he's just about the second most influential man in Sacramento behind Governor Downey."

"You sound like you know him, Pa."

"I've met him a time or two. He's always at the mayors' conferences I got to go to. He knows everybody. He's made speeches to us about all the plans to get California split up into different states."

"So what does it all have to do with us, Pa?"

"It's got to do with you 'cause he asked you to help with the election, Corrie. He's trying to get Lincoln elected."

"But what about you?"

"Well, daughter of mine, you weren't the only Hollister that Dalton talked to last night," said Pa.

"I didn't see you with him," I said.

"It wasn't a long conversation," Pa replied. "And it was private. He took me outside for a minute."

"It sounds secretive—why, Pa?"

"Some things are best not made public until the right time, Corrie. You know how fellas like Royce can twist and turn things to their own advantage if you're not careful."

"Now you've got me dying of curiosity, Pa! What did Dalton say?"

"Well . . . he asked me to run for the state legislature in Sacramento come November."

$\mathscr{P}$a, that's wonderful!" I exclaimed. "Are you going to do it?"

"I don't know, Corrie. I've got lots to think about, just like you. God's bound to cause a heap of changes, like I was saying, we can't see now. It's not something you can do lightly. Naturally I gotta talk and pray with Almeda about it."

"Would you have to move to Sacramento, Pa?"

"I reckon most of the men do, but there ain't no way I'd leave Miracle. I'm not about to pack up everyone to go live in a city. And there's sure no way I'd move there myself or with just me and Almeda, and leave everyone."

"I could take care of the kids, Pa. Zack and I are adults. With Emily and Mike married and down in Auburn, that only leaves Becky and Tad. They're fifteen and seventeen. We can take care of ourselves. You and Almeda can take little Ruth with you to Sacramento and you can become a famous politician. If we have any problems, there's Uncle Nick and Aunt Katie across the stream."

"No, I'm not gonna split up my family for nobody, not for Alexander Dalton, not for my own future, not even for California. Besides, what if you decide to do what he wants *you* to do? Then you'd be gone a lot, too."

"Zack's twenty-one. He's a grown man."

"You know as well as I do that he's itching to be off wherever a horse'll carry him. He and Little Wolf are gone half the time as it is. No, Corrie, if I decide to run, and even if I win, then they'll just have to settle for a congressman who represents his people as best he can by staying with those people and going into Sacramento whenever he has to."

"I wonder how long it'll be before the train comes up that far?"

"I doubt if that'll be for years. There's lots of other places in California growing faster than us. I'm sure I'd have to travel by horse or stagecoach for a good while yet."

"Did Mr. Dalton say why he wanted you to run?" I asked.

A sheepish look came over Pa's face. I'd never seen anything quite like it in his expression before.

"Aw, he did, but you know them politicians—they're always saying things that aren't true to get things how they want them."

"What did he say, Pa?"

"Aw, he just said he and other folks in Sacramento'd been keeping their eyes on me ever since I got elected mayor, and some of them figured I was the kind of man they needed in the capitol to help set the direction for the state in the coming years."

"Of course you're the kind of man the state needs!" I said. I leaned over and gave him a hug. "Pa, I am so proud of you."

Neither of us had noticed the steamer slowing down as we approached the dock at Sacramento.

"Looks like we're to the halfway point," said Pa. "We'll have to decide on our futures later."

We got up and left the boat, walking into the bright warm sunlight of Sacramento in early afternoon. San Francisco was always much cooler, but here in Sacramento, summer was on the way.

If we had come by horseback or had left a wagon or buckboard in Sacramento, we might have made it home by late that same night. But we had taken the stage down, and the return stage north left early in the morning, so we'd have to stay over.

We got our bags and Pa hired a buckboard to drive us to Miss Baxter's Boardinghouse. We always stayed with her whenever we were in the city. By this time, with her keeping tabs on us and all the changes that had come in our family since we first arrived in California with Captain Dixon eight years earlier, she was as good a family friend as we had anywhere in the city.

Once we got ourselves situated at her place, we went out for a walk. Pa said he wanted to show me the statehouse where the legislature and governor had their offices, and where California's government was run from. Since we had all afternoon, we decided to go on foot. As we walked I could tell easily enough that Pa was thinking about what it would be like for him to be involved in what went on in that building. At one point Pa stopped and pointed to a construction site. "See that?" he said. "That's the big new domed capitol they're just beginning." Little did I know how much he would be involved in that building.

We walked for quite a while, back toward the downtown section of town. The day had become warmer and we were enjoying ourselves, talking about what the future might hold for us. As we crossed the street between the post office and station, in the distance I noticed a lady who caught my attention.

"Pa, doesn't that woman coming this way look like Katie?" I asked. "Or am I just imagining it?"

"There *was* something about her that struck me as familiar," Pa replied. He eyed her a little closer as we walked. "If I didn't know better, I'd swear she could pass for Katie's twin sister!"

My curiosity got the best of me. As she approached, I stopped and addressed her.

"Excuse me, but would you happen to know a lady named Katie Morgan Hollister, who lives in Miracle Springs?"

The woman's face lit up. "I sure do," she said. "Katie is my older sister."

"What!" I exclaimed. "But . . . how can—but . . . what are you—?"

The woman laughed at my confusion, and the sound of her laughter left no more doubt that she was related to Katie.

"My name is Edie," she said, "Edie Simpson. Edie *Morgan* Simpson, that is. My husband died two months ago, so I decided to come out to pay Katie a surprise visit while I try to decide what's to become of my life. I take it you know Katie."

"I'm the man she came out here to marry," interjected Pa with a laugh. "Drummond Hollister's the name, ma'am, and this is my daughter Corrie."

"Corrie Belle Hollister, of course! I know your name from Katie's letters. And, Drummond, I am so pleased to meet you too. Katie speaks highly of you both." She extended her hand and gave us each a firm handshake. "How are Katie and Nick?"

"Couldn't be better, ma'am," said Pa. "Erich's gonna turn five next month, and little baby Anne—what is she, Corrie?" he said, turning to me. "A year by now?"

"Fourteen months," I said. "She was born last April, and she just started walking three weeks ago."

"I can't wait to see Katie and meet her family!" said Edie brightly.

"She doesn't know you're coming, ma'am?" asked Pa.

"No. I thought about sending her a letter by Pony Express, telling about Mr. Simpson's passing. But then I thought I might as well just come and see her in person."

"When did you get here?"

"Only this morning."

"How did you come—by ship to San Francisco?" I asked.

"I came overland by the Butterfield coach."

"The ox-bow route, huh?" said Pa.

"Yes, and I felt every bump in the whole punishing trip. I certainly got my $225 worth, and I must say I am very glad to be here at last."

She paused and laughed again. "I took the train to St. Louis. From there the coach went south through Texas, then New Mexico and to Fort Yuma. Luckily the only Indian attack was nearby and the driver outran them to the fort. Then the way led to Los Angeles and north to Sacramento. I arrived only an hour ago. I was just on my way out to locate a suitable lodging for the night."

"Well, think no more about it, ma'am," said Pa. "If you'll show me where your bags are, I'll get them for you. Then we'll get us a ride back to our boardinghouse. You can stay with us tonight, and we'll be off to Miracle bright and early in the morning."

*I*t was late the next afternoon when the stage pulled into Miracle Springs.

We got out, and just in the time it took Pa to get our bags down off the top and walk across the street to the Mine and Freight, half a dozen people came up to greet us and ask about our trip.

"Afternoon to you, Mayor Hollister," said the man in charge of the stage office when he came out to meet the stage. He'd been in town only about a year and still acted as if Pa was about the most important man for miles. I reckon in a way he was, but Pa's old friends still just called him Drum like they always had. But even as they said it, there was a hint of a different tone to it. They knew that Pa had become something special.

As we walked across the street to the office, Edie said, "My goodness, I knew my sister's brother-in-law was the mayor, but I didn't expect *this* much attention. They act like you're a celebrity around here!"

Pa just laughed.

Above the building stood a big sign that read: Hollister-Parrish Mine and Freight Company, a change Almeda had insisted on even though she still ran the business pretty much herself, with my help. The *Hollister* on the sign didn't mean me, of course, but Pa.

My little half sister, Ruth, was three years old, and she was a handful, so Almeda didn't spend nearly so much time in town as she once did. I came into the office on most days; Pa helped out now and then, and Marcus Weber and Mr. Ashton took care of everything else. Almeda wouldn't have needed to come in at all, but she usually made the ride into town once or twice a week, when Pa or I would stay home with Ruth. She was too much of a businesswoman to be content always being at home.

But times had changed in Miracle Springs in the ten years Almeda had been there. There wasn't as much mining and freighting business to be done nowadays, even though Mr. Royce had closed down his competing enterprise. Mining itself had slacked off a lot; most of the men had all the equipment they needed, and Miracle Springs had become less of a gold-rush mining town, and more of a regular community made up of all kinds of people and families.

The business was still called the Mine and Freight, but Almeda and I had gradually started carrying a wider range of goods and merchandise. Now it resembled a general store for all the kinds of work men around the area did—farmers and ranchers as well as miners. We had wood tools and plows and barbed-wire and wagon parts and hand tools, even some harness and saddle equipment and seeds—lots of different things people needed. We were careful not to order goods that any of the other merchants carried; Almeda had strong feelings about such things as loyalty and competition. But if there were things folks needed they couldn't get someplace else, we found a way to get what they needed.

Pa and Uncle Nick still worked the mine several days a week, but not like they once did. They still dug gold out of it, and Alkali Jones was always talking about hitting another rich vein just a little ways farther into the side of the mountain. "Dang if there ain't a whole new lode in there, Drum," I had heard him say again and again. "I can smell it, *hee, hee, hee!*"

Whether Pa or Uncle Nick believed him, I don't know, but the persistence with which he trusted his "gold-sniffer," as he sometimes called his nose, usually brought out a wise-crack or two from Uncle Nick, and a sly wink in our direction from Pa. But he loved Mr. Jones—partly like a brother, partly like a trusted friend, even like a father. He would never do anything to hurt his feelings. Whenever the word *mayor* was used in Alkali Jones' hearing, we'd hear his high cackling *hee, hee, hee!* sooner or later. He still couldn't get used to *dad-blamed ol' Drum being mayor to nothin' but a hill of prairie dogs! Hee, hee, hee!*

Pa and Uncle Nick didn't need to mine. The business did well enough along with the original strike to keep our whole little community of two families fed. But mining was so much in their blood that there was no way they could keep themselves from doing it. I suppose Alkali Jones' predictions of a new vein drove all the men to keep going deep down inside. Hope could be a powerful force. So Pa and Uncle Nick kept poking and picking and sometimes blasting away, and little bits of gold kept tumbling down the stream.

Pa mayored about as much as Almeda kept shop, though most of it was folks coming to him rather than him doing much of anything. He had no office in town. People knew where to find him when they wanted.

"Hey, Marcus," said Pa, sticking his head inside the livery out behind the office, "you got a wagon and a couple horses you could hitch up for us?"

"Yes sir, Mister Hollister," said a beaming Marcus Weber, coming out to greet us. "Your wife's gonna be glad to see you."

"Why's that, Marcus?"

"Little Ruth, she done took a fever."

Pa's face wrinkled in concern as he threw a couple of the bags in the back of one of the wagons. "Anything serious?" he asked.

"I dunno. Miz Almeda, she was just in here a minute yesterday, on her way to the Doc's."

"Hmm . . . then we better get out there as soon as we can," said Pa. "Corrie, why don't you and Edie go back to the stage office and get the rest of the bags. I'll give Marcus a hand with the horses and wagon."

By the time we got back, he and Mr. Weber nearly had the wagon ready to go. We climbed aboard. In two or three minutes, we were off and rumbling through the streets of Miracle and out of town toward the claim.

As much as I could with the bouncing and racket of the horses and wagon, I told Edie about the town—how it had grown and what it was like when we first came in 1852. We'd already told her all about the Gold Nugget and us five kids showing up and Almeda going in to fetch Pa, thinking he was dead and that it was Uncle Nick inside. But now I had a chance to show her everything firsthand. In many ways the town was different than back then—bigger, less raucous, fewer saloons, more stores.

Mr. Royce still had the only bank in town. Pa and the town council had denied Finchwood another petition a year after the first, so they finally decided to open their new bank in Oroville instead. Mr. Royce had lowered the interest rate on all the loans he held to four and a half percent to match Finchwood's. Maybe he wasn't making as much profit as he once did, but folks were much more kindly disposed toward him, and you could tell from his face that he was a happier man for it, too. So nothing more had come of the "Hollister-Parrish Bank."

"It's so different than a city or town in the East," said Edie as we bounced over the bridge and out of town. "So much more primitive."

"You should have seen Miracle Springs eight years ago!" I said.

"Don't get me wrong, Corrie. It looks like a lovely town. Especially compared with some of the rough places the stagecoach went through!" She shook her head at the memory. "My, oh, my! Some of the things I saw! The territories and towns across the plains are called the frontier for good reason—every man carrying a gun! At least Miracle Springs appears to be more civilized than those places. But you really should see the East someday, Corrie."

"We came from the East," I said.

"Oh, where?"

"New York. But only the country part. I've never seen the city."

"Ah, New York is indeed the city of cities!"

"What about Washington?" I asked.

"I've never been there," replied Edie. "There's nothing there, but the government. Why would you want to visit Washington?"

"I'm interested in politics," I answered. "I sometimes write about it in my articles."

"You *write* about politics! Good heavens, that kind of foolishness is for men, don't you know that, Corrie? What could
a young woman like you possibly have to do with politics? We
can't even vote!"

"I'm still interested in what happens to our country."

"The men will decide everything, so what difference does
it make what we think about it?"

"But aren't you interested?"

"Not in men's affairs."

"What about slavery?"

"What about it?"

"Don't you think it's wrong?"

"How could it be wrong when half the country has slaves?
It's not a moral issue of right and wrong, Corrie. It's just part of
the economics of the country. It's how things are, that's all."

"That doesn't make it right," I insisted.

"That's what the northerners are always trying to do—
make it a matter of right and wrong. But it's just different cul-
tures. Slavery is part of the South. Northerners have no right
to condemn something they know nothing about."

For someone who wasn't interested in politics, Edie
seemed to have some definite ideas about slavery. And I
wasn't sure I altogether liked the sound of them.

"You make it sound like northerners belong to a different
country," I said. "Is there really that much difference?"

"When you live in the South, Corrie, there is. The North
is a different country—and not a friendly one."

"You live in the South?"

"Of course. Virginia has always been a slave state, and
always will be. My husband, the late Mr. Simpson, worked for

a large landowner and had dealings with slaves all the time. It's just how things are in the South, and always have been."

"But . . . but doesn't slavery seem wrong to you?" I said again.

"I told you before, it's not a matter of right or wrong. Besides, slavery's in the Bible. Nobody in the Bible ever said it was wrong."

 I'd been so engrossed in the conversation with Edie that I hadn't even noticed that we were approaching the claim.

Suddenly there were Tad and Becky running toward us, followed by Almeda carrying Ruth. I expected to see Zack come out of the barn any second, but he never did.

We jumped down, and there were hugs and greetings and questions. Pa kissed Almeda and stretched his long arms around her and Ruth all at once. "How's my little daughter?" he asked, looking from one to the other. "Marcus said she wasn't feeling too well." He felt her forehead with his big rough palm.

"She was so hot yesterday," said Almeda. "I was worried and took her in to see Doc Shoemaker. "He thinks it might have been a spider bite."

"How is she?" said Pa, looking concerned. "She does feel warm."

"Better today. She's cooled off considerably and seems to be getting some of her spunk back."

All this time Edie had been standing beside the wagon. A brief silence followed, and Pa seemed to suddenly remember our passenger. He turned back toward her and motioned her forward. "But I plumb forgot our guest! Almeda, you'll never guess who we picked up in Sacramento," he said. "This here's Katie's sister! Edie, meet my wife, Almeda."

Almeda came forward and greeted her warmly. "Surely there is some logical explanation," she said, laughing. "This must be more than an accidental meeting."

Edie told about her husband's death and her decision to come for a visit, followed by her version of running into me and Pa in Sacramento. "So where do Katie and Nick live?" she said, looking around.

"Not more than a quarter mile upstream," answered Pa. "Come on everyone, into the wagon. Let's get Edie on to her reunion with her sister!"

We all scrambled back in. Pa gave Edie a lift up into the back with us kids, then took Almeda's hand and helped her up to the seat beside him, with Ruth in her lap. Then he clucked to the two horses, and off we lurched up the road alongside the creek toward the mine, where we would cross over into the woods on the other side.

What a reunion it was! I don't think I'd ever seen Aunt Katie so much at a loss for words. She was so surprised she didn't know whether to laugh or cry, so instead she just stood there with a look of silent disbelief on her face. By the time we left them half an hour later, the two sisters were talking so fast we could hardly understand them. Pa gave Uncle Nick a smile, almost as if to say, *You're gonna have your hands full now with two Virginia women.* Uncle Nick watched us go with a shrug and look that said, *What do I do now?*

When we got back to our place, Tad handed our two bags down to Pa, and we all went inside.

"Well, tell us all about San Francisco and the fancy gathering you two important Hollisters went to," said Almeda, pouring Pa a cup of coffee from the pot on the stove. "We've all been praying for you, and we're anxious to hear how God answered. So . . . did anything exciting happen while you were there?"

Pa and I glanced at each other. Pa gave me a wink, and I burst out laughing.

"What is it?" said Almeda with a curious smile. "*Something* must have happened!"

"Naw, nothing much," said Pa, "not unless you count getting asked to help Honest Abe Lincoln get elected and run for state legislature all within the same hour."

"What!" exclaimed Almeda. "Who asked . . . somebody asked *you*?"

"There was a man named Dalton," I put in. "I didn't know who he was at first, but Pa told me later that he was the most important Republican in the state. He asked me to help with the election in November."

"Help . . . how?"

"Writing . . . I don't know," I answered. "I'm not quite sure what he wanted."

"Corrie's being modest," added Pa. "I told you, Corrie, that you're an important person in this state. There was even some talk," he said, turning to Almeda, "of her making speeches on behalf of the Republican ticket."

"Corrie, that's wonderful! What do you think—are you going to do it?"

"I don't know," I shrugged. "Pa and I talked about it, and prayed together. We were both saying how you never know where something's going to lead. But Pa's news is even bigger! They asked him to run for the legislature in Sacramento!"

"Drummond!" exclaimed Almeda. "Is it true?"

"I reckon they figure there ain't no harm in asking," answered Pa noncommittally. "So ask they did."

"What did you say?"

"I didn't say anything. Just like Corrie, I said I'd think about it. I ain't about to pick up stakes and disrupt my family again. So I don't rightly see as how I could do it. But I didn't tell them anything definite."

"My husband and daughter—the politicians!" laughed Almeda. "I can hardly believe it!"

"You started it with all your notions of running for mayor!" joked Pa. "Now look what you landed me into!"

"And giving me that journal," I added in fun.

"You two aren't fooling anybody. You love every bit of it, and you both know it!"

"Corrie, tell Almeda about the new friend you met there."

"Oh, Pa, why'd you have to bring that up?" I said, blushing.

"What's this?" asked Almeda and Becky at the same time.

"Just some important young man who took a fancy to Corrie."

"Pa, he did not!" I said.

"Don't lie, Corrie," teased Pa. "You should have seen them, Becky," he went on, "together nearly the whole evening. Why, Corrie deserted me, and I was alone for most of the reception."

"Pa! Now it's you who's lying."

"Well, maybe exaggerating just a tad."

"I want to know all about him," said Almeda.

"There's nothing to tell. He's a friend of Mr. Denver's, and he's the one who took me to meet Mr. Dalton, that's all. I'm sure he was just doing what he was supposed to do and nothing more. I'll probably never see him again."

Finally Pa figured I'd had enough of the ribbing, and he turned toward Almeda. "Where's Zack?"

Her face fell and the room suddenly got silent.

"Zack and Almeda had a big argument, Pa," said Tad finally.

"Is that true?" said Pa, his forehead crinkling as he turned toward Almeda.

She nodded. "I'm afraid so, Drummond."

"What about?"

"Something he wanted to do. I told him he'd have to wait until you got back and talk it over with you."

"What was so all-fired important that it couldn't wait a couple of days?" asked Pa.

"I don't know what got into him. He just exploded. I've never seen him like that before. He stormed away, talking nonsense about always having to go along with what everyone else wanted and nobody ever asking him what *he* thought. I don't know where it all came from, but from the sound of it, it must have been pent up a long time."

"I'll take his breeches off and tan his hide but good when he gets home!" said Pa. It was clear he was angry.

"Don't do anything rash, Drum. Zack's not a boy anymore."

"He's *my* boy!"

"He's your son. But he's grown, and whatever this storm is that's built up inside him, it's not something to be taken lightly."

"What was it he got in his head to do?"

"He said he was going to join the Pony Express, Pa," said Tad.

"That true, Almeda?"

"That's pretty much the gist of it. They were offering good money, he said, and he and Little Wolf had both decided to go.

"There were some openings between Nevada and Utah."

"What about Lame Pony? What does he think?"

"I haven't seen him since. It only happened two days ago."

"And Zack hasn't come back?"

Almeda shook her head.

"He's probably up the hill at Jack's. I'll ride out there and see what's up."

Father and Son

Chapter Nine

*N*one of us saw Zack for five days.

Pa went up to Jack Lame Pony's, but neither he nor Little Wolf knew where Zack had gone. Little Wolf couldn't tell him much more than Almeda had, that a fellow they had met had offered the boys jobs with the new mail delivery service and that they had talked about taking him up on his offer. Then Zack had gone home to tell Almeda about it, and that was the last anyone had seen of him.

Then as we were talking, Zack came walking through the door. We hadn't even heard the sound of a horse riding up.

I don't know where he'd been, but he looked dirty and unshaven. He gave me a little nod of greeting, but he didn't smile, and he tried to pretend Pa wasn't there. He probably knew what was coming.

"Where you been, son?" said Pa.

"Out riding," muttered Zack.

"Where?"

"Just around," said Zack, shuffling toward the kitchen area to see if there was anything to eat.

"I was a mite surprised to come home and find you gone," said Pa. "When I'm away I expect you to look after the family."

Zack said nothing. He picked up a piece of bread and bit into it.

"You don't figure you owe no responsibility to the family, is that it?"

Zack mumbled something, but I couldn't make it out.

"What's that you say?"

"I said it ain't my family no more."

"What do you mean by that?" Pa's tone was stern. It was easy to tell that he was getting riled.

"What should you care what I do? You all got your own plans. Corrie's got her writing, and you all think she's pretty great at everything she does. And you're busy being the town's important man. There ain't nothing Almeda can't do for herself. What do any of you need me for?"

"When I'm not here, I want you keeping a watch over things, that's what," said Pa, his voice icy. Zack hadn't looked at any of us straight in the face since walking in. If he was embarrassed about running off, he didn't show it. He just looked mad. I could feel the tension between him and Pa hanging in the air.

"Zack, please," said Almeda in a pleading tone, "I don't want—"

"You don't need me, Almeda. Don't try to pretend."

"Zack, that's not true," she said, turning to him with tender eyes full of anguish. "You know that I do need you—"

"Almeda," Zack said, cutting her off again, "you don't have to try to make me feel good anymore like you did when I was a boy."

"That's no way to talk to your mother, boy!" said Pa. By now he was storming mad.

"She ain't my mother!"

"She's my wife and a woman, and that means you better learn to talk to her with respect in your voice, unless you want my belt around that hind end of yours!"

"So you still think I'm a little kid too?"

"You're my son, and I'll whip you if I need to."

Becky and Tad stared at the two of them; it was all I could do to keep from bursting out crying. To suddenly have two of the people you love most in all the world arguing and yelling at each other was too horrible even to describe.

Zack turned away and laughed—a bitter, awful laugh.

"You find something funny in that?" asked Pa.

"Yeah," retorted Zack, spinning around and leveling that bitter-looking grin on Pa. "I'm twenty-one years old. I'm taller than you. I can ride a horse better than anyone for miles. But you still think of me as a little kid. You don't even know what it's like for me. I got a life of my own to live, and you don't even know the kinds of things I'm thinking about. Everything's about Corrie and Almeda or your being mayor or the Mine and Freight. You got no time for me—you never had. What do you care what I do? You just expect me to be around to take care of things so you can leave whenever you want."

"What's that supposed to mean?"

"You figure out what it means."

"None of that matters. You're not going to the Pony Express without my say-so. Whatever you may think, I'm still your pa. And I still got a right to tell you what you can and can't do."

Zack stared straight into his face, and the next words out of his mouth were so biting I could almost feel them slicing straight into Pa's heart.

"You never knew what it was like for me," said Zack. "You never knew the times I cried myself to sleep when I was a kid, hoping you'd come home. I was frightened without a father. I got teased and made fun of something awful 'cause I was little, and sometimes I came home with bruises and a black eye from trying to defend myself. I used to dream how good it would be to come home to feel the arms of a pa to hold me. I'd beg God to help us find you. But we never did, and I had to grow up alone like that. You'll never know how much you hurt Ma, and how she'd cry sometimes when she didn't know I was watching. She kept loving you and kept praying for you—always asking God to protect you and watch over you. But I finally quit praying, because I was sick of being disappointed."

Zack stopped for a second, trembling with emotion. Then he added, "So I don't reckon you got a right to call yourself my father no more. You may be my pa. But I figure I'm old enough to decide for myself what I want!"

Zack's words came so fast and were so unexpected that Pa didn't know what to do. I know Pa was hurt by what Zack had said, but his response came out as anger.

"However mixed up a job I done of it, I'm your pa whether you like it or not!"

"I'm stuck here with nothing but women and babies and little kids," Zack shot back. "You can go off and do whatever you want, and you figure I got nothing of my own that matters?"

"You got no right to talk about your mother and sisters that way. You apologize to them, or you're gonna feel that belt like I told you!"

"Ha! Your belt ain't gonna come anywhere near my rump! And I ain't apologizing to nobody! It's true, everything I said. I said to myself a long time ago I was getting out of here first chance I got. God knows I spent my muscles and blistered my hands working that mine for you all these years. You don't know how many days I sweated all day long, aching inside just for you to smile at me once and say I'd done a good day's work. But I might as well not even been there, for all you ever noticed! I don't reckon you'll figure you owe me anything for it. Well, that's fine with me. But all that's over with. I met a guy, and he's got a place arranged for me in the Pony Express. And I don't care if Little Wolf's changed his mind, I'm gonna take it. It's the chance I been waiting for to get out of this place!"

He turned and strode toward the door, still without looking at any of the rest of us. But Pa was closer, and took two giant steps and cut him off. He laid a strong hand on Zack's shoulder.

"No you're not, son," he said. "You ain't goin' nowhere without my leave. Now you get back in here, and we'll sit down and talk about it."

"I'm not talking about nothing," retorted Zack. "I've listened to all the rest of you long enough. Nobody ever seemed much interested in talking to me before. Now I'm going, whether you like it or not."

"And I'm telling you you're not."

"It's too late. I signed the papers. I start my first run next week."

"Then I'll go talk to this fella and unsign them."

Zack laughed again.

"You're not leaving home, Zack! You hear me, son? You got duties to this family."

Zack's eyes squinted ever so slightly, and his next words weren't loud but they cut deep.

"Is that how it was when *you* left Ma?" he said icily. "Duties to the family!" He laughed again. "*You* talk to *me* about duty to the family? Where were you all those years when I needed a pa? Even after we'd come all the way across the country to find you, you didn't want us. You denied you even knew us!"

Zack's back was to me as he spoke, and I could see Pa's grip on my brother's shoulder loosen. Pa unconsciously took half a step backward, as if Zack's words had been a physical blow across Pa's face. The rest of us stood in stunned silence to hear Zack accuse Pa like that.

"Well," he went on, "you talk about duty all you want, but I figure I've already about done as much as you ever did. You ran out on us, and even now you're always gone somewhere or another, but still you figure I'll do for you what you never did for me. Well, I tell you, I ain't gonna do it no more! If I go ride for the Pony Express, at least I ain't leaving a wife and five kids like you done!"

He wrested free of Pa's hand. As he did, Almeda approached, her eyes full of tears, and stretched out a hand and gently placed it on his shoulder.

"Oh, Zack," she pleaded, "if only I could make you see how much we all—"

But Zack, still backing his way free of Pa, either didn't hear her tender words of love or misunderstood her gesture. For whatever reason, as her hand touched him, thinking she intended to restrain him further, he reached up and in a swift motion threw her hand off him and took a step toward the door.

Seeing him rebuke Almeda so rudely was all Pa needed to jolt him awake from his stunned silence. Zack's reaction could not have been more ill-chosen.

Pa's eye's inflamed with rage. He leaped forward and struck Zack across the jaw. Yet even as Zack fell, Pa realized what he'd done and pulled back.

His cheek red from the blow and his body trembling, Zack slowly rose. "It's no secret where your loyalties lie," he said. "Everything for the women, but you won't lift a finger unless it's *against* your own son!"

He turned, opened the door, and stalked off, slamming it behind him. Pa half stumbled back into a chair, mortified at what he'd done. His face was white as a sheet.

The house was silent. The next sound we heard was Zack's horse galloping away.

Pa and Tad

CHAPTER TEN

*T*he silence, the tension, the uncertainty the rest of that day and the next was so thick and strong that we all walked around in a numbed state of sadness. Besides Pa, I think Zack's leaving was hardest on Tad. He had been a devoted son to Pa and a loving younger brother to Zack. And now suddenly the two idols of his world had nearly come to blows. He moped around in silence.

Pa managed to keep busy in the barn, going to town a lot, fixing things. He worked harder at the mine than I'd seen him work in three years, taking out his frustration on the rocks.

By the end of the second day, I sensed a gradual change come over Pa, and I was glad to see it. Zack was gone, and how long it would be before we might see him again, no one could tell. But instead of allowing it to destroy what was still left, Pa began to draw Tad closer. I suppose if good can come out of such a problem, it was good to see Pa trying to make use of what time was left him with his younger son to build up the relationship so he didn't hurt him like he had done to Zack.

Of course Tad had been involved in the mine ever since he had found the huge nugget that had changed everything for our family. But on the second day after Zack's leaving, instead of just walking up to the mine to pound away by himself,

Pa said, "Say, Tad, how about you and me seeing if we can dig any gold out of that hill today?"

Tad was still feeling pretty low, but he went with Pa. I don't know if the two of them talked much, and if they did I doubt they talked about the one person who was most on their minds. But they both came back, sweating and tired and dirty, in much better spirits than before. Hard work has a way of clearing out both the mind and the heart when they're cluttered up with feelings that are hard to understand.

The next day they cleaned out the barn together and repaired a section of the corral. Almeda and I could see that Pa was doing what he could to help ease Tad's pain and at the same time trying to give them both something—not to *take* the place of Zack, but maybe *in* the place of Zack's being there. That something was each other.

The two of them kept busy all week—busy, active, working hard, and tired. If they were going to keep thinking about Zack, they were going to have to do it in the midst of work and exercise! They got more gold out of the mountain and stream than they had in any week for three years, prompting Alkali Jones to fairly burst at the seams with his predictions of a new lode *just waitin' to spill out all over the dad-blamed valley, hee, hee, hee!*

The barn and grounds hadn't looked so tidy for a long time. They even took the wagon out into the woods and got started on next winter's firewood supply when summer hadn't even officially begun yet. At week's end, the two of them mounted up and went up into the mountains overnight—the first time Pa had ever gone hunting alone with Tad—and they came back the next afternoon with two bucks slung over the pack mules. For the first time since Zack's leaving, I saw a smile on Tad's face as he was telling us about stalking the one that he himself had shot.

"He was too far away to get a clean shot when we first spotted him," Tad said, his eyes gleaming. "So we had to work our way through the brush and trees to get closer without spooking him."

"You shoulda seen him," said Pa proudly. "He took dead aim right into the flank below his shoulder. One shot was all it needed. The big creature dropped where he stood without twitching a muscle. I've never seen such a shot!"

Tad went on excitedly telling about how they ran across the second one. I glanced over at Pa, watching him quietly. I could tell from the look in his eyes that he knew his efforts all week had paid off, that Tad felt better about Zack. Pa couldn't know it yet, but his efforts accomplished far more than just helping Tad deal with the loss of his brother. The two of them were closer than they had ever been, and were fast friends from that day on.

I knew the pain over Zack, and what Zack had said, went further inside Pa than he was letting on. Almeda knew, too, how deeply he felt it. But Pa was the kind of man who had to sort things out by himself for a spell before he was ready to talk. I was sure he would let us know what he was feeling once he was ready. In the meantime, he seemed to be putting his efforts into helping Tad figure out his frustrations.

Whatever Zack might have said, I saw a loving, unselfish man when I looked at Pa. And I wished Zack could see, as I did, how Pa had been a good father to all of us—at least once we'd arrived in California.

When we first came to California, Zack carried a chip around on his shoulder against Pa for a while, but I thought he'd gotten over all that years ago.

But I guess I was wrong. All it took for me to forgive Pa was to talk with him a few times and see how his own heart ached over the past. I had seen Pa cry and pray and grow, and I knew what kind of man he was—deep down, on the inside. But maybe he and Zack had never talked that way.

As I thought about Zack, I realized that when a person isn't able to forgive someone, a little seed of anger will eventually sprout and grow until branches and roots and leaves of bitterness come bursting out somewhere.

With Zack, apparently the forgiveness didn't get finished, and now he was gone. And Pa was feeling one of the deepest pains a man can feel on account of it.

Meanwhile, other things kept us from thinking only about Zack. The Sunday after Pa and Tad got back from their hunting trip, Aunt Katie and Uncle Nick invited all of us to their place to eat and to have a family visit with them and Edie.

That day suddenly put Zack into the background of our thoughts for a while, and got me thinking about the dilemma of my decision all over again.

A Heated Discussion about Slavery

CHAPTER ELEVEN

*A*fter dinner was over, Almeda and Aunt Katie put Ruth and Anne down to sleep; then the rest of us got to talking.

Pa had been telling Uncle Nick and Aunt Katie about our trip to San Francisco and about my conversation with Mr. Dalton.

"So, are you going to do it, Corrie?" Uncle Nick asked me.

"I don't know," I answered. "I'm just waiting to see what might come of it. I said to the Lord that if it was something he wanted me to pursue, then he'd have to make something happen so I'd know it."

"How could he do that?" asked Edie.

"He has lots of ways," I replied. "I just want to make sure I don't do something *myself*. If I just patiently wait, then there's no danger of making a decision all on my own. When he wants me to move a certain way, maybe in some new direction, then he'll make sure I get the message. He'll send someone or some circumstance to give me a nudge."

"That sounds like a rather passive approach to life," said Edie. "I thought all you Californians were pioneers who didn't wait for anybody but went out and did whatever you wanted to do!"

We all laughed.

"Is that what easterners think of Californians?" asked Almeda.

"That's what I thought before I became one myself!" said Katie.

"I don't mean I just sit by and don't do anything," I said to Edie. "I go on about my life as usual. But in making important decisions, I want to be sure I wait for the Lord to have some say in it, too."

"So if the Lord gives you the nudge you're talking about," Uncle Nick asked again, "then do you figure you'll do it?"

"I like what they're saying about Mr. Lincoln," I said. "It seems important for the country that he get elected. I suppose I'm thinking that maybe I ought to try to help."

"If he wins in November, the whole South will rise up against it," put in Edie abruptly. "A Lincoln victory will destroy the nation."

A moment of silence followed. I think we were all a bit shocked at her strong statement, and no one had expected it of her.

"Is it really that serious?" Almeda asked after a moment.

"Before he died, my husband used to say that if the Republicans nominated Lincoln, and if the country elected him, the South would never stand for it. It's not just the slavery issue, he said, but the whole southern way of life."

"How can that way of life be justified when it is based on such a horrid thing as human beings enslaving others of their kind?" Almeda asked. "In Christ's own words, he came to set people free."

"That is an ideal not necessarily found in this life, Almeda. That's the mistake abolitionists always make— quoting the Bible and talking about God's hatred of slavery when there is nothing of the kind to be found in the Holy Scriptures."

Almeda's strong feelings surfaced. "You cannot mean you actually believe slavery to be just!" she said. "How can there be any doubt, for a serious-minded Christian, that slavery is wrong?"

"There are Christians in the South just as well as in the North."

"They cannot honestly deceive themselves into thinking slavery is *right*! It goes against every truth of the Bible."

"Abraham had slaves. The Ten Commandments mention slavery twice without disapproving of it. Jesus never uttered a word condemning slavery, although it was widespread in the world at the time he lived. Paul told slaves to obey their masters, and even returned a runaway slave to his master."

"It sounds like you met someone who knows her Bible as well as you do, Almeda," chuckled Uncle Nick.

"All of what you said may be true, Edie," said Pa, "but be honest with us. Do people in the South, God-fearing people especially—do they really believe slavery is right, deep down in their hearts?"

"I can't speak for everyone, Drummond. All I know is that church leaders and preachers all through the South are just as staunch *for* slavery as the abolitionists are against it."

"What do you think, Katie?" Pa asked.

Katie hesitated a moment, weighing, I think, how she should answer when the debate was between her own sister and her upbringing in Virginia and her new family, which had no firsthand exposure to the issue at hand.

"You have to realize," she said at length, "that slavery was common practice when I was growing up. We were all taught to accept it as the natural order of things between the races—even, some said, for the good of the Negro people. Since coming to California six years ago, I've hardly thought about it. All the disputes between the states and all the arguments over whether slavery is right or wrong—that's risen to new heights since I left. I don't even know what I think."

"Have you read *Uncle Tom's Cabin?*" I asked Edie.

"Certainly not. Harriet Beecher Stowe is hated in Virginia! That book is full of falsehoods from cover to cover!"

"I have read that its portrayal of slavery is quite accurate," said Almeda.

"Then you must be listening to a northern abolitionist. Everyone in the South knows the book for what it is—a pack of lies."

"I want to know something," I asked. "Why did you say that if Mr. Lincoln wins it will destroy the country?"

"Because he has been speaking out against slavery for two years, ever since he ran against Douglas for the Senate in '58. My husband and the men he worked with say Lincoln is sure to attempt to free the slaves. To do so would ruin the South economically. That's why the southern states would never go along with it."

"What would they do?"

"There is already talk circulating around Virginia of withdrawing from the United States and forming a new country if Lincoln wins."

A few gasps went around the room, including one from Katie herself. We all sat in stunned silence a minute. Because of my articles, we always got the *Alta*. We had read of the growing dispute over slavery between the northern and southern states, and had even seen the word *secession* more than once. But somehow it hadn't struck root exactly how serious the division was until Edie began talking about the southern states *forming a new country.*

Uncle Nick broke the heavy silence with a laugh. He was probably the least well read of any of us, and the idea of two separate countries, a slave South and a free North, struck him as absolutely preposterous.

"That's the craziest thing I ever heard!" he said. "There's nothing in the South that could keep a country together. The South would die without the North!"

I could see Edie getting ready to give Uncle Nick a sharp reply, but Pa spoke up first.

"Don't be too sure of that, Nick," he said. "You know about the big collapse of the banks in New York two years ago and all the financial crises it caused." Pa had read more of the newspapers that came to me than I realized!

"Not much. Didn't hurt us here."

"Well, it hurt the North, and it still hasn't recovered all the way. But the South is booming. Their cotton helped save the northern banks. They can sell all they want in Europe. I tell you, Nick, there's folks saying the South is stronger financially than the North."

"There you go sounding like a politician again!" laughed Uncle Nick. "Where do you get all that stuff, Drum?"

"Well, I figure if I'm gonna have a daughter that writes for the paper, I might as well read it."

"I've read that too," said Almeda. "The North needs the South, not the other way around. If the South were to pull out, they would have plenty of resources. The cotton crop would support it."

"Exactly!" agreed Edie. "Without the South, the North would perish. If Lincoln dared to tamper with slavery, he would be cutting the throat of the very North he thinks he loves so much. The future of the United States lies south of the Mason-Dixon Line."

Again there was silence for a while. At last Katie spoke. "After all this, Corrie," she said, "do you *still* think you'll support Lincoln?"

"I don't know," I said with a sigh. "I suppose there's more to the decision than I thought at first."

*I*t was a hard dilemma.

Now all of a sudden the slavery issue wasn't two thousand miles distant but right in my own backyard, even right in my own family. It had hardly occurred to me before that Katie had, indeed, come from a slave state. We had never talked about it. But now Edie's arrival, and her strong views on the subject, brought the debate closer to home.

In spite of everything she said, in my own heart and mind I couldn't see how slavery could be anything but wrong. It couldn't be right to treat other people the way slaves were treated! I was in agreement with Mr. Lincoln.

But what if it was true that his election could spell ruin to the country? What if his election caused an even more serious rift between North and South than already existed? Did I want to be part of contributing to that? What would it all mean to California?

I found myself wondering about my responsibility as a writer and a Christian in a lot of new ways. If people really were paying attention to what I said, I had to be sure of myself when I put my pen to the paper. What if I said something wrong, something that readers believed and took action on? I would be responsible for misleading them.

Always before, I'd written about things because I was interested in them. That's why I started writing—because it was something I wanted to do for myself. I wanted to express my thoughts and feelings. And there were so many things I wanted to explore! Writing seemed the natural way to express what was inside me, to communicate, even to grow as a person. That's what my journal was to begin with—just a diary of my own thoughts and feelings. It had never been meant for anybody else.

I reflected on Ma, on things she'd said to me. I had always been a reader and more quiet than outgoing. She'd made no secret of thinking I'd probably never get married. She figured I ought to read and write and keep a diary so I could be a teacher when I got older and no man would have me.

I had done what Ma said, even though I sometimes ached when I realized it took her dying to get me started. Writing in my diary back then had been a way of letting the pain out.

I was twenty-three now, and I had books and books of diaries and journals! That first beautiful book Almeda had given me, with *The Journal of Corrie Belle Hollister* stamped across the front of it, had been the first of many such volumes I had filled with memories and recollections and drawings over the years.

At first Pa and Uncle Nick had kidded me about always writing down what I was thinking. But once the articles started, and payments of two, and then four, and then even eight dollars started to come in for things I'd written, they realized maybe it was a worthwhile thing for me to be doing, after all. But even then it was just *my* writing.

Then gradually my writing started getting bigger than just *my* own personal, private thoughts. Especially as I'd written about the two elections back in 1856, I had thought a lot about truth and trying to tell the truth to people. Even from men like Derrick Gregory and Mr. Royce, I had learned a thing or two about truth and being fair. I tried to learn from everybody I met, although men like that probably had no idea they were helping to teach me and show me things, even by their deceit.

Yet I don't think it ever really struck me that anything I might say was important . . . not *really* important. I was trying to learn about truth and being a good reporter, but I figured that it was still mostly for me. Robin O'Flaridy still looked down on me, even after the '56 elections; my story had never appeared, and Mr. Fremont had lost the election. Nothing I had done or said *had* been that important, and I had gone back to writing about people and floods and how things were in California now that the gold rush was slowing down.

Mr. Kemble kept telling me that my articles were getting a wider audience in the East on account of a woman reporter being so unusual, but I didn't think much about it. I knew of plenty of women authors and it didn't seem so unusual. Julia Ward Howe wrote poems, and Harriet Beecher Stowe and Louisa May Alcott wrote, too. I didn't see what was so unusual about what I did. After all, Mrs. Alcott's poems and stories were being published in the *Atlantic Monthly*.

"None of those women are writing for newspapers, Corrie," Mr. Kemble said to me. "That's what I'm trying to tell you. Newspapers influence people. All those other women are just writing stories. They can get as famous as you please, but they're not going to be taken as seriously as a nonfiction *news* reporter."

"*Uncle Tom's Cabin* has influenced a lot of people," I said.

"It's sold a million copies," he replied. "But it's still just a story."

"You can't say Mrs. Stowe isn't an influential writer."

"She is indeed. Her book probably has started more fights and brawls and arguments than any book ever published in this country. But she's still just a novelist. You, on the other hand, Corrie Belle Hollister—*you* are more than a novelist. You are a newspaper reporter. And while it may be true that when you first came in here with little stories about leaves and blizzards and apple seeds and new schools and colorful people you had met, tricking me into thinking you were a man—"

I glanced up at him, but the little curl of his lip and twinkle in his eye told me he was just having fun with me. He never lost an opportunity to remind me of my first byline: C.B. Hollister.

"As I was saying," he went on, "at first I may have published some of your stories as a lark, just for the novelty of showing up some of the other papers with something by a young woman. But I've got to admit you surprised me. You kept at it. You didn't back down from me, or from the odds that were against you, not from anything. You proved yourself to be quite a tenacious, plucky young woman, Corrie. In the process, I'll be darned if you didn't start writing some pretty fair stories and getting yourself quite a following of readers— women *and* men."

He stopped and looked me over as he did from time to time, kind of like he was thinking the whole thing through all over again, wondering how he'd gotten himself into the fix of having a woman on his staff.

"So that's why," he went on after a minute, "you're different, Corrie. Your name might not be as famous as Mrs. Stowe's. A hundred years from now nobody'll know the name Corrie Hollister, because newspapers get thrown away,

SEA TO SHINING SEA

while books don't. But right now, people are listening to what you say, Corrie. I tell you, you've got an influence that you don't realize."

His words kept coming back to me as I debated with myself about what I ought to do, especially after all Edie Simpson had said. It was more than just journal writing now.

What if . . . *what if* something I said or wrote really did influence the election? Even if I caused only one or two people to vote differently than they might have otherwise, it was still a sobering responsibility.

I did a lot of talking to the Lord about it in the days after Pa and I got back from San Francisco, running the pros and cons through my mind, and always remembering Pa's words on the boat. *You never know what might be around the corner, and so you ought to be watching and paying attention as best you can.* I knew Pa was doing the same thing, both about his decision and about Zack's leaving.

Ordinarily I would have talked to him or Almeda. But with slavery and the North-South dispute and the heated difference of opinion about Mr. Lincoln, I thought this was a decision I had to make alone—just between me and the Lord.

After the discussion at Uncle Nick and Aunt Katie's, I was growing more and more sure that slavery was wrong and should be abolished. But I saw more clearly now that there might be consequences—not only to my decision, but to the whole outcome of the election—that no one could predict. It might even mean disputes in our own family.

In my heart I found myself wanting to do it. I wanted my writing to *matter* for the sake of truth. If Mr. Lincoln and the antislavery people and the Republican party represented that truth, then I wanted to be part of helping people know it.

But I had to be sure. So I found myself telling the Lord that I wouldn't do anything further, and that if I was supposed to get any more involved, he would have to make it clear by having somebody contact *me,* or by sending along some circumstance I couldn't ignore. I didn't want to initiate anything more all by myself.

If I never heard again from Mr. Dalton or anybody else from the Republican party, I would take that as God's way of saying no.

The dilemma of whether I should get involved with the election wasn't the only question my mind was wrestling with since hearing Katie's sister's views on slavery. But it was probably the easiest one to resolve.

In the meantime, I found myself thinking a lot about something Pa had told me about Davy Crockett. They had both fought in the Mexican War, and everyone who fought in California admired the men who died in the same cause at the Alamo.

Davy Crockett had been a congressman from Tennessee before he went to Texas, and I had read that Mr. Crockett always told folks in Washington he had based his life on the saying, *Be sure you're right, then go ahead.* I found myself reflecting on those words every day.

I kept saying to myself, "Don't go ahead until you're sure you're right."

I was pretty certain the *cause* was right. Now I just had to wait to see if involving myself in it was what God wanted me to do. Figuring that out, as well as waiting, was the hardest part of all.

I found myself coming away from that afternoon at Uncle Nick and Aunt Katie's with a heaviness in my heart, a confusion—not about the slavery issue alone, but rather how there could be so many different views on the same thing. I wanted to talk with someone about it, but I didn't feel that Almeda or Pa would be the right persons. I respected them as much as ever, but maybe because they'd been part of the discussion, and I knew that Almeda herself held pretty strong opinions on things, I wanted to get an outside, unbiased perspective.

Since it was a spiritual question even more than something to do with issues, I thought of Rev. Rutledge. As a pastor, he not only ought to have answers to spiritual questions, but by now I knew that he didn't usually voice outspoken views on issues people normally differed about. When it came to the Bible, he said what he had to say without fear and without backing down. But he never took sides about politics or on decisions facing the community. Pa would sometimes get riled when he wanted Rev. Rutledge's support for something the town council was getting ready to vote on.

The Rutledges had become our good friends, and we had grown to feel a great deal of respect for Rev. Rutledge since his first awkward days in Miracle Springs. He had changed nearly as much as Pa had. His teaching and his sermons and his outlook on life and Scripture and what being a Christian meant had been important in forming the person I'd grown up to be. There was a lot of Almeda in me, and a lot of Pa. But there were big chunks of Harriet and Avery Rutledge, too. They both had influenced me in different ways.

So on the Monday after the dinner and discussion, I found myself saddling up my horse and riding down into Miracle Springs for a visit with them. School had been out for a week, and I knew that Rev. Rutledge usually spent Mondays at home, so I hoped to find them both there.

Harriet opened the door. "Corrie, hello! It's nice to see you!"

"I wondered if I might talk with you," I said. "Both of you, I mean. Is the Reverend at home?"

"Yes . . . yes, he is. Come in, Corrie—Avery, we have a visitor," she called out as she led me inside and closed the door.

I followed her into their sitting room, where Rev. Rutledge was just rising from his chair, a copy of the *Alta* in his hand.

"Corrie, welcome," he said, giving me a warm handshake. "Harriet and I always enjoy your visits."

"Thank you," I said. "I've come to ask you about something that is troubling me . . . I hope you don't mind."

"Of course not. Troubled souls are in my line of work," he said with a laugh.

"It's not my soul that's troubled, only my mind."

"I was only jesting. You can feel free to share anything with me, with both of us if you like."

"I would like both your opinions," I said, glancing back at the former Miss Stansberry, whom I still sometimes had a hard time calling by her first name. "It's not what you'd call a spiritual problem, but there's something about being a Christian I don't understand as well as I'd like."

"Well, we've been through a lot of growing together, Corrie, you and I, and your whole family," said Rev. Rutledge. "You've spent lots of hours in this house talking and praying with Harriet and me, and it wouldn't surprise me if we've learned just as much from you as you might have from either of us."

"That could hardly be," I said, "when I sit and listen to your sermons on most Sundays. I've learned more from listening to you talk about the Scriptures than you can imagine."

"The best sermons aren't to be found in church, Corrie."

"How do you mean?"

"Do you remember what the apostle Peter said in his first letter? 'Ye also, as lively stones, are being built up a spiritual house.' He's saying that *we* are the building blocks and bricks of the house that God is building. Then the apostle Paul wrote to the Corinthians about our being *living* epistles or letters. 'Ye are our epistle written in our hearts, known and read by all men . . . written not with ink, but with the Spirit of the living God, written not in tables of stone, but in fleshy tables of the heart.'" He paused, then added, "Do you see the connection I'm trying to make?"

"I always like it better when you tell me instead of my trying to guess," I answered with a smile.

He laughed. "People can be stones and letters, according to the Scriptures—*living* stones and letters. In the same way, *people* can be sermons too. And living people-sermons are far more powerful than anything a preacher says in church. I suppose the point I am attempting to make is that *you* make a better sermon just by your life than any thousand sermons I may preach."

"That's nice of you to say, but I'm not sure I believe it," I said. "When you preach, people listen to what you have to say. Nobody pays that much attention to people going around just living."

"Oh, I think you're wrong about that, Corrie. As a matter of fact, I think it is exactly the reverse. People sit quietly when I'm preaching. But most of them aren't really listening, not deep down in their hearts. You might be, and a few others. But most people don't know how to *really* listen and absorb what another person is saying. There's an art to listening that most folks don't know too much about."

"I suppose you're right. But then, what about when people aren't in church?"

"People look as if they're listening in church, when they're really not. In the same way, out in the midst of life, people look as if they're not paying that much attention, but they really *are*. In other words, people listen far more to the living people-sermons around them every day than you would ever know to look at them."

"Hmm . . . I hadn't thought of that."

"Tell me, has Almeda influenced your life?"

"You know she has, in a thousand ways."

"Why is that, do you think? Is it because of the things she's *said* to you, or the person she *is*?"

"Of course it's the second, although she's taught me a lot too."

"Certainly she has. But it's the *living* sermon she *is* that's gone the deepest inside you, isn't it? Her words go only so far as she lives them out. What do you think my sermons would mean to you if you never saw my words at work in what I tried to do in the rest of my life?"

"Not much," I admitted.

"How much did you listen to me when I first came?"

I laughed.

"There, you see. And when *did* my sermons start getting into you?"

"You're right," I smiled. "When I saw the real *you*, when I saw you and Pa trying to form a real relationship."

"That's right. That's the living stone, the living epistle—the real-life sermon at work. So I stick by what I said to begin with—the best sermons aren't to be found in church, and your life is as dynamic a sermon as I'll ever preach. One that people are watching and observing and listening to all the time."

"Do you really think so?"

"You listen to me, Corrie; the Lord has placed you in many situations where you are constantly being a living epistle, a flesh-and-blood sermon to the people you rub shoulders with. You have more influence for him than you realize—and I don't mean only because you write. The person you are is the living sermon. You can believe me—people *are* listening to it!"

I didn't say anything more for a minute. That word *influence* had come up again, and I couldn't help wondering if what Rev. Rutledge had said had any bearing on the decision I was facing.

Trying to Get to the Bottom of Truth
CHAPTER FOURTEEN

"Would you like some tea?" asked Harriet as the room fell silent for a few moments.

"Yes, thank you," I replied, looking up again.

"What I meant to say a while ago," said Rev. Rutledge as his wife went to the stove, "is that we've been through a great deal together, and it's always a pleasure to talk and share with you about anything that is on your mind."

"I appreciate it," I replied.

"So . . . what is troubling you?"

I drew in a long breath of air, then let it out slowly. "It's hard to put into words exactly," I said finally. "We had a family talk yesterday—you knew that Aunt Katie's sister was here for a visit?"

"Yes, I met her yesterday. They were in church."

"She and Katie are from Virginia."

"Right. That's what I understand."

"Well, we all got to talking about slavery and the dispute over it between the North and the South, and I came away confused."

"About whether slavery is right or wrong?"

"Not exactly that. What I found bothering me as I went to bed last night was that all—on *both* sides—think they're right, and they've got passages out of the Bible and seemingly religious reasons for thinking what they do. How can people look at the very same thing and then think completely opposite ways about it?"

"That's been going on for centuries, Corrie. People look at things differently."

"You'd think at least Christian people would be of one mind."

"That's never been the case. Christians have had some of the world's most bitter arguments."

"It doesn't seem right."

"No doubt it isn't. But it still happens."

"Why?"

"I suppose besides looking at things differently, people also have motives of self that get mixed in with what they believe. So the stands they take on things have as much to do with what they *want* as what they believe."

"Christians ought to be able to separate the two, and take their own wants out of it."

"Perhaps they ought to be able to, but not many people can do that—even Christians."

"What about truth? Can there be something that's true down underneath everything? It seems like people ought to be trying to find it if there is."

"It always comes back to truth for you, doesn't it, Corrie?" Rev. Rutledge smiled.

"I think about it a lot. If a writer doesn't have a grasp of the truth, it doesn't seem like there's much to write about. At least that's how I've come to see it."

"Ever since that sermon I preached years ago about Jesus and Pilate."

"You sure got me started thinking with that one!"

"Yes, and apparently you haven't stopped since."

"That's another thing a writer's got to do—keep thinking."

"I'll take your word for it, not being a writer myself."

"It shouldn't be any different for a preacher."

"I suppose you're right."

Harriet came in with a tray of tea and cups. She served us, then sat down herself.

"Well, I don't care if people have always differed and argued, it seems to me that if there's such a thing as truth and right and wrong, Christians especially ought to feel the same about it. I don't understand how two people can both be Christians and believe the exact opposite. One thing can't be right and wrong at the same time. There's no sense to it!"

"Something like slavery?" asked the minister.

"Not just slavery, but that's as good an example as there is. Edie said that Abraham had slaves, and slavery is mentioned in the Ten Commandments, and then she said that according to the Bible, slavery is right. Almeda quoted the verse about being made free and then said that slavery went *against* the truths of the Bible. There they are—both Christians and yet saying the very opposite thing. Doesn't one of them have to be wrong? *Is* there a right and wrong about it?"

"Is it just slavery you're trying to understand, Corrie?" asked Harriet.

"No, I don't suppose it is," I answered. "I do have to decide if I'm going to write any articles about this election between Mr. Douglas and Mr. Lincoln. I suppose that comes down to the North-South dispute and the question of slavery in the end. But right now I'm trying to understand how two Christians can look at the same thing and see it so differently."

A silence filled the small room, and we all took a sip of our tea. I could tell Rev. Rutledge was thinking hard. That was one of the reasons I liked to talk to him, because he didn't give an answer until he had thought about it first.

"You're right about one thing, Corrie," he said at last. "There *has* to be such a thing as right and wrong. Otherwise the Bible and its whole message is meaningless. There has to be such a thing as truth, which is the opposite of falsehood."

"That's what I believe, too. Then why isn't it more clear?"

"Because people get in the way. They don't always see as clearly as they should. Their vision gets foggy and blurred, and then truth and right and wrong get muddled up in the process."

"Mixing in, like you said before, what they *want* to believe?"

"That's it exactly."

"Then if people are going by what they *want* to think instead of trying to get at what truth is, how do you ever get to the bottom of it? It seems like all you'd do is end up debating your different viewpoints."

"That's all most people do end up doing. To answer your question, if you're talking to a person who views things only through his *own* blurry vision of what he himself *wants* to be true, then you probably can't get to the bottom of a question like slavery. You just each tell the other what you think and leave it at that."

"But there we are back at the question I asked to begin with—how *do* you get at what the truth is if you don't know yourself and you want to talk to other Christians about it?"

"The first thing you have to do, I suppose, is talk and pray things over with people who also want to get down to the underneath layer, down to where truth is, even below what they themselves might want or not want. You can't get too far in a discussion unless you share that much at least."

"That's why I like to talk to the two of you," I said. "I know you want to get to things down at that level just like I do."

"I hope I do," sighed Rev. Rutledge. "But it's difficult, Corrie. Every one of us has personal biases and preferences and wants and tendencies that we can't ever escape. Laying those down, even for the sake of trying to find truth, is not an easy thing to do. I constantly try to put *myself* in the background so I can be on the lookout for something deeper."

He paused, but then went on after a moment.

"There is another way of looking at it too, Corrie," he said. "There are two different kinds of truth you can be looking for. Or perhaps I should say two different kinds of right and wrong."

"I don't quite understand that, but I'll keep listening," I said.

He laughed. "Let me see if I can explain it. I've only been thinking this through recently myself. First, there's the kind of right and wrong that's absolute, that's clear in the Bible. It's always the same, it's the same for everybody in every situation. There's no variation to it. Right is right and wrong is wrong. Lying is like that—it's always wrong. Murder, stealing, hatred—those things are always wrong. And of course, in the same way there are right things too that are *always* right, true things that are *always* true. It is true that God made the world. It is true that Jesus Christ lived and died for our sins. It is true that man cannot live meaningfully apart from God. It is true that people are supposed to treat one another with kindness and love. All those things are true no matter what anyone says. If somebody says differently—that God didn't make the world or that it's all right to be cruel—then he would be wrong. These are the kinds of things I call 'absolute' truth or 'absolute' right and wrong. There's no question about them."

"I understand all that. Then, what's the second kind?"

"Well, that's the one I've been wrestling through in my own mind lately. I haven't come up with a good name for it yet. It has to do with things that *aren't* absolute, where the Bible *doesn't* necessarily give a clear view on it, or maybe doesn't say anything at all about it. For example, is it *right* for your father to be mayor of Miracle Springs?"

"I hope so!" I said.

"So do I. And I think it is. But do you remember how the whole thing came about? It was Almeda who got involved first, and yet in the end she decided it was the wrong thing for her to do. You see, running for mayor isn't something you can say is right *or* wrong. It might be either."

"Almeda didn't think it was what God wanted for her."

"Exactly. Because of that it would have been wrong for her to do it, yet at the same time it could be *right* for your father."

"The same thing being right and wrong all at the same time. That could get a mite confusing."

"Once I started looking around, I found so many examples of this I'd never noticed before. Is rain a good or a bad thing? Both. It depends on the situation. Too much and you have a flood, too little and there's a drought. Is it right or wrong for a young lady to be a journalist? It might be either, depending on whether God wanted her to be or not."

I smiled.

"Harriet and I, of course, think that God *has* led you all along the way you've come, and we are very proud of you. That was just an example."

"I see."

"Personal decisions, like writing or being a mayor, are easy enough to see. But there are all kinds of things in the Bible that aren't black and white either. Does everybody come to God in the same way? Is there a *right* form of salvation? Those kinds of questions are very perplexing to a man in my occupation, as you can imagine. Nicodemus came to Jesus by night and the Lord told him about being born again. Paul was blinded by a great light. God spoke to Moses in a bush. Timothy and St. Mark grew up under believing parents. So many differences! There may not be any question about murder, stealing, and lying. But what about all the deep things St. Paul wrote about in his letters? There are so many interpretations about what he meant. Does hell last forever? Will we know each other in heaven as we do now? Is the devil a real being? What does it mean to be dead to sin? Oh, Corrie, you can't imagine all the questions and issues ministers get involved talking and thinking about where there are no clear biblical answers!"

"What do you do to keep from getting confused?" I asked.

Rev. Rutledge laughed loudly. "I *don't* keep from getting confused!" he said. "I talk to my wife, and we both get more confused than ever!"

They both laughed.

"You see, Corrie," Rev. Rutledge went on in a minute, "as long as you keep a balanced perspective on such things, you can't go too far wrong. I am aware that I don't know too much about heaven and hell. But I am perfectly content not to know, because I realize we're not supposed to know such things perfectly. God didn't make them clear in the same way he made lying and stealing and murder clear. Some things are supposed to be absolute, others aren't. Where people go wrong is in adopting some personal view on one of the non-absolute things, and then saying that people who disagree with them are wrong."

"So if we were talking about heaven," I said, "I might say, 'I think we'll know each other there,' and you might say, 'I don't think we'll know each other there,' but neither of us could say the other one was wrong."

"We could say that we disagreed, but we couldn't know absolute right or wrong about it because the Bible doesn't make it clear."

"Hmm . . . that is interesting," I said. "Then it comes down to whether a certain question is absolute, like lying and stealing; or not absolute, like being mayor or what heaven will be like."

"That's what it comes down to, all right—what things fit into which category. That's where most people go wrong and start arguing with other people—they assume *their* views are more absolute than someone else's."

"But there *are* absolutes where someone *is* right and someone *is* wrong?"

"Yes. And on such issues Christians must not waver from the truth. But on all the other wide range of things, we have to give each other freedom to think without criticizing."

A long pause followed. Finally I spoke up again.

"Which kind of question do you think slavery is?" I asked. "Is it right or wrong in an absolute way, and everybody ought to feel the same about it? Or is it right for the South but maybe wrong for the North, and each side ought to respect the other's view?"

"Ah, Corrie, you've landed right in the middle of the hornet's nest with that question!"

"The whole future of the country may depend on the answer," I insisted.

"That may well be, which is why slavery is such a divisive issue. Of course, I personally find the very notion of slavery abhorrent, contrary to everything I see mirrored in the life of Jesus. Yet . . . I know there are Christians, and ministers, in the South who do not see it so. The Baptists, the Methodists, and the Presbyterians have already split over the question, their southern factions believing just as strongly *in* the validity of slavery as their northern counterparts believing it is wrong."

"How can that be?" I said in frustration, back again to the original quandary that had brought me to the Rutledges in the first place.

"People on both sides heatedly and righteously consider it an absolute issue with an absolute right and truth at the bottom of it—their *own*! Neither side will admit to anything except that the other side is absolutely in the wrong."

"What do you think? Is slavery one of the absolute issues, where there *is* a positive right and a positive wrong?"

A long silence followed. At last Rev. Rutledge exhaled a long sigh. I could tell he had already thought long and hard on the very question I had posed but without coming any nearer a conclusion than I had.

"I wish I knew, Corrie," he said almost wearily. "I truly wish I knew." Again he paused, then added, "And I fear for our country unless God somehow reveals *his* mind on the matter to large groups of people on both sides . . . and soon."

*I*n spite of his activity with Tad, Pa could not help but be weighed down by Zack's leaving and by the angry words he himself had spoken. Both Almeda and I knew him well enough to see that beneath the surface he was struggling hard to come to terms with what had happened.

A few days later I found him alone on the far side of the corral checking a hoof on one of the ponies. I walked up behind him.

"Made any decision about Sacramento, Pa?" I asked.

He slowly set the pony's foot back down onto the dirt, then straightened up. The weary and downcast look on his face made him seem ten years older than he was. The loose shoe was the furthest thing from his mind.

"Sacramento?" he repeated, forcing a slight chuckle. "To tell you the truth, Corrie, I hadn't hardly thought about it for a week. What about you? Got any idea what you aim to do yet?"

"No," I shrugged. "I've been thinking about it, but I don't suppose I'm any closer to knowing what God wants me to do than when we came back from San Francisco."

"I reckon getting away from all the hubbub of the city does slow the pace a mite. I suppose that's why I like it here.

I couldn't abide living in no city. That's one thing I think I've decided. Whatever comes, I don't aim to leave Miracle. Zack's right about one thing. I was a fool to leave the only other home I ever had."

"He didn't say that, Pa."

"He didn't have to say those words. He may as well have said it. And even if he didn't say it, it's true anyhow, and I don't intend to make the same mistake twice. I've got a home now, and I'm gonna keep it, even if it means I turn my back on everything any other man would give his eyeteeth for. No, I don't suppose I've thought about it much, but I don't reckon there's much else to do now but say no."

"Zack's just all mixed up now, Pa," I said. "You can't plan your whole future on one outburst."

"It goes a lot deeper than just the other day, Corrie. Couldn't you tell? It had been building up inside the boy for years, and I never knew it. I don't know how I could have been such a blind fool!"

He turned away and leaned over the rail fence. I knew what he was fighting against. I walked toward him and laid my hand gently on his shoulder. He didn't say anything, and after a minute I pulled away, then climbed up and sat down on the top rail of the fence, looking up toward the mine.

"Doesn't seem to me like you ought to blame yourself, Pa," I said after a minute or two.

"How can I not blame myself? Don't seem like there's anybody else I can rightly blame."

"He'll cool off and come back, Pa."

"I ain't so sure, Corrie. You saw that look in his eye. He was determined. And it's sure he's not just a kid anymore. I got a feeling we might not see him for a spell."

"Are you afraid for him?"

"No, that ain't it."

"Like you said, he's not a kid. He's old enough to take care of himself. He's been away before, just like I have. You never seemed too worried about me, and Zack's a man."

"I'm not worried about him, Corrie. Sure, I know Zack's every bit the man I was at his age. He's made of better stuff inside, too. But I can't help feeling a heap of guilt for the things he said. I haven't been the pa to him I should have been. He's right about me running out on you kids and your ma. My life isn't one to be altogether proud of. The boy's got every right to hate me. I deserve it."

He stopped and let out a long sigh.

"But even when he said what he did," Pa went on, "telling me how he'd hurt and saying nothing but what was the truth about me, like a blame fool I just got angry at him. . . ."

Finally Pa's voice broke slightly at the memory of the blow he had given his son.

"God, oh, God . . . how could I?" he said in a more forlorn tone than I'd ever heard. "Telling him I'd take the belt to him! No wonder he was mad. He had a right to be. How could I have been so blind all this time to what he was feeling and thinking?"

He stopped. It was quiet for a minute, Pa breathing in deeply, but kind of unsteadily.

"Zack was always one to keep things inside, more than me, Pa," I said. "When we first came here, he was trying to be more a man than he was. Then he took to hanging around you and Uncle Nick all the time, wanting to be grown up."

"He did grow up too," said Pa. "I don't know why I didn't let him know better how I felt about him."

"You tried, Pa."

"Not enough. But a man just gets so busy and involved with his *own* affairs that he doesn't even know what his kids are thinking. They grow up so blamed fast; suddenly they're adults and they're holding things inside them that you done. But there's no way you can go back and make it right to them."

He paused a moment, then looked up at me earnestly.

"You got anything you're holding inside about anything I've done or said, Corrie?" he asked. "It'd kill me to find out something I oughta know but not find out till it's too late."

"I don't think so, Pa," I answered with a smile. "Nothing I know of at least. You've been about the finest pa a girl could have, and I love you, Pa."

He looked away. There were tears in his eyes, both from what I'd said and from the hurt over Zack.

"Pa," I said, "I feel bad, too. I was guilty of taking Zack for granted myself. I figured Zack felt just like I did about being a Christian, but maybe he had a more independent streak in him than I did. You and I talked about your past, and you confided in me and we prayed together. I suppose I was able to put it behind me more than he did. It made me love you more, but I guess people can react to the same situation in opposite ways, and so what drew me closer to you, he resented. It's not your fault. You can't lash out at yourself for Zack's holding things against you."

"If he had a right to . . . if it was for mistakes I made."

"You said it yourself, Pa—he's grown up now, just like I have, and so he's got to be responsible himself for his reactions. That's part of growing up too, it seems to me."

"Maybe you're right. But how does a man keep from feeling guilty over not giving his own son all of him he might have?"

Neither of us had seen Almeda walking slowly toward us as we'd been talking. She came closer and heard the last of Pa's question. He glanced up, then reached out his hand and drew her toward him.

"Still wrestling with Zack, Drummond?" she said.

Pa sighed and nodded his head. I knew they'd talked a lot about it already.

The three of us were silent for a while; then Almeda began to pray softly. "Oh, Father," she said, "I ask for a special pouring down of your grace for my husband. Comfort his father's heart and ease his pain over his son."

She stopped. There was nothing else to pray. Her simple words had expressed what both of us were feeling right then toward Pa. I was praying silently myself, not knowing what I could say. Then to my surprise I heard Pa's voice.

"God," he prayed in a raspy, quiet voice, "watch over my son. Wherever he is right now, take care of him. Even if he doesn't think I care about him, Lord, show him that you care for him. And if you can, help him to see that I do too. Bring him back to us safe, Lord."

"Amen," Almeda added softly.

Again it was silent for a while. At last Pa and Almeda headed off toward the creek, Pa's arm still around her shoulder, talking softly together.

*T*he summer progressed. July was hotter than June. August was hotter than July. We heard no word from Zack.

"What are you gonna do, Corrie?" Pa asked me one day at breakfast. "That paper of yours is getting fuller and fuller of election news all the time, and I still haven't seen your name in it anywhere."

"Are you going to write for Lincoln or Douglas?" asked Tad around a mouthful of warm biscuit.

"She wouldn't support a Democrat," said Becky. "You'd never go against Mr. Fremont's party, would you, Corrie?"

All summer, Katie and Edie had kept political issues stirred up to such an extent that even Becky and Tad were aware of what was happening. We'd managed to stay clear of any arguing about it again, although Edie and Almeda kept a cool distance from each other because of their strong views on the two opposite sides of the slavery question. I'd never really thought much about Almeda being a "northerner" before. But even ten years in California couldn't take the Bostonian out of her, any more than Edie's recent trip west could take the Virginian out of her.

"I don't know, Becky," I answered. "I suppose I might be able to support a Democrat someday if he was the right man.

But not this year. As far as I can see, Mr. Lincoln's the best man to be president."

"Then why don't you write an article saying so and send it in to Kemble?" asked Pa.

"I'm still a little confused over how Christians can feel so differently about the same thing."

"They do, though, so why don't you just jump into it and give 'em *your* two cents' worth?"

"What if I'm not right?"

"Do you have to be right to speak your mind?"

"It seems like if I'm going to advise people what to do, and tell them how they ought to feel and how they ought to vote, then I *have* to be right. I couldn't do it otherwise."

"Do you still have doubts about how you feel, Corrie?" asked Almeda.

I thought for a while. "No, I don't suppose I do," I answered finally. "I guess down inside I *do* think I know that slavery is wrong. It's just knowing whether I'm supposed to say that in public, and tell people they ought to vote for Mr. Lincoln—that's the thing I'm still unsure about."

"How are you going to know that?" asked Pa.

"I guess I'm waiting for some sign from the Lord, something that tells me he's urging me one way or the other. You've always said to me, Almeda," I said, turning toward her, "that when in doubt about what to do, it never hurts to wait."

"God never will discipline us for going too slowly." Almeda smiled. "I've had to learn that the hard way. We can get ourselves into plenty of trouble by going too fast, but not from holding back waiting for God's guidance."

"What kind of a sign, Corrie?" asked Tad. "Is God gonna say something to you in a dream or something?"

I laughed. "I don't know, Tad. I doubt it. Just circumstances, probably. I feel like I know what's right, and even
what I'd like to do. But I also feel like I need to wait until
he brings something to me, rather than me going out to do
something myself."

"Well, I hope he does it pretty soon," said Pa. "If you wait
much longer without making up your mind, the election's
gonna come and go and leave you behind altogether."

"If that happens, then I'll just figure I wasn't supposed to
do anything in the first place, and everything will be fine."

After breakfast I decided to saddle up Raspberry and go
for a long ride. Somehow the day reminded me of the one
more than two years earlier when I had ridden up to the top
of Fall Creek Mountain on my twenty-first birthday. It had
been a while since I had a good long ride, and somehow the
questions at breakfast put me in a reflective mood.

The sun was well up as I headed off east, and the earth
was already warming up fast. I never got tired of the smell of
sugar pines under the beating of the sun's rays. Especially if
there'd been rain anytime recently, and the earth underneath
a bed of fallen pine needles was moist, the fragrance of the
warming dirt, the dead leaves and needles and cones, and the
live breathing trees were to me the very smell of heaven itself.

It hadn't rained today, of course, because it was the first
week of August, but the smell was almost as wonderful. The
rugged, rough-textured bark of the trees, cracked and splitting,
oozed the translucent sticky pitch that ran up and down the
trunks. It was precious to me, as were all things of the forest, as
indications of the fingerprints of God when he made the world.

I had been thinking for a year or more about the first
chapter of Romans, and found myself almost daily awakening

to its truth, that God's invisible being really was clearly visible and obvious in everything around me—that is, if I had eyes to see him.

The world tells us what God is like. But most folks don't take that truth deep enough to allow the world to really speak actively to their hearts and minds about God's character. I found myself forgetting it sometimes, too. At such times, the world around me only spoke quietly, not with the vibrant reality that the bark was speaking to me today about his creativity.

More and more I thought that God intends for the world to really *speak* to us—loudly, constantly, every day. I believed that God means for our surroundings to be a very close-up way of us getting information about him. The world God made with his own hands should speak to us just as directly and actively as the words of Jesus himself.

As I rode through the woods and meadows, I found all these thoughts running through my mind as they had many times before. I found myself thinking about the barn back at home, and how much it could tell a stranger about Pa, if that stranger took it upon himself to look past the surface appearances of things—how orderly Pa kept his tools, how he lined up the spare saddles, the stables, the feeding troughs, the wagon and buggy, the loft for hay and straw. To a casual observer, none of these things would be especially noticeable. But since I had heard Pa talk about why he had done such and such and question aloud how he should build this part or where he ought to put that, I saw evidences of Pa's personality everywhere as I looked around the barn.

I saw Almeda's personality at home and in her office at the Mine and Freight in town, too—how she kept her desk, the pictures on the walls, the books in the bookcase, how she organized the whole business. She was *there,* just as Pa was in the barn—even if neither of them happened to be there in person. The barn, the office, the house—they all reflected both characters and personalities because they had put so much of themselves *into* them, maybe even without knowing it.

In the same way, the whole world is like God's office, his barn, the room where he lives. His desk and walls and rooms are full of things that are shouting about the person he is. It's up to us to try to discover what those characteristics of his personality are. Every tiniest detail of the universe is full of energetic life.

The bear and the ant *both* reflect the God who made them—the bear, his power and magnificence; the ant, his energy and productivity and unceasing labor.

The sun and the moon *both* are pictures of God—the heat and brightness and life-sustaining force of the sun, and the reflected light that God's being is able to give, even in the darkness when the fullness of his presence is turned away for a time.

The world could no more keep quiet about the nature of God than could Pa's barn or Almeda's office about them. The world is shouting at us, so loudly that in most people's ears it sounds like silence. The thunder of his voice is so huge and so deep that it rumbles past them in awesome silence. They hear nothing.

I reined Raspberry in, slowed to a stop, then dismounted. I hadn't gone far, probably not more than an hour from home, not nearly as far up into the mountains as I had that day two years before.

Most of the ground was brown under the scorching summer's sun. Where snow had lain six months earlier, now the dirt was hard-packed, with dried mountain grasses blowing gently in the rising breeze. Among the trees all was still and quiet. The only sounds were those of the birds overhead and the buzzing of bees and flies and other tiny flying creatures.

I left Raspberry tethered to a pine branch and walked through a thicket of trees into an open meadow. I felt full, happy, overflowing with life. Thinking about God all the way up as I had ridden had filled me with a sense of how good he had been to me.

Suddenly I found myself running . . . running across the grass as fast as I could, running toward nowhere, but urged on by a feeling inside I could not keep back. I wanted to scale the heights of the hills under my feet, I wanted to run and climb to the peaks of the world, I wanted to shout and sing and laugh and cry all at once!

On I ran, my heart pounding, my legs beginning to tire. But the weariness just made me want to run all the more! I wanted to exhaust myself, to run until I dropped!

At last I could not go another step.

I lifted my hands into the air and threw my head back, gazing upward into the empty expanse of blue. Two or three white, billowing clouds hung there in the midst of it, lazily working their way across the sky. I felt great throbbing prayers inside me, yet I had no words to say. There was only a sense that God was nearby, and even that he was looking down on me right then. A closeness came over me that I had never felt before, as if his great arms of love were wrapping themselves around me, even as I stood there all alone in the middle of that meadow, hands held upward toward the sky.

Slowly I dropped my hands back to my sides and turned around and began walking down the way I had run. I was crying, although I did not know when the tears had begun to flow.

I don't think I'd ever been happier in my life than in that moment. I *knew* God my Father was with me, that he loved me, that his tender arms were about me, and that I was his.

"God," I said softly, "I want nothing more than to be your daughter . . . to be completely yours. Oh, God—take away from me any other ambitions or motives or desires than just to let you be my Father every moment. Let me be content that you care for me, as content as I am right now."

All at once the prayers that I hadn't been able to pray a few moments earlier began to bubble up out of me in an endless spring. Thoughts and prayers and feelings tumbled together from out of my heart and mind. Such a desire swept through me to be nothing more, to do nothing more, than what God himself wanted for me. Any anxieties I may have had over the future or what to do vanished. I *knew* God would direct my pathway, as one of my favorite proverbs promised.

I felt so thankful, so appreciative to God for all he had done for me—for the love of life, for the sense of his presence with me, for the peacefulness he had given me. What poured out of me was unspoken thankfulness, and a calm knowing that he *would* direct my steps, that he would keep my life in his hands, and that he would show me what I was to do and when.

I rode Raspberry back toward town and arrived at the house sometime shortly after noon. My spirit was still calm, and I could not have been more unprepared for the surprise that awaited me the moment I walked in the door of the house.

There, talking to Pa, sat Cal Burton!

The Invitation

CHAPTER SEVENTEEN

*I*nside, my knees went weak, and a lump shot up from somewhere down in my stomach up to my throat. Flushed from the exercise of the ride, I knew my face went immediately pale. A faintness swept over me, even as Pa jumped up the moment he saw me come in.

"Look who's here from San Francisco, Corrie!" he said.

I hardly needed Pa to point it out to me! Even in my state of perturbation, I knew well enough who it was!

I took his hand, feeling a slight tremble go through me at the touch, and said, "Mr. Burton . . . but I don't understand . . . what are you doing here?" Never had my voice sounded so high and squeaky! And I had never sounded so stupid in all my life.

He laughed. "I know it must come as a surprise, and I apologize for coming all this way to see you without warning."

"Don't say another word about it," Pa said boisterously. "You're welcome anytime, with or without warning. Out this far from the city we don't stand too much on ceremony."

As Pa was responding to Mr. Burton's apology, I immediately decided that he had come to see Pa. It must have something to do with them wanting him to run for the legislature in Sacramento.

"So are you going to do it, Pa?" I said, turning to him.

"Do what?"

"Run for the legislature."

"What are you talking about, Corrie Belle? What's me running for office got to do with anything?"

"Isn't that what you two were talking about?"

"I don't know where you got a notion like that," laughed Pa. "We were just sitting here passing the time till *you* got back."

The blank look of confusion on my face must have been more humorous than I intended it to be because both men laughed.

"I'm sorry," said Mr. Burton. "I was speaking to you a moment ago, not your father. It's *you* I came all this way to see."

My heart fluttered all over again! "Me?" I squeaked. "What would you want to see me for?"

Pa laughed again. He was really enjoying my discomfort! "Corrie, you just go get yourself a drink of water, then come and sit down with us. Cal here's got to talk to you."

I did as Pa said, and a minute or two later the three of us were seated.

I glanced from one to the other of them. Mr. Burton spoke first.

"What I came for, Corrie," he said, "was to ask you again, on behalf of Mr. Dalton in San Francisco, if you would consider helping us with the Lincoln campaign."

I stared back blankly at him.

"I have been thinking about it," I said finally. "But I just hadn't decided yet what I ought to do."

"Mr. Dalton thought you might not have taken his words seriously before, and he felt a personal visit from me might

persuade you. Let me assure you, he was quite serious. He
. . . we all, that is, would very much like you to be part of the
Republican campaign team."

The color began coming back into my cheeks. I didn't
know what to think!

"What . . . what would I do?"

"We were sure you'd ask that. I've already spoken to
your editor, Mr. Kemble, about your writing a couple articles
in favor of Mr. Lincoln from a woman's point of view. Then
we would like to include you among the speakers at a public
assembly to be held in Sacramento four days from now. A
woman has never addressed such a gathering, in this campaign at least, and Mr. Dalton feels you could have a great
influence. My instructions were to convince you to say yes,
and to bring you back to Sacramento with me."

I sat staring, trying to take in his words.

"Don't just sit there, Corrie," Pa said finally. "The man's
talking to you."

"I . . . I don't know what to say," I stammered.

"Say the only thing you can say, Corrie," said Mr. Burton.
"I was instructed not to take no for an answer. The Republican party will pay your coach fare and put you up in a nice
hotel. The trip won't cost you a cent."

"Well, I have been praying about what to do."

"And do you have reservations?"

"No, not exactly."

"Then it's all settled."

"I'll have to talk to my mother and father," I said.

"Of course. I understand." He rose and shook Pa's hand.
"I'm going to ride back into town. I'm supposed to see the
banker Royce for Carl, and I'll be at the boardinghouse if you

should need me. Otherwise, perhaps I'll drop back by later this afternoon."

"And join us for supper," suggested Pa.

"But, your wife. . . ?" hesitated Mr. Burton.

"My wife will be delighted when I tell her," insisted Pa. "Now it's my turn not to take no for an answer!"

They both laughed, and it was agreed.

Embarrassment Enough to Last a Lifetime

CHAPTER EIGHTEEN

I had been praying about it, like I'd said. But now that the moment of decision had come and I was face-to-face with it, I felt nervous and uncertain all over again. Of course, how much of that had to do with the election and how much had to do with Cal Burton himself, it was impossible for a twenty-three-year-old girl like me to know.

I couldn't help being a little taken with him. He was just about the finest-looking man a girl like me'd ever set eyes on. And so nice—how could I keep from liking him?

As much as I tried to concentrate on things like the election and what I ought to do as a writer, my mind kept filling up with Cal Burton. I wanted to say yes just because of him. All kinds of doubts would rise up, reminding me that I wasn't pretty, that a man like him would never look twice at me. I'd take to looking in a mirror and fiddling with my hair without even realizing I was doing it. When I suddenly woke up to the fact that I was daydreaming the day away, I could hardly stand what I saw in the glass and would turn away in disgust.

One time Pa chanced by the open door of my room and saw me standing there like an idiot, turned sideways, looking at myself. I caught his reflection in the mirror as he walked by, mortified to have him see me like that. I got so flushed my skin burned, and I turned away from the mirror and ran outside. Pa never said a word, but he knew well enough what I was thinking about.

All the rest of that day I wandered about in a daze, trying to concentrate, trying to pray, trying to be rational about it. But it was useless. I'd never figured myself to be overly emotional as women were sometimes said to be. I thought my head was sitting pretty level on my shoulders.

But after this day I didn't know! As close as I'd felt to God that very morning, suddenly he might as well have been a thousand miles away. I couldn't stand it, but I couldn't help it either.

I had to talk to Almeda! But when she got back from town about an hour after Mr. Burton had left, I couldn't get up the gumption to tell her. I had always talked to her about everything, but this was different. I couldn't help being embarrassed for how I was feeling.

Cal Burton came back some time between four and five in the afternoon. I was wandering around aimlessly near the corral when I heard his rented buggy approaching. I had been working in the garden and rubbing Raspberry down, and I was positively filthy from head to foot. I quickly ran into the barn, hoping he wouldn't see me. He reined in the horses in front of the house and went inside. I watched the house for a few minutes from one of the barn windows, being careful to keep out of sight.

A little later, the door opened and Pa and Mr. Burton came out. They were talking away like old friends. Pa really seemed to like Mr. Burton. It was the happiest I'd seen him since Zack left.

Suddenly I realized they were heading straight for the barn! I jumped back from the window and hurriedly ran back into the back part of the building where it was darkest, frantically trying not to make any noises that would give me away. I was just crouching down behind two bales of hay in the far corner of the barn when I heard Pa and Mr. Burton enter by the opposite door. I held my breath and hoped the hay didn't make me sneeze!

"Corrie!" I heard Pa's voice call out. "Corrie . . . you in here?"

A brief silence followed.

"Blamed if she wasn't around just a few minutes ago," I heard Pa say. I thought I heard his footstep coming nearer. He *had* to know where I was! It would be awful if they found me like I was! What would I say? But I hadn't answered Pa's call, so now there was nothing I could do but make *sure* they didn't see me!

Silently I hunched down even more, lowering my face into my dress so if any part of me did show, at least my hair would blend in with the hay and straw around me. Why had I hidden? Now I was really in a pickle!

I heard Pa's footsteps going one way and the other, looking about. "Corrie!" he called out again. I felt like such a deceiver for not answering, but I couldn't make myself say anything now!

Pretty soon they turned and headed back out. "Can't imagine where she went," Pa said. "But come on, Cal, I'll show you the mine, and take you up to see my brother-in-law. Corrie'll be along soon enough. The two of you can talk about your business later."

These last words were faint, because by now they were outside and walking up the stream toward the mine. Slowly I crept out of my hiding place and tiptoed toward the window. I peeked carefully around the edge of it. There they were, thirty yards away, their backs to me, in animated conversation, Pa seemingly telling him all about the mining operation, which Mr. Burton seemed interested in by his questions and gestures.

I stepped back inside the barn and breathed a big sigh of relief. Then first it struck me what I must look like. I was sweating like a horse, my hair was all messed up and hanging all over everywhere, my dress was dirty and had pieces of straw and hay stuck to it all over. I was a mess! Whether I was pretty or not, I was certainly in no condition to meet a man like Cal Burton!

I sneaked back to the window and peeked around the edge. There they still were, almost at the mine now. I needed to go clean up, but I was dying to know what they were saying! What if they were talking about me?

Pa turned and led the way toward the creek. They crossed the bridge and in another minute were out of sight, walking through the trees toward Uncle Nick and Aunt Katie's. Without even thinking what I was doing, suddenly I left the barn and hurried after them, keeping out of sight behind trees and brush, just in case one of them should glance back in my direction.

I made it all the way to the bridge, then stopped. I couldn't hear their voices any longer.

Quickly I ran across the bridge, then ducked out of sight off the pathway again. From there I slowly made my way through the trees toward the clearing, moving from tree to tree, glancing around to make sure no one else was coming who could see me. I slipped around behind the house. Everything was quiet, but I knew they were inside. I crept out from my hiding place and ran to the house, kneeling down behind one of the back windows.

I was safe there. Even if someone came to the window and looked out, they couldn't see me. That side of the house faced the forest, which was close by and generally darker than the front. I strained my ears to listen.

"All this way to talk to our future congressman, eh, Drum?" I heard Uncle Nick say.

"No, he didn't come to see me. I already told you, I'm not at all sure what I'm gonna do."

I heard a woman's voice next, either Aunt Katie's or Edie's.

"He came to see Corrie, of course," Pa answered whoever it was. "And to take her back to Sacramento with him."

Some exclamations went around, followed by some laughter. How mortifying. They *were* talking about me!

Uncle Nick must have made a joke, although I was glad I didn't hear it. Some more laughter and comments went around the room. "I'm sure Corrie will keep her head," said Katie.

Cal Burton was the next to speak. "It's all for the good of the party, I assure you," he said. "They genuinely want her involved, as they do her father, I might add. I promise to take good care of her."

"It's your chance to be a famous man, Drum," said Uncle Nick, going back to the subject of Pa's running for office.

"That's the last thing I want," said Pa. The laughter had faded from his voice, and I figured he might be thinking about all the things Zack had said. The conversation gradually subsided, and I couldn't hear everything. The next thing I did hear seemed to be Cal Burton talking to Aunt Katie and her sister. Edie had apparently said something about having recently come from the East.

"What's it been like there?" Mr. Burton asked her.

Edie laughed. Her voice had an edge to it just like Katie's, and I could hear her distinctly. "How do you mean?" she said. "Between my husband dying and political tensions, I can't say it was an altogether pleasant time for me before coming here."

"I suppose what I meant was more the weather, the scenery. It's been some time since I saw spring come out in that region, and your mentioning Virginia flooded me with memories."

"Why?" asked Katie, drawing into the conversation. "*You're* not from there, are you?"

"And *you* are working for the Republicans?" put in Edie in astonishment.

"You have to take the opportunities that come your way, you know."

I had hardly paused to consider why their three voices sounded so clear. With the next words Katie uttered I suddenly knew— they had been gradually moving closer to the window I was crouched below outside.

"Is it only me, or is it rather hot in here?" said Katie.

When I heard her hand on the window latch. I panicked and ran. But it was too late!

"Why Corrie Hollister," I heard behind me. "What in heaven's name are you doing out there?"

I stopped and turned, trying to look as though nothing was wrong. "Oh . . . I was just coming around the back of the house," I said lamely. "I heard you talking and couldn't help listening."

"Eavesdropping!" said Katie with pretended annoyance. "Shame on you, Corrie!"

There stood Cal Burton right behind Katie, along with Edie, looking out the window at me where I stood like the mooncalf I was! I was so glad the trees kept the light dim. I would have died for him to see me in the state I was in!

"Well, Corrie, don't just stand there," said Katie. "You were coming in, weren't you?"

"I . . . was . . . I mean I didn't want to—"

"Come on around to the door, Corrie," she insisted. "As I understand it, this man came all the way from the big city to see you."

I hastily tried to think of some way to squirm out of the awkwardness and get out of there. But by now Pa realized what the ruckus was about. He came outside as I walked slowly around the side of the house.

"Where you been, Corrie?" he said. "I've been looking high and low for you."

"Just around and about, Pa."

"Well, come on in. Cal's back."

"No, I have to go back home and take a bath before supper, Pa."

"At least come in and say hello."

"Oh, Pa, I'd rather—"

"Come in and be sociable a minute," interrupted Pa. "You can clean yourself up later."

I knew there was no way out of it, so I sighed silently and went into the house with Pa. He may not have minded my dirty dress and mussed hair, but Uncle Nick wasn't about to miss the chance for kidding. For once I wished he'd have kept his humor to himself. Usually I didn't mind, but this time it hurt.

"Corrie Belle," he said, "you're a mess! You look like you just stepped out from wrestling with a dad-blamed hog!"

"Nick! Haven't you got any sense in your head?" Aunt Katie rebuked him sharply. "Now's not the time for saying such things."

I was grateful for Katie's standing up for me, especially since it gave me a quick second to blink back the tears.

"I think your niece looks just as nice as can be, Mr. Belle," said Cal Burton to Uncle Nick. Hearing his voice say such a thing took my breath away for an instant, and I almost forgot the mess I was in. "Hello again, Corrie," he added, turning to face me and holding out his hand.

I shook it, daring a quick glance up into his face. His eyes were looking straight at me. I glanced away almost as fast as I'd looked up.

"Honest, hard-working, robust beauty, Mr. Belle," he said, turning again to Uncle Nick. "Not the kind of thing you see too much in the city, you can take it from me. I'll take a handsome young lady from the country like this anytime!"

"Oh, Corrie," whispered Aunt Katie behind her hand, but loud enough so that she made sure everyone in the room heard her, "you better snatch up this fellow while you can! Men like that don't come along but once in a lifetime!"

Now my face *was* red! I couldn't stand it, being the center of everyone's talk. But everybody just stood there looking at me in my dirt-smeared dress. I could hardly keep the tears back now. It was awful to be stuck there like that!

"So, where have you been, Corrie," asked Pa, "to get such a mess all over you? We got a guest for dinner."

"I know, Pa," I said, trying to stay calm. "I was rubbing down Raspberry. I guess the time got going too fast for me." I wiped the back of my hand across my eyes.

Pa laughed. "You just smeared a streak of dirt across your forehead," he said. "Here," he added, reaching into his pocket for a handkerchief, "you can wipe it off with this."

Suddenly, without even realizing what I was doing, I spun around and ran for the door. I made for the woods as fast as I could, tears streaming down my cheeks.

*S*omehow I managed to get through the horrid day.

After a long cry I went back home, got water for a hot bath, with Almeda's help, and was probably halfway presentable by the time Pa and Cal Burton got back down from Uncle Nick's. Almeda and I talked a little, but I think both of us realized if we talked *too* much about what had happened, I'd start bawling like a baby all over again. So she just loved me as best she could, and let me take my bath and get dressed by myself.

Pa felt bad for what he'd done, I knew that. I did my best to look at him in a way that would tell him I didn't hold anything against him, and that I knew it was my own fault. I didn't want him to have to worry about anything he'd said to me on top of his heartache over Zack.

Cal Burton kept being just as nice as he could be all evening, treating me as if nothing out of the ordinary had happened at all. But I kept my eyes away from his. Down inside I was just too mortified over having behaved like a ridiculous little schoolgirl.

"So, Miss Hollister, what about going to Sacramento to work for Mr. Lincoln?" he asked.

"I've been thinking about it," I said, "but I haven't had the chance to talk with Pa and Almeda yet."

He smiled into my eyes—a smile that almost made me forget how foolish I'd been. "I understand," he said. "I can stay for another day at the boardinghouse in town, and we can discuss it again tomorrow." Then he and Pa spent most of the rest of the evening talking about politics. As interested as I'd been before, I just couldn't seem to concentrate on what they were talking about. I sat there silent the whole time, my mind muddled up with Mr. Burton's eyes, his smile, his deep resonant voice. Then I'd think about running out of Uncle Nick and Aunt Katie's that afternoon, with a dirty dress and crying, with everybody staring after me! It was a miracle I didn't cry again just thinking about it! I did shed a few more tears later, though, lying in bed trying desperately to go to sleep and put the day behind me at last.

I felt just as stupid the next morning, but at least a night's sleep put some distance between the present and my inane behavior. The sun shining into my room helped cheer my spirits somewhat. Besides, whatever I felt like, I had to make a decision about what to do.

I got dressed and walked out. Almeda was just taking the water for Pa's coffee off the stove. I walked toward her. She put the kettle down and drew me to her in a warm embrace. We stood there for a long time without saying a word. I wrapped my arms tightly about her waist and buried my face in her neck. It felt so good to know I was loved no matter what I did!

"What should I do, Almeda?" I said finally, slowly pulling away from her and sitting down.

"About yesterday, or about going to Sacramento?"

"I don't think there's *anything* I can do about yesterday!" I laughed halfheartedly. "No, I mean, should I go?"

"What are you feeling about it?"

"After yesterday it's hard to know. I thought I had things more or less worked out about the election. I was even beginning to look forward to writing something. Now I'm confused again."

"Do you feel the Lord prompting you to go?"

"Oh, I don't know!" I wailed in frustration. "I can't even concentrate enough to pray or to ask the Lord what to do! I don't know why, but it seems like a big decision. I have the feeling that whatever I decide, the results will be with me a long time, maybe for the rest of my life. But God might as well be a thousand miles away for any feeling I have of his presence."

"Do you think he really *is* a thousand miles away, Corrie?" Almeda asked.

"No, I know he hasn't gone anywhere. You've taught me better than that. I know you can't depend on your feelings. God is near, he is still with me—I know that. I just don't feel him, that's all."

Almeda smiled. "I'm so glad to hear you say that, Corrie," she said. "It doesn't concern me to hear you say the Lord seems distant as long as you know he *really* is still right beside you."

"I know it, at least in my head," I answered. "But not feeling him, not hearing his voice anywhere makes a decision that much harder. How can I *know* what his will is?"

"Could he be speaking to you in ways you're not used to?"

"How do you mean?"

"God doesn't always speak to us by giving us a strong urging or compelling to do something. The older we grow as Christians, the more he actually may *not* give us those strong inward voices telling us what he wants us to do."

"Why is that?"

"I have an idea," Almeda answered. "But it's only my own personal theory, nothing I've found in the Bible or anywhere." She gave a little laugh. "So if I answer your question, you can't hold me to it if someday the Lord shows us I'm wrong."

"Agreed," I said.

"Okay, here it is." She paused, took a breath, then launched in. "When we're young, either in age or young as a Christian, there are many things we don't know. Young people have to learn about life. And when you decide to give your heart to the Lord, there are many, many things you have to learn about what life with him is like. The Lord has to tutor us, for a while, helping us learn new habits, new attitudes, new ways of looking at things. He has to train us spiritually. He has to teach us to stand, then walk, then move forward as Christians. In the same way that a parent has to train a child in the ways of life in the world, our Father has to train us in the ways of life in his kingdom. Until we get our spiritual bearings, that training has to be very direct, very close, very personal. There is so much we don't know and that he needs to teach us."

She stopped, and a thoughtful look passed over her face. Then she laughed again.

"Oh, Corrie!" she said. "If you could have seen me that first year or two I was married to Mr. Parrish. There was so much I had to learn, not just about being a Christian, but about being a wife, about living a normal existence. Every day was a new learning experience!

"You see, that's what I am getting at. Both my heavenly Father and Mr. Parrish together contributed to that remaking process in me. But eventually I did change. Eventually I learned the new ways. And now, after all these years, I am truly an altogether new and changed person. I have matured in many ways. As a Christian, as a daughter of God, although he is still with me always—inside my heart and right beside me—I no longer require the same kind of training I did back then. I am God's daughter, but I am also a grown woman. I think God treats me in many cases like an adult rather than a child. Whereas, at first he had to show me *everything,* and had to take my hand and literally guide me through every step of life, he doesn't have to do that anymore. He has trained me, and in the same way that a parent gradually releases a child to walk on his own, I think God begins to release us—not to walk independently of him, but to walk beside him as he has shown us without his having to direct every single move we make. In obedience to him, we walk along the path he has given us to walk, without having to stop to consider every step. Does that make sense?"

"I think so," I said.

"It's very difficult to explain what I mean," Almeda went on. "I don't mean to sound as though I think I want to walk independently, or that I think God isn't there with every step I take. I do try to bring him into all aspects of my life, even more than I did at the beginning. But the more we mature as Christians, the more of our decisions he leaves in *our* hands—knowing that we are walking along the road he has placed us in, and according to the ways and habits and attitudes that he has trained into us."

"In other words," I said, "he might be leaving part of the decision of what I should do in *my* hands?"

"Exactly. If he *didn't* want you to write, I am confident he would let you know it very clearly, and I am equally confident you would obey his voice. But since he *has* led you into writing in the past, I think he will very often let *you* make the decision yourself as to what specific things you write about. He may give you a stronger sense of leading at some times than others. But there will also be times when he will trust you to go either way when you're facing a particular decision, and he will make *either* one work out for the best."

"Hmm . . . that is a new way to look at it."

"God is our Father, of course. We must look to him for *everything*. We can't breathe a single breath without him. We can't take a step without him. Yet it is one of the many paradoxes of the Christian life that he also entrusts to us a sort of partnership with him. As we walk along *with* him, keeping our hand tightly in his, it is as if he says to us, 'My son, my daughter, I have trained you and taught you and placed my life and spirit inside you. Now go . . . walk in the confidence of your sonship. I will always be at your side; if you err or misstep, my hand will be right there to help you up and guide you back into the middle of the path. But until then, walk on with the boldness that comes from having my Spirit inside you."

"Do you think that applies to big decisions too?" I asked. "Things like whether or not I should get involved in this election?"

"I think we always have to pray and ask the Father for his specific guidance," replied Almeda. "Then the time comes when we must make a decision."

"And if we don't seem to hear a definite answer?"

She thought a minute, then answered. "There are two ways, it seems to me, in which God can answer our prayers and direct us. He can open doors, or he can close doors. If we're standing still, facing a fork in the road, facing a decision to be made, he can either open a door going in one direction or close the door going in the other. Or, if we don't happen to see the fork, or don't see *any* possibilities clearly, it has always seemed best to me to keep moving and praying until he either opens or closes a door. I've even prayed something like this sometimes: 'Lord, I don't know for sure if this is the way you want me to go. It *seems* to be best right now, and I *think* this is what you want, so I'm going to keep moving cautiously ahead until you say otherwise. Please, Lord, if this is not what you want me to do, slam the door shut in my face.'"

"Is that what you did before the election four years ago?" I asked.

"I suppose it was something like that, although there was, as I now look back on it, an ample supply of my own wishful thinking involved in what I *thought* was God's leading. Yes, I thought I was going in the right direction, so I moved ahead. But then when God made some things clear in my thinking about my relationship with your father, I knew he was closing the door."

"And so maybe Cal Burton's coming like he has is the Lord's way of opening the door to what I've been in doubt about all this time."

"It wouldn't surprise me a bit," said Almeda.

"I've been thinking about Davy Crockett's saying, 'Be sure you're right, then go ahead.' Maybe I've been expecting the Lord to be more direct than he wants to be."

"There's wisdom in that motto," said Almeda. "Yet on the other hand, we don't always have the luxury of being absolutely sure before we *have* to go ahead. In the absence of any positive leading by God, sometimes we have to launch out according to what circumstances seem to be saying, and prayerfully trust God to open and close doors as we go along."

Both of us were quiet a minute or two, until the door opened behind us and Pa walked in. Almeda glanced up, then her face fell.

"Oh, Drummond!" she exclaimed. "I'm afraid I let your coffee get cold."

"What'd you go and do a thing like that for, woman?" barked Pa, throwing me a wink.

"Corrie and I were talking. I'm sorry."

"Cold coffee from your hand is better than a hot cup from anyone else's," said Pa, walking to Almeda and giving her a kiss.

She handed him the cup. He took a long swallow, then nodded in satisfaction. "Yep . . . not bad at all!"

"So, what do you think, Corrie?" asked Pa. "You recovered from your embarrassing little runaround yesterday?"

"Oh, Pa, don't remind me!" I said. "Mr. Burton probably thinks I'm a complete ninny!"

"Don't bet on it, Corrie. I walked him out to his buggy last night and we chatted awhile. He thinks a lot of you. Seems like all them high-up fellas in Sacramento do."

"No more than they think of you, Pa," I said.

"Naw, Corrie. A man like me ain't that unusual. If I turn down their offer, they'll just get someone else. Who knows, maybe Franklin Royce'll run instead of me! But you—that's different! If you turn them down, who else are they going to get? Ain't too many young women like my daughter Corrie Belle around!"

"Cut it out, Pa," I said. "I was a complete fool yesterday, and you know it."

"Doesn't make me love you any less, or make me any less proud of you. So . . . you decided yet?"

"I don't know, Pa."

"Seems to me that Cal's coming with a direct invitation like he brought—seems like that's just exactly the sign from the Lord you were waiting for."

I glanced over at Almeda.

"An open door?" I suggested.

"Looks like one to me," said Pa, taking another drink of his coffee. "If you ask me, I say you oughta do it!"

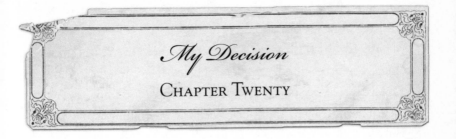

My Decision

CHAPTER TWENTY

I took Pa's advice.

I may have been twenty-three, but I still figured my pa was about as dependable a man as there could be. Even if he hadn't been my pa, I would have heeded his words. His being my father made it all the more important to listen to him and obey him as fully as I could. I'd had plenty of independence at times in the past, but the older I got, the more I found myself wanting to trust his way of looking at things.

Besides, I *wanted* to do it. I was interested in politics. I knew by now that I was against slavery, and that I did want Mr. Lincoln to win the election—maybe not as much as I had Mr. Fremont four years earlier, but enough to be able to speak out and tell folks that's how I felt.

So Pa's words gave me the nudge forward I needed—a nudge, as it turned out, that would make a mighty big difference in my life.

I left the next day on the midmorning stage south to Sacramento. Pa and Almeda and Becky and Tad took me to town to see me off. I was dressed in the traveling suit Almeda had Mrs. Gianini make for me. She said it would help to save my two fancy dresses for special occasions if I had something just to travel in. It was of dark brown patterned wool on the bottom, with a loose white muslin blouse with a short wool wraparound cape if it should be chilly.

When Cal Burton took my hand to help me up into the stage, I nearly wilted, even though my heart was pounding rapidly inside my chest. I tried not to show anything on my face, but sat down, then looked out at my family while Mr. Burton took the seat next to me. They were all smiling and waving and saying their farewells to me as if I were going to be gone a month instead of just four or five days.

"Don't you worry about a thing, Mrs. Hollister," Mr. Burton said through the open window. "I'll make sure your daughter is well taken care of."

"We stopped worrying about Corrie four years ago," laughed Pa, "when she took to gallivanting off all over California by herself on horseback!"

"What's this?" he said, glancing over at me.

"A long story," I answered.

"I want to hear about it. What is your father talking about?"

"The *last* time I got mixed up in an election," I said, laughing. "I hope this one turns out better than that."

The stage jerked into motion. I leaned outside again, and they all waved. I kept looking back, waving as we picked up speed down the main street of Miracle Springs. Something about this departure was different than any other before, even though I had gone a lot farther than Sacramento in the past. Probably the difference had something to do with the man sitting next to me inside the stagecoach.

As we pulled out of town and headed south, I could not keep from thinking of the awful scene after Aunt Katie discovered me outside her window, and wondering if Cal Burton

would say something about it. I didn't know *what* I was going
to talk to him about the whole way!

I shouldn't have worried. He treated me with complete
respect and kindness, never referred to the incident at Uncle
Nick's, and was so easy to talk with I soon forgot my nervousness and began to converse more freely than I imagined
possible with a relative stranger. He asked me about my involvement with the Fremont-Buchanan election, and I told
him about my adventures in Sonora and Mariposa, and what
had happened with my story in the end.

"I never could help feeling less important than the other
people around whenever I was in the city," I said. "And everything that happened back then only made it worse."

"From what I've heard, you've stood your ground against
Kemble more than once, and even made him back down a
time or two."

I couldn't keep from smiling at the memory.

"That doesn't sound like a timid country girl to me."

"I suppose you're right," I said. "I did do that. But down
inside, someone like me still can't help feeling kind of out of
place in a big city and around important goings-on. Like that
gathering in San Francisco that Pa and I went to in June."

"You seemed perfectly at ease to me."

"Oh no—I was so nervous!"

"Why?"

"I guess because I'm not used to all the big-city fancy ways.
I'm more at home on the back of a horse than in a frilly dress."

"You could have fooled me. You looked as elegant that
evening as any young woman I could imagine."

I blushed and glanced down at my lap. Nobody had ever
used the word *elegant* about *me* before! The very thought of

me being elegant would have made me laugh if I hadn't been
so embarrassed at the words.

"So tell me, did you ever get to meet the Fremonts after
all you tried to do on their behalf?" Mr. Burton asked.

"Yes. Ankelita Carter arranged for me to meet them when
they came to California after the election."

"I imagine they were very appreciative of your efforts."

"They were very nice to me," I said. "Jessie Fremont's a
writer too, and so she seemed interested in all I was doing."

"And Colonel Fremont?"

"He said he had mentioned my name to some of his
friends as someone to 'get on your side when the chips are
down.' I laughed at first and didn't think anything more
about it. But now I find myself wondering if it might be true,
after all."

"I imagine if Colonel Fremont said he told people about
Corrie Hollister, then he probably did exactly that. He and
Lincoln were talked about in connection with each other for
a while. You can never tell where your name might be getting
around. Kemble told me that just about everything you write
nowadays finds its way into print in the East. It must make
you very proud to have accomplished so much as a woman,
especially at such a young age."

"I guess I never really stopped to think about it," I said.
"It never crossed my mind to think that I had *accomplished*
anything."

"The women of this country would likely disagree. Someday they'll look back on you as a pioneer of a different kind
than Daniel Boone, and John Fremont when he first explored
the West."

"Me, a pioneer?" I said.

"Of course. You mark my words, the day will come when people will remember your name and be proud of you for what you did."

"Mr. Burton," I asked after a minute, "do you think it is because of something Mr. Fremont may have said that Mr. Dalton asked me to help with the election?"

"I never heard anything to that effect. It's possible, of course. But as influential as he was in helping to form the Republican party and make it a viable alternative to the southern Democrats, the party has begun to move in different directions than those of John Fremont himself. He does not have the influence he once did, as fond as you may be of him. Although you may not know it, your editor, Ed Kemble, thinks more highly of you than he probably lets on in your hearing. Word about Corrie Hollister has gotten around San Francisco and Sacramento without any help from John Fremont."

He paused, then looked over at me earnestly. "There is one other thing I have to reply to about your question," he said. "If we are going to be friends, as I hope we will, you are going to have to call me Cal. I'm only twenty-five. That can't be more than a year or two older than you. If I've taken the liberty to call you Corrie instead of Miss Hollister, the least you can do is drop the Mister."

"I'll try," I said shyly.

"If you ever meet my father, you can use Mr. Burton again. But not until then . . . agreed?"

"Agreed," I nodded with a smile.

A Ride Not to Forget

CHAPTER TWENTY-ONE

We rode for some time without talking again. Cal spoke to a man and woman in the opposite seat, who were on their way from Reno to Sacramento. They, too, had spent the night in Miracle Springs.

When he turned to me again, he seemed to have returned to the subject we had been discussing earlier. "Do you really feel ill at ease in the city, Corrie?" he asked.

"Just when I have to pretend I'm something I'm not," I answered.

"Why would you want to be other than you are?"

"I don't suppose I do. But when you're in the city, around people in fancy clothes who know how the city works and are doing important things, a country person like me can't help but feel that Robin O'Flaridy had it right all along when he said I was just a bumpkin from the sticks."

"O'Flaridy?"

"Never mind," I laughed.

"He really had the nerve to call you that?"

"Robin had enough nerve to do plenty more besides that! Yet sometimes that's exactly how I do feel—especially around important people. When I'm at home and can be all by myself and write, I don't have to worry about what anyone thinks

of me. I can be free with my thoughts and let them flow out
onto the paper. But something like what we're going to Sacramento to do—that makes me real nervous. It makes me wish
I was more used to the city and its ways so I didn't feel like a
bumpkin."

"Let me tell you something, Corrie," he said seriously.
"Don't ever wish to be something different than exactly the
person you are. I've been in a lot of cities, and I've known
many city people. But I don't know that I've ever met a family
quite like yours, or a young lady quite like you, or a man quite
like your father."

He stopped, then turned and looked out the window at
the passing scenery. The silence lasted a long time. When he
finally turned back toward me, I could see a wistfulness in his
eyes, a far-off look—almost longing for something or a painful
memory out of his past. I knew he'd gone somewhere far away
and was now struggling to bring his mind back to the present.

Until that moment, Cal Burton had seemed so high above
me, so confident and sure of himself, mingling with important
people, a friend of politicians and assistant to Mr. Stanford,
one of California's most influential men. All of a sudden, in
the brief second when he turned back from the window and
his eyes met mine, he was an ordinary person just like me, and
in that instant I momentarily forgot about all of the things
that made us so different. All of a sudden he did seem to be
Cal to me rather than *Mister* Burton.

"No, Corrie," he said with a sigh, "don't ever leave Miracle
Springs, or your family. It's too special a treasure. Wherever
you go, whatever you do, however many people you meet, and
however many big cities you visit, don't change. Don't let Miracle Springs and the country and that homestead by the creek

you love so much—don't let it get away from you. You can stand tall alongside anybody, no matter how big or important they may seem to you. You've got something just as important down inside, whether anybody sees it right off or not."

I didn't know how to respond, so I kept quiet.

"So you've got nothing to be nervous about," he added after a moment. "When we get to Sacramento, you just be who you are, and that will be enough for anybody."

"I'll do my best," I replied.

"So tell me," Cal said, brightening up again with that wide smile of his, "what's it like to write? How do you do it? How'd you ever get started writing for the *Alta*, anyway?"

"I started out just keeping a journal," I said. "I wrote down things I felt, things I thought about. I just did it for myself at first."

"How'd you start writing for the newspaper, then?"

I told him about the blizzard of '55 and the story I wrote about it. "After that," I said, "I just kept doing it a little more, thinking of things to write about, getting braver about sending things to Mr. Kemble."

"And getting braver about facing him and speaking up to him, too, from what I understand."

"What do you mean—how do you know about that?"

"Dalton had me do some checking up on you," Cal answered. "Kemble was half mad, half proud of you when he told me about your facing him down and arm-twisting him into paying you eight dollars for an article he wanted to buy for a dollar."

I laughed. "How I could have been so brash back then?" I said. "At nineteen, to think I should get paid what a man did. I don't know whether it was bravery or stupidity!"

"It must have worked. You made a name for yourself. You've written a lot of articles, Kemble likes you, and you've made a little money at it, I would imagine."

"Forty-three dollars, altogether," I said.

"Is that all?" exclaimed Cal. "I would have thought it would be hundreds!"

"I got only eight dollars that once. Most of the time Mr. Kemble still pays me between two and six dollars an article, and I've written only fourteen or fifteen articles he's published. Some of them are so short I get only a dollar."

"Then you must not write for the money."

"Oh no, it's not that at all."

"What then?"

I had to stop and think a minute. "It's a lot of things," I said finally. "People, nature, thoughts, ideas, feelings . . . I don't know if I could really explain it, but what's inside me has to come out in words. When I think something or notice something or have some kind of an insight about the world, to be able to communicate that to someone else is the greatest feeling on earth."

"Are you an intellectual, Corrie Hollister?" Cal asked, with a serious and pensive look on his face. For an instant I thought he might be poking fun at me, but then I realized he honestly was trying to figure out more about me.

"An intellectual?" I repeated in surprise. "You must be joking!"

"You're certainly a thinker, almost a philosopher in a way."

"A philosopher! That's even more strange to hear you say. Didn't you hear me a few minutes ago—some people think I'm a bumpkin from nowhere."

"Ah, but they don't know you like I am beginning to," replied Cal, his eyes open wide in a knowing expression. "But you don't deny that you're a thinker, do you?"

"I don't suppose I could be a writer without being a thinker at the same time," I answered finally.

"There—you see . . . a philosopher! A philosopher is just someone who thinks and has his own way of looking at things and then writes them down for other people to think about too. Isn't that what you do, in your own personal Corrie-Belle-Hollister-from-Miracle-Springs sort of way?"

"Maybe you're right. But I don't think of it like that. I just look at things, at the world, to observe people. Then I write about what I see, describe it, and maybe try to figure out what it means."

"Tell me what *you* mean."

"Maybe it's just from living in the country. But I have this feeling that everything is supposed to *mean* something. There are two ways we can look at something—just as it is on the surface or on two levels at once—what it looks like *and* what it is saying about life and the world. Do you know what I mean? Don't you have the feeling that the whole world is talking to you all the time if you just had sharp enough hearing to listen?"

"I've never thought of it before."

"Oh, but it is!"

"Give me an example."

I thought for a minute. "There's the creek outside our house. Sometimes I lie awake in my bed at night and just listen to it singing and babbling away down the hill toward the town in the dark. Or sometimes I sit beside it on a sunny day, with my feet in the water, watching for an hour as the clear water tumbles and splashes over the rocks. I love that creek! And don't you see why? It's so much more than just water. Its splashy, wet noises are constantly bringing messages down from the mountains—telling tales of snow and winter, of secret places where it has been, under the hills where huge vaults of gold exist that no man has ever seen, telling about falls it has cascaded over and about the fish and otters that play in its deep pools. Oh, it's got so much to tell if you only stop and listen to its voice. But best of all, when you kneel down and put your lips to it in the early spring when it's icy cold, and you drink in a mouthful, then it tells about life itself and how God made it, such a simple thing to look at, as the very sustainer of everything that lives and grows. The water that comes down that creek is nothing short of a miracle."

Cal laughed. "You are indeed able to see a great deal in things that most people look right past."

"But that's not nearly all," I said enthusiastically. "If there has been a heavy snow up in the mountains and then a week of warm weather comes, the stream will grow and grow, almost hourly, until it thunders and roars and rushes down with foamy swiftness. Then the stream can tell stories about the science of water itself—how it is gathered up into the sky from the ocean, to wait and accumulate together in clouds, finally to descend back to the earth in snows and rains, hitting the earth and soaking into it and wandering to and fro in streams and springs, sometimes pausing in lakes, until it finds its way back to the ocean again. I sometimes think of all these mysteries as I sit and watch and listen to the water as I did yesterday."

"Now I know I was not mistaken!"

"About what?"

"About your being a philosopher."

"Nonsense!" I replied. "It's all there for anyone to see. That's what I love so much about the country, about life. *Everything* is just as full of marvels and secret mysteries as the stream. Just the other day I was looking at the bark on the pine trees in the woods and found myself thinking about the mysteries of how the trees grow and gather nourishment from the ground. Nothing is without a meaning, almost a personality— *if* you know how to look for it and what you are looking for."

"And what is the meaning, the mystery, the significance of it all, Corrie?"

"Why, that God made it, of course."

"I don't see what is so mysterious about that. Everybody believes that. Everything has to be *made* somehow, by someone."

"The mystery is in what it tells us about God. He put himself into every tiniest thing."

"Even an ugly old gray rock?"

"Of course. His hand can't touch anything without leaving his fingerprints behind—even on the simplest of rocks."

"Hmm . . . you do have a way of looking at things differently than most people. Is this how you write, too?"

"I don't know," I laughed.

"Have you ever written about streams and pine trees?"

"No. I just think about things when I'm watching them. Sometimes they find their way into things I write, but mostly they just get into my journal where nobody else sees them."

"You mentioned your journal before—tell me about it."

"I keep journals of things I do and think about. Sometimes I draw pictures in it or respond to books I've read. When I'm writing in my journal, I don't have to be as careful as if I'm writing an article, so I just let it be as personal as I want."

"You said journals. How many journals do you have?"

"I've filled up five—no, let's see . . . yes, five. I just started my sixth book in the almost eight years I've been keeping a journal."

He drew in a sigh, then turned to glance out the window. The pause in conversation suddenly made me realize how much I'd forgotten my nervousness and how much talking I'd been doing. A fresh wave of embarrassment swept over me.

"I can hardly believe it. I must have babbled on for ten or fifteen miles!"

"Please, don't fret about it," said Cal, turning slowly back to face me. His voice was soft and reflective. "I enjoy listening to you, Corrie. It takes me back to a simpler time in my own life when some of those things were important to me, too."

"Did you once live in the country?" I asked.

"A long time ago," he answered, and again that same wistful look filled his eyes, and I heard the longing in his voice that I had detected earlier.

"I'd love to hear about it," I said.

A long silence followed. I could see a look of pain cross his face, and he turned to gaze outside for a while again. When he finally spoke, it was only to close the door into himself that he had opened just for an instant, and only a crack.

"Maybe someday, Corrie," he said slowly. "But I don't think I'm up to it right now."

We were just coming to Auburn, where the stage stopped for half an hour to pick up one more passenger, get the mail, and give the passengers time for coffee and food if anyone wanted it. Cal asked me if I'd like to join him in the restaurant for something to eat, but I said I'd rather just walk around and stretch my legs. After I'd answered him, I realized I was a little hungry, yet somehow I'd thought maybe he'd rather be alone after the way our conversation had ended. I opened my bag and pulled out the apple I'd brought along and munched on it as I walked up and down the main street of Auburn.

When we climbed back into the stage, Cal's gaiety had returned. It was more crowded now, but he was just as genial as ever, talking to the others, helping the elderly lady who had gotten on at Auburn to adjust to the bumps and noises, and speaking to me again in a way that put me completely at ease.

We talked back and forth, gradually working our way around to the reason for the ride in the first place.

"What am I supposed to say when we get there?" I asked him. "I've never made a speech before in my life."

"Are you nervous?"

"Of course. How could I not be?"

"Don't worry about a thing, Corrie. All you have to do is be yourself and people will love you."

"I've got to do a little more than that," I said. "I have to say *something*."

"Sure, but it hardly matters *what* you say. What the people are coming out to see is a woman standing up there—and a pretty one!—with the men. Standing up and saying, 'Vote for Lincoln.'"

I don't know what got into me, but suddenly I lost my shyness and out of my mouth popped the words, "Come on, Cal. I'm not pretty, and you shouldn't lie like that."

The instant I said it, I wanted to retract the words! But he just laughed. "You are something, Corrie Hollister!" he said, still laughing. "Not afraid to speak your mind one bit. But you won't object if I disagree with you, will you? You're going to stand up there, and folks are going to say to themselves, 'There's one beautiful young woman, and I'm going to listen to what she has to say!' So there, Corrie—like it or not. I'm not taking back a word of it!"

Now I was embarrassed again!

"But is it really true that it doesn't matter how good a speech I make?" I asked, trying to turn the discussion back toward Sacramento.

"Doesn't matter a bit. We want you there because of who you are, that's all. Dalton and the others know you're not a speechmaker."

"There's a big difference between speaking in front of people and writing down thoughts on paper when you're all alone," I said.

We bounced along for a while, then Cal asked me, "Why are you interested in politics, Corrie? How did you get involved in the first place?"

I stopped to think. "I suppose it was my mother's decision to run for mayor of Miracle Springs," I answered after a bit. "Actually, she's my stepmother—Almeda, you know. And it turned out she *didn't* run, but my pa did instead. It all happened in 1856, and we were so involved in it as a family, how could I help but be interested? So I wrote a few articles about the Miracle Springs election. Then with the presidential election going on at the same time, and Mr. Fremont being a Californian, well, I just kind of got drawn into it."

"But why did you *stay* interested? Why did you get *so* involved with the Fremont cause as to risk your life and do all you did, especially when you'd never met the man?"

"I don't know; I suppose it seemed the right thing to do."

"The *right* thing?"

"Yes. The more I found out about everything, the more I knew I had to stand up for the truth, and to write the truth so that people would know how things *really* were."

"Truth . . . hmm."

"For me there's no other reason to write at all. That's what everything's about—all of life, in fact."

"Like the Miracle Springs Creek?" suggested Cal.

"Yes," I said. "The creek, the election in '56, what kind of person I want to be. It's all about truth. The creek's got truth in it, if you know where to look for it. It seems to me that life's about learning to be a true person. That's what being a Christian is to me—not knowing a lot of religious things, but becoming a *true* person, a true daughter of God. That's what my writing's about too—learning to find life's good things, life's *right* things, life's *true* things—and then writing about them in a way folks can understand, in a way that gets down inside them. Whether I'm writing about creeks or trees or politics, I've got to make sure inside myself that it's *truth* I'm writing about."

Cal was very thoughtful for a minute. "An unusual approach to political reporting," he said at length. "And so," he added, "have you satisfied yourself that supporting Lincoln is the right and true thing to do?"

"I had to spend a lot of time thinking and praying about it," I answered. "It wasn't an easy decision. But, yes, I'm satisfied now that it's what I'm supposed to do, and so I'll give myself to stand up for the truth as I see it just as much as I did before with Mr. Fremont. What about you? Isn't that why you're in favor of Mr. Lincoln?"

Cal thought for a moment. Then a smile spread across his face. "My boss, Mr. Stanford, would not take it too kindly if I didn't," he said. "He is one of California's leading Republicans!"

"Why did you go to work for him," I asked, "if it wasn't because you believed in what he stood for?"

"Leland Stanford believes in himself," laughed Cal, "and his businesses and his railroad and making money."

"But surely you believe in *him?*"

"Of course I do. But I'm afraid it's on a more pragmatic level than because he stands for the truth. I hope you won't hate me, Corrie, but I believe in Mr. Stanford because I believe he represents the future, and therefore offers me the greatest opportunity to be in step with the future when it comes. Truth doesn't seem to me as important in this case as who holds the key to the future. Does Leland Stanford, or does former governor Latham, or does Congressman Burch with his idea of a separate California republic, or do the Breckinridge southern Democrats, or does Governor Downey, or does the state's new golden-tongued orator Thomas Starr King? Where does the future lie, Corrie? That seems to me the question. That is why I have cast my lot with Mr. Stanford and his cause. He'll be governor one day, mark my words. His railroad will span the continent. He may one day even live in the White House. And I want to be standing beside him if he does!"

"What about Mr. Lincoln? Do you believe in him in the same way?" I asked.

Cal's face turned thoughtful. "I can't say as I do, Corrie," he answered. "I think the North is very weak, both politically and economically. In a financial battle between North and South, the southern states would win hands down. With regard to the future of this nation, I do not see the North leading the way. For now it seems to me that the West is where the true future exists."

"*For now?*"

"Change that. Let me just say I came to the West because I saw the future moving in this direction."

We rode along for a while in silence. The three other passengers were occasionally making some attempts to carry on a conversation, but I think they were mostly listening to us. Whenever Cal and I stopped talking, it generally quieted down as if they were waiting for us to continue. Finally I picked the discussion up again.

"Is it all right if I ask you the same question you asked me?" I said. "Why did *you* get involved in politics?"

"A fair enough question," answered Cal. "I'll see if I can give you as straightforward an answer as you gave me."

He paused, thought for a minute, then went on. "The answer is very simple really—politics has been in my family as long as I have. Does the name Stephens mean anything to you?"

I shook my head.

"It's my mother's maiden name. My uncle, her brother, spent sixteen years in Congress in Washington, until just last year, and had served six terms in his state legislature before that. He is such a political creature that his very name raises images of the founding of the country itself—Alexander Hamilton Stephens."

"So it was in your blood?"

"In more ways than one. And I began to love it early in my life. I was only eight when my uncle packed his bags for Washington, but I remember it as distinctly as if it were yesterday. When we went up to visit him there, the sense of power the place exuded got into me, and I knew I wanted to be part of it someday too. My uncle was a Whig. But he was a pragmatic man too, and he taught me to look for opportunity wherever and however it came. And so now here I am working for the new Republican party, which didn't even exist eight years ago."

He laughed at the thought.

"Don't you see, Corrie? It's all about opportunity! That's what politics represents to me. It's where the power is, where the future is. That's why my uncle said to me, 'Cal, the future's in the West. If you want a life in politics that'll take you to the top, seek it in California. That's where tomorrow's leaders are going to come from.' So I took his advice, and here I am!"

"You're involved in politics and with Mr. Stanford for where they will *take* you?"

"Do I detect a slightly negative tone?"

"I just wanted to know," I answered. "I never thought of that before, at least in relation to myself. I don't envision my writing *taking me* anywhere—at least not in the way you mean it."

"Your reputation is growing in importance. That doesn't mean anything to you?"

"I never think about it. I want to grow *inside,* as a person. But I never think about becoming important."

"Well, I do. I want to *be* somebody. I want my life to count. Don't you see, Corrie? People like you and me, young men and women with ideas and enthusiasm, we're going to be tomorrow's leaders of the country. Doesn't that excite you? Don't you want to be part of it?"

"I've never thought of it. What about what you said two hours ago about the simpler life? You told me never to leave the simple country life behind. It even sounded as if you wished you could go back to it yourself. Now you're saying that I ought to want to be important."

"I grew up in the country too," said Cal. "I suppose part of me looks back on my childhood with a kind of longing. But once the lure of politics began to get hold of me, with all the opportunities it afforded, I vowed to myself that I would use every opportunity, every situation, to the fullest."

"To the fullest . . . in what way?"

"For where it could take me, what it could do for me— for taking advantage of the opportunity in whatever ways I was able."

I fell silent, and we didn't pick up the same conversation again. Cal had certainly given me a lot to think about. We were both on our way to Sacramento to be involved in Mr. Lincoln's campaign together, and yet our reasons and motives seemed very different.

They had offered to put me up in a big hotel in Sacramento, but I said I preferred to stay with Miss Baxter in her boardinghouse.

The meeting was scheduled for the afternoon after we arrived. I must have taken an hour to get ready. Just pulling the dress over my head and trying to button the buttons with my trembling fingers was so hard I finally had to ask Miss Baxter to help me. The dress was a light brown cotton, with full sleeves, navy piping around the collar and lapels, and a matching navy ribbon around the waist. I wished Almeda had been there to help me get it all just right and brush my hair and tie it up with its ribbon. But Miss Baxter was a fine substitute. It was so nice to have a woman there to share the anxious moments with me!

Cal came to pick me up in a fancy buggy and complimented me on how I looked. But I was still dreadfully nervous.

A platform had been built downtown near the capital buildings and decorated with red, white, and blue banners. Flags were flying, and a band was playing peppy patriotic songs. Quite a crowd had already gathered, and wagons and buggies were still pulling up. It reminded me of the festive day in Miracle Springs back in '52, but one look around told me this was a much bigger and more important event. All the men were dressed in expensive suits, and just the looks on their faces told me they were probably important men in California's politics.

Most of them were, too. Cal introduced me to more than a dozen people that day, and I can hardly remember a single one of them. I was so nervous before and so relieved after my brief time up on the platform that my mind was blank of everything else.

There were going to be speeches on behalf of all three of the candidates for president. In addition to me, Mr. Stanford and some other of his friends, Mr. Dalton and a famous orator named Edward D. Baker, all spoke for Abraham Lincoln. The Republicans were in the minority in California, as they were in the rest of the country. Up until this time, in the national elections California had always sided with the party that favored slavery. But now in 1860, when the line came to be drawn so clearly between North and South, and between slavery and antislavery, the Republicans hoped to break this record and bring California around and make it a free, pro-Union Republican state.

The split of the Democratic party, Cal told me, would help more than anything to make this possible. After the nomination of Stephen Douglas by the moderate wing of the party, the southern faction set up John Breckinridge as a candidate as well. On this day in Sacramento, many prominent Californians came out in favor of both men.

Governor Downey gave a speech in support of Douglas. I was surprised at how many famous western politicians were in favor of the southern cause and slavery. Former Governor Latham supported Breckinridge, although he wasn't there that day because he was now serving in the U.S. Senate representing California. California's other senator, William Gwin, formerly from Mississippi, did happen to be present, and spoke on behalf of the southern cause and candidate Breckinridge. John Weller, also speaking for Breckinridge, actually brought up the issue of the South seceding from the Union. I couldn't believe slavery could be so important to the South that they would actually try to start a new country rather than to see the slaves set free.

I had my journal with me, and I tried to write down some of what was said. But all the newspapers told about the speeches anyway, and I got copies the next day so I could read them over again. Weller said this: "I do not know whether Lincoln will be elected or not. I will personally urge every Californian to vote instead for John C. Breckinridge of the Southern Democratic party. I do know this, that if our efforts fail and if Lincoln is elected, and if he attempts to carry out his doctrines, the South will surely withdraw from the Union. And I should consider them less than men if they did not."

One speech got the biggest applause and was written up in all the newspapers of the state during the next few days—the one delivered by Edward Baker. He had been defeated a year before as candidate for Congress and then had gone up to Oregon where he had been elected to the Senate from the new state. He had come down to California and had been called upon to speak on behalf of the Republican party, freedom, and the election of Abraham Lincoln. People said afterward it was one of the greatest political speeches ever delivered in California. Baker said:

Where the feet of my youth were planted, there, by Freedom, my feet shall stand. I will walk beneath her

banner. I will glory in her strength. I have watched her, in
history, struck down on a hundred chosen fields of battle.
I have seen her friends fly from her. I have seen her foes
gather round her. I have seen them bind her to the stake.
I have seen them give her ashes to the winds, regathering
them again that they might scatter them yet more widely.
But when they turned to exult, I have seen her again meet
them, face-to-face, resplendent in complete steel and
brandishing in her strong right hand a flaming sword, red
with insufferable light. I take courage. The people gather
round her. The Genius of America will at last lead her
sons to freedom.

After Baker's speech I wasn't any too anxious to walk
up there on that platform, with four or five hundred people
standing all around listening, and open my timid little mouth
to try to say something. What could I say that could compare
in any way with what Mr. Baker had said?

But there was no getting around it. And eventually I
heard Mr. Dalton start to introduce me. I sat there listening
to him, my whole body sweating and shaking, terrified at the
ordeal that was about to come.

"Ladies and gentlemen, fellow Californians," he said, "you
have heard from eminent statesmen today, from senators and
governors and political leaders and men of industry and com-
merce. But I now want to introduce to you a young lady of
perhaps equal reputation in some circles, a young lady whose
simple and honest words have been read in newspapers from
one shining sea of this great land all the way to the other; a
young lady who, I must tell you, is a bit nervous about all this.
She is a country girl, yet her words ring with truth whenever

she sets pen to paper. Therefore I know what she says to you today comes directly from the heart. Ladies and gentlemen, I give you Miss Cornelia Belle Hollister."

I stood up. I glanced at Cal, sitting beside me, and he gave me a smile of encouragement. I walked up the steps and to the front of the platform.

I stood there for a moment. Everyone was quiet, all eyes looking up at me, waiting.

"I've never made a speech before in my life," I began. "I don't know if this will even qualify as one now. They told me all I had to do was say what I felt and thought about things, and that would be good enough. I suppose I can do that."

My voice sounded so tiny, like a little mouse! All the other men had loud, deep voices, and I sounded like a little girl. I didn't think the people more than ten feet away would be able to hear a thing I said!

"I've been thinking a lot about this election," I said after clearing my throat and trying to speak up a little louder. "I had to think about which side I'd be on and what I ought to do about it. I can't say as I'm a Democrat or a Republican, and it hardly matters much since I can't vote anyway."

A small wave of laughter spread among the men who were listening. There were a good number of women there too, and by now most of them had come forward as close to the platform as they could. They were all watching me intently.

"I don't know Mr. Lincoln or Mr. Douglas or Mr. Breckinridge, for that matter, who I just found out today is running too. To tell you the truth, I don't really know too much about any of the issues except for the issue of slavery and freedom. But if you want a woman's point of view, that's just about the most important issue of all. And that's the one I spent nearly all my time thinking over when it came to this election.

"The conclusion I came to is that freedom is a mighty important thing in this country of ours. The Constitution talks about it, and I guess it seems to me that if people in the United States of America can't be free, then I don't know where else in the world freedom's going to find a place to grow. Some of the Democrats might say that the freedom the Constitution talks about doesn't apply to Negroes because they aren't people in the same way as the rest of us are, so they don't have the same right to be free. But I don't agree with that. I'm a woman, and I don't have the right to vote. But that doesn't make me feel any less of a human being, and I don't figure too many Negroes feel like they're less than human, either.

"It looks to me like freedom's a thing that's got to apply to everybody, or else it doesn't mean much. It's got to apply to women and Negroes, to rich people and poor people, to folks in California just like it does to folks in Alabama or anywhere else. Some of these men we've been listening to today have said you ought to vote for Mr. Douglas or Mr. Breckinridge because it'll be better for the South, and the whole country, or because Mr. Lincoln's made so many strong remarks about being against slavery that the South will be so mad if he gets elected, there's no telling what they might do.

"All of that doesn't seem to have anything to do with freedom, if you ask me. The Democrats have been the party that supported slavery all these years. Now the Republicans are trying to change that by standing for freedom. It seems to me that's about the most important thing of all. I don't know much about money and the economy and all that. But if folks in these United States aren't free, then it doesn't seem to me that our money means much, or the word *freedom*, or our Constitution either.

"Four years ago I tried to write some things to help Colonel Fremont get to the White House, because he was against slavery too, just like Mr. Lincoln is. He got defeated, and I figured my efforts had been wasted.

"But now I've got a chance to try to do something again, and I hope the people of this country will do better by the cause of freedom for our people than last time. That's why I decided, after thinking about it a good long while, to support Abraham Lincoln. No, I can't vote. But if I could, I'd vote for Mr. Lincoln, and it seems to me you all ought to vote for him too."

I turned and walked back down the steps and sat down. I was sweating and trembling from head to foot. I never heard any of the applause, but Cal told me they loved it, especially all the women.

The next morning, on the *front page* of the Sacramento *Union*, I was shocked to read the headline over a two-column article: BAKER, DOWNEY, WELLER, HOLLISTER ADDRESS SACRAMENTO ELECTORATE. And toward the end of the article, they actually quoted from *my* speech!

$\mathcal{B}$y the time all the festivities of the day were finished, I was exhausted, not just from having given the speech, but from everything that had followed—talking to people, shaking hands, greeting a long line of women well-wishers who treated me like some kind of hero for "the cause," as they put it, although I had no idea what cause they were talking about.

I had tried to keep smiling and stay friendly, but by the end of the afternoon I was *so* tired. Cal stayed at my side nearly the whole time, encouraging me, telling me what to do if I got confused, picking up the conversation for me if I didn't know what to say. All day long I kept meeting people, most of whom I can't even remember. But they all looked important.

Then he took me and showed me inside some of the capital buildings, including where the legislature met. "Here's where your father will be one of these days," he said, and I thought to myself that they shouldn't count on it because Pa was an independent man who was used to making up his own mind and not having anyone else do his thinking for him. But just the thought of Pa in the midst of all these fancy, dressed-up men brought a smile to my lips. I couldn't imagine *him* making a speech in front of that great big Assembly hall! And if he did, he'd no doubt shake things up once in a while!

"What's so funny, Corrie?" Cal asked.

"Oh nothing," I replied, still smiling to myself.

"You've got something on your mind. You can't hide that."

"I was just thinking about what it would be like if Pa *was* to come here," I said.

"I hope he does," replied Cal. "This place could use more men of his caliber."

Finally, around six o'clock, Cal took me to dinner at a place called Livingstone's. We drove up to the front of Livingstone's, and Cal jumped out of the buggy, took my hand, and helped me down to the street, while someone else hopped up and drove the horses around to the back. Then Cal slipped his arm through mine and led me inside. I don't know if I'd ever felt so out of place in my life! If this was what it was like to be a *lady*, I wasn't sure I liked it.

Livingstone's turned out to be a fancier restaurant than I had ever seen—even nicer than the International House, where Almeda had taken me on our first trip to San Francisco. Mingling around the front door were several men in tuxedos and women in silk dresses. The flash of diamonds caught my eye now and then. Once we were inside, I realized all the more what a glamorous place Cal had brought me to. I heard music playing from somewhere, and the waiters were dressed up to look like preachers.

I was so nervous, I felt like I was going to stumble and fall over my dress with every step. And Cal was close to me, our arms linked together, my dress brushing up alongside him, my arm and shoulder touching his as we slowly made our way to our table behind one of the fancy-dressed waiters. As I sat down, Cal went behind me and helped scoot my chair in.

I'd never been treated like this, and I hardly knew what to do! Just the thought of Robin O'Flaridy made me laugh inside at the comparison. Cal was such a fine and gentlemanly *man*! I took stock of the white linen tablecloth, the candle in the middle of the table, the wine glasses and silver, which all made me think: What is Corrie Hollister doing *here*?

I might have been California's best-known woman reporter, but I couldn't make heads or tails of the menu. Cal helped me order. I had roast lamb with some fancy kind of potatoes with cheese mixed into them. It was tasty, but I didn't have much of an appetite. I don't know if it was because of how tired I was, but I could eat only about half of what the waiter brought me.

"You stole the show today, Corrie," said Cal across the table.

"I did not," I responded. "You heard all those other men, and the clapping after Mr. Baker's speech!"

"Those men are all politicians. Edward Baker's on his way to Washington. Speechmaking is the business of men like that. I'll wager Baker's given several hundred speeches in his life—all smooth, polished, every word just as it ought to be. But *you*—your speech was different. It was from the heart . . . it was just *you*! I saw Dalton's face as he was watching."

"What . . . what was he thinking?" I asked, wondering what he meant.

"He was sitting back in his chair with just the hint of a smile on his face. He knew well and good that he'd found the right young lady."

"He didn't say anything to me afterward."

"Alexander Dalton can be a funny man at times. But he knows politics like no one in this state. And you mark my words, you will hear from him again. I tell you, Corrie, there were some people there today paying more attention to you than anyone else who got up on that platform the whole day."

"I don't believe a word of it," I said, although I looked down at my plate in embarrassment at the same time. I couldn't help feeling pride at his words. I suppose part of me knew he was just trying to make me feel good about the day, yet another part wanted to believe he was sincere and wouldn't say anything he didn't really mean.

"Well, there's nothing I can do to convince you," said Cal sincerely, "even if I do know these men and their kind better than you do." He paused, then put his fork down and looked across the table at me. "But I will tell you this, Corrie," he added, "and even if you can't believe the other, I hope you will believe this. You were not only the prettiest speaker in all of Sacramento today, in my humble estimation you were also the most eloquent. If Abraham Lincoln does not carry California, it will be only because the men of this state were too deaf to heed the words of his most ardent supporter."

The rest of the evening was lost in a fuzzy blur. Even as I lay in bed hours later, I could hardly recall the specifics of it in any pattern that made sense. By the time I tried to write about it in my journal as I bounced along in the stagecoach going home, it had nearly all escaped me. The feelings inside lingered, but what we had done, where we had gone, what we had seen, and the words we had spoken—I could recall none of them.

I do know that Cal showed me nearly all of Sacramento— Sutter's fort, some of the old original houses still standing from the 1840s. We got out and walked along the river just about the time the sun was setting and the half moon was coming up. Then we rode again in the buggy, for hours it seemed, until the city was dark and night sounds faintly echoed about in the distance.

It was very quiet and still when at last Cal pulled the horse up in front of Miss Baxter's. The only sounds were the crickets in the trees lining the streets. Even the occasional shouts from the saloons down in the center of town were so faint as to be drowned out by the thunderous chirping of the tiny creatures overhead.

Cal got down, tied the reins to the fence, then came over to my side, held up his hand to take mine, and helped me down to the street. I was finally getting used to such treatment, although it still brought about a fluttering sensation all through me. But I wasn't prepared for him keeping hold of my hand as he led me up to Miss Baxter's porch!

We walked toward the house slowly, in silence. When we reached the porch, Cal stopped, still grasping my hand, and turned toward me.

"Corrie," he said, "this has been one of the most pleasurable days I have spent in all my life. You are an engaging and wonderful young woman."

He looked deeply into my eyes. The light from the moon reflected from his, seeming to draw me right into them. My heart was pounding so hard, I thought the whole boarding-house must hear, and that windows would begin opening any moment to find out what the racket was!

Then he slowly drew my hand up, bent slightly, and kissed the top of my hand as he held it between his fingers. I just stood there, compliantly watching as his lips rested for just a second on my hand. Yet inside, my heart and brain were exploding with the sounds of a thousand waves crashing against a stormy shore.

He raised his head, released my hand, and softly uttered the words, "Good night, Corrie."

Then he turned and was gone. I remained standing on the porch, watching him bound up into the carriage seat, and briskly urge the horse into action with a flick of the rein and a click of his tongue.

I was alone, in the silent darkness of the Sacramento night. Alone with only the sound of a million crickets in my ears and ocean waves somewhere down in my heart.

I can't remember opening the door and walking inside the house, or climbing the darkened stairs to the room I always stayed in whenever I came to Sacramento. I cannot remember taking off my bonnet, nor getting out of my long dress and tossing it across the chair. Somehow I got into my night clothes, although I don't recall that, either.

When I next came to myself I was lying on my back in the soft bed, moonlight streaming through the window into the room. Just lying there. Thinking, yet not thinking. A smile on my face, my heart full, yet my mind empty. Full of feelings, yet none that could be expressed in words.

The only words I was aware of were those three that kept repeating themselves over and over and over . . . *Good night, Corrie.*

I don't know how long I lay there. But somehow, eventually, my eyelids closed with heaviness, the sound of the waves and the crickets gradually subsided, and sleep slowly stole over me.

The Two Letters

CHAPTER TWENTY-FIVE

*I*t seemed kind of dull at home for the next couple of weeks. I couldn't find much energy to interest myself in anything. I went on long walks and rides and pretty much kept to myself. I doubt I did anybody much good when I went into town and tried to busy myself with Mine and Freight business.

Marcus Weber looked me over with his big drooping eyes of concern every day I came in, and finally, when he couldn't stand it any longer, he burst out one day, "What in tarnation be ailin' you, Miss Corrie? Blamed if I just can't stand to see you lookin' so sad!"

I smiled, but from the reaction on his beautiful, tender black face I could tell it didn't reassure him much. "Nothing, Marcus," I said. "I am just fine. Just a little tired."

I know he wasn't convinced. He looked me over for another several seconds, with an unspoken expression of concern flooding across his humble features. He gave me a nervous fatherly hug, and I almost thought I detected a tear in one of his eyes. Then he turned and went back out to the livery. In those brief moments, I felt my heart's eyes could see down into Marcus far deeper than his mere words expressed.

It was such a revelation. I could see how much he really loved me! To be loved like that, when you realize how deep it goes into somebody *else's* heart, has to be one of the most humbling things in all of life.

Pa acted the same way, looking at me with concern, asking if I was sick, telling me I ought to be eating more or I was going to waste away. Almeda didn't say much; she just smiled at me a lot, and gave me more than my share of motherly hugs whenever she had the chance. She knew what it was and knew that I had to work through it as best I could on my own.

A couple of letters arrived early in August that helped me get back on my feet and quit thinking so much about Cal Burton. I couldn't stop thinking about him altogether, but having something to *do* at least got my brain and hands occupied with activity.

The first was a letter to Pa from Alexander Dalton. He said the time was getting very close when Pa would have to make up his mind about whether to run or not. He stressed again his assurance that Drummond Hollister was exactly the kind of man the state of California needed, and his confidence that if Pa made up his mind soon, there would be victory in November. He would handle the whole campaign and all the details, he said. It would not cost Pa a cent. All he had to do was give his consent and perhaps make two or three speeches between Miracle Springs and Sacramento—Grass Valley and Auburn, and maybe one or two other towns besides.

The second letter was addressed to me. My heart jumped for a moment, but then settled back into place when I saw the familiar handwriting of my editor at the *Alta*. Not so long ago, a note or letter from Mr. Kemble would send me into a positive tizzy. Now I found myself opening it almost with disappointment. His words, however, were sufficient to bring a tingle to my skin.

You always continue to astound me, Corrie Hollister. I never gave you two cents' worth of a chance of succeeding in this business, but you've been writing for me for six years and are one of the most well-known reporters I have. And now you've taken up speechmaking and politics besides! Is there anything you don't do?

In any case, I have heard the reports from Sacramento where, as I understand it, you were quite impressive. My Republican friends are badgering me for an article under your byline in support of the Lincoln-Hamlin ticket. Dalton says he will pay half if I will offer you enough myself to encourage you to set your pen to paper again as you did, unfortunately in vain, for the Fremont cause. He also assures me that, for the right article, he could almost guarantee publication in most of the major eastern cities. We would like an article of some length, which men and politicians would heed as well as the women who make up your customary readership. This is the title we would like to use: "Why Abraham Lincoln Should Be President—A Woman's Point of View."

Can you do it? We will pay you a total of ten dollars. We would need the finished article by September 15 in order to get it to the East and published within the first week or two of October.

I remain, sincerely yours,

EDWARD KEMBLE

A Bold Decision

CHAPTER TWENTY-SIX

I don't know what Pa intended to do about the letter he had received, but I needed something to occupy my mind for a while, and I liked what Mr. Kemble had suggested. I started on the article right away.

I had no sooner begun when thoughts of Zack began to intrude into my mind. Maybe it was from seeing Pa wrestling with his decision, and knowing Zack was part of what he was thinking about in it all. There still had been no word from or about Zack, and even though we didn't talk about it much, we were all worried.

I couldn't help feeling personally involved. I didn't feel responsible for his leaving, but I did feel that maybe I'd let Zack down too, that a lot of the things he'd said to Pa applied to me as well. I even felt that some of what I'd done, the opportunities I'd had and the attention I'd received, all went into making him feel less important. It wasn't true, of course, but his outburst surely made it seem like that's how he felt. I thought we were about as close as a brother and sister could be, and then I found out that he was hurting about all kinds of things no one knew about. It wasn't right for him to suffer like that, and I began to feel that it was important for me to do something about it.

At first I thought of writing Zack a letter. What better way to get in touch with him? He'd have his hands on it in just a few days!

Then I realized what a stupid idea it was. He might have his hands on it, but a letter would just be stuck inside a mail pouch in his saddlebags, and he would never see it! We had no idea where he was staying, so there was no way to address a letter actually *to* him.

All the while I was working on my Lincoln article, Zack kept running through my mind. I'd see his face, first laughing, then serious. I'd see him riding on a horse like the wind. I recalled our first coming to California and how he'd tried so hard to act grown up. I remembered the pain I could see underneath the brave exterior. I remembered how he and Pa had a hard time at first, but how they had become friends—or so I'd thought. I remembered the first gun Pa gave him that Christmas and how proud Zack had been, and how much he'd loved working at the mine with the three men.

So many memories kept rising and falling into my thoughts, all now clouded over with the pain and hurt of his bitter words of anger the day he'd left.

One day a daring plan came into my mind—in its own way almost as daring, I suppose, as Zack's going off as he had. I went to talk to Pa about it.

"What would you think," I asked, "if I was to go find Zack?"

"Tarnation, girl!" he exclaimed. "How you figure on doing that?"

"I'll follow the Express route east till I get to Zack's leg."

"You're gonna ride along with the Pony Express! You're a decent rider, Corrie. But you ain't gonna keep up with *them* skinny young wild men!"

"I don't have to keep up with them, Pa," I said. "I only have to follow the route. I figure I'll go from station to station, asking as I go about Zack. Somebody's bound to know of him, and somewhere along the line I'll run into him."

Pa rubbed his chin and made like he was thinking. "It's a foolhardy enough notion for my daughter to have thought of," he said after a while, breaking into a grin.

"Is it all right, Pa?" I asked eagerly.

"'Course it ain't all right. This is crazier than any of your schemes four years ago!" Pa's tone was lighthearted, but I could tell he meant it, too.

I laughed kind of sheepishly.

"What do you want me to say?" he went on. "That I like the idea? It's dangerous out there."

"We have to find out about Zack sometime, Pa," I said.

"Yeah," Pa sighed. "And I reckon by now you *have* proved yourself, and I trust you. But I don't like the idea of you being out there alone. I don't like it for a second, and I don't see how I could do anything but try to keep you from it just like I did Zack."

"But I'd only be gone for a short time, Pa. Not like what Zack wanted to do—not to take a job."

Pa sighed. "I'm as anxious about Zack as you are. Why don't you take the stage?"

"The stage doesn't follow the same route till it gets to Wyoming."

"The wagon trail?"

"There are no wagon trains going east this late in the year. I wouldn't find anybody to hook up with that way, either. Besides, the California Trail goes north of the Express route. There's no way I can see to find him except to go straight out to Placerville and Carson City and then straight across Nevada toward Salt Lake City."

"I tell you, it's dangerous territory, Corrie. Your ma died out there from the heat. You know that better than I do. There's Indians, desert, sometimes no water."

"That was almost ten years ago, Pa. It's more civilized now. There are horse-changing stations every twenty or twenty-five miles. There are people, food, water, a place to rest. If I just told them my brother was a rider, they'd be hospitable enough, and even let me sleep the night."

Pa thought again. "Yeah, I reckon that's so," he said. "Still, I don't much like the idea of you being that far from home alone."

All of a sudden *another* wild idea struck me.

"Why don't you come with me, Pa?" I said. "Let's go find Zack together!"

Pa's face remained blank, not twitching so much as a muscle. But his eyes betrayed that somewhere deep behind them, his mind was spinning fast to take in the words I had said and to figure out what to do about them.

"You know his being gone's eating at you, Pa," I said after a minute, "just like it is me. Let's both go out there and find him and tell him we're sorry for not letting him know how we felt, and tell him we love him."

Still Pa was silent, thinking it all over. He stood there for a long time, looking out into the distance. Finally he turned to me.

"You think he'd listen to me?" he said softly, the pain and uncertainty all too clear in his voice.

"Of course he would, Pa," I said. "What son's going to turn his own pa away?"

"Seems like that's just what he wanted to do."

"Oh, Pa, no he didn't. He was just feeling pain and confusion. He didn't know what to do with it all. I think you got in the way, that's all."

"But I was the cause of it all."

"No you weren't, Pa. Kids blame their parents for all kinds of things that are really no one's fault but their *own*. They just don't want to look down inside themselves, so they blame the nearest person around."

"Did you ever do that, Corrie?" asked Pa. He and I had lots of personal talks together. But when he said those words, there was an earnestness in his voice I'd never heard before. Never in my life had I seen a man so vulnerable as Pa was at that moment, so stripped of all the barriers men usually put up to shield themselves from other people. I felt I was looking all the way to the bottom of Pa's very soul, where there was a tender human being just as capable of feelings and suffering and questions and pain and worry as any woman or any child. It's not the kind of thing most kids ever get the chance to see in their parents, but I saw it right then in my pa, and it pulled me all the deeper into him and made me love him all the more.

He was looking at me intently, almost as if he were afraid of the answer I would give him.

"When we first got here," I said, "there were a couple of times I felt hurt, Pa. But Ma had just died. I was so confused about everything, and I was only fifteen."

"Did you blame me for what happened?" Pa asked, still with the earnest, transparent, questioning probing in his eyes.

Again, I thought hard. "I can't say as there wasn't any pain, Pa," I said. "That was a hard time for all of us. But no, after we were together awhile, I never blamed you, Pa. I got to know you too well. I got to know what was inside that heart of yours. I found out how much you loved Ma, how much you loved all of us and missed us . . . and how much you loved me. How could I blame you for anything, Pa, once I really knew who you were . . . once I knew how full of love you were?"

Pa was still gazing straight at me with those manly, loving, almost pleading eyes of his. But as I was speaking they had slowly filled with tears. His lips remained unmoved, but in those sparkling eyes I could see his relief.

We just stood, holding each other's gaze for a minute. Then finally Pa did smile, and as he did he took me in his arms, drew me to him, and embraced me with a strength that almost squeezed the breath out of me.

"Thank you, Corrie," he said, his voice just the slightest bit quivery.

"Yes, Pa," I whispered.

"I'm sorry for the pain you felt."

"It's long past now."

"Not for Zack," he said.

"For me it is, Pa. And you have to remember that I know you better than he does."

"It means more to me than you can know, Corrie, that you believe in me, and don't blame me. That means more to a man than his kin can ever realize."

We stood for another minute or two in each other's arms. "I love you, Pa," I said finally.

Just a moment more we stood; then Pa withdrew his hands from around me, pulled back, and looked at me, his blinking eyes drying again. He smiled broadly.

"Then let's you and me go find Zack!" he said.

The Pony Express

CHAPTER TWENTY-SEVEN

The idea for the Pony Express came from a business-man by the name of William Russell, who hoped that the government would pay his company—Russell, Majors, and Waddell—to have mail delivered speedily coast to coast. He proposed that they be paid one thousand dollars a week for two trips in both directions. The government never did pay for the service, and the costs involved turned out to be as high as ten to fifteen thousand dollars a week instead.

Before the Pony Express began in April of 1860, mail took twenty-five days to go from the East Coast to California—*if* the stagecoach didn't break a wheel, run into snow, or get attacked by Indians! Compared with how isolated California had been from the rest of the country in the early 1800s, even that was mighty fast. But when the organizers of the Pony Express said they would take mail between St. Joseph, Missouri, and Sacramento in ten days or less, everyone was amazed and wondered if such speed was possible.

Naturally, with Zack's fondness for horses, we had been curious and had followed the development of the idea with interest. Like all the papers, the *Alta* carried detailed stories about the first few mail crossings. Even in the midst of all the political news of 1860, some of the Pony Express riders became nationally known heroes. I read all the news articles that had been written for over a year now about it. Zack had sent off for some pamphlets too, and I had saved all the articles I'd read from different papers. So now with Pa and me planning to go find him, I pulled out everything I'd accumulated and read through it again.

Actually, the idea wasn't really Russell's at all, because there had been something like the Pony Express during the Roman Empire. And in the 1200s, Kublai Khan, the emperor of China, had a huge system of communication with stations stretching all the way from China to Europe, and with as many as four hundred fresh horses at every station, and thousands and thousands of messengers.

But for the United States the idea was new. And with mountains and deserts and Indians and bandits and no roads and no station houses, it was all a pretty big undertaking for Mr. Russell's company to get started. We had been reading about it in the papers for months before the horses actually began carrying mail.

There were to be eighty expert light riders riding between eighty relay stations, and making use of four to five hundred fast and hardy top-quality Indian horses. Forty of the riders would be stretched out in a line going east, the other forty in a line going west—all of them going back and forth both ways from their home base. It turned out later that there were two hundred riders in all—eighty in the saddle at all times, and the others resting between rides and replacements.

The mail would be carried by a leather cover that fit right over the saddle, called a *mochila*. There were four pouches on all four corners of the *mochila*, each of which had a lock on it.

The keys were kept only in St. Joseph and Sacramento—the two end points of the Express—and at Salt Lake City in the middle.

From California, the route of the Express went to Placerville, up over the Sierra Nevadas and down into Carson City, Nevada. From there it went straight across the high desert of the Great Basin and over the awful salt flats to Salt Lake. That was the only real city along the way, and was about a third of the whole distance. From Salt Lake the riders went gradually north up into the Rockies, past Fort Bridger, through South Pass, and to Casper, Wyoming. Then they started south, to Fort Laramie, and down onto the plains of Nebraska, following the same routes as the Mormon Trail and the Oregon Trail, down to Fort Kearny, into northeastern Kansas and to St. Joseph. The whole distance from Sacramento was 1,966 miles.

So many eager young boys wanted to join the Pony Express, right at first that they could have probably been hired cheaply. But Russell, Majors, and Waddell decided to pay them over a hundred dollars a month—high pay for anybody! As time went on, though, even that much money wasn't enough to keep some of them riding for the Express!

I don't know how God-fearing the owners of the company were, but they must have had some religious beliefs, because every rider that signed on, besides being given a lightweight rifle and a Colt revolver, was also given a Bible to carry with him. Riders also received the clothes that became the "uniform" of the Pony Express—a bright red shirt and blue dungarees. I never did understand, given as much trouble as they had with the Indians, why they made the riders dress so brightly!

Before he was hired, every rider had to sign a pledge that read:

I do hereby swear, before the Great and Living God, that during my engagement, and while I am an employee of Russell, Majors, & Waddell, I will, under no circumstances, use profane language; that I will drink no intoxicating liquors; that I will not quarrel or fight with any other employee of the firm, and that in every respect I will conduct myself honestly, be faithful to my duties, and so direct all my acts as to win the confidence of my employers. So help me God.

At least if Zack had to leave home, I was glad it was to work for a company with high standards of morality like that. I just hoped all those who signed that pledge kept to their word and lived by it!

Pa and I Take to the Trail

CHAPTER TWENTY-EIGHT

With the history it had and the reputation the Pony Express had already gained, when Pa and I left Sacramento it was almost as if we were following in the footsteps of George Washington. It seems odd to talk about California and the West as being part of history when everything was so new out here. But if the gold rush and the Pony Express didn't make us westerners part of history, nothing ever would.

A fellow named Sam Hamilton rode the first leg between Sacramento and Sportsman's Hall. The Express left Sacramento every Tuesday and Saturday. Since we had arrived late Monday, we stayed at Miss Baxter's and decided to leave at the same time. Pa was excited, and wanted to see how long we could keep pace with him.

But Sam was a skinny little fellow, and his horse not much bigger. To give them an advantage when trying to outrun Indians, each animal's load was limited to 165 pounds—20 pounds for the mail, 25 pounds for equipment, and 120 pounds for the rider. Zack must have lied about his weight, because I knew he weighed at least 130 or 140 pounds. But little Sam Hamilton might have been only 110!

When we took off down the street out of Sacramento, Hamilton was a block ahead of me and Pa before we'd gone a mile! He glanced back, lifted his hat in final greeting, gave us a shout of *Good Luck,* and gradually disappeared in a cloud of dust. Finally Pa pulled up his horse, turned around at me laughing, and said, "We gave it a gallant effort, Corrie! But there ain't no way we're gonna keep up with him for even two miles!"

"And if we keep running our horses like this," I yelled as we reined them down to a gentle canter, "they won't make it past Placerville!"

Already the dust cloud surrounding little Sam Hamilton was fading into the distance. I could hardly imagine that the mail pouch he was carrying would be in Missouri in ten days or less!

Pa and I slowed up and walked for about ten minutes, Pa breaking out in laughter every so often at how ridiculous it was for us to think we were going to keep up with the Express rider. Then we eased our two horses on into a trot. If we didn't move at a little bit of a pace, we would never get to Nevada.

We were obviously not going to make it to a station house every night, so we would spend some nights alone out on the trail. With Pa along, I felt as safe as if we had our own private detachment of cavalry. There would not be any danger of Indian attack until well into Nevada, and we hoped by then to have had some word about Zack.

The weather proved better for us than it had been back in April for that first "Pony" run. It was beautiful climbing up high into the Sierras, although the trail was narrow and rocky in places, with huge cliffs on the edge falling away into deep gorges and canyons. I couldn't imagine how Warren Upson had made it through here at all in the snowy blizzard of that first run!

"Listen to this, Pa," I said as we sat around our campfire on our second night out. I had been reading an account of the first runs of the Express from some papers I'd brought along, keeping track of what had happened as we followed along the same route. "It was snowing here on that very first run."

"Hard to make their time in a blizzard."

"But they did it! Want me to read it to you?"

"Sure," said Pa, sipping his coffee. "I ain't going nowhere. Maybe I'll fall asleep with you reading to me!"

I began: "Everything had been arranged on that first day for the two riders to leave St. Joseph and Sacramento at the same time, one heading east, the other heading west. . . ."

I stopped for a second, then said, "I wonder what it was like when the two batches of mail passed each other. It must have been somewhere in Wyoming."

"Getting a little ahead of your story, ain't you?" said Pa.

"But don't you wonder if the riders stopped and chatted or if they just blew by each other with a shout and wave?"

"To tell you the truth, I never thought of it."

"How I wish I could have been there to watch it!"

"I'm gonna be sound asleep before you have that mail pouch out of Sacramento! Now you got my curiosity up—come on, read me the story, girl."

"Yes, Pa," I said with a smile. "First let me read you a short little notice out of the *Alta*."

My paper had been involved in the Pony Express right from the beginning, and we had been watching it closely all year, especially after Zack's leaving. But only the names of the most well-known riders were ever mentioned, so we had never seen anything about Zack. The April 3 edition of that year had an article on the festivities about the first rider leaving San Francisco, and that's what I read to Pa.

> The first Pony Express started yesterday afternoon, from the Alta Telegraph Company on Montgomery Street. The saddlebags were duly lettered "Overland Pony Express," and the horse (a wiry little animal) was dressed with miniature flags. He proceeded, just before four o'clock, to the Sacramento boat, and was loudly cheered by the crowd as he started. . . . The express matter amounted to 85 letters, which at $5 per letter gave a total receipt of $425.

"Didn't you tell me that first fellow wasn't even a Pony Express rider at all?" said Pa.

I laughed again. "He was just a messenger who worked at the paper," I answered.

James Randall told me later how much he'd wished he could go farther. But he only rode three blocks to the waterfront, and then got on the steamer for Sacramento with San Francisco's part of the mail. It was in Sacramento that the route of the Pony Express *really* started, despite Mr. Kemble's attempt to make San Francisco and the *Alta* seem like the most important parts of the whole thing!

"You ever gonna get back to that story you started out of the *Bee?*"

"I'm trying, Pa." I picked up the first paper again and finally read to Pa the whole article.

> Sam Hamilton was the first rider out of Sacramento on April 3. He rode sixty miles to the station at Sportsman's Hall, where he handed off the *mochila* and leather

pouches to Warren "Boston" Upson, who had to cross the treacherous Sierra Nevadas. There had just been a fresh snowfall, and a new storm was on the way. The very first day out from Sacramento proved to be one of the most dangerous. Warren found himself in the middle of a blinding blizzard crossing over the mountains, having to walk his pony on foot part of the way, and many times nearly losing the trail. At last he made it safely to his station house at Friday's Station, right on the California border.

Robert Haslam took over next, riding across the perilous Great Basin to Fort Churchill, Nevada. This was one of the worst parts of the whole route, with many mountain ranges, rivers which often disappeared into "sinks" in the ground and were hard to follow, and broken canyons, rocky terrain, wild animals, rattlesnakes, a critical lack of water in summer, snow in winter, and Indians besides. The long distance across Nevada and Utah was the most hazardous of all.

"Not much wonder why Zack found himself an opening there," Pa interrupted. Neither of us said it right then, but it also explained why we were so worried about him. Already, in the first five months of the Express, there had been numerous attacks reported, and several killings of station people. Some whole stations had been burned to the ground.

I put down the Sacramento paper to read the account from a Salt Lake City reporter who told about the midpoint of that first run. Many of the riders in Utah were Mormon boys who knew the difficult terrain in both directions out of Salt Lake City. Although this was not an exact halfway point, it was close enough to be considered the major intersection between eastbound and westbound mail. The first riders reached Salt Lake within two days of each other. The *Alta* later ran the article that had appeared in Salt Lake in the *Deseret News* on April 11.

The first Pony Express from the West left Sacramento at 12 p.m. on the night of the third inst., and arrived on the night of the seventh, inside of prospectus time. The roads were heavy, the weather stormy. The last seventy-five miles were made in five hours and fifteen minutes in a heavy rain.

The Express from the East left St. Joseph, Mo., at 6:30 p.m. on the evening of the third and arrived in this city at 6:25 p.m. on the evening of the ninth. The difference in time between this city and St. Joseph is something near one hour and fifteen minutes, bringing us within six days' communication with the frontier, and seven days from Washington—a result which we, accustomed to receive news three months after date, can well appreciate.

The weather has been very disagreeable and stormy for the past week and in every way calculated to retard the operation of the company, and we are informed that the Express eastward was five hours in going from this place to Snyder's Mill, a distance of twenty-five miles.

The probability is that the Express will be a little behind time in reaching Sacramento this trip, but when the weather becomes settled and the roads good, we have no doubt that they will be able to make the trip in less than ten days.

After putting down the *Alta* reprint, again I read from the *Bee* as Pa listened.

Up through the Rockies out of Salt Lake, then through South Pass, past the famous landmark Independence Rock, and across the Platte River to Fort Laramie. This is the major stop where riders could feel a sense of civilization again. Fort Laramie is one of the major trading posts and army headquarters of the Rockies region, where trappers, Indians, emigrants, and travelers all mix with one another.

From Fort Laramie down to the Cottonwood Springs Station and into Nebraska, the riders regularly pass stagecoaches and wagon trains, as their route follows already well-worn paths. Through woodlands gradually descending down into the plains and across buffalo and antelope country, riders are again likely to encounter Indian lodges or tepee villages, until they arrive at Fort Kearny in Nebraska, which was originally built to protect travelers along the Oregon Trail.

Across Nebraska and Kansas at this time of year, the trail is heavy with wagon trains. The Kickapoo Indians of Kansas are mostly peaceful and friendly farmers who had learned to get on very well with the white man, and thus gave the Pony Express Riders no trouble. And across the Missouri River from Kansas lay the final destination of the eastbound rider—St. Joseph!

The first two runs arrived at their respective destinations at almost the same time. From St. Joseph to Sacramento it had taken nine days and twenty-three hours—one hour ahead of schedule. The eastbound trip had taken one hour longer—exactly ten days!

I laid down the paper. If Pa wasn't asleep yet, he would be soon. It was dark and the fire was getting a little low.

Everything was quiet except for the night sounds—mostly crickets. I put a couple more pieces of wood on the fire and watched them spark and flare up. Then I settled down into my bedroll, watching the flames but reflecting back on that day when the first Pony Express rider from Missouri had reached Sacramento and then gone on to San Francisco.

What a celebration there had been that April 13! I wish we could have been there, but we heard about it as if we had been. Both the Senate and the Assembly of the legislature adjourned and the whole city turned out to welcome Sam Hamilton, returning from Sportsman's Hall, where he had been waiting for Warren Upson to return with the eastbound pouches. Sam was given a hero's welcome as he hurried to the steamer to take the mail on downriver to San Francisco. He didn't arrive there until the middle of the night, but that didn't stop the torchlight celebration, band music, fire engines, cheering, booming of cannons, and speechmaking, including one from my editor, Mr. Kemble! The people of San Francisco rejoiced, for it seemed that their isolation from the rest of the world was over.

It was a significant year for the Pony Express, with so much news going on between North and South, and over the election. The news that was carried back and forth between East and West was now less than a week and a half old, instead of nearly a month old! The news people were most excited of all. An article in the *Sacramento Union* read:

> Yesterday's proceedings, impromptu though they were, will long be remembered in Sacramento. The more earnest part of the "Pony" welcome had been arranged earlier in the day. This was the cavalcade of citizens to

meet the little traveler a short distance from the city and escort him into town. Accordingly, late in the day, a deputation of about eighty persons, together with a deputation of the Sacramento Hussars, assembled at the old Fort, and stretched out their lines on either side along the road along which the Express was to come.

Meanwhile, the excitement had increased all over the city. The balconies of the stores were occupied by ladies, and the roofs and sheds were taken possession of by the more agile of the opposite sex, straining to catch a glimpse of the "Pony."

At length—5:45—all this preparation was rewarded. First a cloud of rolling dust in the direction of the Fort, then a horseman, bearing a small flag, riding furiously down J Street, and then a straggling charging band of horsemen flying after him, heralding the coming of the Express; a cannon, placed on the square at Tenth Street, sent forth its noisy welcome. Amidst the firing and shouting, and waving of hats and ladies' handkerchiefs, the pony was seen coming down J Street, surrounded by about thirty of the citizen deputation. Out of this confusion emerged the Pony Express, trotting up to the door of the agency and depositing its mail in ten days from St. Joseph to Sacramento. Hip, hip, hurrah for the Pony Carrier!

Zack had said he would be riding somewhere between Nevada and Utah. As Pa and I rode along over the next couple of days, we hoped we would find him before we got too far. From Sacramento to Salt Lake was about six-hundred eighty miles!

The first ad I had seen for hiring Express riders was in the *Alta* earlier that year. It read: WANTED—young, skinny, wiry fellows, not over 18. Must be expert riders, willing to risk death daily. Orphans preferred. Wages $25 a week.

Zack must have lied about his age too. I heard about one Express rider named David Jay who was only thirteen, and another named William Cody who was fifteen. I don't know why they wanted them so young. A boy that age wouldn't know how to take care of himself if his horse broke a leg or if he got captured by Indians. Of course, they didn't want them to do anything but ride, and eventually they replaced the rifle with a knife. They weren't supposed to stop to fight the Indians who chased them—only outrun them! Maybe they wanted boys who had no family and who were so young that when they got killed, no one would miss them too much.

I suppose for that much pay, a lot of boys would love the adventure of the Pony Express. A hundred dollars a month *plus* board and keep was a lot of money!

They earned it, though. They rode all day and all night, changing horses every twenty or twenty-five miles over the most desolate stretches, every ten miles where it was more civilized. The places where they just changed horses were called swing stations. Each rider would ride three or four or even five horses, and then would stop at a station house where another rider would take over. Most of the time they rode seventy-five miles, usually on three horses. That took them seven or eight hours, and by that time they were ready to stop for food and sleep.

We got to Friday's Station at the Nevada border, and then down into the Carson valley of western Nevada. At the next station house, we met "Pony Bob" Haslam. Even though he was hardly more than a boy, he was already a legend from all the adventures and narrow escapes he had riding across Nevada. We spent the night there with the station keeper. Pony Bob was expected the next day in from the east, and the man kept us up half the night telling us of Bob's exploits over the last five months. When we told him we were looking for Zack Hollister, a shadow passed over his face.

"You know Zack?" Pa asked.

"Heard of him. Don't know him, though," the man replied.

"Why did you frown when I said his name?"

"On account of where I last heard he was riding."

"Where's that?" said Pa with concern.

"Nevada-Utah border. It's hot enough to be hell over there this time of year, Mister," the man said. "And the Paiutes is nasty as ever. Can't see as how I could let you and your daughter go over there and be able to live with myself later."

"I gotta see my son," said Pa.

"You stand a better chance of seeing him if you just wait for him to come home than for the two of you to head out across the Basin."

"Surely they wouldn't hurt two people just passing through," I said.

"Look, Miss," the man said, squinting his eyes at me. "Them Paiutes has been on the warpath since last May. There's over eight thousand of them. They got guns. They'll kill anybody, no matter whether they're innocent or not. They been attacking all over Nevada. We've lost half a dozen stations. I tell you, the two of you'd be dead before you was two days out."

I looked over at Pa, my eyes wide. I didn't like the sound of this!

For the next half hour or so, Pa and the station man talked about the Express and the Indians. I think the man was as anxious to have somebody to talk to as he was interested in convincing us not to go any farther into Nevada. Living out there mostly alone like they did, the two or three men at the station houses got tired of each other mighty quick and were plenty happy to see visitors—especially out in the middle of nowhere like in Nevada!

Pa later said to me that this particular fellow had talked so much because I was a pretty young lady, and he was trying to impress me with every tall tale he could think up to tell. I told Pa I didn't believe a word of it, but he insisted he wasn't pulling my leg. The truth of it is that the man did have tales to tell that made my blood shiver right inside me.

Pa even told him I was a newspaper writer and that he ought to be careful what he said or it might find its way into print someday. The man looked at me kinda funny, probably not believing Pa any more than Pa said *he* believed half his wild stories. But in any case, the man grew even more talkative after that.

"I tell you, Mister," he said after pouring each of us a cup of coffee, "if I was you, I'd turn straight around and head back the way you come. Word is them blamed Paiutes is headed this direction again."

"Again?" said Pa.

"Yep. They was all over here three, four months back. Major Ormsby took over a hundred men from Carson City and went out after them and was beaten back so bad they had to retreat to the city. Three weeks we was without the Express at all."

"What happened?"

"Finally the army got them back up into the mountains, helped by a snowstorm—in the middle of June, if you can believe that, little lady!" he added, turning toward me with a chuckle. "Since then it ain't been too bad at this end. But they keep raiding to the east, and, like I told you, word is they been heading back this way."

I took a sip of the coffee out of the tin cup the man had handed me. I couldn't keep from wincing. It was the bitterest, foulest stuff I had ever tasted! He must've crushed the beans with a hammer and then soaked them in water for a week, then boiled the water and called it coffee! I didn't care much for coffee anyway, but that thick, black syrup was awful. Pa was a regular coffee drinker, and I saw even him grimace slightly with his first drink. But he took a big gulp, swallowed it down bravely, and even had a second cup when the man offered it a little while later.

"Yeah, it's a wonder they keep any riders between Carson and Salt Lake," the man was saying. "Most of the originals have quit or been wounded or injured by this time anyway. But they keep on finding adventure-crazy young fools who'll hire on—meaning no offense to your son, Mister—but it takes a special breed of young rapscallion to put up with the dangers those boys face every day and every night out alone on the trail."

"Zack's a good rider," said Pa. "Maybe that'll keep him outta the way of—"

"They're *all* good riders, Mister!" interrupted the man. "Them that ain't—why, they'd be dead inside o' two or three days. They don't ride for the Express unless they're the best riders this side of the Ohio valley. It ain't good riding that keeps 'em alive in this foolhardy business."

"What is it?" I asked.

"It's pluck, little lady. It's determination, it's courage, it's guts, it's bravado. It's being able to look death in the face and not blink. You ever heard of Nick Wilson?" he asked, looking back toward Pa.

Pa shook his head.

"The blamed fool had a will to live beyond what any mortal oughta have to have. They left him for dead a couple of times, but he lived to tell what happened. Takes a lot of that too—a will to live."

He looked at us, almost as if baiting us to *ask* what happened before he would continue.

"We're listening," said Pa finally, taking another sip of the horrid coffee.

"Young Nick got to the relay station at Spring Valley, but there weren't nobody there. No sign of the keeper. Everything looked in order. No sign of attack. The relay horses were grazing near the cabins. So Nick, he didn't waste no time asking questions—he just jumped off his mount and started to saddle himself up a new horse.

"All of a sudden if he didn't hear a dreadful screaming whooping war cry that's the fear of every Express rider. He pulled out his Colt and started firing at the Indians that was heading toward the corral to steal the rest of the horses. The blamed fool took off chasing them to try to scare them away! But just then, from behind a tree close by, another redskin drew aim at Nick and sent a stone-tipped arrow right at him. Nick never saw him till it was too late. The arrow hit him above his left eye, and the arrowhead went right into his skull, halfway into his head. And there Nick fell and lay, right there among the trees.

"The Indians made off with all the horses, and figured they'd killed the young kid. But two men happened along a few hours later, found him, and saw that he was still alive. They tried to get the arrow out, but couldn't. All they managed to do was loosen the shaft from the stone tip, but there the arrowhead stuck, tight as ever. Weren't nothing much they could do, so they dragged him into the shade, then rode off to the next relay station to tell somebody they had a dead rider and an untended station.

"The next morning, two men came back from the station, figuring to bury the dead rider they'd been told about. Blamed if they didn't find Nick lying there, still breathing faintly! They didn't figure he'd survive the trip, but they hoisted him up across a saddle and carried him back with them to the Ruby Valley Station.

"But that kid had no hankering to die just yet. He stayed alive long enough for them to get a doctor to him. He cut out the arrowhead and bandaged up the gashing wound as best he could. He hadn't woke up since the arrow slammed into his head, and no one could figure why he kept breathing! But he did, and after a few more days he woke up and looked around and asked what all the fuss was about. I ain't lying to you, Mister, when I tell you that Nick was up and riding his stretch o' the Express line in less than two months!"

"What about his wound?" I couldn't help asking.

"Yeah, well, it weren't none too pretty, and that's a fact. Ol' Nick, he don't see too good outta that eye, and he still keeps a patch over it to hide the ugly hole. But blamed if he can't still ride with the best of 'em!"

Pa took in a deep breath, no doubt thinking of Zack. But the man hardly gave us a chance to get our wits back together before he was off again.

"Pony Bob, though," he said. "He's my favorite o' the riders. Why, that young fool, he don't know the meaning of the word *fear*. And he don't know the meaning of tired, neither! He's saved more lives than his own, and ridden more than his share of dangerous miles. You recollect what I was telling you about pluck, little lady?" he asked, looking at me.

I nodded.

"Well, Pony Bob's made of the stuff, I can tell ya that! Why, one time he was riding along lickety-split, and rounding a bend suddenly found himself squared off face-to-face with a war party of thirty mean, blood-thirsty Paiutes! He reined in his pony, sat there a minute, this one young kid staring back at an ambush from one of the most savage tribes west of the Sioux. I tell ya, them Paiutes has killed and massacred and burned to death more settlers and workers for the Express than all the other tribes put together!

"After sitting there a spell, that young rascal just drew out his revolver, and then just ever so slowly urged his pony

200 MICHAEL PHILLIPS

on. He just stared straight back into their faces, walked right up to 'em, gun held out just beside him. And without a word being said, them Indians watched him ride right through their midst and just keep going.

"Now *that's* guts!" he said, laughing and showing what teeth he had left. "Them redskins was probably so surprised that he'd challenge them right to their faces like that, they couldn't help admiring him!"

The station tender himself was almost as good a subject for an article as anything he was telling us. His name was Claude Tavish, which he only told us after Pa asked him. He had broad shoulders and big, muscular arms, which was probably a good thing for all the work he had to do around the place—building and repairing things, blacksmithing, fixing meals for the riders, and tending their horses and getting them saddled and ready. He said he had a helper who came out the four days a week when the riders came through in both directions.

Mr. Tavish had probably been a blacksmith before, and that's how he got so strong. But now he was starting to get a little fat. His hair was getting thin, too, and gray around the edges. He didn't look as if he worried too much about what he looked like. His face had four or five days' worth of beard stubble on it, and the graying whiskers stood out on the brown face. He had a pleasant enough expression, and a nice smile except for the two or three missing teeth. But he seemed tired, from more than just the work—almost as if life itself was exhausting him.

If we could have gotten him to stop talking so much about all the Express riders he knew, I would have liked to ask him about his *own* life. I had the feeling that behind all the tales he was telling us was probably a sad story of his own—maybe a family dead, or left behind. I couldn't help but wonder why he was out here like this, all by himself in a dangerous job, at his age. It was plain he liked people by the way he wanted to visit with us. But here he was miles from anybody. He reminded me a little of how Alkali Jones might have been at fifty, but without the same gleam in his eye. His eyes did sparkle some when he was talking, but behind the sparkle was a look that made me suspect there was pain somewhere back in his past.

All the time I'd been observing *him*, he had been talking about Bob Haslam. "Fortitude, that's what he's got—enough for a dozen riders! Why, during the Paiute War, he started off his ride one day with a seventy-five-mile stretch to the Reese River Station. That's all a rider's suppose to have to do in a day, but on account of the Indian trouble, there weren't nobody to hand the mail off to, and all the horses had been requisitioned by the army to fight back the Indians. So Pony Bob, he just kept on riding, hoping for better luck fifteen miles away at Buckland's. But there his replacement refused to ride from fear of all the war parties out on the loose.

"Pony Bob had already been riding some nine or ten hours, but there wasn't no one else to carry the mail. So with a fresh horse, he took off again, an' had to pass through three more stations without finding another rider to replace him. He'd ridden 190 miles almost continuously!

"An' what should be the news awaiting him? Only that the rider from the other direction had been badly hurt in a fall. Pony Bob got himself an hour and a half of sleep before they woke him up to make the return trip. Off he rode again, only to get to the first station that he had left several hours

before to find all five of the crew murdered by Indians and all
the horses stolen. He kept right on, all the way to Buckland's,
where he slept nine hours, waiting for nightfall when there
would be less danger from Indians. Then he continued on
through the night, outrunning a party of Paiutes who spotted
him once, and finally arriving back here after 380 miles!

"I tell ya, I was glad to see the lad! I made him the finest
meal I knew how to make, and put him to bed and told him
to sleep for a week! He'd only lost four hours from the scheduled time after riding practically four days on ten hours' sleep!
Quite a kid! The company gave him a special hundred-dollar
prize after that."

"Sounds like he's a fellow you oughta talk to and write an
article about, Corrie!" said Pa.

"You'll meet him in the morning!" said Mr. Tavish. "He's
due in sometime afore noon."

"How long will he be here?" I asked.

"Day or two. If there ain't no Indian trouble, he'll ride out
East again day after tomorrow evening."

"Might there be Indian trouble . . . this close to California?" I asked, growing nervous again.

"There's been reports of Paiutes scouting this way. But
don't you worry none about Pony Bob. He can outrun anyone. Why, there was another time when he rode into the Dry
Creek Station and found the whole staff murdered. He kept
going to Cold Springs, and the station was burned down and
the dead body of the station keeper lying in the ashes."

As he spoke, Mr. Tavish stopped momentarily and drew
in a deep breath. "Funny how fate works, ain't it?" he said re-
flectively. "When I first was hired by the Express, I worked the
Cold Springs Station, but then I got transferred here. Other-

wise, that woulda been me laying there with a Paiute arrow sticking out of my chest."

He paused again. "But ol' Bob, he kept on riding. Wasn't nothing much else he could do, I don't reckon. When he came to Sand Creek, he told the station tender all he'd seen and managed to get him to leave with him. That night the Sand Creek Station was burned down, too.

"Those were a bad couple of months back the early part of the summer! It's better now, but there ain't no one I'd rather was coming our way than Pony Bob. If there is trouble, he'll know of it and be far enough ahead of 'em to warn us."

He stopped again, and the station room was quiet for a minute or two. I looked around and began noticing all the stuff hanging up and sitting on shelves or in crates everywhere. The floor was dirt. Several bunks were built right into the far wall, and besides the bench Pa and I were sitting on, there wasn't much else in the way of furniture. Just a table, one chair, and empty crates turned up on end for people to sit on. There was a big wood stove for cooking with shelves full of supplies—flour, sugar, coffee, cornmeal, hams and bacon, containers of dried fruit and meat, tea, coffee, beans. All around the rest of the room were scattered an assortment of other things they might need—tools, brooms, candles, blankets, buckets, medicines, borax, tin dishes, turpentine, castor oil, rubbing alcohol, even sewing supplies. The alcohol was only for treating wounds or injuries. No drinking of any liquor was allowed at any of the Pony Express stations. Of course, there were lots of guns and rifles and ammunition around too.

Outside there were a couple of other buildings—a blacksmithing forge, a stable and barn. They had to have everything on hand that might possibly be needed for any situation—

Indian attack, lame horses, broken legs, loose shoes, wounds, injury. At most of the Nevada stations, the ground was so dry that there was no grass for animals to graze on, so they had to have a large supply of oats and other feed on hand, too.

"Where'd you say your boy was at?" Mr. Tavish asked Pa.

"Not sure. Far as we know, out toward Utah."

Mr. Tavish gave a low whistle. "That ain't good, Mister. He musta come in after the Indian troubles quieted down. They brought in lots of new kids in July to replace the ones that left. When'd he join up?"

"Early July. He said he'd heard there was openings out toward eastern Nevada."

"Openings is right!" laughed Mr. Tavish. "The whole blame line from Carson to Salt Lake was open! Weren't hardly nobody left."

The look on Pa's face was not a happy one. My heart sank just to hear the station man's words.

"Well, can't be helped now," he went on. "If your boy's alive, he's alive. If he's dead, I'd probably have heard about it. So we'll wait on Bob tomorrow and see if he knows anything. One thing's for sure, Mister, you ain't gonna take the little lady here no further east than right here. If you was fool enough to go by yourself, there wouldn't be much I could do to stop you, though I wouldn't give a plugged nickel for your chances out there alone. But with a young lady—nope, I just wouldn't let you go another mile past here."

Pa and I looked at each other. I guess this is where we'd be spending the night!

"You ever heard of Billy Cody?" Mr. Tavish asked.

"Nope," Pa answered. I nodded my head that I had.

"What'd you hear about him?" asked Mr. Tavish.

"Only that he wasn't much older than a boy," I said.

"Cody's just like Pony Bob! Guts of a man inside the body of a kid. I hope your brother's like that . . . for his sake. Otherwise, even if he is still alive, he ain't likely to stay that way for long. But let me tell you about Cody," he went on.

"They gave him an extra bit of mail one time, a box of money that had to get through. Now the Indians, they'll attack anybody or anything just to be ornery. But the bandits and thieves with white skin, they're more particular. They're after loot. Well, I tell you what happened—there'd been reports of a couple outlaws in the region where Cody was riding. And with him having to carry cash money, it was a dangerous situation. So Cody, he hid his *mochila* and mail cases under an extra leather blanket. Then he filled a couple of extra pouches with paper so that if he was held up, the robbers would think they had the real thing.

"Well, sure enough, blamed if Cody didn't get stopped as he was riding through a narrow ravine. The two bandits had guns on him and told him to get off his horse and put his hands in the air. He obeyed. One of the men rode closer, put away his gun, and reached out to grab the fake mail pouches from Cody's horse. But instead of waiting for them to take it and hope they'd leave without discovering them to be worthless, Billy suddenly flung the whole blanket up in the man's face, drawing his gun at the same instant, and shot the thief. The other man fled. Billy jumped on his horse and took off after him."

Mr. Tavish stopped in his story long enough to give a great laugh.

"That's the kind of kids out riding this part of the Express territory," he said. "Kids that can send grown men to flight!

Yes sir, I hope the young fella you're looking for can take care of himself like that!"

I shuddered. Just the thought of Zack having to shoot at or possibly even kill someone was enough to turn my stomach. I could hardly stand the thought that he was mixed up in such a violent thing as the Pony Express seemed to be.

I knew Pa was thinking the same thing. He and Uncle Nick had run with a much rougher crowd and had fought in the Mexican War. But I suppose it seemed different to Pa, thinking about his own son. Things he went through himself, he didn't want his kids to have to face. And however young Bill Cody and Pony Bob and all the rest of them were, to me and Pa, Zack still seemed too young to be part of all this.

The rest of that night we listened to more of Claude Tavish's stories, although by the time supper was over, Pa'd managed to get him talking about something besides the Pony Express. It turned out Mr. Tavish had fought in the Mexican War too, and that kept him and Pa busy till late talking about their recollections. At least it took our minds off worrying about Zack.

I mixed up some biscuits to go with beans and a ham hock Mr. Tavish had boiling on top of the stove. He raved and raved about those biscuits, even though there wasn't anything to them that he couldn't have done himself. He didn't have any baking powder to mix in, so they were flat and hard. But he kept saying he hadn't eaten anything so good in years. "Anything tastes better if a woman's hand's gone into the making of it," he said. "A man and woman can put all the same ingredients in a bowl, and mix it up, and cook it just the same, and feed whatever it is to a passel of hungry miners or cowboys or anybody else. They'll all cuss and complain at the man for his lousy grub, but they'll rave and carry on at how wonderful the lady's food tastes. I always figured they weren't treating me none too fairly, but after tasting them biscuits of yours, little lady, I reckon I know what they been getting at all these years. There just ain't no denying that a woman's hand's got something special in it."

"They taste about the same as always to me," I said. "But thank you all the same, Mr. Tavish."

I listened with interest to the two men talk, because now every story that came out gave me new glimpses into Pa's past during those years before we were together again.

"Where was you at?" Pa had asked Mr. Tavish.

"Buena Vista, where else!" answered the station man.

"You *were* at the center of it all," said Pa. "Me and Nick never got that close to Santa Anna."

"Lucky for you! He was a mean cuss—came at us with fifteen thousand men. But he hadn't counted on Zachary Taylor! No sir. Us with our five thousand just waited in the mountains for them to attack. Dreadful night, I can tell you— wind, rain, hardly no sleep. But it must have been worse for them Mexicans, because the next day we sent 'em running!"

"Tell me," asked Pa. "What did the men think of President Polk?"

"I don't know, what's to think? He was president and we was following orders," answered Tavish.

"Did they think the war was a good one? What about slavery?"

"What about it?"

"Did you talk about how what you were really fighting for was to have more slave states in the country?"

"Tarnation, no! We were just fighting the Mexicans. We didn't know what it was about. Why, did you fellers in California talk about all that?"

"No," said Pa thoughtfully. "Back then I didn't know what it was about any more than you did. I was just curious, that's all."

When we went to bed that night, I lay in my bedroll on one of those hard wooden bunks. I couldn't get right to sleep, and as I listened to Pa and Mr. Tavish snoring, all his stories about the Indians came back into my mind. I should have been more concerned for Zack, but instead I grew more and more terrified for myself! I remembered his words about how savage the Paiutes were, and how they were headed our way, and how many people they'd killed.

Then I started to realize how far out in the middle of the desert we were—twenty or twenty-five miles past Carson City—and how we were all alone. Pretty soon every little noise I heard made me jump, and I started imagining that the place was surrounded by fifty or a hundred Indians, sneaking up on us quietly in the night, to kill us!

In the distance a wolf's cry rang out. I practically jumped out of my skin! My heart was racing, and I couldn't imagine how Pa and Mr. Tavish could just sleep so calmly through it all. All sorts of little noises I hadn't noticed before seemed to be coming out of the night—creaks and groans from the cabin, an occasional whistle of wind through a crack, now and then a bird or other animal, a sound from the stables, the bark of a wild dog, and always the howl of the wolves far off in the mountains.

I had been out on the trail alone many times, but never had I been so scared as I was tonight.

Never had the morning sunshine looked so good! The wind had died down and whatever the spooky noises had been during the night, they had gone away too. The place was calm and cheery; even Mr. Tavish looked more chipper as a result of his company and the discovery of a comrade from the days before the gold rush and California's statehood. The dull, sad look in his eyes had given way to something almost like enthusiasm.

"Well, little lady, what's you and me gonna rustle up for breakfast?" he greeted me warmly. "Flapjacks?"

"We need eggs for that," I said. "And milk."

"We got no milk, but I just may be able to lay my hands on two or three eggs," he said with a wink, "*if* my hens have been the good girls they oughta have been during the night. You just wait here, and I'll go check the coop."

He disappeared outside, and returned in about three minutes, face beaming, with two brand-new eggs in each hand.

"We'll make us up the finest batch of flapjacks this side of the gold diggin's!" he announced, and immediately began taking down pans and dumping flour into a bowl. I don't know what he needed me for!

"Here, little lady," he called out after a minute. "You take over here. We want 'em to have that female touch. I gotta go draw us some water. You get 'em cooking on the griddle there. You'll find syrup and grease up there on the shelf to the right. While we're at it, what say we fry us up some bacon to go with 'em?"

I nodded and smiled my agreement. Mr. Tavish left the cabin just as Pa came back in.

"What's Tavish so all-fired beaming about?" asked Pa with a grin.

"I don't know, Pa. Talking about the war last night seemed to perk him up."

"And the presence of a young lady on the premises might have had something to do with it!" added Pa.

Whatever it was, when the stationmaster returned ten minutes later, not a speck of gray stubble was left on his clean-shaven face. He also put on a new clean shirt for breakfast. In the meantime, his young helper, a Mexican boy named Juan who lived a few miles away, had come to help him prepare for Pony Bob's arrival. By then I had a good stack of pancakes ready, with several more on the griddle. Mr. Tavish rang his bell, and the four of us gathered around the table while he offered a simple prayer of thanks. Pa and I sat down on the bench. Juan pulled up one of the crates, and Mr. Tavish took over at the stove to watch the flapjacks and the last of the sizzling bacon. He wouldn't hear of me doing any more now. I was his guest, he said.

We had barely started eating when the sounds of galloping horses caught our attention. Mr. Tavish's smile faded. There were too many horses for it to be a Pony rider!

He threw down the metal spatula with a clang onto the stove and ran to the door. He opened it for a second, then slammed it shut with a thud and pulled the iron bolt down across it.

"Indians!" he cried. "Juan . . . get the rifles and ammo!"

Even before anyone had the chance to ask him if he was serious, one of the two windows of the cabin shattered, its glass tinkling down the wall onto the dirt floor. At almost the same instant, an arrow slammed into the opposite wall.

Mr. Tavish ran to it, yanked it out of the timber, examined it for a second, then swore under his breath. "Paiutes!" The despair in his voice filled me with a dread such as I had never felt before, and hope I never ever feel again in my life!

I looked around for Pa, but there was only time enough for our eyes to meet briefly. In that second, a multitude of unspoken thoughts passed between our hearts. But there was no time even for a word, for the next instant Juan was *shoving* a rifle into my hand, and Mr. Tavish was showing Pa where to crouch down behind one of the windows. I took the gun without even thinking, and before I knew it I was huddled down a little ways from Pa. Things happened so fast there was no time for me to stop and realize, *I don't want to kill anyone . . . even an Indian!*

I don't know how much time passed. It could have been an hour. It could have been five minutes for all I know. There was a lot of gunfire, both inside and outside the cabin, and several more arrows flew through the windows, both of which were broken. After one of them, I heard Pa shout, "Corrie, you keep your head down, you hear!" His voice held such a fearful yet commanding authority, I didn't dare crane my neck up anymore to try to see what was going on. I'd never heard such a sound in his voice before!

The Indians must have had guns too, because there were far too many gunshots to be coming from just the three guns inside. The rifle I still held in my hand was silent!

"Use that carbine, little lady!" Mr. Tavish called out at me, but I didn't have words to answer him. I just kept lying there on the floor, trying to stay out of the way. Pa was shooting out the window at the attackers. It all seemed completely natural at the time. Only later did I realize that he was trying to *kill* someone with that gun he was firing.

"I was praying to God the whole time," he told me later, "that I *wouldn't* have to kill no one. But when his family's in danger, a man does things he might not do otherwise. And if I had to kill to keep them Indians away from you, Corrie, I would have done it and asked God if it was right or wrong later. I'd have done just about anything to keep their savage hands off you, including getting myself killed trying."

In the meantime, it seemed as if we were all going to be killed!

Thwaack! An arrow flew through the window above my head, coming at a low angle, and stuck into the adjacent wall next to me only about five feet away. Pa glanced over at it. His face was white, and he was sweating.

"I got me one . . . I got one!" shouted Juan.

"Keep down, you little fool!" yelled Tavish, who was crouched down reloading his rifle. "Just because you shoot one Indian don't give you no reason to stick your head up like that and give 'em an easy target. When you've picked off fifteen or twenty, then you can shout about it!"

His rifle reloaded, Mr. Tavish turned back to the window, one knee bent to the ground, raised the gun to his shoulder, squinted his eye along the barrel, and started firing rapidly again at our attackers, his gun resting on the bottom ledge where broken glass was strewn about.

He only got off a couple more shots; then all of a sudden Mr. Tavish screamed out in pain. I looked over just in time to see him falling backward to the floor, an arrow sticking out of his shoulder.

The gunfire in the cabin ceased. Juan and Pa looked at each other as if wondering what to do now. The next instant, however, Juan was firing from his vantage point with renewed vengeance.

"Corrie, get over and see what you can do for him!" yelled Pa.

"What do I do, Pa?"

"I don't know. See how bad it is. Get a towel or something and keep it from bleeding!"

Pa turned back to the window and started shooting again. I crept over to where Mr. Tavish lay. His shirt was torn and red, and the warm blood was dripping down and soaking into the dirt. His face was white, but he managed to give me a thin smile.

"I'm sorry, little lady," he whispered. "I didn't mean to get you mixed up in nothin' like this."

"How is . . . is it bad?" I asked.

"I'll live. Them Paiutes ain't gonna get rid of Tavish so easy, but—" He winced in pain. "Blame if it don't hurt somethin' fierce, though!"

"What should I do?" I asked. Thinking back, I realize that I didn't hear any more gunfire after that. For the next two or three minutes, the whole world centered around me and Claude Tavish. "Should I try to . . . to get the arrow out?" I asked, shuddering involuntarily even as I said the words.

"I don't know if you can," he answered, closing his eyes and breathing in a slow deep breath as if preparing himself for the ordeal. "But the thing's gotta come out."

"What should I do?"

"Look in there and see how far it's stuck in. If it didn't get all twisted or lodged against a bone, you oughta be able to yank it straight out."

I bent over a little closer, trying to see.

"Get in there with your fingers, little lady! A little blood ain't gonna hurt you. Ain't no way you're gonna find how deep it's gone unless you get in there and wipe some of the blood away and see where the tip is."

I leaned closer toward him, but I couldn't see a thing. His shirt was all red and the wooden shaft of the arrow disappeared inside it. I reached out and gingerly touched the arrow right where it went into his shirt, but the same instant pulled my hand back.

"Get in there, little lady!" This time Mr. Tavish's words were a command. "You want me to bleed to death? Get in there, and if the arrowhead ain't all the way inside, then you give it a good hard pull!"

Again I probed with my fingers, tearing at the hole in his shirt to make it bigger. There was so much blood I still couldn't see. I didn't even stop to think what I was doing at the time, but later from seeing the blood all over me, I realized that I grabbed the hem of my dress as I crouched there beside him and used it to wipe away some of the blood so that I could see the wound better.

Less than a minute had gone by since he'd fallen. The blood was still warm and wet and oozing from his shoulder. I tore a bigger hole in his shirt and wiped back the blood as best I could. Then I felt all around the arrow with my fingers. The sensation of feeling his wet bloody flesh, with the arrow sticking out, was too horrible to describe. I turned away, my stomach retching. I gagged two or three times, but luckily didn't throw up. I turned back to him, took a deep breath, gritted my teeth and lips together to keep my stomach down where it belonged, and tried to examine the wound again.

I felt all about. My hands were all bloody by this time, but by now I was determined to get the arrow out. I could feel the jagged hole the rough arrowhead had made. I forced my fingers to move around it, feeling at the base of the arrow. Down low, just at the skin line, I could feel the top end of the stone arrowhead. Feeling that hard piece of stone inside his soft flesh made me gag again.

"Is the head exposed?" asked Mr. Tavish.

"It's right at the edge of your shoulder," I said.

"It ain't all covered up?"

"No, I can feel the top of it."

"Good. You pull it out."

I shuddered again, clenched my teeth, and grabbed hold of the arrow with both hands and pulled.

My hands just slid up the shaft, but it remained as tightly lodged in Mr. Tavish's shoulder as ever.

"Blood's as slippery as grease!" he said. "Wipe off your hands first."

I grabbed at the end of my dress again, wiped off my hands as best I could, then wiped off the shaft of the arrow, trying to clean if off right down to the wound.

I clutched at it again, down low right on his skin. This time I could feel my dried hands take hold against the wood. I closed my eyes, then yanked upward for all I was worth.

Mr. Tavish let out a horrible yell, rising up off the ground as I pulled, then falling back down again. The sound of his voice made me let go. When I looked back down at his face, he was breathing rapidly in obvious pain. But the arrow was still stuck in his shoulder!

"Good girl," he whispered, though his eyes were closed. "One more time and we'll have it."

I swallowed hard, then grabbed the arrow again. This time I determined I wasn't going to let go. I pulled again, but this time when I felt the resistance of the arrow sticking into him, I held on all the tighter and gave one mighty tug.

I fell backward, the arrow in my hand.

This time Mr. Tavish hadn't screamed out, although I had felt his body rise up again as I yanked. He was lying on the floor, his eyes still closed, breathing rapidly. I can't even imagine how painful it must have been for him. I don't know why he didn't just faint from the agony of it.

"Now go over to the cupboard behind the stove," he said, still in a faint, quiet voice. "Behind the black pot there's a bottle of whiskey. You go get it . . . but keep your head down."

He must have sensed me hesitate, because I saw his eyes open a crack.

"There's alcohol there on the shelf," I said.

He forced a smile. "Don't want alcohol," he said. "I want whiskey."

Still I hesitated.

"I know . . . I know, little lady," he said. "But them rules is to keep the kids in line and not for the likes of old fellers like me. You won't tell Mr. Russell, will you? Besides, I only keep it for medicinal purposes."

I got to my feet and ran over to the cupboard. The bottle of whiskey was right where he said it was. He must have had a number of wounds to treat recently, because the bottle was less than half full. I took it back to him and pulled out the cork.

Without a moment's hesitation, Mr. Tavish reached out with his uninjured hand, took the bottle from me, and took a long swig that used up half the remaining contents in one huge swallow. Then he handed it back to me.

"Pour it into the wound," he said. "You gotta get it right in the hole, or I'll die of gangrene before the month's out!"

I put the mouth of the bottle to the hole in his shoulder and poured it in. His face twisted up in an awful look of pain. He sucked in a wincing breath through his clenched teeth, his eyes shut tight. He held his breath for what seemed like a long time, then slowly let it out in a long sigh as his body relaxed.

"Once more, Corrie," he whispered. "Pour it in again."

I did, and he winced sharply just like before, though this time it didn't seem to be quite so bad.

"Now go get a towel. Soak a piece of it in whiskey and stuff it in there and try to bandage me up as best you can so's I don't keep bleeding."

I don't know when the shooting had stopped. Like I said, I hadn't noticed anything but Mr. Tavish. But suddenly it did seem awful quiet. I stood up to go find a towel. But as I turned around, my heart sank with an altogether new terror.

There stood an Indian with a rifle pointed straight at Pa!

I stood paralyzed with fear while three or four more Paiutes climbed in through the broken windows, training their guns on the rest of us.

The Most Unusual Breakfast in the World

CHAPTER THIRTY-ONE

They must have known they'd gotten one of us when only two guns were firing at them instead of three. Then when Juan stopped to reload, the Indian had jumped through the silent window, and the next second Pa was staring down the barrel of a Paiute gun.

Pa could have tried to shoot him, of course. But then they'd both have been dead, and there would have been a dozen more Indians following right after the first. Not only would it have been pointless, Pa didn't want to shoot anyone anyway. I saw him glance over at me, all blood-stained like I was, as he set his rifle down. I knew he would have killed to save me if he needed to. But now it looked as if we were all going to die together! And the look of futility on his face said there wasn't much he could do about it.

By now one of them had opened the door, and more Indians were pouring into the cabin, some holding bows, others rifles, talking in a strange language, making gestures and signs, looking around, taking stock of the inside of the station. They didn't seem to pay any attention to my being a woman, which I know was the main thing on Pa's mind. I don't suppose I looked all that attractive to them in the condition I was in!

A few of them started taking things—some tools and supplies, what food they could carry—while two of the others talked among themselves. Then one of them gave what sounded like an order, and another ran outside and returned a minute later with several strands of buffalo rope. He threw one of them to his companion, and the two of them grabbed Juan and Pa and started to tie them up. Then one of them approached me, grabbed at my arm, and pulled me over against one of the two support timbers in the middle of the cabin. He yanked my hands behind my back and tied me up too. He was none too gentle, and he smelled horrible. I tried not to cry out, but he hurt my wrists as he twisted the rope around them and yanked it tight.

I don't know what danger they thought Mr. Tavish was going to be in his condition, but one of them dragged him by the feet over next to me, then pulled him viciously to his feet and tied him up behind me. We could feel each other's hands but couldn't see each other.

"I'm sorry about this, little lady," Mr. Tavish groaned softly. "These blamed Pai—"

A blow across the side of his head and face put an end to whatever he had been going to say.

Meanwhile, the Indians who were taking things seemed to have gotten all they wanted out of the cabin and had left. Outside we could hear movement and rustling. The door was still open and I could see them dragging brush and bales of straw from the stables over toward the station. Out one of the windows I could see the same thing going on.

"What are they doing?" I whispered when the one who had been tying us up went over to check on the knots around Pa and Juan.

"Fixing to burn down the place," Mr. Tavish whispered back. "It's their favorite way—surround the place with kindling and firewood and set it ablaze."

"What about us?" I said in horror.

"It's the Paiute way of burning the white man at the stake. The good-for-nothin' savages!"

"They're going to leave us inside?" I gasped.

"Leave us inside to burn, take us outside and put arrows through our hearts—their kind ain't too particular how the white man dies."

"Pa!" I wailed.

"Be brave, Corrie," I heard Pa answer, even though I couldn't see him from the direction I was facing. "Just remember—this ain't the end of it. Our Father will take care of us, even if—"

He never finished. I heard a big *whack,* and I squirmed at my ropes, straining around to try to see Pa. I managed just to see him out of the corner of my eye. His head was hanging limp, a red gash from the butt of the Indian's rifle already swelling up from above his ear down into the upper part of his cheek. The blow had knocked him unconscious.

I found myself wishing they'd do the same to me. If I was going to get burned up, I'd rather be asleep!

There was still a lot of activity outside, but it looked as if they had just about got the cabin all surrounded with dry material that would ignite in just a few seconds. Then it got very quiet. The Indian who had seemed to be in charge walked out the door and was gone for two or three minutes. When he finally came back in, the look on his face was one of taking a last look around to make sure he hadn't missed anything. A handful of others followed him in, then stood back waiting. He walked slowly about, indicating now one thing, now another, with a grunt and a few words. The others picked up whatever he'd pointed to and took it outside. They grabbed up several blankets on a shelf that had been missed before, a shovel, an axe, an unopened bag of beans.

The leader walked slowly around the table, eyeing it carefully, then over to the stove, where he first noticed the flapjacks and bacon still frying away. By now the two large pancakes on the griddle were black on the bottom, and the thin strips of bacon burned to cinders. But the smell seemed to attract his attention. He glanced back at the table, then again eyed the stove, this time lifting the lid off the pot of coffee, which still sat there steaming hot. The smell seemed to appeal to him. He smiled, replaced the lid, took a tin cup from the shelf behind the stove, and poured out a cup of the black brew.

As he sipped at it, he must have thought more of it than I had the previous evening, because he smiled again, then called to his companions, apparently asking them if they wanted some. They all set down the things they'd been carrying outside and approached him, grabbing cups wherever they could find them, and pouring coffee for themselves.

The five or six Indians left in the cabin talked and laughed as they sipped at Mr. Tavish's strong coffee. Then before I even realized what was happening, they all sat down around the table, using *our* plates and eating up the flapjacks that *we* had cooked!

There they were, getting ready to burn the place down, and us along with it, and they were celebrating by eating *our* breakfast!

After some discussion, they finally figured out that the syrup was sweet and tasted good on top of the pancakes. They poured it on, then tore the pancakes in half with their fingers, picked them up, and ate them. It was the messiest breakfast I had ever seen in my life, and if I hadn't been about to die, I probably would have laughed myself silly. As it was, I didn't know whether to laugh or cry or look the other way and try to ignore their uncivilized antics.

But they were impossible to ignore. By now they were making quite a racket. The pancakes and bacon were gone in a few minutes, and they had syrup and grease all over their faces and hands. Then they got up and started rummaging all through the cabin to see if there was anything *else* they could find to eat! One of them grabbed up the bottle of syrup and drank down the rest of it, then set it back down on the table with a crash and a loud laugh. The rest were helping themselves to more coffee, spilling half of it in their haste. One had discovered a tin of dried venison, which all the rest now came and started to fight over.

Then suddenly, in the distance, a bugle sounded, followed by the pounding gallop of approaching horses.

All activity inside the cabin stopped immediately, and they looked around at one another. Immediately, I realized that the Paiutes had heard the sound, too, and were scared by it. They dropped everything and ran for the door. Within fifteen seconds, amid shouts and unintelligible cries, we heard their ponies galloping away in the opposite direction, followed by pursuing gunfire.

Pony Bob!
CHAPTER THIRTY-TWO

*I*t wasn't the cavalry at all who had rescued us!

Pony Bob was early in arriving on his run from the East. He'd seen signs of the Indians from far off and had ridden in shooting and firing up a storm.

He was a courageous young boy, that much we already knew, but I doubt if he really expected to scare off twenty or thirty Paiutes all by himself. But he had help that we didn't know about when we first heard him approach. All he'd been trying to do was distract the war party long enough for that help to arrive. Fortunately for everybody, he didn't have to wait for it before he got into the cabin to untie us.

We heard his horse gallop up and stop, and a few seconds later he ran inside.

"Am I glad to see you!" Mr. Tavish whispered weakly. "Get us outta these ropes, Bob!"

Pony Bob was already slicing through the cords around my hands and Mr. Tavish's with a knife. The instant I was free I ran over to Pa and threw my arms around him.

"I love you, Pa!" I said, not able to keep from crying and not the least bit embarrassed about my tears. I hardly even realized that he was still bound hand and foot and couldn't have hugged me back if he'd tried!

Pony Bob was just what I might have expected. Small, thin, six inches shorter than Zack, and with a recklessness, almost a mean streak in his young eyes. He didn't look as if he was afraid of anybody or anything. Whether it was courage that drove him, or just that he didn't have anyone in this life he cared about enough to stay alive for, I couldn't tell. His face showed little trace of a beard, but his eyes had the hardness of a man of fifty. In Mr. Tavish's eyes I had seen the dull pain of loneliness; in young Bob Haslam's I saw only emptiness.

"Everyone outside!" gasped Mr. Tavish, even before Pa and Juan were free. "We gotta pull the straw away from the station. One flaming arrow and the place'll go up like a dry brushfire in a hot wind!"

He staggered outside, and with his uninjured arm began dragging back the brush and straw the Indians had piled up. In a minute all four of the rest of us had joined him.

"By now they'll know they was run off by only Bob. They'll either be back or will try to set the place off from where they're hiding!"

"In two or three minutes the army'll be here," said young Haslam.

"What?" Mr. Tavish said, breathing hard and gritting his teeth against the pain.

"Ormsby's out from Carson. He heard they'd attacked the Widow Cutt's place yesterday. I'd seen signs of the raiding party all the way in the last ten miles. I ran into his troop of men five or six miles back and told him I thought they were heading for the station. They're right behind me."

"Blamed if you ain't better'n a whole hundred cavalrymen!" said Tavish, his face flushed with fever and exertion.

The next instant a shot rang out, followed by the sound of a bullet ricocheting off an iron wagon wheel next to the station house. It had come from the direction the Indians had gone.

"Them Paiutes is back!" cried Tavish. "Everyone inside!"

We rushed into the station. Pony Bob bolted the door. Pa, Juan, and Bob grabbed rifles and sent several volleys of fire out through the windows, hoping to discourage the war party from trying the same thing again. Mr. Tavish, still bleeding, made me help him get a rifle up onto the window ledge where he could rest it against his good shoulder.

But the shooting didn't last long this time.

Again we heard a bugle call, followed by thunderous hoof-beats. A minute later Major Ormsby's troop of forty men roared past after the Paiutes, who were back on their horses and making for the mountains as fast as they could. We never saw them again.

Once the cavalry had passed, Mr. Tavish sank into the one chair, and Pony Bob packed and dressed the wound.

"The army's bugle didn't sound anything like what I heard before you came," I said to Pony Bob when he had finished bandaging Mr. Tavish's shoulder.

He and Mr. Tavish laughed.

"That's because Pony Bob's weren't no army bugle, little lady. Back when the Express started, they gave every rider a horn so as to announce his coming to the station. Wasn't long before everybody knew we didn't need 'em. You can see the dust five miles away, and hear the horse's hooves a mile away, so what use was the horn? But Pony Bob, he just kept his. How come, Bob?"

"Aw, just for fun," replied Bob. "You never know when you're gonna have need of something like that."

"If the army ever heard someone trying to imitate their charge with a little tin horn like that, they'd take it from him and trample it flat!" said Mr. Tavish.

"Anyhow, the Indians believed he was a one-man cavalry charge," laughed Pa. "So I'm mighty glad you saved it, son. Say, you know a Zack Hollister?"

Pony Bob's face grew thoughtful. "Yeah, I think I heard of him," he answered after a minute. "Rides over to the east. Ain't never run into him myself, though."

"These folks come from California looking to find him," put in Mr. Tavish. "You reckon they could make it to Utah, Bob?"

"Not unless they want to go through what you've just been through every day—and that's *without* a station to hide in and no cavalry within miles."

"You reckon the Paiutes are going on the warpath again?"

"They're everywhere out there. I was lucky to make it through. You want my advice, Mister," said Pony Bob to Pa, "you'll saddle up and head for Carson and just keep right on going past the Sierras. If Zack Hollister's your kin, there ain't much you can do for him now. But if you aim to keep this pretty girl of yours alive, you'd best take my advice."

"When's the safest time to leave for Carson, you reckon?" asked Pa.

"Right now," answered Mr. Tavish. "Ormsby's driven the savages up into the hills. They won't bother nobody for some few days, and he and his men will be moving back that way, so if there was trouble, they'd be on the trail with you."

"We ought to do what they say, Pa," I said. "If we are ever going to find Zack, it doesn't seem as if this is the time to do it."

Pa thought long and hard for a few minutes. He knew we had to go back, but he was torn with wanting to find his son.

Finally he nodded. "Well then, Corrie, I reckon you and me had best saddle up our horses and get our things together."

"You could make Carson, or maybe even Friday's Station before nightfall," said Mr. Tavish.

"I'm obliged to you for everything, Tavish," said Pa, shaking the station man's good hand. "All except for nearly getting us killed, that is!"

"You come back and visit again, Hollister," he said, smiling weakly. "And bring the little lady with you. She's a right fine nurse, along with being a cook and a newspaper writer!"

"You take care of yourself!" said Pa.

"And get a doctor to fix up your shoulder," I added, giving Mr. Tavish a one-sided hug. "I don't want to worry about anything happening to it."

Pa and I were on the trail back in the direction of Carson City in less than twenty minutes.

We rode for the rest of the morning in silence, interrupted only by Pony Bob as he passed, finishing up his run to Carson. We had probably started fifteen or twenty minutes ahead of him, but he caught up with us in no time.

We heard him coming behind us and stopped to turn around. At first all we could see was swirling dust in the middle of the desert valley floor, although the sound of the iron-clad hooves could be heard thudding loudly against the rocky trail. We squinted to watch as the cloud of dust grew steadily larger. Then a black speck began to appear in the middle of the cloud, which gradually sprouted arms and legs and came alive with movement. Across the endless level of the Carson sink, the cloud of dust grew, the now-defined horse and rider in its midst obscuring mountains and desert and sky. A show it was—magnificent to behold!

He was nearly upon us, and we watched in nothing less than awe, as if history itself resided in the four locked pouches of the *mochila* coming from the East and bound for the Pacific. Had I been able to pull out paper and pencil, to stop the motion of Pony Bob and his steed, I would have tried to capture in a drawing what I felt as he flew past. As it is, however, the scene must lodge only in my memory, for it was over in a few brief seconds.

As he thundered by, I saw the blur of four powerful black feet, Bob's arms and the reins and the bandanna around his neck all flying, and in the center of it all the huge black head of the horse, his eyes flaming, his nostrils wide to suck in all the air he could, mouth foaming, his powerful frame bulging and pulsating with muscular strength. He was by us in an instant. Only Bob's whoop of greeting, and long drawn out *Haaalllisteeeerrrrr!* lingered echoing in the wind with the suddenly retreating hoofbeats.

Like a blur, it was gone. Man and horse flew by our wide-eyed faces like a thunderstorm borne on a swift wind, then receded into the distance ahead . . . tinier, tinier, until Pony Bob disappeared in a dust cloud against the blue of the horizon. Except for the lingering whirlwind of dust, I might have believed that the whole thing had been the dreaming fancy of an overactive imagination.

But it was no dream. Pa's next words woke me out of my reverie. He had been astonished by the sight as well.

"Tarnation!" he exclaimed. "That boy does know how to ride! I reckon Tavish was right when he said they're *all* good riders!"

We rode for an hour after that without either of us saying anything. After all we'd been through, our anxiety over

Zack, and even wondering where the band of Paiutes were, there was plenty to think about. I was thinking about the attack that morning, Zack, and the Indians. But Pa hadn't been thinking about those things at all I found out.

"I think I'm gonna do it, Corrie," he said after a long, long time of quiet.

"Do what, Pa?"

"Run for the legislature."

"You are? Why, Pa, that's . . . that's wonderful!" I exclaimed.

"You really think so?"

"Yes—I was hoping you would!"

"Why's that?"

"Because you're a fine man, Pa, and I want everyone to know it. What made you decide?"

"I can't rightly say," replied Pa. "Something about what happened back there just—I don't know, Corrie, it just made me think it's the right thing to do."

"Does it have anything to do with Zack?"

Pa thought for a minute. "I'm not sure. I guess I just got to figuring that everybody's gonna die sometime. We came closer than I'd like to think back there! But if I am gonna die, then I oughta have done something worth remembering before I do. Raising my kids right is probably about the most important thing a man can do, and I ain't done such a good job of that."

"Please, Pa, I don't like to hear you talk like that."

"All right, Corrie. Let's just say that *one* of my sons doesn't think much of my fathering. Maybe the rest of you still look up to me. But you're all nearly grown. Why, little Tad's gonna be a man himself in another year or two. So I figure my fathering days are nearly over—except for little Ruth, of course.

Whether I've done a good or a bad job of it, maybe I oughta
be looking for something else worth doing that people will
remember Drummond Hollister for. You don't always get too
many chances to do something important, so when one comes
along, a man's gotta look at it and decide if he wants to do it,
or before he knows it, the chance is gone and might never
come back."

"A man *or* a woman," I added with a smile.

"Right you are there, Corrie. Which is why you've got to
take your opportunities with writing and with this election,
and why maybe I've got to take mine with this political thing
Dalton's offering me."

"I understand, Pa."

I really did. I had been thinking along the same lines
for the last couple of months—not having to do with dying
or doing something important, but having to do, as Pa and
Cal had both said, with taking the opportunities that came
your way.

In some ways the decisions facing both Pa and me were
similar too. And the choices we made were bound to have a
big effect on our futures.

Things started to happen pretty fast after we got back from Nevada. Pa's decision to run for the California House of Representatives was like yanking up the boards to let the water from a stream into a sluice trough. Once the water started flowing, it rushed through fast! I know it didn't take our minds off Zack and the danger he was in, but it kept us busy enough that we didn't have to mope around and think about it.

We stopped in Sacramento long enough for Pa to meet with Mr. Dalton and tell him what he decided.

"I'm pleased to hear of your decision, Hollister," Mr. Dalton said.

"I still don't have much notion of what I'm supposed to do," Pa said sheepishly. I knew he felt awkward around smooth politicians like Alexander Dalton.

"You just leave everything to me. All you have to do is try to spread the word around your area that folks need to vote for you. Since you've already run for mayor a time or two, it ought not to be too difficult."

"We'll make up some more handbills, Pa," I suggested, "just like last time."

"Good girl!" said Mr. Dalton, giving me a gentle slap on the back. "I like how she thinks, Hollister," he added to Pa. "Political acumen must run in the family! Like I say, you just leave the rest of the territory north of Sacramento to me. I'll be in touch with you and let you know everything you need to do."

Pa nodded his head agreeably. "And as for you, young lady," he went on, turning to me, "that was some article you wrote!"

"You read it?" I asked, half embarrassed, the other half astonished.

"Did I ever! So did the rest of the state. It appeared three days ago in the *Alta,* and another half dozen papers have already picked it up. I don't suppose I should be surprised after that speech you gave here in town about freedom. Some of the people I'm in touch with are already starting to say you just might be one of the best weapons Abraham Lincoln has in this state. In fact, because of that speech of yours, the Rev. Thomas Starr King, who was in the audience that day, has decided to become even more actively involved than he had planned. He wants to work with you!"

"That's my Corrie!" exclaimed Pa proudly. I tried to hide my embarrassment. I didn't know Mr. Dalton that well, but ever since the first time we'd seen him in San Francisco I couldn't escape the feeling that he sometimes exaggerated how he said things just to make me feel good, so that I'd be more inclined to do what he might want me to do later. I suppose politicians had to do that sometimes, but I hoped what he said about Mr. King was true. I liked Mr. Dalton well enough, but I didn't like having to wonder what he *really* thought. It seemed to me a man's words ought to be exactly what they were—no more and no less. In his case, I always had the feeling they were just a little bit more than he truly meant.

Nevertheless, I was just vain enough to enjoy his compliment anyway. I hoped there was *some* truth in his words, and that my article would do some good.

"In fact," he was saying, "there are two more large rallies we've got scheduled—one right here in Sacramento and another in San Francisco. I hope you'll be able to join us both times."

I shrugged noncommittally and glanced at Pa, but the expression on his face didn't give me any help.

"I realize it's a great distance to come," he added hurriedly. "But we'll pay for all your expenses, of course, just like before. And you can know that you're having a great impact for the good of our country and its future . . . for liberty, just as you said in your speech!"

"I'll think about it," I answered him.

"I've already talked to Cal about bringing you down for them." He paused, and when he went on I wasn't sure I liked the sly look in his eye or the tone of his voice. "He's taking good care of you, I understand," he said.

I nodded.

"Since you and he seemed to, ah . . . hit it off, as it were, I took the liberty of asking Leland—that's Mr. Stanford—to allow me to borrow young Cal now and then to help out with the election, and to make sure my favorite young newspaper writer is kept just as happy as she can be."

Again he smiled, with a look I didn't altogether like. Now I was sure his words said more than he meant. I knew, after all the years he'd been involved in important things, that I *wasn't* his favorite newspaper writer. But he'd said it just as plain as

day. You couldn't actually call something like that a lie, but it
certainly wasn't the whole truth. I didn't think Mr. Dalton was
intentionally trying to deceive me. He probably considered
it a nice thing to say. But it still wasn't the truth—the *whole*
truth, anyway. I don't suppose Alexander Dalton was the kind
of man who had made truth the same kind of priority as I had.
I hoped it wasn't politics that had made him the way he was.
I didn't want Pa to get like that if he went to Sacramento—
saying one thing but always having a slightly different meaning to it that he *didn't* say.

"You like Cal, don't you?" Mr. Dalton asked, seeing me
hesitate.

"Yes," I answered, blushing a little.

"Good, good! People like to see a nice young man and
woman standing up for principles and involving themselves in
the nation's affairs. I'm very happy to hear that we'll see you
again up on the platform representing the Republican party!"

"I don't think you heard my daughter, Mr. Dalton," said
Pa. "At least, I never heard her say for sure what she was going
to do."

"Did I misunderstand?" he said, looking at me bewildered.

"I said I would think about it," I said. "And I will."

"Fine! That's all I can expect. I will have Cal get in touch
with you about the details."

Warning Signs
Chapter Thirty-Four

I did speak both times Mr. Dalton had told me about.
How could I say no when Cal practically begged me? And
why would I have *wanted* to say no, anyway? I wouldn't have
turned down another chance to be with Cal.

The most memorable part of September, however, wasn't
the two speeches I gave. They weren't much different than
the first, although I wasn't quite so nervous even though there
were more people listening. But after we were through in San
Francisco, instead of going straight back home, Cal invited
me down to Mr. Stanford's ranch south of San Francisco in a
little town called Palo Alto.

"He raises horses," Cal said. "There's a big ranch house
where you'll be very comfortable. I'll show you his estate.
We'll saddle up two of his finest horses, and I'll show you the
peninsula. It's beautiful country!"

"I . . . I don't know," I hesitated. "I suppose it would be all
right. It does sound fun." Inside, my heart was beating wildly.
It sounded like a dream come true—a fairy tale!

"How will we get there?" I asked, not even knowing what
I was saying.

"I've got one of Mr. Stanford's finest carriages here in the city. I'm heading back down to the estate bright and early in the morning. Say you'll join me!"

"But . . . how will I get back here, and then home?"

"Don't worry, Corrie. With a man of the world like me to take care of everything, you need have no concerns. I'll see to your every need!"

In the thrill of the moment, I totally believed him. Not until later, as I lay in bed that night, did I realize that something about his words had struck a tiny chord of dissonance somewhere inside my brain.

Just then, as we were still talking about it, Mr. Dalton walked up. He greeted me kindly, congratulated me on a job well done, as he put it, and then turned to Cal and began speaking more quietly and more seriously. It was clear they didn't intend for me to listen, but they made no particular attempt to keep me from hearing, either. Men have a way of ignoring women when they want to, and paying attention to them when they want to. And when they're ignoring them, they seem to think they're not there at all, or that their minds don't work because they're not being paid attention to. But women are generally smarter and more aware of things than men realize. In this case I *was* listening, and I found their conversation very interesting, even though I know they probably thought my head was off in the clouds someplace.

"One of Senator Gwin's *Breckinridge* people is making trouble for us down in the South," Dalton was saying. "There's talk of a Breckinridge-Douglas coalition to smear Lincoln, to insure that *one* of the two Democrats wins California. Apparently they've sent someone up this way to spread the lies into northern California, too."

"What's his name?" asked Cal.

"Jewks . . . Terrance Jewks."

"Where is he? How do I find him?"

"Their people are said to be putting him up someplace in the city."

"Don't worry about a thing," Cal said after a while. "I'll take care of it. If he's in one of the San Francisco hotels, I'll find him."

"You know what to do?"

"I've run into just this sort of thing with Mr. Stanford. I've got ways of handling his sort."

"Leland tells me you are very resourceful," said Mr. Dalton, a grin breaking over his face.

"My goal is to be useful," replied Cal, returning the smile.

"Nothing more?" queried Dalton. "Leland is a powerful man, a man whose star is on the rise."

The look on Cal's face told that he knew exactly what that meant.

"All the more reason for me to serve him faithfully," said Cal, "as well as the whole party. To answer your question—yes, I know what to do. And I've got just the people to do it. Believe me, Mr. Jewks will not prove troublesome. He'll wish he stayed in the South and left northern politics to the Republicans!"

"Good. I knew I could count on you," said Dalton. The two shook hands, and I was left alone with Cal again.

"What was that all about?" I asked.

"Nothing . . . nothing, Corrie, my dear. Just the details of politics."

"It didn't sound too pleasant."

"Politics sometimes gets a little messy, Corrie. You must know that. Your father is a politician."

"He's mayor of Miracle Springs," I replied. "I don't know that I'd call him a politician."

"Well, he soon will be, from what I understand," Cal persisted. "Once he's sitting in the statehouse in Sacramento, his hands will get dirty, too."

"Not Pa's," I insisted.

Cal laughed. "Don't worry, Corrie. I'm not talking about anything serious. But it can't be helped. Your pa will explain it to you someday. In the meantime, you and I don't have to worry about all that! How about me taking you out for a fancy first-class dinner and a night on the town to celebrate your speech today? Then I'll get you safe and sound back to Miss Bean's later, and pick you up tomorrow morning for Palo Alto!"

Cal made me feel special, more like a real woman than I'd ever imagined I'd feel. I don't suppose I really believed half the sweet things he said to me. Yet I wanted to believe them so badly that I convinced myself to ignore the uncomfortable warning signs.

Besides, Cal Burton was not the kind of man a girl says *no* to. And I didn't really *want* to say no, after all.

Memories on Horseback

CHAPTER THIRTY-FIVE

*P*alo Alto was all Cal promised it would be . . . and more!

Mr. Stanford and his wife treated me as if I were the most honored guest they'd ever had on the estate. I could hardly believe that a short time ago I had been out in the desolate land of Nevada nearly being burned alive by Indians, and now I was hobnobbing with one of California's wealthiest men—and, according to Cal, one of its most influential politicians too!

The Stanford estate was completely different from the primitive Fremont estate at Mariposa. Mr. Fremont was also rich, of course, but he spent so little time in California, and Mariposa was so far away from everywhere else that he never did much to fancy it up. But I could tell instantly that the Stanfords intended to live on their new estate a long time. Besides politics and railroads, Mr. Stanford loved horses, and told me it had always been a lifelong dream of his to raise them. Now that he had a place and the means to do it, he intended to make his dream come true, right there in Palo Alto.

Mr. Stanford was a good friend of John and Jessie Fremont, and once Cal explained to him my connection with the campaign of 1856, he told me many interesting things I hadn't known.

"John Fremont may have lost the election in '56," he said, "but as far as I'm concerned it was a great victory. For a man to come so close to becoming president only four years after the formation of a new party is remarkable, in my opinion, and we Republicans owe him a great debt of gratitude. We'll win this year with Lincoln, thanks to people like you throughout the country, Corrie. The John Fremont campaign four years ago laid the groundwork for this year's victory."

"Was he considered as a candidate again this year?" I asked.

"By a few people. But to be honest with you, there wasn't a great deal of support for him at the convention. Lincoln represents the rising new tide of the party, Corrie, although John's name was bandied about for vice-president. I wouldn't be surprised to see him with a cabinet appointment in the new administration, however. Lincoln thinks highly of him, from what I understand."

Just then Cal walked in.

"The horses are all saddled, Corrie. Shall we head out over the hills and see what kind of adventure we can find?"

"You be sure to take her up to the top of the ridge, Cal," said Mr. Stanford. "On a clear day like this, Corrie, from up there you can see out to the Pacific to the west, down into the bay to the east, and, if it's clear as crystal like it gets after a rain, you can just make out a bit of San Francisco at the tip of the peninsula. It's the most stunning view in all of California, if you ask me. And it's right here on my estate!"

"I'll be sure she sees it," said Cal.

"I probably won't see you again, Corrie," he said. "I've got a meeting with the Crocker brothers this evening, and tomorrow I have to get up to Sacramento early to see Judah,

Huntington, and Hopkins on some railroad business. But you enjoy the rest of your stay, and you let my wife or Cal here know if you need anything."

"Thank you, sir," I said. "You are very kind."

It was still fairly early in the morning when we set out. Cal led the way at a leisurely pace, westward from the house and barns, down through a grassy little valley, and then up the gradual incline at the far end. The grass was dry and brown at this time of the year, and the hills were gently rolling, with oaks scattered thinly about. The air was not hot, just pleasantly warm. There was no breeze yet.

Gradually the climb grew steeper, though still nothing like the mountains I was used to back in the foothills country around Miracle. There was no trail, but the grass was almost meadowlike. We wound around gnarled old oaks, crossed several small streams, came across little glens that interrupted the upward ascent, and if I had let myself daydream, I could have easily thought we might crest a small rise and see the snowcapped Sierras in the distance. It was hard to believe we were actually going in the exact opposite direction.

Finally a clearing spread out before us, with a rise about four or five hundred yards farther that seemed to taper off at its crest into a flat plateau.

"There it is!" said Cal.

"What?"

"The top. That's the summit."

"The summit!" I repeated with a laugh. "That makes it sound like a mountain."

"Okay, maybe it's not a mountain peak. But it's the highest hill for thirty miles in either direction. It's the one Mr. Stanford told me to show you."

"I'll race you there!" I cried.

"You're on!" Cal yelled back, giving his horse a slap on the rump and lurching into a gallop.

I let him get about twenty yards out in front, just enough of a lead for him to look back to see me sitting at the starting point calmly. Then I dug my heels into the mare Mr. Stanford had let me pick out earlier in the morning. I had liked her looks immediately, and had tested her speed a couple times on the way up, so I was confident of what kind of mount I had under me.

By the time Cal looked back again I had closed half the distance between us, and drew alongside him before we were halfway to the top. I didn't even look over, but just leaned forward against my mare's neck and whisked by. I reached the top, reined in the mare, and was sitting calmly in the saddle regaining my breath by the time Cal galloped up alongside ten or fifteen seconds later.

"What took you so long?" I asked, grinning.

"Let me answer with a question—where did *you* learn to ride like that?" laughed Cal. "You put me to shame."

"I'm just a country girl," I answered. "I told you I've been riding for years. When you don't live in a city, you learn to ride."

"Maybe it's you who ought to be riding for the Pony Express instead of your brother!"

"I might if they let girls join," I said.

"Don't you dare! We need you too much in this campaign!"

Now that the race to the top of the hill was behind us, I had a chance to look around and see where we were.

"It's absolutely breathtaking!" I exclaimed.

Spread out, not above us as the Sierras would have been, but rather below us like a distant blue infinite carpet stretch-

ing all the way to the horizon, was the Pacific Ocean. The day
was perfect. The sky was nearly as blue as the sea, with a few
billows of clouds suspended lazily here and there. As we had
come up over the ridge, the gentlest whisper of a breeze had
met us, and now as I drew in deep breaths I could smell just
the faintest hint of the ocean's fragrance.

I stretched all around in my saddle, looking down upon
the long blue fingers of San Francisco's huge bay in the other
direction, just as Mr. Stanford had described it. Then I turned
north to see if the city itself was in view. It hadn't rained in
the last several days, but it was just clear enough that I *thought*
I could see fuzzy glimpses of it. If it wasn't the actual buildings
of the city I saw, perhaps it was just the rounding part of the
end of the peninsula, with my imagination filling in shapes
where I knew the city was.

"Look over that way," said Cal, pointing northeast.
"There's the mouth of the Sacramento River emptying into
the bay. And Sacramento eighty miles away," he added,
swinging his arm a little to the right.

As I watched Cal describing the view, I saw a subtle
change come over him when he began talking about Sacramento. The capital city, it seemed, possessed a greater significance for him than all the rest.

"What is it about Sacramento that's so special to you?"
I asked.

"Opportunity, Corrie," he said after a long silence. "Just
like I told you before . . . opportunity."

I thought back to Pa's talk on our way to Carson City;
he had said that sometimes we have to take the chances that
come our way before it is too late. But I had the feeling he
and Cal meant two completely different things. Pa seemed

to be saying that we ought to be mindful of the opportunities God puts in our path. Cal seemed to be saying something else, although I wasn't quite sure what it was yet.

"Look around you, Corrie," Cal went on, turning in his saddle. "Look out there—what do you see?" He pointed due west.

"The ocean," I answered.

"What else do you see?"

"The sky," I said, half in question.

"What else?"

"I don't know, Cal . . . the clouds?"

"No, Corrie! Down there is the end of the land, the coast of California . . . the *end* of the country, the last piece of the United States, the edge of the whole continent!"

His face was lit up as if he had revealed the whole riddle of the universe. He kept looking at me as if expecting light to break in upon my mind at any second.

"Don't you see what that means?" he asked finally.

"Uh . . . I guess I don't," I said.

"It means the end of one kind of opportunity and the beginning of a whole new era in our country's history—a whole era of *new* opportunities!"

Again he stopped and scanned all around, at everything we could see. Slowly we began walking our horses along the plateau of the ridge.

"You see, Corrie," Cal began, "for the last century, the whole thrust of opportunity in this country was just to *get* here—to reach the Pacific. This was the frontier. It had to be explored, then tamed. Lewis and Clark, Jedediah Smith, even your own John Fremont back in his exploring days—they were men whose passion was just *getting* here, to this very place, to the Pacific coast. Then all those who came after them—trappers and traders and homesteaders and cattle ranchers, and families by wagon trains—they were coming here just to *be* here—to come west, to live, to settle, to make lives for themselves. Do you see what I mean? *Getting* west was the opportunity in itself! Then came the gold rush, and men and women poured in by the hundreds of thousands. Now California and Oregon are states, and one day Nevada and Washington will be, too. We've reached the end, the end of the frontier, Corrie. The country's come as far west as it can go. California's been tamed and settled. And here we stand, right at the very end, gazing down to where California meets the Pacific."

We rode on slowly; then he stopped and suddenly jumped down off his mount, gazing down toward the ocean below us.

"Do you know where the *next* era of opportunity lies, Corrie?" he asked.

"Where, Cal?" I said.

He hesitated just momentarily, then wheeled around, stretched his arms widely out into the air as he faced eastward, and cried, "Out there! Back where we've come from—toward the East and everywhere between this spot right here and the same spot overlooking the Atlantic coast somewhere in New York or Maryland or Georgia! It's what we *do* with this land now that we've conquered it and explored it. We've spent two hundred years just getting to this spot, Corrie. Many people shed their blood so that you and I could stand here and look out upon that expanse of blue. In the next century, fortunes are going to be made and empires are going to be built by those who lay hold of the opportunities afforded them.

"Men like Leland Stanford *came* west. That was their first opportunity. He came from Wisconsin with his four brothers and set up business in Sacramento. Getting here was his first opportunity, which he took hold of, and it made him a rich man. But he didn't stop there. Then he turned his eyes back *over* the country he had crossed, and he began to take hold of new political opportunities—the opportunity of power. He ran for governor of this state. Even though he lost, Leland Stanford is still looking for new frontiers to conquer. He came to the Pacific, but now he is seeking to *return* to the East by rail—a new opportunity. I have no doubt that he and his friends *will* one day build a railroad back to the East where they all came from, and grow even more wealthy and powerful in the process.

"Oh, Corrie, don't you see what I'm getting at? It's in the statehouses like Sacramento where these opportunities of the future originate—where the laws are made. It's there where the powerful people gather, where the money flows from. Politics, money, and influence—they are the opportunities of the *next* century! Those with vision to see such things will go far."

He turned around, his eyes glowing as he looked up at me. I sat still on the mare, listening to every word he said.

"From the Pacific to the Atlantic," I said, halfway to myself, reflecting on what he'd said a minute ago.

"Sea to sea . . . shore to shore! That's it exactly!"

"There's only one thing I don't understand, Cal," I said. "Why then do you want to have anything to do with someone like me? I'm hardly the kind of person you're talking about."

"But you are, Corrie! I knew that right from the first, when I heard about you and then when I laid eyes on you. Not only were you a beautiful young lady, all dressed up at the Montgomery Hotel in San Francisco. You also have done just what I'm talking about. You came west. The first frontier was just *getting* here and joining back up with your father and uncle. But no sooner had you done that than you turned back around and set your sights on higher goals. You started writing; you took every opportunity that you could, and now your writing is being read all the way back across the country. And the very Pony Express pouches that your brother carries across the mountains and desert have newspapers in them with *your* articles and speeches written down for folks in the East to read. You know the Fremonts and Mr. Stanford and Mr. Dalton. Don't you see, Corrie—in your own way, you're going to be an important person someday too, just like Leland Stanford!"

"That doesn't sound like me, Cal," I said.

"But it is, Corrie. You should be proud of it!"

"I never set my sights on having high goals. I never tried to *take* opportunities so I could get well known. That kind of thing never entered my mind, Cal."

"It happened all the same. And now look at you—who would deny that you're better off for all of it. For a *woman* to have done all you have, at such a young age . . . it's remarkable, Corrie! I tell you, you ought to be downright proud!"

I suppose it was idiotic of me to keep questioning him. He had been so nice to me, and a short time ago I had thought I was in love with him. Maybe I still was. I had even persuaded myself that his attentions came from feelings he perhaps shared. But I had to know.

"Is that why you want to have something to do with me?" I persisted. "Because I might be an important person someday?"

"No, of course not," he answered quickly. His voice bore a roughness, a defensiveness I had never heard before, as if such a blunt question had caught him momentarily with his guard down. It wasn't the kind of thing young women asked when men were showering them with praise.

"That is, not if you find such a motive to be offensive," he said smoothly, recovering his old composure. "I cannot deny that your accomplishments and reputation add to the charm I find so compelling about you. But even without them, I would still find you attractive above any other of the young ladies I have known. Do you believe me, Corrie?"

"I would like to."

"Then *do* believe me," he implored. His voice was so sincere; how could I possibly not believe he was in earnest? "Come, Corrie . . . get down. Walk with me." He reached up his hand and helped me down off the mare. When my feet were on the ground, however, he did not let go. My heart fluttered to feel his hand around mine, but I was too flustered to make any attempt to pull it away.

"Ah, Corrie," he said at last, "so much lies within our grasp—young persons like us, with life and opportunities and exciting new times for the country ahead of us!"

We walked on. My mind and heart were spinning in a dozen directions at once. I'd always thought of myself as rational and level-headed, but not now. Not with Cal Burton.

"Be part of it with me, Corrie," he said after a minute or two. "Let's find our opportunities together, and take advantage of them! You and I—we can be the Lewis and Clark of the next generation. You'll be a famous writer someday. And I'll—well, who knows how far we can go, Corrie, or what we can achieve! We can go back across this continent in the footsteps of Leland Stanford and men like him, and maybe even start to make our own marks in the history books of this country! What do you say, Corrie?"

I know I was being a fool, but I couldn't help asking one more time, "But . . . why me, Cal?"

"Don't you know, Corrie? Haven't you figured it out from all I've been telling you? It's because I care for you, Corrie—I care deeply. That's why, with us working together, there wouldn't be anything we couldn't do, couldn't achieve, couldn't get if we set our minds to it!"

Cal's closeness and the excitement in his tone overwhelmed me. I felt like running! I pulled my hand out of his and took off across the grass as fast as I could go.

"Hey . . . where are you off to?" called Cal behind me. I heard him start to chase after me, but I ran all the faster. I ran until I was tired, then slowed and let him catch up with me.

When he did, he threw his long arm around my shoulder and gave me a squeeze, then let go as we turned and started walking back to where the horses were nibbling at the brown grass.

We mounted back up and started slowly down the hill.

We rode down to the seashore, stopped and ran along the sandy beach, explored a watery cave, then galloped the horses miles along the sand before climbing back up inland, over the ridge of the peninsula again, and down through the woods and meadows. Even though we didn't arrive back at the Stanford estate until late in the afternoon, in spite of all the exertion and the long ride, I didn't seem to be hungry.

Dinner wasn't exactly "formal," but I did put on a different dress than the one I'd ridden in all afternoon, and Cal made his appearance in a black coat and ruffled white shirt with bow tie. He was indeed a handsome young man, and seeing him all dressed up reminded me of how taken I had been with him that night in San Francisco back in June.

When I went to bed that night, I lay awake a long time, dreaming of horses and sand and oak trees and the shining sun dancing and reflecting off the shimmering white and blue surface of the ocean. But mostly I dreamed of a tan face with brown hair flying above it in the breeze, and eyes of a blue so deep that even the sky above and the Pacific below seemed pale by comparison.

How Many States?

CHAPTER THIRTY-SIX

When I got back to Miracle Springs several days later, the two speeches I had made already seemed far in the past. But knowing nothing about my trip to Palo Alto, Pa and Almeda were full of questions about the political situation.

"You heard anything more from Mr. Dalton?" I asked him.

"Got a letter just yesterday," Pa answered. "He asked how the handbills that you had suggested were coming along—"

I had forgotten all about them—we were going to have to get busy in a hurry!

"*And,*" Pa went on, "he said he'd arranged for me to speak at a town meeting over in Marysville next week."

"What do you think, Corrie?" asked Almeda.

"What's more important is what *you* think," I answered.

"I think it's wonderful!" she said with a big smile. "I had no idea what I was starting when I got the notion of running for mayor. Now look what it's caused—Drummond Hollister running for state office!"

In California, the presidential election of 1860 in California had as much to do with the dispute between North and South as it did anywhere else in the country. The battle for supremacy of the nation, and which region was going to hold the reins of power, *was* the election of 1860. In addition to the slavery issue itself, the election would determine who was going to direct the course of the future of the United States of America.

The South had controlled the government in Washington for thirty years. But all of a sudden, a major change seemed at hand. But the South did not intend to give up without a fight. The battle was to be waged on November 6, 1860.

California was one of the only states, however, where the dispute over control between North and South went on *inside* the state. California was now the second biggest state next to Texas, almost nine hundred miles from top to bottom, running north and south. The top of California next to Oregon was parallel with New York, and the bottom border ran right through the middle of Mississippi, Alabama, and Georgia. It was only natural, I suppose, that there would be debate *within* California as to which side its loyalties ought to lie on.

Even during the Mexican period in California before the gold rush, there had been a spirit of sectionalism between the northern and southern halves of the state. Especially once the gold rush came, those in the south didn't like all the activity of the north. When statehood was being discussed in 1849, many southern Californians did not want to be part of the new state and proposed dividing California in half at San Luis Obispo. They wanted to be able to go on with the slow pace of their old way of life, without being forced to be part of the frantic, growing, alien north where people were pouring in and towns were growing into great metropolitan areas overnight. Those in the south felt it unfair that they should have to pay taxes and support a state government that was located in the north and that was expensive and heavily weighted toward the needs and concerns of the north. The south was so sparsely settled, it would even have preferred not to be a state at all, just as long as it could be separate from the north.

Statehood came to the whole state, but the desire to split the state into northern and southern halves continued as a volatile issue all the way through the 1850s. A huge movement in Los Angeles and throughout the south in 1851 tried to develop enough support to break away and form a new state. In the next two years, the southern legislators in Sacramento tried to call a constitutional convention that would divide the state. But since the north controlled the state legislature, such attempts were defeated.

Finally, in 1855 a bill was introduced into the California Assembly that at first called for a new state named Columbia to be formed. Then later the bill was changed to split California into three states. A new state called Colorado would be made of the area south of San Luis Obispo. A new state called Shasta would be made of the far northern part bordering Oregon. And California would remain as the central region of the three states.

That bill never passed, but the idea for making separate states continued, and even gradually began to be supported by some northerners. Another bill was introduced in Sacramento in 1859, again for two states, and again with the separation at San Luis Obispo, creating a new territory south of that to be called Colorado. This time there *was* enough support for the idea to pass both the state senate and the state assembly in Sacramento.

But the legislature couldn't split the state apart all by themselves. There were two other groups of people who had to be part of the decision, too—the federal government and the people who lived in the part of California where they wanted to create a new state.

So the legislature wrote up a bill that would create a new territory to be called Colorado—*if* two thirds of the people in that region south of San Luis Obispo approved of the plan, and *if* the Congress in Washington, D.C., also approved. The bill passed in the state assembly 33 to 15, and in the state senate 15 to 12. Then a special election was set up late in 1859 for the people of southern California to vote themselves on whether they wanted their part of the state to be formed into a new territory called Colorado.

They surely did! The people south of San Luis Obispo voted 2,457 to 828 in favor of dividing California in half, and calling their half Colorado.

Therefore, in January of 1860, Governor Milton Latham formally sent the results of the bill and both votes to President James Buchanan, asking for the U.S. Congress to approve the division of California.

No approval had yet been given, however. The rest of the nation was too taken up with other momentous events that year. The election between Lincoln and Douglas and the dispute between the southern states and northern states all made a local squabble within distant California seem a little insignificant to the politicians in Washington. Not only was California far away from the rest of the country, it was made up mostly of Spanish-speaking Mexicans in the south and gold-hungry miners in the north. At least that's what Pa said folks in the East thought about us.

"What does that have to do with splitting up the state, Pa?" Tad asked when we were all sitting talking about it a couple of weeks later.

"Nothing directly, son," answered Pa. "It's only that back in Washington I reckon they figure California's a mite different than other states, and that maybe they just oughta leave it alone to do what it wants."

"But if California wants it, all they have to do is approve it," said Becky.

"Well, there are certain kinds of things where the federal government's just not anxious to interfere. It's called *states' rights*. This country got its start as a collection of independent states that pretty much did what they pleased. The government in Washington was set up just to ride herd over the whole conglomeration, while the states went on deciding things for themselves. That's why it's called the United *States* of America instead of something else."

"You sound like a politician, Pa!" laughed Becky.

"Of course he's a politician!" said Almeda. "That's what being mayor is all about."

"I mean he sounds like a speechmaker."

"Like Corrie!" said Tad.

"I'm no speechmaker, Tad," I said.

"What about it, Drummond?" said Almeda. "Did that speech you made in Marysville last week go to your head? You *are* starting to sound a little high-falutin' for the likes of simple country folk like us."

"Now you cut that out, Almeda!" joked Pa. "You all know well and good I ain't about to start sounding like no doggone politician from Sacramento or Washington. I was only trying to answer Becky's question."

"Is states' rights why there's slavery some places, and it's against the law in others?" asked Tad.

"Right you are, son. That's it exactly. It's up to the states to decide for themselves."

"What about right and wrong?" I asked. "It seems as if on an issue like slavery there ought to be more to it than everybody deciding what they want to do. That's why I decided to support Mr. Lincoln, because of right and wrong."

"But who's to say what's right and what's wrong? You've listened to Katie and Edie, Corrie. They *don't* see anything wrong in slavery, because they were both brought up in the South. That's why the government in Washington has always stayed out of such disputes. They don't want to get into the business of deciding right and wrong, so they let the states decide whatever *they* want to do."

"Then, why don't they let California split into two states?" asked Tad.

Pa looked at him a minute, then shook his head with a puzzled expression.

"The truth of the matter, son, is that I'm blamed if I know," he answered finally. "Maybe they just ain't got around to approving it."

"If you're elected to the Assembly, Drummond," said Almeda, "what stand are *you* going to take?"

"On what?" asked Pa.

"On the split of California. Are you going to continue to push for it next year if President Buchanan doesn't act on the measure before the election?"

Again Pa grew thoughtful. "If I do get elected to the Assembly, which I still doubt, then I'll have to figure out what I'm gonna do about a lot of things. Right now I can't say. I can't see much reason to be against dividing it up, but I got no objections to keeping it the way it is, either."

"If they won't let California do what *it* wants to do," said Becky, "then why do they let the states do whatever they want to do about slavery? It doesn't seem fair."

"Politics isn't always fair, girl, any more than the government always does what's *right*, like Corrie was saying. States' rights isn't a doctrine of governing that always makes things turn out fair. It just happens to be how this here country got put together in the first place. Besides, Buchanan's a Democrat and a southerner. Letting the states do whatever they want—that's just how the southerners want to keep it, so they can keep having their slaves and growing their cotton. No Democrat's gonna change that."

"A Republican might," I suggested.

"Yeah, you're right, daughter, a Republican just might. That's why the Democrats and southerners are so all-fired worried about this election. They figure if Lincoln's elected, it just might be the end of states' rights altogether."

"Why can't it all just keep going how it is?" asked Tad. "Some states could have slaves if they wanted, others don't have to."

"Yes, Pa," added Becky, "why can't there keep being states' rights no matter who gets elected?"

"That's what the southerners want," put in Almeda. "But Abraham Lincoln has made no secret of his revulsion toward slavery."

Pa turned to me. "Corrie," he said, "where's that paper that had your article about the election in it? Seems I recollect reading a speech of Lincoln's there."

"I'll get it, Pa," I said, jumping up.

"You see, Becky," Pa went on, "Mr. Lincoln figures we just can't keep going forever with half of the states one way, the other half the other way. He says it's tearing the country apart, making people hate each other, making it so the government can't do anything but argue and dispute and can't get on with the business of helping make the country what it ought to be. He says that we *got* to be what our name says—*united.* One way or the other—either all for slavery or all against it. We can't keep being split up like we have been. And now that there's more northern states than southern, the southerners figure that if he's elected, he's gonna try to take the *whole* country the direction he wants to go."

"Against states' rights?"

"They don't figure Mr. Lincoln cares so much for states' rights as much as he wants to do what *he* thinks is right."

Just then I returned with the paper.

"Here," said Pa, reaching out and taking it from me, "just listen to this. I'll read you part of the speech and you can see for yourselves what Mr. Lincoln says about it."

He rustled through the *Alta* till he found the speech on the second page and began to read.

In my opinion, the agitation over the issue of slavery will not cease until a crisis shall have been reached and passed. A house divided against itself cannot stand. I believe this government cannot endure, permanently half slave and half free. I do not expect the Union to be dissolved—I do not expect the house to fall—but I DO expect it will cease to be divided. It will become all one thing, or all the other. Either the opponents of slavery will arrest the further spread of it, and place it where the public mind shall rest in the belief that it is in the course of ultimate extinction; or its advocates will push it forward, till it shall become alike lawful in all the States, old as well as new—North as well as South.

"I didn't understand that, Pa," said Tad.

"He's just saying that it's got to be all one way or all the other. Slavery's either got to be legal everywhere throughout the whole country, or else it's got to be thrown out completely, including in the South."

"What about the states that are talking of seceding, Drummond?" asked Almeda seriously. "Do you think it could actually happen?"

"No way to know, Almeda. One thing's for sure—people can be mighty stubborn and dead set against change, whether they're right *or* wrong."

"But if some states want to secede, should they have the right to?" I asked. Ever since I had decided to get involved in the election, I'd been thinking about this question because I knew it was on Abraham Lincoln's mind. I still hadn't been able to figure out even what I thought about it.

"That's the question of 1860, girl," said Pa. "It ain't so much just about slavery, but whether states' rights gives some of the states the right to pull themselves out of the United States of America altogether. If California can't split in half without the government's permission, then can some of the southern states go off and do whatever they want to do without permission either? I don't reckon anybody knows the answer to that question yet. But if Mr. Lincoln gets elected, I don't much doubt that some of 'em are gonna put it to the test and see what comes of it."

Pa surely was sounding like a politician! From a fugitive to a gold miner to a father to a mayor . . . and now he was talking about the future of the whole country as if he was personally involved in what happened.

And as a candidate for the California State Assembly, I guess he was, at that!

*I*n a way, the question that California politicians had been debating was just a small version of the same issue politicians in the rest of the country were wrestling with.

Should California, where the interests of the northern and southern sections were much different, be one *state* or two? And should the whole country be one *nation* or two? How far did states' rights go, anyway?

Trouble had been brewing between the North and South for a long time. There had been strong outcries against slavery for almost thirty years—going clear back to the preaching of Charles Finney in the 1830s as well as that of many others. The American Anti-Slavery Society was formed in 1833. William Lloyd Garrison had begun a radical antislavery newspaper called *The Liberator* two years before that stirred up sentiments on both sides all over the country. More societies were formed. Books were written. And dozens of preachers denounced slavery from the pulpit.

But none of that could do anything to put an end to slavery. The Congress in Washington, D.C., made the laws. And since Congress was controlled all that time by the Democratic party, which was mostly made up of men from the South, they continued to uphold the right of each individual state to have slavery if it wanted—which, of course, all the southern states did.

When the Republican party formed in the early 1850s, the Democrats and southerners weren't too worried. But it grew so rapidly—with new states and territories all being more inclined toward northern interests, and with antislavery preaching continuing to grow—that by 1856 the Democrats realized they *should* be worried. Buchanan had been elected over John Fremont only by a hairsbreadth. If two of the northern states had gone for Fremont instead, he would have become president. The governor of Virginia, Edie had told us, had been thinking of secession even back then if Fremont had been elected.

Now, in 1860, southern leaders *were* worried!

In the North, there was strong and growing opposition to the hold of the South. But the southerners had no intention of giving up their power without a fight. There were growing threats throughout the year that a number of the states of the South would simply secede, or pull out of the Union. The South was financially strong, and if it had to, it would simply form its own new nation. But it would *not* give up slavery, nor give up its right to make its own decisions.

But the election of 1860 was not as simple as Democrats against Republicans, North against South, slavery against abolition. In fact, there were *four* candidates for president. Douglas, the Democrat, was not even a southerner at all. He was from Abraham Lincoln's home state of Illinois, and was the U.S. senator from Illinois. He had defeated Lincoln for that position in 1858 after their famous series of debates.

Many southerners, in fact, didn't like Douglas. He wasn't strongly enough in favor of slavery to suit them. But most

Democrats, by 1860, realized that Lincoln was absolutely sure to win if they nominated a proslavery southerner to run against him. So at the Democratic convention earlier in the year, a majority had nominated the northerner Douglas, figuring that a northern candidate was their only hope against Lincoln.

That only angered the Democrats from the deep South. Win or not, they wanted a candidate who stood *for* slavery! So they organized a convention of *their* own and nominated their Democratic candidate, Buchanan's vice-president, John Breckinridge, from the slave state of Kentucky.

Now there were two Democrats running against Lincoln!

Back in the spring, a whole new party had been formed, called the Constitutional Union party. They hoped to find some middle ground between both the Democrats and the Republicans, and stood above all else simply for loyalty to the Union itself. They hoped to attract support from Union-loving conservatives in the South. The ticket for this new party was made up of two U.S. senators, one from the North, one from the South—John Bell of Tennessee for president and Edward Everett of Massachusetts for vice president.

So those were the four candidates: Lincoln for the Republicans, Douglas for the Democrats, Breckinridge for the southern Democrats, and Bell for the Constitutional Union party.

It was a hard-fought campaign. Douglas traveled up and down New England calling on people to preserve the Union and speaking against secession—sounding almost like Lincoln himself—trying to get the northern vote while retaining southern Democratic support. Even as prosouthern as he was, Breckinridge tried to convince the voters that he, too, was opposed to secession.

In California, as in the rest of the country, the Democrats had been in control, and there was a large prosouthern sentiment throughout the state. But the split of the Democratic party also split California and its leaders. Governor Downey declared his support for Douglas. Former governors Weller and Latham and Senator Gwin declared their support for Breckinridge. And Mr. Stanford and his business and railroad associates Huntington, Cole, Hopkins, and Charles and Edwin Crocker made up the most well-known of the Republican leadership within the state.

It was remarkable to me how much prosouthern, proslavery support there was in *northern* California. Except for the possibility that a lot of Californians had come from the South, I couldn't understand it. I hadn't understood it back in 1856, and I still didn't understand it in 1860. If the Democratic party hadn't been split in its loyalties, I don't think Mr. Lincoln would have had a ghost of a chance in California.

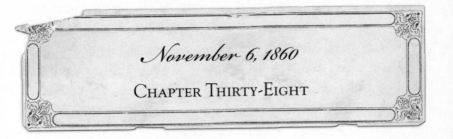

$\mathcal{W}$e made up the handbills for Pa. This time it was important to distribute them not just around Miracle Springs but everywhere possible in the whole section of the state north of Sacramento in the Assembly district Pa hoped to represent. Pa was running as a Republican, and though there were several other candidates—one other Republican and three Democrats all together—we hoped that he might have a chance to win. For the flyer I wrote a story that told all about Pa and who he was, adding quotes from some people in Miracle Springs saying what a good mayor he'd been.

Then I wrote an article for the handbill, like the speech I'd given in Sacramento about freedom and the future of the country. It probably didn't have much to do with Pa and whether he'd be a good legislator or not, but I hoped it would help. I didn't want to say *too* much, because if people knew that a Hollister was writing telling people to vote for a Hollister, it might not seem altogether unbiased.

Edie was still with Aunt Katie, and in spite of our differences about slavery itself, she thought it was exciting about Pa's running for office, even as a Republican. She offered to help, and the rest of us were ready to do anything we could, too. It was a lot of work, but we split up and took handbills to all the towns for thirty or forty miles around Miracle Springs—wherever we could get to on horseback and back in a day, or to the towns Pa or I passed through on our way to Sacramento. We even gave them to Marcus Weber when he had deliveries to make.

In every town we posted a copy of the handbill up on the town announcement board, or if they didn't have one, on a post somewhere near the center of town. Then the rest we'd leave at the General Store if they'd let us. Most of the folks knew something about Pa and were happy to pass out the flyers to their customers.

I didn't make any more speeches, although Pa did at a couple more towns where Mr. Dalton had made arrangements for him. He was having lots of the smaller northern newspapers print articles about Pa, too, and he told us just a week before the election that Drummond Hollister was the most widely known and recognized name of the five candidates.

I got several letters from Cal in the month preceding the election, although I didn't see him again. I wrote to him several times, too, and asked him about what I'd overheard between him and Mr. Dalton concerning the anti-Lincoln move in the southern portion of the state. *It's all taken care of, Corrie,* he wrote back in his next letter. *Forget you heard a word about it.* In fact, he expressed surprise that I remembered the incident.

It was a minor annoyance, he went on to say, *which we took care of. I have every confidence our Mr. Lincoln will carry the day in northern California.*

The long-awaited day finally came on Tuesday, November 6. Pa and Uncle Nick went to vote, but of course it was days before the ballots were all collected and counted, and two weeks before we found out what the results were throughout the rest of the country. That Pony Express rider carrying the election news was one of the most eagerly anticipated since the Express had begun. They didn't have to ride all the way to Sacramento for the news to reach us, because by that time a telegraph had been installed between San Francisco and Churchill, Nevada. The San Francisco papers carried news of the election results on November 19.

The Democratic strategy of two candidates hadn't worked. And the independent had done much better than predicted, carrying three states. Douglas had received the second-highest number of votes behind Lincoln, but only carried Missouri and split New Jersey with Lincoln. Breckinridge got only 18 percent of the total vote. But because of his strong support in the proslavery South, he carried eleven southern states.

The final votes were: Lincoln 1,866,000, Douglas 1,383,000, Breckinridge 848,000, and Bell 593,000.

Abraham Lincoln received 40 percent of the total, not nearly a majority. But because he carried all the northern states and seventeen states in all, his electoral vote was a huge majority. The final electoral results were: Lincoln 180, Breckinridge 79, Bell 39, and Douglas 12.

Abraham Lincoln had been elected the next president of the United States!

A Dreadful Way to End a Year
CHAPTER THIRTY-NINE

*B*ut would the United States stay *united* for much longer? Almost immediately after the election it began to look as if the answer was no!

The South was now clearly and unmistakably the minority. The once-powerful region that had controlled the nation had been defeated. Many mixed sentiments ran through the hearts of loyal southerners—pride, honor, fear of what the North might do. And stubbornness, too. They feared that their traditional and cherished ways of life would now be destroyed, their lands taken, their fortunes and businesses ruined. Their pride had been assaulted. Many southerners felt themselves superior, and that *they* were more capable of ruling the nation no matter what the election might have said. Now the mammon-worshiping materialists of the North were in power, intent on destroying the southern culture forever, and replacing it with their Yankee ways.

Their honor was at stake. They would not, they *could* not submit to such humiliation. They must save the South, even if they had to create a whole new republic to do it!

It did not take long for the southern states to act. They had prepared for this moment for more than a year should

Lincoln be elected. One month after the vote, on December 6, 1860, South Carolina voted to withdraw from the Union.

Rapidly the governors of the other southern states called special sessions of their legislatures to vote on similar measures. They wanted to act hurriedly, while a sympathetic and Democratic James Buchanan was still president. What Abraham Lincoln might do once he took office on March 3, no one knew. And the southern states didn't want to wait to find out!

I suppose that in the South during these tense months, there was a feeling of excitement, as if they were part of a historic and honorable cause, out of which a new and noble nation was about to be born. But in the rest of the country, news of what South Carolina had done caused only gloom. Why, we all wondered, would they try to tear the country apart?

We still hoped nothing might come of it. South Carolina had always been the most radical southern state. Back in 1832 when Pa hadn't been much more than a boy, South Carolina had gotten defiant and had threatened to do the same thing. But President Jackson had answered heatedly and had said he'd send in the army if he had to. South Carolina had backed down.

Many people held the opinion that they could be forced to back down again if Buchanan would act, and act promptly. But President Buchanan's party had been defeated. He had only three months more to serve, and he had never been a swift decision maker. The result was that he did nothing, and left events to take their course. He would just wait and let the new president worry about it.

In the meantime, the South became stronger and stronger in their resolve that they would *never* back down again.

As bad as all this was, it wasn't the worst news to come to Miracle Springs as 1860 came to an end. Two weeks before Christmas, a letter arrived addressed to Pa. The handwriting was a barely legible scrawl, but his name and "Miracle Springs" could be made out on the envelope. The letter inside was no easier to read. It was a single sheet of paper.

HOLISTR,

I hope this here letter gits to you. I give it to Pony Bob an tol him to give hit to the next feller an to git hit to Sacremeno an that somebudy there'd no how to git it to youe. This aint no good kin of letter to have to writ to nobudy nohow, an I hate to be the one to have to do hit. But I figger youd rather hear hit from a freen than from somebudy you never heerd of. What I got to say jis this, Holistr, an Im sorry as a man kin be, but word came to us las week that yer sons horse come wanderin into the stashun without nary a trace o the kid. The mail was ther but no rider. Thats all we heerd. I sent Pony Bob back out ther an tol him to fin out sumthin mor, on account o youe bein my freen an all. I didnt want to writ you til we cud tell you jist what happen. But Bob he didnt git no more informashun, an nobudys heerd hide or hare o the boy sinse, and its been more na week now, an this time o yere nobudy kin live out in them hills past tu or thre days. Im sorry as kin be, but hit dont look good fer yer boy. Hits been snowin there tu. An the blame Piyutes. Give yer little lady my best, and tell her Im sorry tu.
Tavish

The whole rest of the week a spirit of gloom hovered all about the claim. When all the folks in town heard about it, a quiet settled over all of Miracle Springs. Pa was held in mighty high regard by everyone, and so was Almeda. The fact that Zack had been riding for the Pony Express had made people proud in a way. His disappearance affected everyone.

Rev. Rutledge prayed for Zack in church the next Sunday, and of course everybody came up to us to offer their sympathy and to say they'd be praying for all of us.

Mr. Royce was among them. "I'm sorry to hear about the boy, Hollister," he said, shaking Pa's hand. "I really mean that."

"I know you do, Franklin," replied Pa.

"The kid had spunk. Almost as much as your girl there," he added, glancing toward me with as much of a smile as Franklin Royce was ever likely to give anyone. "He was the one who saved my money and your wife's property back when the Dutch Flat gang was causing so much trouble. No, I'm not likely to forget that. If anybody can take care of himself out there, it's your Zack."

"I'm much obliged to you, Royce," said Pa.

As time went on, it was almost worse not knowing. It would have been easier to deal with and get past if we had just heard he was dead. But to not know, and to have to think of him lying somewhere with an arrow in him, or frozen in a snowdrift in some ravine—that was the worst part.

The only bright spot in the last month and a half of the year was that Pa was elected to the California State Assembly. But nobody felt much like celebrating. Least of all Pa.

Secession!

CHAPTER FORTY

*C*hristmas of 1860 was certainly not a very festive day.

Almeda and Aunt Katie tried to make it as happy as they could. There were presents and we had a nice dinner with the Rutledges at our house. But Pa felt so downcast over Zack, and everyone shared his misery.

Pa now had two things to feel guilt-ridden about—driving Zack away in the first place, and then turning back when we were there instead of going on to find him—Indian danger or not!

"If only I hadn't been such a coward," Pa said a dozen times. "I might have got to him and talked him into coming back home with me. But that handful of Indians made me hightail it outta there like a scared jackrabbit!"

"There were more than a few, Pa," I reminded him. "We both almost got ourselves good and dead."

But nothing I or anyone else said could perk up Pa's spirits. And who was I to blame him? I'd have felt terrible, too. I *did* feel terrible, but not so bad as if I'd been his father. Maybe Zack was being rebellious and independent by running off as he had. But Pa didn't have the luxury of the man in the New Testament, knowing he had been a good father and yet not being able to do anything about his son's foolish youthfulness.

Maybe Pa had been a decent father to Zack; maybe he hadn't. He sure had been to me. But the fact was, he didn't think so, and he believed the accusations Zack had shouted at him the day he'd left.

So it was a lot harder on him than the father in the Bible who just had to wait patiently for his prodigal son to come to his senses. Pa had to carry guilt along with everything else, guilt for having caused all the trouble and heartbreak himself. Now thinking that Zack was probably dead, but not knowing, and knowing he might *never* know for sure—it was just an unbearable load for poor Pa. All the rest of us could do was love him and pray for him. But we couldn't make it go away.

As always, news from the East got into our papers about two weeks after it actually happened. During that first week of the new year of 1861, we began to learn of events that did not portend good news for the future. President Buchanan still hadn't done anything to block or counter South Carolina's action. Neither had he nor anyone else made any hard attempts to resolve the crisis with a compromise of some kind. These failures led to the most serious news of all: one by one, starting with Mississippi on December 20, the rest of the southern states began to secede from the Union too. Next came Florida, then Alabama, Georgia, Louisiana, and finally, later in January, Texas.

Still President Buchanan did nothing. Abraham Lincoln remained powerless until he would take office on March 3. Was nothing to be done to save the *United* States of America from becoming the *Disunited* States?

As they seceded, the southern states had taken possession of federal properties inside their borders. South Carolina could not immediately seize Fort Sumter in Charleston harbor, however, because it had no navy and because the fort was held by seventy-five Union soldiers.

But South Carolina wanted the fort. Now that the new independent little country was over a month old, it was beginning to feel itself strong and important. So a committee was sent to Washington to negotiate with the United States on behalf of the nation of South Carolina to have the fort transferred to the former state.

President Buchanan refused to give up the fort. Finally he got angry and sent an unarmed steamer down the coast to Fort Sumter with more troops and supplies. South Carolina military troops fired on the ship and forced it to turn around.

It had been the first act of war. Yet even though northerners and we in the West were shocked and astonished at what the South was doing, there was still no real sense of the danger and peril yet to come.

Even if President Buchanan had *wanted* to force South Carolina and the other states back into the Union, there would probably have been little he could have done. The regular army of the nation was only fifteen thousand strong, and most of those men were out West protecting settlers and wagon trains and Pony Express riders from Indians. It would have taken months to get the army back to the East—and doing so would have left the West to the Indians!

Everyone loathed what the South was doing and said it was illegal and against the Constitution to do it. Yet no one actually wanted to *fight* to stop them from doing it.

But tempers and emotions were gradually running hotter and more violent and unpredictable.

Meanwhile, the southern states were wasting no time. As northern politicians scurried around trying to set up meetings and find compromise plans, the seven states that had seceded were busy forming a new government. From the beginning, they had planned to organize a whole new nation as soon as secession had been accomplished—a new nation based on the principle of states' rights. And it was important that they do so immediately . . . *before* Lincoln's inauguration!

Therefore, delegates from the seven states met in February in Montgomery, Alabama, and founded a new nation. They called it the Confederate States of America. And they didn't waste time with an election—the delegates themselves chose Mississippi Senator and former Secretary of War Jefferson Davis as their new president.

A New President Comes to Washington

CHAPTER FORTY-ONE

*T*he new southern nation was confident, and in early 1861 better organized and more united than the rest of the United States. All was not lost quite yet, however, because eight more slave states of the upper and border regions of the South had remained loyal to the Union and were determined to give Lincoln a chance.

All this time, President-elect Abraham Lincoln had not revealed to the country what he intended to do about the crisis. Would he attack South Carolina? If so, with what troops? Would he try to find some new compromise nobody had thought of yet? Would he just wait and let events go as Buchanan had? Or would he accept the new nation, and go on as president of just half the former country?

No one knew. So everyone in *both* countries anxiously awaited Lincoln's inaugural speech, scheduled for March 4, to find out what his new policy was going to be.

In the meantime, out in California, there was a lot of support for the South. The South Carolina fever for secession ran all the way west to the Pacific!

But for some reason, by the time it reached California, those who felt the state ought to secede didn't necessarily want to join the Confederacy. They wanted California to pull out of the Union to start a *third* independent republic. If the North and South couldn't solve their squabbles, why should California be joined with either of them?

A year before, former California Senator Weller had proclaimed: "If the wild spirit of fanaticism, which now pervades the land, should destroy this magnificent Union, California will not go with the South or the North, but here upon the shores of the Pacific will found and establish a mighty new republic."

"It's plumb fool ridiculousness, Almeda!" exclaimed Pa, looking up from the newspaper.

"What is it, Drummond?" she'd asked.

"I'm just reading here in the *Standard* that this fellow Butts is calling for a convention to found a Pacific Republic. Who is he, anyway—do you know, Corrie?"

"Judge Butts is the editor of the Sacramento *Standard*, Pa."

"Well, he's got no business interfering in politics, if you ask me."

"You better learn to get along with him when you go to Sacramento," laughed Almeda, "or you might find yourself tarred and feathered in that paper of his!

"It was just a month ago that you were laughing about that proposal by John Burch proposing the formation of a Pacific Republic."

"That's because I thought it was a joke—California, Oregon, New Mexico, Washington, and Utah forming a new country! But I think Butts is serious!"

"He is serious, Pa," I said. "The *Herald*, the *Gazette*, the *Democrat*, the *Star*—they've all come out in favor of western independence."

"What about your *Alta?*"

"The *Alta's* pro-Union all the way," I said. "You don't think I'd keep writing for a Democratic paper, do you?"

"Well, if this one Republican has anything to say about it when I get to Sacramento, California's gonna stay put right where it is—in the Union, and supporting Mr. Abraham Lincoln when he gets to be president!"

All through the elections Lincoln's opponents had made fun of his appearance—tall, thin, and gawky, with rough features and a big beak nose. He was said to sleep in the same shirt he gave speeches in, and from listening to some reports I would have thought he still lived in the backwoods log cabin where he was raised. Even after his election he was not considered "sophisticated" enough for Washington society.

But people were in for a surprise. Lincoln might not have been handsome or cultured, but he was a strong man, a shrewd politician, and an authoritative leader—just the right man to be president at such a time, and certainly better than James Buchanan. Abraham Lincoln would not do nothing. Whatever he did, it was sure to be decisive.

Lincoln left his home in Springfield, Illinois, for Washington in late February. He traveled by train and took eleven roundabout days to get there, stopping all throughout the states of the North to visit people and make speeches and let them see their new president. Everybody wanted to know what he was going to do about the Confederacy, but he wouldn't reveal his policies yet. His speeches were light—some even thought them frivolous. People began to get the idea they had elected a simpleton to the White House. He seemed almost unaware of how serious the crisis was.

At Westfield, New York, he asked the crowd if a young girl by the name of Grace Bedell was present. She was brought up to the rear of the train where he was speaking. Then he told the listening crowd that she had written him during the campaign to tell him that he would look much handsomer if he grew some whiskers. Then he stooped down with a smile. "You see, Grace," he said, "I let these whiskers grow just for you."

When he attended the opera in New York City, he did the unthinkable by wearing black gloves instead of white. High society was aghast at the thought of having such an oafish man living in the White House and in charge of the country.

In Philadelphia a private detective named Allan Pinkerton came to the president-elect with the news that he had learned of a plot to assassinate him when he changed trains in Baltimore. Lincoln would have paid no attention, except that a little while later another report came to him of the same thing.

So Lincoln let Pinkerton take charge of getting him to Washington safely. He was put up in a sleeper that had been reserved by one of Pinkerton's female detectives for her "invalid brother." They passed through Baltimore at three in the morning and reached Washington just about daybreak.

When it was discovered what had happened and that Lincoln had at one point in the journey draped a shawl over his shoulders so as not to be recognized, all kinds of mocking and cruel stories and jokes and cartoons were printed in the newspapers, especially in the South. This was the man, they said, who was going to lead the nation! People were beginning to think he was an incompetent, ignorant clown.

But Lincoln had just been beating around the bush with his lighthearted speeches. In fact, he knew exactly how serious the crisis was. He had been planning for it for four months.

The Pony Express was gearing up to speed Lincoln's inaugural address to California the moment it was delivered. I wished Zack had been able to be part of it!

It took three days for the speech to reach St. Joseph by train from Washington. Then the Express took over at an amazing pace. The speech was brought down the Main Street of Sacramento from St. Joseph in an all-time speed record: seven days and seventeen hours. Two of the riders, trying to make up for delays, actually rode their horses to death.

The speech, which Pa read to us all from the March 17 edition of the *Alta* when it arrived in Miracle Springs on the eighteenth, was certainly not the speech of a weakling or a simpleton. It was clear right away what kind of man had been elected president, and I was glad that I'd done my part to help him win California's four electoral votes. It wasn't much, out of the 180 he'd received, but I was glad they hadn't gone to anybody else.

"The Union is older than the states," he said in his speech, "and was founded to last forever. Secession is illegal, a revolutionary act." Then the new president went on to tell what he planned to do.

He did not intend to be rash, he said, or to do anything sudden or forceful. He would proceed with patience and caution for a time. And that right there, Almeda said as we listened, was the clue that showed he had no intention of putting up with the so-called new country forever—he would be patient *for a time.*

But he *would*, he went on to say, do all in his power to enforce all federal laws in *all* the states, and he would keep firm hold of federal property. Everyone knew he meant Fort Sumter.

He was not considering any forceful retribution, and there would be no threat to the constitutional rights of the states that had left the Union. If they wished to return, they could. But the government *would* act to defend itself.

Then he brought up the horrible prospect of what would happen if the southern states *didn't* come to their senses and come back to the Union. He spoke straight to the South when he said whose fault it would be.

"In *your* hands, my dissatisfied fellow countrymen," he said, "and not in *mine,* is the momentous issue of civil war. The government will not assail *you.* You can have no conflict without being yourselves the aggressors. You have no oath registered in Heaven to destroy the government, while *I* shall have the most solemn one to *preserve, protect, and defend it.*"

The closing words of his speech showed that he still wanted to believe that the people of the South deep down felt as loyal to the country as he did. Maybe their radical leaders didn't. But surely the great masses of southerners didn't really want what was happening.

"We are not enemies," he said, "but friends. We must not be enemies. Though passion may have strained, it must not break the bonds of affection. The mystic chords of memory, stretching from every battlefield and patriot grave, to every living heart and hearthstone, all over this broad land, will yet swell the chorus of the Union, when again touched, as surely they will be, by the better angels of our nature."

Pa in Sacramento

CHAPTER FORTY-TWO

*T*hose were times of peril, those first few months of 1861.

The only trouble was, no one knew how dangerous they really were. No one expected what came afterward. No one knew how bad it would be. If they had, they probably would have done things differently.

As it was, time kept passing, and everybody on both sides got more and more determined *not* to give in. They all thought *they* were right and everyone else was wrong. Sometimes that may be true, but it can still be a dangerous way to look at things. Admitting you might be a little wrong yourself is hard for most folks, but it seems like the easiest way to avoid conflicts later.

Pa had gone to Sacramento to get sworn in to the new Assembly in January of 1861. He was gone a week that first time. When he came back he was so full of stories and enthusiasm he hardly stopped talking for days. I had never seen him like that! Almeda couldn't get over him; she laughed and laughed just to listen to him. It seemed such a short time ago that he'd been just an ordinary soft-spoken man trying to make a gold strike. Suddenly he had a family and a vein of wealth right on his property, a new wife and a business. Before he knew it, he was mayor of a town, then a state legislator.

"If a simple man like Abraham Lincoln can go from a log cabin to splitting wood rails to being president," said Almeda one day, "then I don't see any reason why you can't, too!"

She made the mistake of letting Alkali Jones hear her! He'd been working at the mine with Uncle Nick, Pa, and Tad, and had just walked into the house for lunch. Whenever Pa came back from Sacramento business, he worked at the mine for the next two or three days. "Makes me feel back to normal," he said, "to get wet and dirty and get my arms and back aching again. Too much sitting around talking like they do down there in the capital, it just ain't natural. A man's gotta sweat from hard work, at least three or four times a week, or things just get out of order. I gotta be working if I'm gonna think right!"

"Drum fer President!" cackled Mr. Jones, walking in on the tail end of what Almeda had said. "That's a good'n—hee, hee, hee! I can die in peace now, I've heard jist about every dad-burned tall tale a body could dream up! Drum fer President—hee, hee, hee!"

"You don't think I could do the job, Alkali?" said Pa seriously, giving the rest of us a wink.

"Oh, I ain't sayin' no such thing. Fer all I know, you'd march straight down t' them southern rascals an' look 'em straight in the eye and say, 'Now look here, you varmints! You're breakin' a passel of laws, an' worse'n that—you're all actin' like a bunch of dang fools. Now git back t' your homes; let your slaves be the free men they got a right t' be, and cut it out with all this blamed foolishness of tryin' t' start a country of your own. It ain't gonna work no how!'"

By now we were all in stitches from laughing so hard. Of course, that just spurred Mr. Jones all the more to keep going.

There wasn't anything he loved better than being at the center of stories high on imagination and low on facts.

"Yep," he kept going, "you jist might make a president that'd git folks in this country t' stand up an' take notice of the kind of guts and grit it takes t' live out here. Drum for President—hee, hee! That's what them there fools back there need, all right—a Californian with the guts t' make them rascals back down and git off their dang high horses! Hee, hee, hee!"

"What would you do if you *were* president, Pa?" Tad asked.

Pa got a real serious expression on his face. The room grew quiet, and we all waited to see what he'd say.

"You mean about the Confederate states, boy?" he said finally.

"Yeah, Pa. How would you make them not do what they're trying to do to the country?"

"Well, I reckon the first thing I'd do is send my vice-president down to Montgomery to talk to 'em, to look 'em straight in the eye, and to horsewhip some sense into 'em."

"Who would be your vice-president, Pa?" asked Becky.

"Why, I thought you knew, girl," answered Pa. "Alkali, of course!"

"Please, Drummond," said Almeda this time, wiping the tears of laughter out of her eyes and trying to be serious. "I really am curious what you would do."

Again Pa thought long and hard.

"I don't reckon I can answer what I *would* do if I was in Washington without saying what I *am* doing right down there in Sacramento," he answered finally.

"What do you mean by that?" asked Uncle Nick, drying his hands off with a towel and walking over toward Pa.

"Just what I said, Nick. I mean, my first business is right here and right now. I tell you, there's as much foolishness coming out of some of those southern sympathizing Democrats in Sacramento as in those renegades setting themselves up as so all-fired important down in Montgomery! It makes my blood boil just to think of it. That's why I had to get back here to Miracle and swing the sledge a few times against some good hard rock."

"How you figure it, Drum?" asked Mr. Jones. I'd never taken him as one much interested in politics, but the look on his face was serious. This dispute between North and South had *everyone's* attention!

"We sat down for our first session," said Pa. "Half of the new members, like me, had no idea what was going on or what to do or how the place even worked. Then this guy named Zack Montgomery stood up. He talked half the morning about how we needed to break away from the Union ourselves. Later I heard there was a senator named Thornton doing the same thing over in the Senate room. The Democrats are trying to get California to do the same thing as South Carolina!"

"Surely it's not a serious threat?" said Almeda, in both amazement and shock.

"You gotta realize, Almeda," said Pa, "the Democrats still outnumber us Republicans in the state. Breckinridge and Douglas together got a heap more votes than Lincoln. A lot of politicians in this state think Lincoln's a buffoon, and they're not ashamed to say so. Lots of 'em don't have that much loyalty to the Union. They figure California's the only thing that matters, so let Lincoln and the eastern states do whatever they please. Why, there's a feller named Charles Piercy who voted for Douglas—he's not a slave man, has no particular loyalties to the South. But he stood up, just a few seats away from me, and he said he'd written up what he called a resolution condemning the Republicans as altogether and solely responsible for bringing on the secession crisis. Then he walked up to the front and handed the piece of paper he was talking about to the Speaker. Then Piercy turned around to face the rest of us—and this was after Montgomery's fiery speech—and said, 'My fellow assemblymen, for this reason, I feel most strongly that we Californians will never entirely be able to support our new president. I am urging you, therefore, to stand with me in backing the formation of a mighty Pacific Republic, as advocated by our colleague, Mr. Montgomery, earlier today. Our former governor, Mr. Latham, now in the Senate in Washington, has long been in favor of such a proposition, and would no doubt return to help us in the formation of a constitution and provisional government.'"

Pa stopped, then added, "Those are probably not his exact words, but something like 'em. Speechmaking words! And ridiculous words, if you ask me!"

"What did the rest of you do?" asked Uncle Nick.

"There were some folks saying 'Hear, hear!' and agreeing with him, but others stood up when he was done and said just what I was thinking, that it was downright foolishness. One fella got up and even brought France into it."

"France?" repeated Alkali Jones. "What do them foreigners have t' do with us?"

"Well, this fella said that if we tried to set ourselves up in a new country over here, this far away from the other states, with a thousand miles of coastline and less than a million people and no army, he said we couldn't defend ourselves against anybody—especially with the North and South at each other's throats. He said Napoleon would come right in and gobble us up and make us into a Pacific France."

"Napoleon's dead, Pa," said Becky. "Mrs. Rutledge was just teaching us about him and a place called Waterloo last month, before Christmas."

"Napoleon the Third, Becky," I said. "He's the other Napoleon's nephew. He's the emperor of France."

"Well, whoever the varmint is, let him try t' come in here an' make trouble! We'll show him what kind of stuff Californians is made of!"

"With what, Alkali?" said Pa. "We got no army, and hardly no militia to speak of. We're barely a state, much less a country that could fight off somebody like France!"

"So what happened next, Pa?" asked Becky.

A funny look came over Pa's face. Almeda recognized it immediately. "I can tell when you're holding something in, Drummond," she said. "Now tell us, what happened?"

"Well, all of a sudden I found myself on my feet," Pa answered, as if he was embarrassed to remember it.

"Good for you, Drum!" exclaimed Uncle Nick. "You gave 'em all what for, didn't you? I knew you had it in you!"

"No I didn't give 'em what for, Nick!" Pa shot back. "What do you think, that I wanted to make enemies there my first week in the capital?"

"You must have said something," said Almeda, her eyes eager to hear what had happened.

"I reckon I did," said Pa slowly. "The second I realized what I was doing, I got afraid and wanted to sit down something fierce. But I went ahead with what I'd been thinking, and I just told 'em all that I figured since we'd elected Mr.

Lincoln, he deserved for us to at least give him a chance of seeing what he could do. I said we oughta let it sit a spell. Gettin' too hasty's always a way of hangin' yourself, I said. I told 'em I'd always made a practice of trying to take important decisions slow. You don't usually get in trouble from goin' too slow, I said—that is, unless you're in a gunfight. They laughed a little when I said that," said Pa, chuckling as he remembered it. "But you *can* get yourself in a heap o' trouble by rushing into something you ought not to have done. So I finished up by saying I figured we oughta wait and give the president our loyalty, and see what happened."

The room got quiet when Pa finished.

All at once Almeda started clapping, and then the rest of us joined in, just as if we'd been sitting there in the state Assembly room actually listening to Pa's speech.

"Now cut that out—all of you!" scowled Pa. I don't think I'd ever seen his face red before, but it was then. "It wasn't no big thing!"

I glanced over at Almeda. Her face was fixed intently on Pa with a look of admiration and love, and tears stood in her eyes.

"What happened next, Pa?" asked Tad eagerly.

"Well, boy, some of the folks did just what you done— they started clapping, and I sat down pronto and wished I could just sink right down into my chair and hide. I gotta tell you, I felt a mite foolish!"

"What about the resolution, Pa?" I asked. "Did you decide anything?"

"Naw. Politics is mostly talking, Corrie. There ain't much *doing*, only yammering about everything. I reckon we'll be voting on what to do one day, but I don't know when. Most likely we'll just keep talking for a long spell, and I'll keep getting my fill of it and have to spend more time up at the mine crushing rocks just to keep from going looney from all the words that don't accomplish much of anything!"

It was quiet for a long time. Finally I asked Pa the question that had been on my mind ever since he had come back home from Sacramento.

"Did you see Mr. Burton when you were there?" I said shyly.

"As a matter of fact, I did, Corrie. He congratulated me on my getting elected and told me to give you his fond re-gards. Those were his words—his fond regards. *And* he told me to give you this. I was so anxious to get up and pound them rocks in the mine that I nearly forgot."

He reached inside his coat and took out a rumpled letter, then handed it to me.

My face flushed with embarrassment, but that didn't keep me from snatching the letter and getting up to go to my room to read it.

Everybody else got up too. Just as I was going into the bedroom, I heard Alkali Jones behind me, opening the door to head back outside. He was muttering and chuckling to himself.

"Drum fer President . . . hee, hee, hee!" he was saying. "Blamed if he ain't startin' t' sound like one, at that."

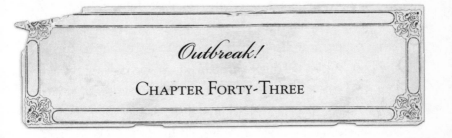

*S*hortly after the inauguration, I received another letter, this one from Mr. Kemble.

"You get to writing, Corrie!" he said. "There's foolishness and plots and subversion afoot all over this country. The Union's in trouble, Corrie, and we've got to have a strong, supportive position. Half of California's papers are advocating everything from throwing in with the Confederacy to the Pacific Republic."

He had enclosed a clipping from one of the other San Francisco papers, which read:

> We shall secede, with the Rocky Mountains for a line, and form an Empire of the Pacific, with Washington Territory, Oregon, and California, and we shall annex all of this side of Mexico. We don't care a straw whether you dissolve the Union or not. We just wish that the Republicans and Democrats at the capital would get into a fight and kill each other like the Kilkenny cats. Perhaps that would settle the hash.

Mr. Kemble finished his letter: "It's time for the *Alta* to take its stand, and you along with it. The Union needs us all, Corrie!"

He hardly needed to tell me how desperate the situation was! Every day I'd been reading, not only in the *Alta* but in other papers as well, about everything that was happening in the East. With the Pony Express making news only two weeks late, everything that was going on felt so real and urgent. I saved all the papers so I'd know just what was happening, and that when I did write things, I'd have my facts straight. If I was going to help Mr. Lincoln and the Union, I had to make sure what I wrote was right and true. I didn't want anyone to be able to complain that the young lady newswoman from California wrote nothing but female emotionalism and that she didn't know what she was talking about. So I tried to understand the events that were going on and keep track of everything as it happened.

The time to have saved the country was back in November or December of 1860. If only Mr. Lincoln had been able to become president right after he was elected! But by the time he set foot in Washington, the Confederacy was already better organized than his new administration! The Republicans had never been in power before. So Mr. Lincoln had to set up an entire executive branch of government from scratch—a cabinet, and all kinds of other appointments. While he was busy having to be an executive and an administrator, the Confederacy was growing stronger and stronger every day.

Not only was the Confederacy stronger right at first, they were confident that Lincoln and the northern states could never stand against southern might. The South had economic strength, strong ties with foreign governments because of the worldwide demand for cotton, and the best politicians in the land. Now that leadership was all in the South. Washington had a group of bumbling midwesterners and Republicans who had never governed a nation before. In addition, the South had strong financial reserves in her banks, while the North was financially strapped. Perhaps most importantly, the South had the best generals.

By the time Lincoln took office, the Confederacy had a permanent constitution, a treasury, an army, a navy, a post office, and a legal system. Its organizers had been busy. A completely functioning government had been created and was in full operation. Southern leaders had not a doubt in the world that Lincoln would be powerless to oppose them. What could he do? The Confederacy existed, and he could not undo it! If he tried to use force with the two or three thousand army troops he might muster from the Northeast and Midwest, the results would be laughable. The South would beat them back so fast it would make the tall, lanky rail-splitter from Illinois wish he'd never run for president!

Pa returned from his next trip into Sacramento right at the end of February with serious and disturbing news. Suddenly the dispute between North and South wasn't so far away!

A plot had been discovered, he told us, by a group of southern supporters, to take control of the government of California!

"Knights of the Golden Circle, that's what they called themselves," he said. "Once they had control of Sacramento, they were going to send an armed force down into Mexico where they would seize control of Sonora."

"They could never have gotten away with it!" exclaimed Almeda.

"They had powerful men from the South behind it," said Pa. "They had fifty thousand guns on the way to California by

the southern route. The knights had sixteen thousand supporters. They might have been able to do it if we hadn't got
word from Washington. They were going to set up an independent republic of the Pacific. Their first move was to grab
the Presidio to hold the entrance of the Golden Gate, then
the rest of San Francisco's forts, Alcatraz, the mint, the post
office, everything of the government's. Then they were going
to join the Confederacy!"

"I can't believe it—in California! Who was behind it?"

"Buchanan's secretary of war, John Floyd. He left Washington, joined the Confederacy, and from what we hear had
been arranging for the shipment of guns even while he was
in Washington. I tell you, Almeda, it's a dangerous situation.
The South has supporters everywhere!"

If 1860 had been a dangerous year in the history of the
country, as I'd heard the men discussing at the celebration
at the Montgomery Hotel, then 1861 was the year when that
danger climaxed and exploded. It didn't take long after Mr.
Lincoln's inauguration. The day after it, in fact.

On March 5, Mr. Lincoln was told that the army men at
Fort Sumter were running seriously low on supplies and food.
Unless they received more soon, they would have to abandon
the fort. If that happened, South Carolina would take possession of it, and their victory would make the new outlaw
nation seem all the more legitimate.

Mr. Lincoln determined not to let that happen. Fort Sumter was a symbol of the authority of the United States government and its army. It *had* to remain in Union hands. Even
though a ship with provisions had been fired upon and turned
back in January, Lincoln decided to send several ships this
time, as a relief expedition.

Early in April, therefore, he informed authorities in South Carolina that the ships were on their way.

At last the leaders of the new Confederacy showed how confident they were. They didn't want to let the ships get to Fort Sumter, or else it would reduce *their* authority in the world's sight. They wanted to prove how strong they were. In their eyes, a foreign nation controlled a Confederate harbor. So they decided not to wait for the ships to get there. They would attack Fort Sumter first and take control of it before the relief force arrived. They would show whose authority was greatest!

The Confederate commander at Charleston took an order to the Union commander at the fort demanding that he surrender Fort Sumter at once. He refused.

On the morning of April 12, therefore, the Confederate commander opened fire on the fort and blasted it with cannon balls and gunfire all that day and into the night. The small detachment of Union soldiers with scant supplies was helpless. If they didn't yield, they would all eventually be killed. On the next day they gave up and surrendered.

Suddenly the North came alive. Everyone who heard the news of the attack was outraged. It was finally clear—there was no more hope of compromise!

The president and the country had been patient long enough. The honor of the flag had been flagrantly attacked; the Rebel outlaws must be punished! As with one loud unanimous voice, the public demanded retribution against the South. There could be no two separate nations! The Union must be saved. The United States of America must be preserved . . . no matter what had to be done!

The New York *Tribune* carried the news:

Fort Sumter is lost, but freedom is saved. There is no more thought of bribing or coaxing the traitors who have dared to aim their cannon balls at the flag of the Union, and those who gave their lives to defend it. Fort Sumter is temporarily lost, but the country is saved. Long live the Republic!

News of the firing on Fort Sumter reached San Francisco on April 24, twelve days later. The very next afternoon a great crowd assembled at Portsmouth Square. Patriotic pro-Union speeches went on for a long part of the day, amid applause and cheering. It was not a day in San Francisco to express support for the South!

Immediately President Lincoln sent out a call for seventy-five thousand volunteers, and orders went out to the regular army troops stationed at the Presidio to be sent to the East. Lincoln's message did not actually say the word. He said that the troops and additional volunteers were needed to deal with certain "combinations too powerful to be suppressed by the ordinary course of judicial proceedings." In other words, all hope of compromise was dead.

But whether he said it or not, everyone knew that the United States was now at war.

With itself.

$\mathcal{E}$veryone expected the war to be short.

The South was so sure of a quick victory they thought all that would be necessary was for them to raise an army of volunteers and march north to take Washington, Philadelphia, and New York, and that would be the end of it. There was not even a need to sign up troops for lengthy assignments. The Confederacy made the enlistment period just twelve months. That would be more than enough time. Young men and boys throughout the South volunteered in droves. They were so feverish to join the Confederate army there weren't enough guns for them all.

Four more states promptly seceded—Virginia, Arkansas, Tennessee, and North Carolina. Although they were bound to the South in many ways, the states of Missouri, Kentucky, Maryland, and Delaware all decided to stay in the Union.

In the North, the volunteer army grew just as rapidly. More practically minded as to the true depth of the conflict, the North enlisted its young soldiers for three years. Within weeks Lincoln's request for seventy-five thousand men had been passed. By the middle of the year, the Union's army was five hundred thousand strong. President Lincoln ordered a

naval blockade of the whole southern coastline so that ships
with provisions could not get through.

Loyalties in California were more divided than ever, now
that war between the states had actually come. Pa came home
from a session in Sacramento in May with what he considered
good news.

"Well, we finally put all that new republic and western
confederacy talk to rest," he said. "Piercy and Montgomery
and all their crowd oughta be silenced for a while!"

"What happened?" asked Almeda.

"We Republicans finally got our *own* resolution on the
floor—a resolution strongly supporting the Union and Mr.
Lincoln's government."

"Did you speak again?"

"You bet I did! And this time I wasn't embarrassed. I got
up there and I said what I had to say!"

"And it passed the vote?" I asked.

"You're doggone right it did—49 to 12. California's on the
Union side of this thing once and for all, and for good!"

"What did it say?"

"Just a bunch of fancy sounding words to say, 'We're behind you, Mr. President.'"

"But what were the actual words?"

"I'll see if I can quote them: 'The people of California
are devoted to the Constitution and the Union now in the
hour of trial and peril.' Some kind of political gibberish
like that!"

But despite the vote in the California legislature, there
still was more southern support in the state than was altogether comfortable. Many high office-holders had once been
southerners. Not long after the war started, a group of San

Francisco's city leaders wrote to Secretary of War Cameron in Washington about their concerns. Since he was editor of the *Alta*, Mr. Kemble was part of that group. He later let me read a copy of the letter.

> A majority of our present state officers are undisguised and avowed Secessionists. . . . Every appointment made by our Governor unmistakably indicates his entire sympathy and cooperation with those plotting to sever California from her allegiance to the Union, and that, too, at the hazard of civil war.
>
> About three-eighths of our citizens are from slaveholding states. . . . These men are never without arms, have wholly laid aside their business, and are devoting their time to plotting, scheming, and organizing. Our advices, obtained with great prudence and care, show us that there are upwards of sixteen thousand "Knights of the Golden Circle" in the state, and that they are still organizing, even in our most loyal districts.

Whether blood would ever be shed in California as a result of the North-South loyalties that were so divisive, it was still too soon to tell. We all hoped not and hoped that the pro-Union stand of the legislature, in spite of what these men had said about Governor Downey, would ultimately influence the rest of the state to support the government of Lincoln and Hamlin instead of that of Davis and Stephens.

But in the meantime, the first major exodus *out* of California since the gold rush began to occur. Young men began making their way east to volunteer for the fighting that was sure to come, some to join the Union army, others that of the Confederacy.

I hadn't seen Cal for quite some time, even though I hadn't stopped thinking about him. There had been letters from time to time, but it wasn't nearly the same.

Then all of a sudden one day, there he was in Miracle Springs! I was working at the Mine and Freight when the stage rolled into town. And as I stood staring blankly and absent-mindedly through the backward letters of the word P-A-R-R-I-S-H painted on the window, suddenly there he was stepping down out of the coach.

I couldn't believe my eyes! I blinked a time or two. I must have been dreaming, I thought. But when he turned momentarily in my direction, I knew there could be no mistake.

The next second I was out the door and bolting across the dirt street—not very ladylike, but I wasn't thinking of propriety at the time!

"Cal!" I called out, clomping along in my office boots, my dress flopping about behind me, and holding on to my bonnet to keep it from flying off into the dirt. "Cal . . . !"

He turned from where he had been saying something to the driver and smiled at me in greeting. Before I knew what I was doing, I'd run right up to him and almost threw my arms around him. Luckily I caught myself in time.

"Whatever are you doing here?" I exclaimed, gulping for breath.

"What else would I be doing in Miracle Springs," he said, "but visiting my favorite writer and person, Cornelia Hollister?"

Hearing my full name from his lips sent a tingle through me, and I was glad I was already flushed from the run across the street!

"But why?"

"You don't think visiting you would be enough of a reason for a man?" he said with a grin and a wink.

"Oh, Cal, don't joke with me. You must have come for some other reason. Did you come to see Pa about some Republican business?"

He laughed. "Ah, Corrie, but you are inquisitive. Well, you're right, I *did* come on Republican business—but not to see your pa. I tell you, I came to see *you*!"

"I . . . I don't understand."

"I'll tell you everything. But don't you want to wait until the dust from the stage settles? Perhaps we could have dinner together. Is there someplace—?"

"Of course! You'll come home and have supper with us tonight!" I said enthusiastically. "Everybody will be happy to see you again!"

"I had in mind someplace where we might be alone," said Cal.

I blushed in earnest.

"Am I embarrassing you, Corrie? I do apologize. It's only that I have something very important to talk over with you— something I want to discuss in private, something that concerns our future."

What was he saying? My head was spinning, frantically trying to think what to say, what to suggest. Before I could get
another word out, Cal spoke up again.

"Now that I think about it," he said, "I suppose it would
be fitting to include your father—your whole family, in fact—
in the announcement I have to make."

"Announcement, Cal . . . what announcement?" I faltered.

"Oh, you'll just have to wait to hear with the rest of them!"
he laughed. "I gave you a chance to hear the good news by yourself. But now you'll just have to share it with everyone else!"

He finished his statement, then just stared at me with his
blue eyes and a big grin.

"So . . . do I consider that a formal invitation to supper?"
he said at length.

"Uh . . . uh, yes," I stumbled out. "Yes . . . of course."

"Tonight?"

"Yes."

"Well, then . . . I know you've probably got work to do
over at the office. So I'll just keep myself busy, look around
the town awhile, maybe have a drink. And Carl asked me to
pay a visit to Mr. Royce as long as I was coming this way. Shall
I meet you out at your house this evening?"

"Uh . . . yes," I said. "I reckon that'll be just fine."

"I'll hire a buggy and be out."

He turned and began to walk away. I was still standing
there in a daze. "No . . . wait, Cal," I said, finally coming to my
senses. "Ride out with me. I have Almeda's buggy here. Come
over to the office around five o'clock."

"I'll be there," he said cheerily.

Still I just stood there watching him walk over to the
boardwalk and then toward Mr. Royce's bank.

I wasn't much good at the office the rest of the afternoon. I couldn't concentrate on anything, and it was all I could do to keep away from Marcus and Mr. Ashton. If they took one good look at me, they'd start asking all kinds of questions about whether I was sick or something. This was one time I did *not* want two old unmarried men fussing over me. So I spent most of the afternoon in Almeda's office with the door closed. But I didn't get a single thing done!

All I could think about were Cal's words, going over and over and over again in my mind.

The announcement I have to make . . . someplace where we might be alone . . . in private . . . something that concerns our future . . . our future . . . OUR future . . .

The ride out to the claim later that day with Cal at my side was nearly torture! He was talkative and friendly, as always, but I was about as interesting as a wet dishrag! It was the longest ride home from town I'd ever had.

I wasn't any better at supper. Pa and Almeda and the others were delighted to see Cal, of course, and he was charming and friendly, laughing and nice and hospitable. He congratulated and praised Pa, saying he always knew his star was on the rise.

They talked about politics mostly, and a lot about the problem with the Confederacy and Fort Sumter.

"Do you think there'll actually be fighting, Cal?" Pa asked.

"It seems impossible to avoid it now, with both sides so dead set against any kind of giving in."

"It's just awful," said Almeda. "The thought of Americans killing Americans is horrible! It oughtn't to be happening!"

I just sat waiting, trembling inside. How could they talk about politics and the war when was Cal going to make his *announcement?*

I didn't have too much longer to wait.

"But the hostilities between North and South isn't why I've come to Miracle Springs," he said when there was a lull in the conversation. "I have some exciting news to tell you all—news that I felt merited a personal visit."

I sat staring straight down at the table, too scared to look up. Somehow I knew, though, that Cal was looking at me.

He paused, and the others waited for him to continue.

"You both know, Mr. and Mrs. Hollister," he finally went on, "how fond I am of your daughter."

I glanced up. They both nodded.

"So fond of her, in fact," Cal said, "that I knew from the very start, right from that evening we all met back in San Francisco, you remember, Mr. Hollister, just about a year ago—I knew that here was a young lady I wanted to be part of my future. I knew too that I wanted her to meet my boss, Mr. Stanford. I just had a feeling about her—a feeling which, I am happy to say, turned out to be a positive omen of things to come."

Again he stopped briefly and drew in a breath. Then he looked over at me, reached out and placed his hand gently on top of mine, and began again.

"Just a few days ago, Mr. Stanford made public his candidacy for the governorship of California. And, Corrie, he asked me to come out here to ask you personally if you would be part of his campaign—a campaign to take control of the great state of California on behalf of the pro-Union Republican party."

He stopped. His face was bright with expectation as he gazed at me. I knew he probably thought I would be overcome with gratefulness. I was overcome, all right—but with an entirely different emotion!

"That . . . that is the announcement you told me about in town?" I asked softly, trying to keep my voice from cracking.

"Yes. Isn't it exciting, Corrie? It's the opportunity I was telling you about . . . the future. For us to be part of together, just like I was saying when we were together in Palo Alto. An exciting future full of opportunities that we can share!"

But I only heard about half his words before I was up from the table and running to my room. I lay down on my bed and sobbed quietly. How could I possibly have been so stupid?

But even as I lay there, I remembered the other time Cal had been here, and what a fool I'd made of myself, sneaking around in the woods with dirt all over me. I could *not* let something like that happen again!

I quickly jumped up off my bed, ran to my washbasin, which still had some water in it, dashed a little on my face, dried with a towel, sucked in a deep breath, and turned around to walk back out and face the music. I would be brave and put the best face on an awkward situation I could.

I returned to the table. "I'm sorry for leaving so abruptly," I said. "I was just overcome for a minute, and had to be alone. But I'm fine now."

I sat back down and gave Cal the biggest smile I could manage to muster. I hoped my red eyes didn't betray me.

"You can tell Mr. Stanford that I'd be honored," I said. "I would very much like to do what I could to help him."

"Good . . . wonderful!" exclaimed Cal. "I know that will please him a great deal."

With the business out of the way, the conversation again drifted toward politics. It seemed that was just about the only thing folks talked about these days. With a war imminent, there was a great sense of uncertainty and tension, even in far-off California.

Then the door opened and Uncle Nick walked in with his family. Cal immediately jumped up, shook Uncle Nick's hand, and greeted Aunt Katie warmly. Everyone took seats and the conversation resumed.

After about five minutes, suddenly a puzzled expression came over Cal's face. "Say, where is your sister?" he asked Aunt Katie. "Edie was her name, was it not? I had hoped to see her again too."

The room was silent a moment.

"She left for the East," Katie said. Her tone reflected the sadness she and all the rest of us had felt at Edie's parting.

"When?" asked Cal.

"Right after the Sumter incident," replied Uncle Nick.

"She said she had to go—that with the South under attack, she had to be where her home would always be."

An odd look came over Cal's face. What Aunt Katie had said seemed to strike deeply into him for some reason.

"We tried to get her to stay," said Uncle Nick. "Told her it was the South doing the attacking, and that if it did come to war, there couldn't be no safer place for her than right here."

"She hardly had any family left, anyway," said Almeda. "We told her we loved her and that we'd try to be family to her now that her husband was gone. But once news about Sumter came, she changed. She was distant after that. I knew she wasn't at home here."

"Nothing we said could change her mind," said Katie, starting to cry quietly. Almeda was sitting next to her and put her arm around her to comfort her. "I asked her what if we never saw each other again. But she just kept saying she had to be with her new country. It was almost as if we were suddenly strangers."

Katie could say no more. She broke down and wept.

Cal hadn't said another word, and the faraway look remained in his eyes for some time. He seemed very thoughtful and distracted and didn't say much the rest of the evening.

The outbreak of war between the North and South was bound, it seemed, to touch everyone in the country closely, sooner or later.

Already the pain was starting to come into people's lives.

*J*ust like Abraham Lincoln, Leland Stanford faced two Democrats in running for governor—a southern Democrat and a Union Democrat. The campaign was a short one, lasting mainly just through the months of July and August.

Stanford had lots of supporters in the state besides me. Once I began to realize just how much support he did have, in fact, I wondered why he had thought of me at all.

Thomas Starr King, now a strong ally, traveled throughout the state speaking for Mr. Stanford. And as everybody was finding out, he was one of the best orators in the whole country. A group of San Francisco businessmen who were normally Democrats backed Mr. Stanford, too. Like him, they were strong supporters of the Union even if they hadn't voted for Mr. Lincoln. A man named Levi Strauss was one of the most famous of these men, and since they were all influential, a lot of people took their advice when it came time to vote.

One person who *wasn't* so enthusiastic, though it made me mad at the time he told me, was a certain individual out of my past I'd tried hard to forget—Robin T. O'Flaridy.

I had seen his byline occasionally—he called himself *R. Thomas O'Flaridy.* When we ran into each other one day in the *Alta* building, he took me aside and spoke softly to me.

"Corrie, do me a favor and take one last bit of advice from an old friend," he said.

"An old friend?" I said, laughing. "After all you've pulled on me?"

"All in the past, Corrie," smiled Robin. "Part of the business, you know. Surely you've forgiven me by now."

"Oh, I suppose. How could I hold a grudge against a struggling fellow writer."

"Struggling?" he repeated. "Did you see my piece on the new wharf?"

"Yes, Robin," I answered, "and a great article it was, too."

"That's better."

"So," I said, "what's the advice you have for me?"

A serious expression came over his face. For a moment it almost confused me because it was so very different than the normal Robin O'Flaridy look I had grown accustomed to.

"How much do you know about Leland Stanford?" he asked.

"I don't know . . . quite a bit, I suppose," I answered.

"I mean, how well do you *really* know him? How well do you know what kind of person he is?"

"I . . . I thought I did. I've spent time with him. I like him. He's very kind to me."

"Perhaps. But I have a hunch, Corrie, that he may just be using you for his own ends."

"What! How can you possibly say such a thing?" I was annoyed.

"He's a businessman, Corrie. I've been around this city long enough to know some things. The whole deal with the railroad—I tell you, Corrie, it's not as clean and innocent as it seems. There are huge amounts of money involved. Huge,

I tell you, and your friend Stanford and his cohorts are right in the thick of it."

"What are you insinuating?" I asked coolly.

"I'm not insinuating anything other than that the railroad's not primarily about politics—it's about money. I have the feeling Stanford only wants to be governor to line his own pockets and get richer than he already is. I know about these guys, Corrie—him, Hopkins, Crocker. They're businessmen, not politicians. All they are is a new breed of forty-niner, a new kind of gold miner. Some might even call them claim jumpers."

"How dare you, Robin? I won't even listen to you. Who would say such a thing?"

"Ever heard of Theodore Dehone Judah?"

"Of course I've heard of him."

"He might agree with me."

"I don't believe a word of it. Why are you telling me this, Robin? Are you working for the Democrats in this election?" Again the same peculiar look came over Robin's face.

"Look, Corrie," he said, "I'm only concerned for you. Believe me, I just don't want you to get hurt."

"Why do I have such a difficult time believing your sincerity?" I said sarcastically. Immediately I regretted the words. The look on his face changed to one of pain.

"I'm sorry, Robin," I said. "I didn't mean it."

"Well, Corrie, I *do* mean it. Concern for you was the only reason I said anything about it at all."

"All right, Robin . . . thank you."

"Just watch your step, Corrie. That's all. And be careful about that Burton fellow too."

"Cal?" I said.

"I'm not so sure about him either. I've heard—"

"I'll watch my step, like you said, but I won't listen to you say a word against Cal," I interrupted, getting irritated again.

Robin seemed to think better of pursuing it, and he said nothing more. But the look on his face remained with me all the rest of the day. Strange as it was to say, I had the feeling he really was sincerely thinking of me. But then, I thought he was being sincere that night when we'd escaped from Sonora together, too, and he had double-crossed me!

I didn't think much more about what he'd said and continued working for the campaign as before. Mr. Stanford himself traveled through all the northern part of the state—through all the mining regions, from Weaverville up north on the Trinity River all the way down to Sonora in the south. Naturally he came to Miracle Springs too, where I got to stand beside him and speak to my own hometown.

I didn't really do all that much for him, but Mr. Stanford took me with him to lots of the smaller places like Miracle Springs, introduced me to people as if I were more important than he was, and always let me say a few things, either about him or about Mr. Lincoln or the need to be loyal to the Union. He treated me so kindly, and told me—whether it was true or not—that I was helping his campaign a great deal.

The other campaign of that summer was not such a pleasant one. It was taking place twenty-five hundred miles away—and was not a political campaign, but a military one.

The attack on Fort Sumter had taken place in April. But for the next two months nothing happened. Both North and South were busy recruiting, training, and building up their armies. I later heard that the moods of the general public were very different during this time.

In the South, wealthy landowners and the leaders who had organized the Confederacy were all confident—confident that right was on their side, certain that they were doing the just and honorable thing, confident in their strength, sure of victory. Somebody I later interviewed told me it was a self-righteous kind of confidence. God and the Bible were on their side, so how could they do anything but win? The young soldiers of the southern army, though not so religious or philosophical about it, mostly felt the same way.

But hundreds of thousands of people in the South, however, neither leaders nor soldiers nor landowners, were shocked by what had happened. They believed that slavery was permissible. They believed in the ways of the South, in southern culture and their southern heritage. But whether it was worth waging a war over, such people had grave doubts. Surely, they thought, some more sensible solution or compromise could be found than to have to kill over it! Though most of these people remained loyal to the Confederacy, many of them wondered if their own leaders—Jefferson Davis and Alexander Stephens and General Beauregard, who had attacked and toppled Fort Sumter, and General Robert E. Lee and Thomas Jackson, and all the political leaders who had defected from Washington in favor of the Confederacy—weren't doing just as much to destroy the South as the evil Yankees and their sinister head, Abraham Lincoln. These people were scared.

As for the slaves in the South, most of the ones I talked to later didn't have the slightest notion that all the fighting was for them. They were at least the outward symbol of why the Civil War was fought, but they didn't know it. *Freedom* for them might as well have been a word in a foreign language. Even if they had freedom, they wouldn't have known what to do with it. In the meantime, their lives went on as they always had—a life of drudgery, toil, and hopelessness.

Above the Mason-Dixon Line, however, the mood was far different. People there were mad. It was time the South was put in its place, slavery put an end to, and the country made one again. The South could not be allowed to get away with attacking the very foundation of Freedom itself—the United States government. They wanted something done. They called for retribution, for punishment of the South.

Therefore, when news came that the new Confederate Congress was going to meet for the first time, and not down in Montgomery, Alabama, but up in Richmond, Virginia—only 110 miles south of Washington—the anger of the North rose to explosive heights. The call went out—the southern Congress must not be allowed to meet on July 20!

The New York *Tribune* took up the banner and repeated what it called the "Nation's War Cry" in every edition it printed: *Forward to Richmond! Forward to Richmond! The Rebel Congress must not be allowed to meet there on the twentieth of July! By that date the place must be held by the National Army!*

President Lincoln, as well as everyone on both sides, thought that the war would be short. Here was a chance, he believed, to deal a quick and decisive blow to the upstart Rebel army *and* cripple the new government of the Confederacy by taking control of its new capital—all at once!

But standing in the way, between the northern army and Richmond, were thirty thousand Confederate troops. Lincoln gave the order to advance, defeat the Rebel army, and move south to take Richmond.

The battle of Bull Run near Centreville, Virginia, took place July 21.

The two armies were approximately equal in size. All kinds of maneuvering went on among the generals of both sides, trying to trick the other. But down on the fields where shots were being fired, young inexperienced boys who were hardly trained and who had never fought before were shooting guns and killing one another! Which side would panic first?

It turned out that the southern leaders were more skilled in battle tactics than those of the North. After hours of fighting on that hot summer's day, by attacks and counterattacks, they fooled the blue units of the Federal army into thinking they had more reinforcements than they really did. The boys in blue panicked and finally turned around to flee. The gray units surged forward after them.

A full retreat was on, all the way back thirty miles to Washington! The severity of the conflict was still so little understood that hundreds of northerners had ridden out toward the battle in buggies and carriages to watch. These sightseers crowded the roads, making the safe retreat of the army all the more difficult. Suddenly toward them came a streaming mass of fugitives! They turned and fled in panic too, as back to the capital rushed tens of thousands of soldiers and citizens, with the victorious and shouting Confederate army behind them!

The South had won the first major battle of the campaign. Many brave young Union soldiers had been killed.

Fortunately for the North, the southern leaders did not press the victory and keep going. Otherwise they might have taken Washington itself. For either side, Bull Run *might* have ended the contest early.

But it would not.

This was no small conflict that had any chance of being resolved politically or easily or quickly.

A full-fledged *war* had begun. The North was shocked by the southern victory. But the defeat at Bull Run only made them all the more determined. Lincoln sent out a call for more men.

Everyone was beginning to realize that this was going to be a long and difficult war.

The War in California

CHAPTER FORTY-SEVEN

California wasn't the only state split over loyalties to the North and South. In June, after Virginia had joined the Confederacy, the western part of that state broke away and formed a new state, loyal to the Union, called West Virginia.

When news of it came, I found myself wondering if such a thing was bound to happen to California one day.

The election for governor, however, would serve to put the dispute to rest. It was a campaign fought not just along Republican-Democrat lines, but North-South as well. A famous lawyer named Edmond Randolph made fiery speeches against Mr. Stanford. He was outspoken in his calling for Confederate victories in the East, and after Bull Run he claimed that the South would put an end to the war any day. "If this be rebellion," he cried in a speech that I heard when I was in Sacramento with Cal and Mr. Stanford, "then I am a rebel. Do you want a traitor? Then I am a traitor."

There were far more Democrats in California than Republicans. But the split between them kept being the most important factor of all. The Democrats got almost 64,000 votes in September. Mr. Stanford got only 56,000.

But since he was running against *two* Democrats, he was elected governor even with a minority!

I expected Cal to be happier over the victory than he was. This was one of those "opportunities" he was always talking about. He was going to be personal assistant to the governor of the state! He had talked about it before with such a light in his eyes that I would have thought nothing could please him more. He had made it seem like getting to the nation's capital was his greatest goal, and that Mr. Stanford would be the one to take him there. But the southern victory at Bull Run seemed to shake him, and even after the election, he was still quieter than usual. We were all worried when we heard the army had been defeated and had to retreat. But Cal seemed more upset about it than I could understand.

Mr. Stanford was so behind the North, the Union, and Mr. Lincoln that the Republican victory ended once and for all any possibility that California would support the South or would withdraw from the Union to form a new republic of some kind. Talk of a third country, and even talk of splitting the state, diminished. The War between the States was the most important thing on everyone's mind, and the Pony Express deliveries with papers from the East were anticipated eagerly to find out if any more battles had been fought or if anything else had happened. Nothing much did happen, though, throughout the whole rest of that summer and fall.

But just because Mr. Stanford was now governor did not mean support for the southern cause stopped altogether. It just meant the state would officially be pro-North. So all the supporters of the Confederacy—and there were lots of them!—had to go into hiding. They had lost their chance to take California into the Confederacy with the vote. So they turned instead to hidden and underground plots and schemes. There was news every week, it seemed, of some new threat that had been exposed, even threats of plots to take over California for the South.

All kinds of secret societies of southern sympathizers sprang up. Mr. Kemble told me there were as many as fifty thousand people involved, but I don't know if that was true. They caused mischief, but after the middle of 1861 there weren't any serious uprisings.

The debate over which side was "right" in the war continued. William Scott, the pastor of one of San Francisco's largest churches, the Calvary Presbyterian Church, openly preached his belief in the Confederate cause. He outraged many people in the state, including my editor, Mr. Kemble, who knew him personally.

Besides men, money was something the Union army needed more than anything. The North was not as economically strong as the South, and to feed, clothe, and pay an army was expensive.

California was too far away to help with any actual fighting. It was too small a state to be able to provide very many men. But there *was* one thing that California had more of than any other state in either the Union or the Confederacy.

That was gold. California *could* help President Lincoln finance the war, if nothing else.

The Unitarian pastor Thomas Starr King, who had become a good friend of Governor Stanford, turned his speaking skills and popularity in a new direction. He began to organize a fund-raising drive in California in order to send money to Washington.

Of course whenever money is involved in anything, there is always the chance of deception and robbery. Since the first gold miners had started pulling gold out of the rivers and

streams of California in 1848, there had been claim jumpers and thieves. Now, with southern supporters carrying out
their designs more secretively, and with their bitterness over
losing California's support for the Confederate cause, there
was worry that they would try to steal what Mr. King was able
to raise.

According to Mr. Kemble, a quarter of all San Franciscans
favored the Confederacy. There were even more down south
in Los Angeles. After Mr. Stanford's election as governor, a
lot of secessionists moved down there and kept calling, even
then, for California to split in half, with southern California to
become a slave state and join the Confederacy. The Los Angeles *Star* was so seditious and against the Union that Governor Stanford had it banned from the mail so that it couldn't
even be delivered and read in the northern part of the state.

There weren't enough people in Los Angeles or the
rest of southern California, however, to worry about actual
trouble—all the mischief they could do was in writing. And
because they had no gold, they couldn't do the Confederacy
much good, either.

A Rider

Chapter Forty-Eight

The day was one I'll never forget. Never *could* forget!

It was late August. A hot summer's day. Hot and still. Wherever the wind from the Sierras was, it had gone to sleep that day and felt like it intended to sleep all through the afternoon. It was so still I could hear the flies buzzing about. And hot . . . so hot!

Pa had been back from Sacramento for three days. He'd been gone a week and a half, his longest stay in the capital yet. But Tad had gone with him, and they had a wonderful time together. When he wasn't on legislative business, he showed Tad all around Sacramento, and Tad had hardly stopped talking about everything they had done together. He had gone with Pa once or twice to Assembly meetings too. When Pa first saw Alkali Jones the day after they got back, he was telling him about the trip.

"I reckon it's time you changed that motto of yours, Alkali."

"Which one's that?"

"About the presidency."

"You mean Drum fer President—hee, hee, hee!"

"That's the one. But you gotta change it now."

"How so, Drum?"

"Politics has gone and bit my son right square between the eyes. You gotta change it to *Thaddeus Hollister for President.*"

Tad's face beamed at the words.

"Hee, hee . . . Tad fer President! Yep, you're right, Dram— sounds a heap more likely with his name instead of yours! Hee, hee, hee!"

But during the days since he had returned, I could see a downcast spirit coming over Pa. It had nothing to do with Tad, only that his good time with his younger son had brought back to mind the lingering doubts over the fate of his elder. We'd heard nothing about Zack all this time.

Something was different about that day besides it being so hot. There was something in the air. There was no breeze rustling the trees. But there seemed to be an invisible wind about, invisible in the way that you couldn't see it or feel it or hear it. Kind of a wind of the spirit, not a wind of the air. It was a sense, a feeling that something was coming, but you couldn't tell what.

We all felt it, I could tell. As the day wore on, I could just see a look in Almeda's and Becky's and Tad's faces that they felt it too. We found ourselves looking at one another with expressions that had no words. It was a feeling of agitation, of anticipation, as if something was at hand but nobody knew what it might be.

It was a sense of expectation, the kind of feeling people get before a big thunderstorm. Everything changes. A differ- ent kind of warmth is in the air. The breezes start kicking up, and although they don't feel too powerful, you know they are only the fingery edges of the blasts that are coming. You *feel* the storm on its way. The air smells different. Before long, the blackness begins to appear over the horizon, steadily getting

larger and filling more of the sky, and you know your senses
have not betrayed you.

This was a day like that. But there were no breezes, no
stormy fragrances, no hints of anything in the sky other than
blue going on forever in every direction.

The little breezes kicking up the leaves for a moment
and then letting them settle back into place, the feeling of
changes in the atmosphere . . . they were all happening inside.
Every once in a while I'd catch Almeda standing at the door
or window looking out, with her hand over her eyes, peering
into the distance as if expecting something. Then she'd turn
away with a confused expression, as if wondering herself why
she'd paused to look outside, not even knowing what she was
looking for.

Nobody was saying much. The day wore on, getting hotter, and everyone grew more and more quiet. Something was
coming. No one knew what.

Pa tried to work at the mine some. But it was too hot.
After lunch Pa went out again, walked lazily up the creek,
running thin and low now in the late summer.

It was one of my times to stand at the open door looking
out, with *my* hand over *my* eyes. I watched him walk up toward
the mine, kicking at the rocks with his feet, one hand in his
pocket. He disappeared from sight. A few minutes later I heard
noises from the area of the mine. But they didn't last long.

I was still standing there, looking out aimlessly, not feeling
like doing anything, when Pa came into view again, walking
back down the path, this time toward the stable. Apparently
he had given up on the mine again. His shirt was drenched in
sweat, under his arms and down the middle of his chest. But
he didn't need the work to sweat. It was plenty hot to sweat

just standing doing nothing. I was sweating too, in the shade of the house and open doorway.

Closer Pa walked. It was quiet. I could hear his feet shuffling along, too tired now even to kick at the little stones along the way in front of him. Everything was so still. Only Pa's rhythmic, shuffling step broke the stillness and the silence.

I found my eyes riveted on his slow-moving feet, watching them come toward me in the distance. The soft sound of his boots along the dried dirt entered my ears in perfect cadence. *One . . . two . . . right . . . left . . .*

Over and over—right, left . . . thud, thud.

Still my eyes fixed themselves on the motion, but gradually I became aware that something was wrong with the sound. There were still Pa's feet walking along as before, but the rhythm had been interrupted. It had changed. There were too many sounds for only two feet. I heard the noise as of a footfall when Pa's two feet were on the ground and in the air not making any sound.

And . . . the sound itself was wrong.

It wasn't a thud, thud, thud anymore. Now I heard *clomp . . . clomp . . . clomp* mixed in with the shuffling thuds of Pa's boots.

It sounded like a horse.

I shook off my dreaming reverie and turned my eyes in the opposite direction. A horse was approaching from the direction of town. Of course, that was the other sound I'd heard.

Who could it be? I squinted my eyes. . . .

"Somebody's coming," I heard Becky say from inside the house behind me.

"Who is it, Corrie?" Almeda asked from the kitchen.

I kept squinting, trying to see. I could tell it was a man, but all I could really make out was a hat and a light brown beard.

I stared. The horse plodded along as slow as Pa had been walking. But steadily he came closer.

Suddenly an incredible sense of recognition seized my heart! But . . . but it couldn't be!

I spun my head around and my eyes again sought Pa.

His slow step had become a rapid pounding of his boots along the path. He had seen the rider too! He was running toward him!

Unconsciously I started out the door. I looked toward the road. The rider was close now . . . there could be no mistake!

He was climbing down off his horse. I was running now too! "Zack!" I cried. "It's Zack!" I yelled back toward the house.

Out of the house the others came, following me as we ran as fast as we could toward the road.

Pa reached him first.

I stopped, ten yards away, weeping with happiness. I felt the others come up behind me, but I could not take my eyes off the scene of reunion being played out before my eyes. I felt Almeda's arm slip around me as she watched, too.

Zack had slipped off his horse, but he hadn't been able to take more than a step or two before Pa reached him. The father threw his big arms around the son and held him tight, weeping freely and without shame.

Slowly I saw Zack's hands stretch around Pa's back and return his close embrace.

The two stood silently holding each other for a long minute. The only sounds to be heard were the throbbing of six hearts in joy.

Whole Again
CHAPTER FORTY-NINE

When the two released each other, the first words were Pa's. "Welcome home, son!" he said.

The spell of the moment was broken.

The rest of us rushed forward. For the next several minutes Zack was showered with hugs and kisses and questions and laughter. He could hardly get in a word!

"Nice beard, Zack!" said Tad.

"You little runt . . . you grew up while I was gone!" returned Zack, giving Tad a good-natured push. "And you, Becky!" he added. "When did you get to be such a beautiful, grown-up woman!"

Then Zack looked over at me. He didn't say anything at first, just gave me a long hug. Every time I tried to speak, I started crying, and all my words stuck in my throat. "Oh, Zack," I finally managed, "I'm just so glad to see you!"

"Almeda," said Zack, hugging her next.

"Oh, Zack . . . we love you so much!"

Pa had been standing back, wiping his eyes and trying to steady himself. Now he stepped up again, this time offering Zack his hand.

"How about a handshake of welcome, Zack?" he said. "A handshake between men . . . man to man!"

Zack said nothing. He just reached out and took Pa's hand. The two stood again, grasping each other firmly by the hand, gazing intently each one into the other's eyes. It was all we had hoped and prayed for! You could tell in that one moment that they understood each other, and that all was forgiven.

"Why did you grow the beard, Zack?" Becky asked after a minute.

"It's a long story," said Zack, releasing Pa's hand.

"Where you been?" This time the questioner was Tad.

"Another long story!" laughed Zack.

"How did you get back?" I asked.

"That's long too, but the why of it isn't so long," he answered. Then his face turned serious, and his eyes took on a very faraway expression. In that moment he suddenly looked older, like a true man. If I hadn't known better, I would have thought he was my older brother.

"Are you going to tell us the *why,* then?" I asked.

"I'll tell you everything," he replied, "when the time is right."

"Give the man a chance to get the dust off his feet, Corrie," said Pa. "Come on, Zack, son . . . let's get that horse of yours put up. Then what do you say me and you go up and give a *howdy* to your uncle!"

"Sure, Pa . . . yeah, I'd like to see Uncle Nick, too."

The two turned and headed toward the barn. Even though Zack was an inch or two taller than Pa, Pa threw his arm up around Zack's shoulder as they went. Zack's other hand hung down at his side, lightly holding the leather reins of his horse, which followed behind.

Almeda, Tad, Becky, and I stood there watching them go.

Just then Pa stopped and turned around. "Almeda!" he called back. "You start figuring on how to fix up the best vittles we ever had! Corrie, you make up a heap o' those biscuits o' yours. We'll invite the Reverend, and Nick and Katie—I know they'll all be anxious to see Zack. We'll have us a great time!"

He turned again, and he and Zack continued on, talking as they went.

The four of us finally walked back toward the house. "Well, Tad, your brother's home," said Almeda. "What do you think?"

When I heard Tad's answer, the tone of his voice surprised me. It wasn't just the deep baritone quality of it, but rather the maturity of what he said. It was obvious Tad was a young man at peace with his place in the family and secure in where he stood with his father.

"I'm so glad for Pa," Tad said quietly. "Something's been missing for him ever since Zack left. I did what I could to help, but I reckon a man like Pa's never gonna be quite whole when one of his kids is at odds with him. 'Course I'm glad for Zack, too. He needed Pa more than he ever could admit, probably more than I needed him, because I was younger when we came here."

He paused. "Actually," he added, "I guess I'm just about as happy as I can be . . . for *both* of them!"

Unlikely Rescue

CHAPTER FIFTY

A good part of the rest of that day Pa and Zack spent together. There was a lot of getting used to each other again to get done. And of course lots to talk about. But there was time for that now, and everything didn't need to be done all at once.

I could tell when I had a couple minutes alone with Pa later in the afternoon, just from the light in his eyes, that he'd been able to tell Zack the most important thing that had been on his mind all this time—that is how sorry he was. It was obvious from one look at Pa that a huge burden had been lifted from his shoulders.

We celebrated that night to make up for the last Christmas twenty times over. There was food and laughing and singing and more of Alkali Jones' crazy stories than we could have believed in ten nights of merrymaking together, much less one.

It was so strange seeing Zack with a beard! His talk, his mannerisms, his whole bearing had changed. Being out on his own had made him more confident, more independent. Zack entered into the celebration, but when I looked intently into his eyes when he wasn't watching, I could see a certain reticence too, almost a shyness at being the center of attention, and knowing that he'd caused such a fuss. I don't know that

I'd call it embarrassment exactly, but it was like embarrassment in a different sort of way. Humbleness and humiliation aren't the same, though a lot of folks mistakenly think they are because their first three letters are the same. The one is always a good thing. The other isn't bad or good in itself, but can be either depending on what you do with it, and whether you let it make you humble in the end.

It had taken real humility for Zack to come home. It would probably take him a good long time to sort through the impact that act of humility would have on his manhood. Pride doesn't die easy, but humility is the only sure weapon against it. Zack had now become man enough to draw the sword against it himself, I could see the battle in his eyes . . . and I knew he was winning it!

It was well past dark before we all managed to coax Zack into telling his story. It was clearly hard for him, because of how bitter and painful his leaving home had been. But when Pa and I told him how we'd gone looking for him and what had happened, it perked him up and gave him a good place to start his tale without having to dwell on the past.

"Well, I was riding the last two stretches of Nevada and the first Utah leg," he began, "depending on the schedule, and depending on how the others were doing."

"Pony Bob told us how unpredictable it was sometimes," I said.

"It's *always* unpredictable with Bob!" laughed Zack. "That man attracts trouble like a dog draws fleas! I never rode two or three hundred miles at a time, but there were days when you'd have to keep going to another station or two."

"Were the Indians bad?" asked Becky. "Were you afraid?"

"You bet I was scared, girl!" said Zack. "The only fellas who weren't were the crazy ones, and we had a few of those, too."

"Did you ever shoot an Indian, Zack?" asked Tad.

"I shot *at* 'em, Tad, but never shot none. You don't think I'd want to hurt somebody, do you?"

"What if they came after you?"

"They did. But the Express had the best horses in the country, and no Paiute could keep with us for five minutes. So I'd just kinda stick my Colt up over my shoulder and fire back in the air and hope it'd frighten 'em away. Even if it didn't, all I had to do was stay in the saddle five minutes and I'd be out of their sight anyway."

"What if they were in front of you?"

"Then I had a problem."

"What would you do?"

"I could turn around and make a run for it. But then the mail didn't go through. Or I could head out into the desert and try to get around them. But then they'd have the angle on me, and I might ride an extra twenty miles, only to find them still there! Or I could do like Bob Haslam did a couple of times and ride right through the middle of them and hope they didn't kill me."

"What did *you* do, Zack?" asked Rev. Rutledge.

"Well, I tell you, Reverend, it only happened to me once. Funny that you should be the one asking me about it, because when it did happen I thought of you."

"Me!" said an astonished Rev. Rutledge.

"Yep. I just stopped dead in my tracks. And there they were up about a hundred yards ahead of me, right in the middle of my pathway. I just sat there in my saddle, and I started praying, and that's when I thought of you. I thought back to a sermon you preached once about problems. You were saying that sometimes you gotta face your problems head-on.

Then other times, circumstances were such that you had to go around your problems to get to the other side. But there was one thing you could never do, you said, and that was ignore your problems and do nothing and hope they would just go away. They never will, you said."

Everybody in the room started laughing.

"That's just what I did," Zack went on. "I couldn't help myself. Sitting there on my jittery pony, staring at twenty hostile Paiutes, I started laughing. I couldn't stop. All I could think of was that sermon of yours, and I said to myself, just like I was talking to you, 'Shoot, Rev. Rutledge, that advice of yours doesn't do me a blame bit of good! You must not have had Indians in mind when you came up with that!'"

We were all laughing so hard by now we could hardly stop. Rev. Rutledge and Harriet had tears in their eyes—they were laughing hardest of all. Alkali Jones' *hee, hee, hee!* was nearly one continuous cackle!

"I even tried what you said you couldn't do. I stopped laughing long enough to close my eyes and count to ten. I thought that just maybe they *would* go away, that it was a dream, a winter's mirage. It was so cold last December that I thought maybe my brain was frostbit. But when I opened my eyes again, they were still there. And I still had to do what you said in your sermon—either go through them or go around them. But I gotta tell you, Rev. Rutledge, I found myself wishing I'd paid better attention that day, because I thought maybe you *had* said something else that I just couldn't remember!"

"No, that was it, Zack, my boy," said Rev. Rutledge, wiping his eyes. "Through them or around them, that's all I said." He was still chuckling even as he spoke.

"Well, I'd heard of Pony Bob riding through the band of Paiutes. But for all I knew, this might be the same band! And even if it wasn't, they were sure to have heard about the incident just as sure as I had. And they certainly weren't about to let themselves be suckered into just sitting there and letting through a lone horseback-riding kid a *second* time! No, I figured my chances were about zero in a thousand of coming out the other side alive if I tried to tackle *this* problem head-on. This looked to me like a clear case of needing to go *around* the problem!"

"What did you do, Zack?" asked Almeda. She was sitting on the edge of her chair as if she was afraid for him all over again.

"It was in a mountainous area of some pretty nasty terrain. Spread out to my right was a huge flat plain, broken up by gulches and creek beds, and little ravines, mostly invisible from looking across the top from where we were. On the other side of the trail, it turned rocky and steep immediately, working its way up to a high plateau that ran parallel to the road below. So what I figured to do was hightail it out across the plain like I was trying to outrun my way clean around them. I figured they'd light out on an angle to cut me off as I started my swing around to outflank them. So my plan was to ride out into the plain a ways, then dip into a wash suddenly and get out of their line of view. I hoped that they would keep riding toward the plain and that I could double back, maybe staying low in a creek bed or wash, and get back to the road and head back up the other side and lose myself in the huge boulders of the hillside without them spotting me. Then I could work my way all the way up to the top of the ridge and ride along until I was out of danger, and then find my way back down to the trail.

"It worked perfectly at first. I lashed my horse off to the right. They took out after me at an angle across toward the plain. I rode for thirty or forty seconds, then dipped into a creek bed, stopped, and waited. I got off the horse, and crouching down crept up to the edge. There went the band of Paiutes off into the plain, expecting me to appear again any minute still riding in the same direction. I crept back down, remounted my horse, and doubled back, staying in the lows and hollows and washes until I was almost back to the trail. Then I climbed up and out and galloped quickly across the trail and up into the mountainous terrain on the other side. Within another minute I was out of sight and safe. But I still had to work my way up to the top and around back on to the trail or else I'd run into the war party again.

"Up I went. It got steeper and steeper, more rocky and treacherous. The footing was bad. There was loose shale here and there, and wet because it had been trying to snow. I was still frightened and so was pushing the horse pretty hard, which was probably my mistake. By now I was so far away from the Indians I probably would have been safe, but I kept pushing. Both my horse and me were exhausted. And that's how the trouble came. I was just too tired. I'd already been riding six hours that day, and it was another three hours to the next station.

"I was three-quarters of the way up to the plateau, and I came to a little ledge that dropped off steep on one side but was flat enough for a trot along its surface. But it was narrow, only about a foot wide. I urged the horse into a trot, but it was so narrow, and with the cliff on one side I could tell she was spooked. It was stupid of me, but I lashed her on instead of paying attention to what she was trying to tell me. We got moving again pretty good, but then all of a sudden the ridge gave way right in front of us.

"It was only a jump of maybe four feet across to where it picked up again. On the flat at full gallop she'd have taken it so easily in stride I wouldn't even have felt a bump in my saddle. But she was tired. I urged her over it. She hesitated, then reared and stopped dead in her tracks. I was so tired I was barely hanging on, though I didn't realize how shaky I was in the saddle.

"Off her back I toppled, and I landed sideways on my leg. I felt the pain instantly, but I didn't have time to think about anything, because I'd fallen to the right, and I just kept falling, away down the slope off the ridge, over and over, banging against rocks, sliding down the moving shale. It was a long fall, I knew that, though I didn't know much else. I was only conscious of spinning and crunching and bouncing . . . and pain. Pretty soon, even as I was still rolling and falling, everything drifted into blackness, and my senses just faded away. I thought I was dead."

He stopped and took a deep breath, reliving the whole incident for the first time. Even just telling it had shaken him all over again. Little beads of perspiration were on his forehead. The rest of us were still. It was pretty late by now, and dark and quiet outside—all except for the crickets and an occasional owl somewhere.

"When next I knew anything it was still black. I woke up real slow, you know how you do sometimes, faint images, blurry sensations that don't mean anything. That's how it was. It was dark, and all I was aware of was an odor, faint at first, but something I recognized, and a sound that I couldn't figure out.

"I tried to make sense out of things. I tried to remember. Then the fall came back to me, and how I had faded out of consciousness while falling down . . . down . . . down.

"Suddenly I knew the smell. It was smoke! And the sound—it was the crackling of a fire. That was it—a fire and smoke!

"I was coming back into consciousness, but only slowly, and I was still half dazed and confused. My first thought was, *That's it, I really did die . . . and I'm in hell! I'm in hell because of what I said to Pa, and how I left home!*"

I looked over toward Pa as Zack was talking. He was hanging on every word, as if he was living every moment of it with his son. I could tell these last words smote his heart. He winced slightly, but kept looking straight at Zack, waiting for him to continue.

"Then suddenly I felt the sharp pain in my leg. I don't know how I could have a rational thought in the state I was in, but I remember thinking, *I can't be in hell if my leg hurts, because if I was dead my body would still be lying in that ravine back there where I fell.* Then gradually my eyes started to focus, and I saw some light from the low flickering of the flames. Everything else was black. I couldn't see anything except the red orange of the flames.

"I struggled a little, then tried to sit up. 'Lay still, son,' a voice said out of the night.

"My eyes shot wide open in terror at the sound. I couldn't see who had spoken, but I know my eyes were big as a horse's! It wasn't a nice or a gentle voice, very deep, almost gravelly. And it had plenty of authority. It wasn't the kind of voice you disobeyed. Again the thought flitted through my brain about being in the fiery place. I didn't even want to ask myself who the voice might belong to!

"I did what the voice said and lay still for a long time, wondering what would happen next.

" 'What's your name, son?' said the voice again.

" 'Uh, Zack . . . Zack Hollister,' I answered. It was nice to find out *my* voice still worked. 'Where am I?'

" 'You're safe, that's where. You had a bad fall back there.'

"Now things were starting to come back to me. I remembered the Indians, the climb up the hill, and the fall. Now I knew why my leg hurt.

" 'But . . . my horse . . . the mail,' I said. 'I gotta get the mail through. Where's the horse?'

"The next thing I knew, the voice was laughing. If I thought it had been gravelly before, the laugh was a rockslide. If your cackle is mountain water tinkling over pebbles, Alkali," said Zack, turning to Mr. Jones with a grin, "then the laugh I heard out of the blackness was made out of boulders rumbling down the mountain after an earthquake. I never heard such a deep voice or such a throaty laugh.

" 'That horse and whatever mail was on it is long gone, boy,' the voice said. 'We're miles and miles from where you fell, and your horse was miles away before I got to you, anyway.'

" 'The Paiutes . . . did the Paiutes get her?' I said in alarm.

" 'Can't tell you, son. I wasn't looking for your horse. I had my hands full just dragging you back up out of that crevice you got yourself into. As for the Paiutes, they know better than to bother me. I saved enough of their lives to keep me in their good graces for fifty years to come.

" 'But . . . but where am I?' I asked.

" 'Like I said, miles from where you fell. You're safe, that's all you need to know.'

" 'But I gotta get back . . . back to my route. They'll be worried about me. I gotta see about the mail.'

"Again the deep laughter came out of the dark.

" 'Son,' the man said, 'You're not going anywhere. Your leg's broken in two places. You're miles from the Express line. And even if you had a horse and were healthy, we're snowed in.'

" 'Snowed in! Where are we? Why is it so warm?'

" 'It'll all make sense in the morning. You hungry? You oughta be—you been out for two days.'

" 'Two days! What have I been doing, just lying here?'

" 'That's right. I dragged you up here, splinted your leg, made you as comfortable as I could, and then just waited. I could tell you were a strong little rascal, and that you'd wake up. So—you hungry?'

" 'Yeah, I reckon I am,' I said.

"He handed me something in a bowl. I could hardly see, but it smelled good. I picked out some chunks of meat in a kind of gravy and started eating it. I didn't realize how hungry I was until the smell of that stew hit my nostrils and I tasted the meat. The bowl was empty inside of a minute.

" 'More?' said the man.

" 'Yeah,' I answered, handing him the bowl. 'What is it?'

" 'Rattlesnake.'

"I gagged and turned away.

"I heard the laugh again from the other side of the fire. 'What's the matter, son? You never eaten snake before?'

" 'No, and I got no intention of eating it again!' I said.

" 'You'll die if you don't. It's about all I eat most winters up here, so you better get used to it.'

"'Where do you get them?' I asked. 'Ain't no snakes in winter.'

"'Ah, you just have to know where to look. And I do. I find them hibernating in their dens. They're sleepy and cold. I kill ten, maybe twenty of them if I go out and spend a morning at it. Skin and gut them, cut up the meat, slash it in the snow to freeze it. Keeps me in meat all winter long. Just take out and cook whatever I need.'

"'That's all you eat, and you stay alive all winter? This is the high desert,' I said. 'No man can stay alive out here, in summer or winter.'

"He laughed again. 'You must figure I'm a ghost then,' he said. 'I've been living off the hills here for eight years. There's food in the winter, water in the summer. Plenty for a man to live on—if the man knows how to find the provision the Maker put in the desert. No big secret to it.'

"Well, we talked a while longer, and gradually I drifted back to sleep. When I woke up again it wasn't black anymore. But it wasn't light either. There was just an eerie glow coming from one direction, and total blackness from the other.

"I shook myself awake, more quickly this time. My leg hurt, but I felt so much better. Despite how repulsed I had been at the thought of it, the snake meat had given me back some energy. I managed to pull myself up to a sitting position and look around. My host and rescuer, whoever he might be, was nowhere around.

"It was obvious to me now that I was inside a huge cave, and I heard footsteps coming from the inside of the mountain. The instant I heard the footsteps I was terrified. If he'd wanted to kill me or eat me or skin me alive to put in his rattlesnake stew, he'd had two or three days already to do it, but I was scared anyway.

" 'Sleep good, son?' he said, coming toward me and sitting down opposite me on the other side of the fire. The sound of his voice reassured me. It sounded friendlier in the light of day, if this dreary half light could be called day. But when I set eyes on the man, my first impression did not make me feel good about my future safety. This man *looked* like the kind who might skin a kid like me and freeze my meat to go along with his rattlesnake stew.

"His face was long and thin, with sunken cheeks and high cheekbones. His whole frame was slender, but not what I'd call skinny, and that's how his face was too. No fat, just muscle and bone and hardiness. He looked strong and tough, like he'd been in a few tangles and probably had given the other fellow the worst of it. He had lots of hair, going in all directions, but not as bad or as gray as yours, Alkali, and a full beard. His beard was black. I couldn't tell a bit how old he was. A beard always makes a man look older, but in the darkness of the cave, this fella could have been anywhere from thirty to fifty. He still had all his teeth, and every once in a while one of them would catch a shine from the flames.

"He tossed a log on the fire, and sparks danced up from the disturbance.

" 'Where do you get wood around here?' I asked.

" 'Spend my summers gathering wood for winter, spend my winters storing snow water down in the cave for summer. Everything you need's out here, son.'

"I looked in the other direction, toward the light. We were some thirty feet from the opening of the cave.

" 'Why is the light so pale?' I asked. 'Is the sun just coming up?'

"The deep laughter came again. 'Don't you know what you're looking at there, son?' he said. 'That's snow—solid snow! Only lets in a bit of light.'

"'Snow?' I said. 'But why is it there?'

"'We're snowed in! I told you that last night. There's twenty feet of snow over the whole mouth of the cave. You're not looking at daylight, son, you're looking at a snowbank . . . from the inside!'

"Well, he was right. I didn't see the real light of real day for two weeks, when we dug our way out after it had half melted down. But we got snowed in three more times before winter was over."

"*We?*" repeated Almeda. "How long did you stay with this man?"

"All winter and spring. Until just three weeks ago, in fact," answered Zack.

"What did you do all that time, son?" asked Pa.

"Mr. Trumbull—Hawk's what he goes by. It's a name the Paiutes gave him when he first made friends with them. Hawk Trumbull's his name.

"He never did tell me his real first name. Anyway, Hawk taught me everything he knows. He took care of me, fed me, did everything for me until I could get back on my feet, babied me like a mother hen, making sure my leg healed proper, fixing new splints for it all the time. Then when I could walk again he took me out and showed me how he lives, how to survive, where the food and water was. He taught me all about animals and the weather and the mountains, showed me where the water comes and goes above ground and below ground, showed me all his caves—"

"How many does he have?" asked Tad in astonishment.

"I don't know. I don't suppose I ever stopped to count. Eight or ten, maybe. We'd store different things in different places, use them at different times—that is, *if* a bear wasn't occupying one."

"Zack!" exclaimed Almeda.

"It only happened once," he laughed.

"What did you do, shoot it?" asked Harriet.

"No. Hawk doesn't like to kill unless he has to, unless it's life or death. No, that time we took sort of a backwards approach to your husband's advice. We stood out of the way and let the problem go past us!"

"Sounds like you owe the man your life, Zack," said Pa.

"I owe Hawk more than my life."

"How do you mean?" asked Rev. Rutledge.

"He taught me how to live, how to survive, how to see things most people never have a chance to see, and never would see even if it was stuck right in front of their noses. He's more than just a mountain man. After a while I came to realize he was almost a rough wilderness poet at heart. He was always trying to get me to look past the obvious, to look beyond what things seemed to be on the surface. That was true when we went looking for water that had disappeared into a sink somewhere. It was true when we would watch the movement of eagles up in the sky and try to detect from them what might be going on ten miles away on the ground. He was always looking *into* things, he said. Everybody had two eyes, he said, but to really live you needed *four*—two outside and two inside."

"A remarkable-sounding man," said Almeda.

"Best friend I ever had," said Zack.

The house fell quiet. It had been an amazing story.

"Actually, I reckon that ain't quite true," Zack said. "He's the one who helped me see I had an even better friend than him, and had for a long time."

"Who, Zack?" asked Becky.

Zack didn't answer her directly, but just went on talking about Trumbull.

"Once he began to find out about my background, and I began to tell him about you and Miracle Springs and what my life had been before he picked me off the mountainside, he started trying to make me use my extra set of eyes to see inside myself. He helped me see a lot of things I never saw before, things about all of us, this family of ours, and—"

He stopped, hesitating. His voice had gotten quiet. It was obvious this wasn't easy for him, especially in front of so many people.

"Mostly he helped me to see," Zack went on in a minute, "a lot of things I had never seen or understood about me and Pa. Once Hawk realized how it had been when I'd left, he asked lots of questions, wanted to know how I felt about things. He probably knows you about as good as any man alive, Pa, but the two of you have never met. He told me some things about myself that weren't too pleasant to hear, even though I knew they were true. But he was a straightforward, honest man, and I knew I could trust him. So I had no choice but to believe him. And so I had to look at myself, at some of the foolish things I'd done, like running off halfcocked like I did, and blaming things on Pa that I had no right to blame on anyone.

"He made me look down inside myself, just like he made me look at things in nature. He made me look at my anger. He told me that I'd never be a man until I learned what anger was supposed to be for. And that I'd never be a man until I learned to swallow my pride and come back and say I was sorry. He said I'd never be a man till I learned to live *with* the people closest to me. 'Only takes half a man to be able to live out in nature all by yourself,' he said. 'I don't doubt that I've done a pretty fair job of teaching you that. So, Zack, my boy,' he said, 'now it's time you learned to be a whole man, a complete man. It's time you went back. Take the half of being a man you learned out here and put it to use being the other half a man. Don't make the mistake I did of never going back. I went away when I was young, and I learned a lot of things. I know how to live in the wilds. But I'm still only half a man. It's too late for me now. I've drifted for too long and too far away. And most of my people are gone now. But it's not too late for you, young Grayfox.'"

"Grayfox . . . who did he mean? Was that you, Zack?" asked Tad.

Zack smiled—a smile with worlds of unsaid words behind it. "Yeah, Tad, it was me."

"Why'd he call you that?"

"After I'd been there a spell, that was my name up there."

"It sounds like an Indian name, Zack," said Almeda.

Again Zack smiled, the same melancholy, distant, happy, sad, full, grown-up smile he had before. "Yep," he said, slowly nodding his head. "That it was. Given to me by the Paiutes."

"Why . . . what does the name mean?"

Another long silence followed. As I watched Zack, I could tell that his memories, even for such a short time ago, went into deep regions within him that perhaps none of the rest of us would ever see. But I hoped to see into those places inside my brother—maybe even write about them someday . . . or to show him how to write about them himself.

At last he sighed deeply. "That's a long story. Maybe even longer than this one," he said. "Someday I'll tell you about it. But right now I gotta finish this one."

"You go right on ahead, son. We're all listening," said Pa, his voice full of tenderness.

"Well, Hawk and me, we talked about a lot of things," Zack continued, "and he kept on gently tugging at me, helping me to see what I needed to do. But I just couldn't bring myself to do it. I knew I needed to let somebody know I was all right. I figured that one way or another you had probably got word by then that I was missing and would be worried. But though I intended to get word to you, somehow the time passed faster than I realized, and I just never did anything about it.

"One day we decided to go down to the valley. There were a few things Hawk needed. I'd never gone down with him before. I preferred to stay up in the mountains, even after my leg had healed and after the spring thaw came. I was at peace up there, and something inside me didn't want to go back. I felt like a new person out there alone, breathing in the high mountain air, knowing that even as desolate as it was, it was a land I could call my own.

"But this time I decided to go down with him. I figured it was time I let the Express people know I was alive so they could get word to you. We rode to one of the stations, both of us on Hawk's old mule. They couldn't believe it was me, but I told them the whole story. There was even a week's back pay from months before still in an envelope with my name on it!

"They had a couple of newspapers around, extras that the guys had brought to leave off at the stations along the way to keep the station men up on the news. That's how I first heard about the war and everything back in the South.

"I was sitting there having something to eat. Hawk was talking to the station man on the other side of the room. I absently picked up a copy of a Sacramento paper. I don't know what I was thinking—maybe that I'd run across something Corrie had written.

"I just was glancing through it, I think it was a paper from May sometime, and a line caught my eye that said something about a resolution passed by the legislature supporting the Union. To tell you the truth, I don't know why I starting reading it. I didn't know anything about the conflict going on. But it had been so long since I'd read anything, I was just reading the whole paper.

"Then all of a sudden my eyes shot open and stopped dead on the page. I couldn't believe the words I'd read! "According to Assemblyman Drummond Hollister, who was interviewed briefly after the vote . . ."

"*What!* I shouted to myself inside. It couldn't be!

"But I kept reading . . . "The new legislator from the mining town of Miracle Springs, where he has served as mayor for the past four years, has been an outspoken pro-Union voice in the Assembly. . . ."

"I didn't need to read another word!

"I jumped up and ran over to Hawk, shoving the paper in his face. He didn't have a notion what I was talking about. But all I could say was, 'Look! Look . . . right there. That's my pa!'

"I was so overcome that I had to be alone. Still clutching the paper in my hand, I stumbled out the door and toward the stables and the barn where all the equipment was. I wandered inside and sat down on a bale of hay. Even here, so far away from home, I couldn't escape it. Suddenly everything I saw—every leather strap, every smell, from hay to leather to manure to wood to horseflesh—reminded me of home. Everything Hawk had been saying to me over the last two months came back to me.

"In that moment, sitting there, I saw it all so clearly— what I had done, how closed off I had been to all the love Pa had always tried to give me . . . the best friend I'd ever had, and always had, just like Hawk had told me.

"I opened up the paper again and looked down there toward the bottom where the article was. Over and over I read those words about *Assemblyman Drummond Hollister.* And all I could think was what a good man that *new legislator* was, a better man and a better father than any of those people in Sacramento could possibly realize. Better than I'd realized till right then! And the one thing I knew more than anything else was that I *had* to see him again. And I didn't want to wait! I had to see him now. I wanted to go home!

"I was crying by then. I was embarrassed at the time, but I'm not ashamed to admit it now. There were tears falling all over that newspaper page, but I couldn't take my eyes off the words."

Half the room was crying by now to hear Zack tell it—at least Almeda, Becky, Harriet, and I were. I have a feeling the men were choking back tears as well.

Zack looked over toward Pa, drew in a deep breath, and then spoke again.

"I tell you, Pa," he said, "I was so proud of you when I read those words . . . so proud of who you are! I just wanted the whole world to know you were *my* pa! And I had to tell you! I had to tell you . . . how much—I had to tell you how much . . . I love you, Pa."

Both of them were on their feet by now. This time it was Zack who approached and put his arms around Pa, bending down slightly to rest his face against Pa's shoulder, weeping like the boy-turned-man that he now was. Pa's strong gentle hands reached slowly around his son and pulled him close.

Almeda rose and went to them, followed next by Rev. Rutledge. In another minute we all stood together, weeping, hugging, sniffling, and sending up lots of silent prayers of rejoicing.

As we gradually fell away two or three minutes later, Rev. Rutledge broke the silence.

"So, what happened next, Zack?"

Zack drew in a long breath to steady himself.

"I went inside, asked if I could buy a horse for the $25 in the envelope, in up-front payment, and I'd send them the rest.

"Seeing as how it was me, the station man said, and considering what I'd been through, he didn't figure Russell, Majors, and Waddell ought to mind too much.

"I said my good-byes, and I had to fight back the tears again when Hawk took my hand and shook it. But within the hour I was headed west . . . and here I am!"

*Z*ack was home!

It was hard to get used to. Every time I stopped to realize it, a wave of joy swept over me.

It seemed as if life ought to stop, but it never did. There was still a war going on in the East, plots and counterplots in the West. Pa still had to keep going to Sacramento . . . and there was still Cal.

The very next morning, Pa came upon Zack with soap all over his face. "What in tarnation are you doing?" he exclaimed.

"Shaving off my beard, Pa."

"What in thunder for?"

"I figured if I'm going to come back to civilization, I ought to look civilized. Besides. I figured you'd want it off."

"Well, you figured wrong. I like it!"

"You do?"

"Sure I do. Makes you look like me when I was your age."

"You want me to keep it?"

"Well, it's up to you, son. But I sure think a man's beard looks good on you."

"Okay, Pa," said Zack with a smile. He couldn't have been more pleased!

In mid-October a letter came to me, in an envelope from the office of the governor of California. My heart skipped. I was sure it was from Cal, but I was mistaken. I can't imagine a letter from such an important person as the governor being a disappointment, but I have to admit that one was.

Dear Miss Hollister,

I apologize to seem to be always asking you favors. But when a man in my position discovers a person who is loyal and competent, with a handsomeness and intelligence to match, he does not find it easy to replace her. So I am coming to you cap in hand to once again ask for your help in a matter of extreme importance to the future of our nation. As you know, the soldiers of the Union have grave needs, and we of California are doing everything we can to help them. A major fund-raising effort is underway, led by my friend and yours, Mr. King, in order to raise and send to President Lincoln's forces as much cash and gold as possible. California, as I'm sure you can appreciate, stands in a unique position to be able to help in this regard.

It is my hope that you will consider allowing me to appoint you co-chairwoman of a new organization which is being formed to work alongside Mr. King's efforts, to be called California Women for the Union, and whose principal activity will be raising funds for the Federal troops. Your name is one that is recognized and respected among the women of this state, and your efforts on behalf of the Union will, I am certain, not go unnoticed.

I am, your humble servant,
LELAND STANFORD
Governor

A hastily added note was attached to the letter. It said, "As always, my faithful Cal Burton has told me he will help you in this assignment in any way which might be beneficial to you. I look forward to hearing from you. LS."

I hardly knew what it would involve, but how could I not accept? I did want to help the Union. And when somebody as important as the governor asks for help, it seemed my patriotic duty to say yes. I wrote back the next day saying I would do it, but said that he would have to make sure somebody told me what was expected of me. I was willing, I said, but totally ignorant of what the appointment might entail.

In the meantime, another major event in the life of the country was taking place. It had nothing to do with the war, but, because of Zack, and because of what Pa and I had been through, it came a little closer to home.

The Pony Express was about to go out of business after just eighteen months in operation.

The Pony Express had never made a profit for Russell, Majors, and Waddell. They had from the beginning hoped for government financial help but never received it. Once the war began, the amount of mail had dwindled, since many army troops were transferred from the West back to the East, and the army had been a heavy user of the mail services. But on October 24, 1861, something else happened that made the eight to ten days to take news from coast to coast eight to ten days too long. Suddenly the Pony Express was no longer the fastest way to transmit news.

On that day, in Salt Lake City, two teams that had been working from California and Nebraska for six months met and joined the telegraph wires they had been stringing up across the country. The instant those wires were connected, Washington and San Francisco were able to communicate directly with each other over nearly three thousand miles—not in days but in minutes!

Unfortunately for him, Governor Stanford was away at the time. But in his place the chief justice of California sent this message to President Lincoln along the new telegraph wires:

> In the temporary absence of the Governor of the State, I am requested to send you the first message which will be transmitted over the wires of the telegraph line which connects the Pacific with the Atlantic states. The people of California desire to congratulate you upon the completion of this great work. They believe that it will be the means of strengthening the attachment which binds both the East and West to the Union, and they desire in this—my first message across the continent—to express their loyalty to the Union and their determination to stand by its Government in this, its day of trial. They regard that Government with affection and will adhere to it under all fortunes.

The riders of the Pony Express had ridden well over half a million miles. Only one rider had been killed by Indians, although a number of station attendants had lost their lives. Only one pack of mail was lost. Whatever its financial losses, in many other ways it had been a great success. But two days after the completion of the telegraph, the Pony Express officially discontinued its service.

All across the country, and especially in California, there were articles of praise and tribute for the Pony Express, now that it was gone. The *Alta* printed several, too. I had written a story about my experience with Pa at Tavish's station earlier, but now I wished I could have written one of these tributes. Mr. Kemble would have let me, but I wasn't a good enough writer to do the kind of articles that were being written. In November, in the Sacramento *Bee*, for example, one tribute read:

> Farewell, Pony: Farewell and forever, thou staunch, wilderness-overcoming, swift-footed messenger. Thou wert the pioneer of the continent in the rapid transmission of intelligence between its peoples, and have dragged in your train the lightning itself, which, in good time, will be followed by steam communication by rail. Rest upon your honors; be satisfied with them; your destiny has been fulfilled—a new and higher power has superseded you.

> This is no disgrace, for flesh and blood cannot always war against the elements. Rest, then, in peace; for thou hast run thy race, thou has followed thy course, thou has done the work that was given thee to do.

Raising Money for the Union
CHAPTER FIFTY-TWO

After the battle of Bull Run in July, there were no more battles fought in the war all the rest of that year, except for a minor skirmish here and there. Both sides now realized that the enemy was stronger than they had thought, and they spent the next six months and all winter getting their troops ready, strengthened, and trained. Both presidents and their staff of generals devised great battle plans intended to knock out the opposing forces, whatever it took.

The year 1861 had been only a beginning, the calm before the storm. It seemed that 1862 would probably be a devastating and bloody year for our country.

Therefore, fund-raising became all the more important. The Union army would need lots of money. Early in 1862, a movement was begun back in Boston to help the Union effort, and it became the focus of the nationwide effort to raise money. It was called the Sanitary Fund, although I never understood why it had such a funny name. Thomas Starr King and the other leaders in San Francisco—including me—had been raising money to send to Mr. Lincoln. We immediately organized a local branch of the Sanitary Fund.

I had a hard time thinking of myself as a leader, but I was *called* a chairwoman of the California Women for the Union.

So, when the Sanitary Fund started operating in earnest, Mr. King asked me if I'd be willing to work with him as the head of the ladies' auxiliary of it. Mrs. Herndon, a woman I'd been working with on the other committee, would take that over herself. We both agreed.

As chairwoman of the Ladies' Sanitary Fund, I had to go to Sacramento and San Francisco a lot—more than Pa, in fact. He started giving me a bad time about being busier with politics than he was.

"It's you that oughta be in the legislature, Corrie," he said one day. "You spend so much time in Sacramento talking to folks about money, I oughta just turn over my seat in the Assembly to you!"

Pa sometimes had some far-fetched notions, but that was about the most far-fetched one I'd ever heard. The idea of a woman holding a political office like that made Almeda's running for mayor seem like nothing!

He was right, though—I was gone from Miracle Springs more than I was there, it seemed. And I hardly had any time for writing anymore—other than writing asking people to help the war effort and give whatever they could. But most of it was done in person, sitting in front of a group of people with Mr. King or one of the other men involved, listening to them give a rousing speech. They would always give me a nice introduction, saying who I was and making it sound as if I were more important than I was. And then I'd stand up and talk for three or four minutes too, urging the women especially to help out however they could.

We traveled around the northern part of the state, either by stage or in a special carriage arranged for us, or close to Sacramento by train, and spoke at lots of places. Besides being an orator who could hold people spellbound, Mr. King was a great organizer too, and he set up church meetings and town-hall gatherings and outdoor assemblies and political and patriotic festive events. Before the year was half over, San Francisco, they told me, had become the highest contributing city in the whole country to the Sanitary Fund.

We were all proud of the two hundred thousand dollars we had raised, and determined to do even better through the rest of the next year. Most of the gold was taken by ship around by Panama steamer. The stagecoach lines would have been too risky, since the Butterfield route went right through the Confederacy and was controlled by the South. Even as it was, there was always danger of the money falling into the hands of Confederate privateers.

Miss Baxter in Sacramento and Miss Bean in San Francisco each set aside a room just for me called "Corrie's room" because I stayed with them so often. Both became even better friends than before.

Cal was involved in the fund-raising too, so I saw him every time I came to the cities. We'd have dinner together most evenings when there wasn't a function to attend. More than once I turned to Miss Baxter and Miss Bean as a substitute for Almeda in trying to figure out how I felt about Cal. Neither of them had been married, but they understood about being a woman, and that was all I needed. I had never been married either, but I was finding out that I was more of a woman than I sometimes would have wished for!

Sometimes Cal would act strange, and it would worry me. I'd immediately think I had done something wrong. But if he didn't like me, why would he keep inviting me out to dinner or for a ride or walk in the evening? Often he grew quiet and distant, and his moods confused me. I would have expected him to be happy, living permanently in Sacramento, working alongside the governor, having to do with important things.

Whenever I'd ask him what was on his mind, he'd laugh and try to shrug it off lightly. But I could tell it went deeper than he was letting on. Finally I came to the conclusion that it was the war itself. The war had everybody on edge; the future was uncertain, and no matter how much money we raised, the Union might lose. Nobody liked to think it or say it out loud, but after Bull Run, we couldn't help having a gnawing worry that the South *might* win! What if Jefferson and Stephens became president and vice president of the whole country? What if we *all* became part of the Confederacy one day? What if slavery became as common in New York and Minnesota and California and Oregon as it had been in Alabama and Mississippi?

The very thought was too horrible to dwell on!

But facts were facts. The South had won the only major battle of 1861. And as the fighting of 1862 opened, even the mighty Union navy, which had been attempting to blockade the South, suffered a terrible defeat at the hands of the new southern ironclad warship *Merrimac*. She sank two ships her first time out, and the North's own ironclad ship, the *Monitor*, was powerless to inflict any damage upon her.

Cal had spoken about opportunity, but now that his opportunity had come and he was assistant to a governor who might run for president someday, all of a sudden it all seemed about to be destroyed. If the South won, everything would be lost for him. The Republicans—and Mr. Stanford along with them—and everything we had fought for and believed in would be destroyed. If the Union fell, so would Cal's hopes.

There would be no *opportunities* left for someone like him who had so vigorously defended the Union. People like us who had worked for the Union might even be considered criminals!

As I thought about it, it became less of a mystery to me why he was downcast. I wanted him to get to have everything he'd dreamed of and hoped for. I was concerned about the outcome of the war, too, but I personally didn't have as much at stake.

I was excited when news began to reach us about Federal victories in the West along the Mississippi. It was especially exciting to hear that General Grant was leading the Union forces! I wished I could see him again.

Even after the horrible battle at Shiloh down in Tennessee in April, where neither side had been victorious, the march of Union troops toward New Orleans and Grant's control of the Mississippi River seemed to give reason for optimism. I was sure Cal's spirits would pick up.

"No, Corrie," he said, "the Mississippi's a thousand miles from the nerve center of it all. The war will be determined between Washington and Richmond, decided by who controls the two capitals. Only one president is going to emerge on top, Corrie. And right now, whatever your General Grant may be doing in the Mississippi Valley, Jackson and Robert E. Lee are threatening Washington. I tell you, Corrie, I don't expect Lincoln to last out the year!"

His voice sounded different as he spoke. Was he afraid? There was a quivering nervousness in his tone, and a light in his eye.

Through the spring of that year, as the war intensified and news continued to reach us of more battles, more bloodshed, more young lives lost, Cal grew more and more agitated. More was on his mind than just raising money for the Union, but he wouldn't say what. He didn't invite me to dinner as often either.

He seemed to be busy with other things, and often left right after our fund-raising meetings, and I wouldn't see him again for days. I didn't mind too much, but I was worried about him.

*L*ate in May of that year, Mr. King asked me if I would be willing to travel to a few small communities and conduct some fund-raising meetings by myself.

He wanted me to go up into the foothill regions, the gold communities that I was familiar with, but not just near Miracle Springs—also down toward Placerville. I told him I'd be willing just so long as he told me what to do and arranged everything.

Railroads were much in the news that year. There had been all kinds of politics and debate; the companies had already been created, and a bill was before Congress in Washington to finance the building of a railroad from coast to coast. All the people of Sacramento, especially Governor Stanford, had been deeply involved in it for quite a while already. But California actually had only one railroad in operation—the Sacramento Valley Railroad, running out toward the foothills in the direction of Placerville.

I took the train out from Sacramento for the few meetings Mr. King arranged for me, where I spoke and got pledges from people for the Sanitary Fund. I didn't actually take any of the money back with me; it would be sent to the committee's headquarters in Sacramento later.

Traveling by train was exciting! I could hardly imagine being able to get into the passenger car behind a great black locomotive and ride right across the mountains and all the way to the East. But from the way everyone was talking, that day wasn't so far away. In fact, the route that had been decided on would go close to Miracle Springs. It was called the Dutch Flat Route and would run in the valley just on the other side of the hills from Miracle Springs. I wondered if we'd be able to ride up on the ridge and hear it chugging along someday!

During my few days of fund-raising, after I gave my short speeches about the Union and the war and the need for money, people would come up afterward and want to talk to me. And not just women; men would come up too, asking me questions and just wanting to talk in the most friendly way.

Most of these people didn't want to talk about politics or the war, but about personal things. A lot of them had read my article about the flood, or something else I'd written, even years before, and they'd want to talk about that. Then they'd tell me what *they* were thinking about, or what was on *their* minds. Everywhere I went, women would come up and invite me to supper with their family. After the first night, I didn't have to stay in another boardinghouse for the whole trip.

If it wasn't too crowded or noisy, some of them even confided things to me, problems they were having, and one or two asked my advice and what they should do. Before long I realized that my little trip out from Sacramento had more to do with individual people and what was going on inside their hearts and lives and minds than it did with raising money for the Sanitary Fund.

The most eye-opening realization of all was that the people coming up to talk to me afterward were more interested in *me* as a person, in Corrie Belle Hollister, than they were in all the things I may have been talking about. They seemed to see in me someone they could understand and who might understand them, someone they could talk to, even confide personal things in.

I came away with lots of new ideas about how my involvement in politics might have more to do with the people I ran into than it did with the bigger issues that seemed more important at first glance. Suddenly I found myself imagining people's faces, and thinking about what I could say to them and how I might be able to help them in some way. I found myself thinking more about people than politics.

I had always tended to think of myself as young and insignificant. Even with all I was doing now, I still wasn't "important" like the men were. Yet these few days changed the way I looked at myself.

It wasn't about importance . . . it was about people. It was about looking into their eyes and seeing a friend, a person who could understand and care. I found myself wondering if perhaps that wasn't the greatest "opportunity" I could ever have, the greatest "open door" of all.

I found all these things going through my mind as I stood on the last morning waiting for the train to arrive. I had completed my final fund-raising talk the night before at a church in a small foothills town. The morning train would take me back into Sacramento, and from there I would take the stagecoach back home to Miracle Springs.

The sun was well up in the sky, and it was a bright warm spring day. As I stood there on the wooden platform, holding my leather case that Almeda ordered for me out of a catalog, I thought of the changes that had come and were coming to our country, and of course the changes that had come to my own life as a result. All my past flitted by in a few moments, and I could not help but wonder about the future—if it would hold as many changes and surprises as had the past. I remembered my talk with Pa about how circumstances sometimes take us down roads we don't anticipate.

That had certainly happened to me, even just since Pa and I had talked about it! My decision to get involved in the election two years ago *had* caused things to happen in my life that wouldn't have otherwise. Here I was, raising money for the Union! Mr. Kemble and I had talked about making a book out of some of my earlier journals, about our coming to California back in 1852. That was another change on the horizon, another opportunity, as Cal would call it.

As I stood there, hearing the whistle of the train in the distance as it began to come into the station, I felt as if I were standing between my past and future—looking back, seeing the past, and waiting for a future that nobody can ever see.

I glanced toward the slowing train as it approached. Even the train itself, and these tracks right in front of me, would before long stretch all the way out of sight to the east, over the Sierras, and beyond. The very tracks themselves seemed to symbolize to me the endless stretching out of life—going in two directions. Just like the tracks, our lives stretch out behind us, reminding us of all the places we've been, all the experiences we've lived. But it also stretches out in front, and we don't know where that train track leads! We just have to get on the train and find out.

I knew where this train was going. It would take me back into Sacramento. But where was my life headed? It had been an exciting ride up till now. But I wondered where the tracks would lead me next.

A Disturbing Encounter
CHAPTER FIFTY-FOUR

*L*ate summer and fall brought more bad news from the East.

The Confederate forces had scored a stunning victory in August, matching only fifty-five thousand men against the Union's eighty thousand in a battle that was called the *Second Battle of Bull Run.*

In September, General Robert E. Lee invaded the North in force, crossed the Potomac out of Virginia and into Maryland. Not only did Lee want to get the fighting out of Virginia, his home state, so as to protect the badly needed crops for the harvest season, but he also hoped that his army might make Maryland want to secede. With Maryland in the Confederacy, the Union capital of Washington would be right next door.

He did not succeed. But neither did he fail. The standoff, and resulting battle in the valley of the Antietam Creek south of Hagerstown, was the bloodiest engagement of the war. More than twenty-two thousand young men were killed, and neither side gained an advantage.

So much blood was being shed! There was both grief and determination throughout California—determination to help the Federal forces against an increasingly hated foe. It was all so needless! And the South was held accountable for the destruction and the dreadful loss of life.

He tried not to show it, but I know this news deeply disturbed Cal. He expected the government of the North to fall any day, and his future with it.

Not long after these two battles, an appeal came to Mr. King from the Boston headquarters:

The Sanitary Fund is desperately low. Our expenses are fifty thousand dollars per month. The sick and wounded on the battlefields need our help! We can survive for three months, but not a day longer, without large support from the Pacific. Twenty-five thousand dollars a month, paid regularly while the war lasts, from California would insure that we could continue with our efforts. We would make up the other twenty-five thousand here. We have already contributed sanitary stores, of a value of seven million dollars, to all parts of the army. California has been our main support in money, and if she fails, we are lost. We beg of you all, do what you can. The Union requires our most earnest efforts.

Immediately, Mr. King, Mrs. Herndon, Cal, and I—along with a few others—met together to plan a renewed round of meetings to gather together even more funds to help save the Union.

By the end of 1862, Mr. King's efforts had been so successful that nearly five hundred thousand dollars, mostly in gold, had been raised for the Sanitary Fund, more than half of it from San Francisco alone. I was proud to have been a part of it!

Usually we conducted our meeting and gave speeches. Then afterward Mr. King would pass a collection box, just like at a church service, and let people give what money they could right there on the spot. But most of the money came from pledges, and then Cal and I and some of the others would go around picking them up for the next several days. We took the money to the bank we used for the Sanitary Fund, and later sent it off to Boston by steamer. Businessmen or mining companies sometimes made their contributions in actual gold or silver bars. One time I went to a prominent San Francisco banker's office, expecting to receive a check for the pledge he'd made to Mr. King. He loaded me down with twelve pounds of gold and fifteen pounds of silver, worth almost six thousand dollars!

When Cal saw me struggling out of the bank to our carriage, he burst out laughing.

"I only got a little piece of paper," he said. "We went collecting at the wrong places."

"Next time," I panted, "I'll pick up the check, and *you* go retrieve the bullion!"

In spite of my difficulty, Mr. King was pleased.

Cal, still reading every scrap of war news he could lay his hands on, was acting disturbed and fidgety. Once he got so angry after one of our meetings that he nearly came to blows.

A man I had never seen came up to him out of the crowd and started talking rudely to him.

"Got everything going your way now, eh, Burton?" said the man derisively.

"Get out of here, Jewks!" Cal answered back in an angry tone. "What business do you have here, anyway?"

"Your business is my business now, Burton—if you get my drift."

"I don't, and I don't care to!" said Cal, trying to shove his way past the man.

"Watch yourself, Burton," he said, laying a hand on Cal's shoulder.

When Cal grabbed the hand and threw it off, I was afraid they were going to start fighting! I'd never seen such a look in Cal's eyes before, and it scared me.

"Come on, Corrie," said Cal, taking my hand and pulling me along after him, "let's get out of here."

"Who was that man?" I asked once we were away from the bustle of the crowd and walking toward our carriage.

"Nobody—just a troublemaker."

"I recognized his name when you spoke to him. What was it—I've forgotten now."

"Forget it, Corrie. He's nobody, I tell you—forget you ever saw him!"

In the expression on Cal's face, I glimpsed a flash of the look he'd leveled on the man in the crowd. He'd never looked at me like that before, and I didn't like it. Neither of us spoke again right away. We still had another meeting to attend that afternoon, but there was a chill between us all day. Later that evening, Cal said he had to go someplace. When I next saw him, everything was back to normal. He took me to dinner and was even more charming and flattering than ever.

Deceitful Spy

CHAPTER FIFTY-FIVE

The end of 1862 approached.

I was looking forward to being home for Christmas. It had been a busy and tiring year. Besides everything else that had happened, Mr. Kemble had gotten in touch with Mr. Macpherson, an editor from Chicago, and he *did* want to publish some of my earlier journal writing into a book. That, along with the war, Zack's homecoming, and my involvement with Mr. King and Mr. Stanford and Cal, made me ready for a good long rest. After all, I had to update my journal with a whole year of keeping track of everything that had happened!

But before that, we still had one major fund-raising gathering to conduct in Sacramento—the biggest of the year, Mr. King said. We hoped to raise as much as sixty thousand dollars for one huge donation to the Sanitary Fund at the end of the year to put us over the half-million-dollar mark for the twelve-month period.

The meeting was scheduled for December 13, announced all the newspapers. There was a band, and Mr. King did all he could to make it festive so hundreds and hundreds of people would come. There were brightly colored banners and patriotic posters and handbills to get people to feel loyalty and enthusiasm for helping the Union. At the last minute I overheard Cal telling Mr. King he wouldn't be able to attend. He said he had some important business to take care of, but that he would be available all the following day to help gather what had been pledged. I was standing ten feet away, but I don't even think he saw me, he was so distracted. When he left Mr. King, he walked off through the crowd of gathering people without so much as a word to me. He hadn't even looked around to find me.

I have to admit, my mind wasn't on the talk I would have to give in about an hour. I couldn't help feeling hurt.

Suddenly without even thinking about what I was doing, I hurried through the crowd in the direction Cal had gone. It didn't occur to me that I was actually "following" him, I just found myself leaving the assembly under the great canvas top that had been erected for the purpose, and walking toward the business section of Sacramento. About a hundred feet ahead of me, Cal was walking briskly along the boardwalk.

I continued behind him, keeping alongside the buildings, stopping in front of a store window now and then. I would die if he turned around and spotted me!

I hated myself for spying on him like I was! But I couldn't stop. The drive inside to find out what he was doing was stronger than my good sense.

With trembling step, and even more trembling heart, I kept inching forward, ever closer—mesmerized with mingled fear and agony, yet unable to tear my eyes away from the figure in front of me.

He stopped and made motions as if to glance around.

Terrified, I ducked quickly into an open doorway.

"May I help you, Miss?" said a voice surrounded by laughter.

I looked up to discover that I hadn't walked into a store at all, but a men's barber parlor. Immediately I felt my cheeks and neck turning red.

"Uh . . . no, I'm sorry . . . I must have made a mistake," I mumbled, backing out.

I glanced up the street. Cal was just disappearing inside a building.

I ran across the street and dashed into an alley. I leaned up against the building, then sneaked a look out and over to the other side to try to see where he had gone.

I couldn't see through the window because of the glare of the sun reflecting off it. But the gold lettering painted on the glass was legible enough. WESTERN UNION it read in big letters. Underneath, in smaller script were the words *Transcontinental Telegraph Service*.

I stood there waiting.

Suddenly I realized what a fix I was in! What if Cal came out and went back toward the meeting? I'd be stuck there and unable to get back without him seeing me! If the meeting started and I wasn't there, how would I explain myself?

I glanced out again. Maybe I should make a quick dash back across the street now. But it was too late—there was Cal coming out of the telegraph office!

I yanked my head back behind the building. I breathed in deeply, but couldn't get my breath. I was sure he'd know I was there and walk straight over to confront me.

What in the world are you doing here, Corrie. Spying on me, eh! No good can come of that! My mind played out the terrible possibilities.

Slowly I tried to look out around the edge of the building, not even thinking that my bonnet would lead my eye out into the open by at least six inches.

He was still there! I kept watching. Then he turned and continued on down the boardwalk the way he'd been going before. Several steps along he glanced down at a small scrap of paper he had in his hand, held it in front of him for five or ten seconds, still walking, then crumpled it up and tossed it into the street.

Suddenly I found my eyes following the wadded-up scrap instead of Cal, who walked on, rounded a corner, and disappeared.

My heart was pounding. *Did I dare?* What if he came back around the corner and saw me?

I waited another several seconds until I couldn't stand it any longer!

Suddenly I was out of the alley and running as fast as I could across the street in the direction of the Western Union office. I reached the other side. There it was! I ran the five or ten more yards, stooped down, grabbed up the piece of paper, clutched it in my hand, and sprinted back toward the meeting, hardly aware of the noise my boots were making along the boardwalk.

Faintly I heard some yells as I passed the men's parlor, but I just kept going. There was only one sound I dreaded hearing behind me—Cal's voice calling out my name!

There was the canvas tent, the grassy expanse where people were standing and sitting. The meeting hadn't yet begun!

I slowed to a walk, breathing in huge gulps of air into my lungs. I skirted around the edge of the crowd, trying to calm myself down.

Just then the band started to play. I knew Mr. King would expect me up on the platform any minute. I breathed deeply again. I had to calm down! I would never be able to say a word about anything in the condition I was in.

I had to go join the others. But first I had to know what I had in my hand. I unclasped my fingers and unfolded the tiny piece of paper. I was trembling so violently I could hardly focus my vision on the few handwritten words that met my gaze.

The message was brief and made not the slightest bit of sense to me: F-BURG OURS STOP NO TIME TO LOSE.

"Corrie . . . Corrie, where have you been?" I heard a voice say behind me.

I nearly jumped out of my skin. Thinking it was Cal, I fumbled with my hands quickly, trying to make them disappear someplace in the folds of my dress.

"What are you so jumpy about?" asked Mr. King, walking up as I turned around. "It's not like you."

"Oh . . . oh, nothing," I faltered. "Just nervous, I suppose."

"Come, now—that's not my Corrie Hollister. We've got to be at our best. Shall we go? They'll be expecting us momentarily."

He led the way and I followed toward the platform where chairs were set out for us. I managed to get through it, but that day's speech was not one of my best. I kept thinking of the message written on that scrap of paper: *F-BURG OURS . . . NO TIME TO LOSE.*

It Can't Be!

CHAPTER FIFTY-SIX

*C*al never returned.

When the meeting was over, I was anxious to be out of there and get back to Miss Baxter's.

I was walking away from the platform when a man accosted me.

"Mind if I speak to you a minute, Miss?" he said. I looked up to see the man Cal had gotten so angry with a few months back. My first feeling was one of fear. He saw it.

"Don't worry, Miss Hollister. I mean you no harm."

I continued walking. I wasn't in much of a frame of mind for talking, especially to that man. But he fell in and started walking along beside me.

"Name's Jewks, Miss Hollister . . . Terrance Jewks."

I nodded.

"Where's your friend Burton?" he asked.

"I don't know. He wasn't at today's meeting," I answered.

"So I saw. How much do you know about him?" he asked.

"Enough, I suppose," I said, still on my guard.

"I hope he treats you better than he did me."

"What do you mean by that?" I asked.

"Just that he seems to take pleasure in ruining people."

"How so?"

"Only that a certain Democrat with a bright future ran into your friend and found himself in the hospital for three weeks, and with lies spreading about him the whole time. Lies enough to put an end to my political career."

"What does Cal have to do with it?" I asked, stopping to look at Mr. Jewks.

"He has everything to do with it. He was the one who did it to me."

"I don't believe you," I said.

"If it wasn't him personally, he was behind it. It may have taken me a while, but a few months ago I finally found out who it was that hired the thugs that pulled me out of my San Francisco hotel and left me for dead in an alley. That's when I came looking for him."

"Cal would never do such a thing," I said.

"Not even to win an election? Come now, Miss Hollister, you must know him better than that."

All of a sudden the conversation I had overheard between Cal and Alexander Dalton snapped into my mind. Of course—this must be *that* Terrance Jewks!

"Why are you telling me this?" I asked, finally more attentive to Mr. Jewks. "I'm a Republican and pro-Union. You're a Democrat, as I understand it."

"Perhaps I'm just concerned for a nice-looking young lady, and I don't want her to get hurt like I was."

"Perhaps. But why do I have the feeling there is more to it?"

Jewks laughed. "You are a shrewd one, Miss Hollister! Honestly, I would like to keep you from trouble if it's possible. But along with that, I have two other motives. One is simple revenge for what your friend did to me. I'm sure you can understand that."

"I don't happen to think revenge a worthy motive," I said, "but I suppose I do understand it. What's the second?"

"Let's call it a change of heart."

"How do you mean?"

"I was a Douglas Democrat. Didn't care too much for Lincoln, but I was no southerner. Once the war broke out, I realized my loyalties were with the government, not with the South. I'm from Ohio originally. I voted for Douglas, and I'm still a Democrat. But the North has got to win this war or else the United States is all over—a dream of democracy that didn't work."

"I still don't see what any of this has to do with Cal . . . or me."

"A change of heart is what I called it," Mr. Jewks went on. "I had one, once the war started. And so did your friend, Mr. Burton. I've been following him, checking up on him, asking questions of people, using some of my old Democratic contacts. Spying on him, you might say, finding out things, without telling the folks exactly how I stood myself now, if you understand me."

"I'm not sure I do," I said slowly.

"Then let me put it to you plain, Miss Hollister, and you can use the information however you think best." He paused, took a breath, and went on. "I used to have lots of friends in the other camp. Breckinridge people. Once the war broke out, then especially after Stanford was elected, they all went underground. Had to keep out of sight. But I kept tabs on what was going on and didn't let my new loyalties be known. All the time I kept an eye out for who'd had me beaten up and what I might do about it. I found out the *who* several months ago, like I told you. And the *what* I might do to him, I just got to the bottom of this week."

He stopped.

"I'm listening," I said.

"Miss Hollister . . . your Cal Burton is a member of the Knights—the Knights of the Columbian Star."

"But who . . . what. . . ?" I faltered.

"It's an offshoot of the Knights of the Golden Circle."

"No . . . it can't be!"

"It is, Miss Hollister. Believe me."

"But . . . I don't understand."

"It's really quite simple—your Cal Burton is a southern sympathizer."

"I don't believe it!" I finally burst out.

"I finally have the proof," Mr. Jewks added. Worse even than being a sympathizer—the man's a spy for the Confederacy!"

Confrontation, Heartbreak, and Betrayal
CHAPTER FIFTY-SEVEN

The rest of that day was one of the most awful of my life.

I couldn't believe what Terrance Jewks had told me—or *wouldn't*. I was too mixed up and confused to know the difference.

I don't even know what became of the hours between my interview with Jewks and nightfall. I walked for miles, I suppose, slept in my room at Miss Baxter's, stubbornly trying to convince myself it was all a lie. Hadn't Jewks himself admitted that revenge was his motive? How better to get revenge on Cal than to turn me against him! It was a cruel hoax, an attempt to ruin Cal's reputation, and maybe even bring scandal upon Governor Stanford.

Jewks was just being a loyal Democrat. *He* was the southern spy, and his assignment had been to undermine the credibility of one of California's most loyal Unionists, the assistant to the governor himself!

It all made perfect sense! And I was Cal's weakness. They had probably been spying on me, too! I had been part of their plot all along! I had to warn Cal, and warn the governor that right here in Sacramento there were forces trying to destroy them!

But at the same time, I couldn't get rid of an uneasiness in the pit of my stomach. Cal's strange activities . . . the odd looks on his face that would come and go. I knew there must be an explanation! He would tell me everything about Jewks and set my mind at rest completely. That was the only thing to do. I had to talk to Cal tomorrow. I'd confront him with Jewks' accusations. I'd tell him everything that Jewks said. He'd probably laugh the whole thing off!

Despite my attempts to reassure myself, I slept fitfully through the night. My mind told me I had nothing to be anxious about. But my stomach was quivery regardless.

The next day, the fourteenth, was a full one for all of us, contacting people, collecting money and checks and gold, confirming pledges that had been made, banking the contributions. Mr. King had called a meeting that morning to make all the arrangements and give us our assignments. It was the first time I had seen Cal since the previous afternoon. He looked and sounded like always.

We spent most of the afternoon together about the committee's work, all except for about half an hour. He knew there was something on my mind. I wasn't very good at concealing it. But we didn't have an opportunity to talk until later.

When we finally did, I just burst out and told him everything Mr. Jewks had said.

"I know it's not true, Cal," I said, nearly breaking down. "But I had to tell you so you'd know."

"Of course it's not true," he said with a lighthearted laugh. "Jewks is nothing but a two-bit politician, and a liar on top of it!" He laughed again, but the laughter sounded forced, and a little too quick on the heels of his words.

"A troublemaker, that's all he is," he added, denying the accusation too forcefully for me to feel altogether comfortable. "Probably a spy himself!" Again he laughed. But he looked straight at me as he did. I think he realized in an instant that I knew he was bluffing. I may not have been the prettiest or the smartest or the bravest person in the world, but I was able to look into someone's face and know which way the wind was blowing through their mind. I suppose up till then I hadn't made too good use of that ability with Cal. And right at that moment, I would have given anything *not* to have known what was behind his forced laughter and bravado.

Cal's laughter died away. He kept looking at me, kept watching my face for signs of what I was thinking. Then he looked away and glanced down toward the river from the little patch of grass where we were sitting. I knew him well enough to know that he was revolving things over in his mind, trying to decide what to say. Then he glanced up at me again.

Still neither of us said anything. I hadn't realized how much my face must have betrayed my doubts. But it must have, because he quit trying to deny everything. After another minute or two, a smile slowly spread across his face. A melancholy, cynical smile.

"Ah, Corrie . . . Corrie," he sighed. "You are naive."

I didn't understand his tone.

"What do you mean, Cal?" I said.

"You see the world so simply, so black and white. There's no gray for you, is there, Corrie—no in-between? Right and wrong, that's all there is."

"I . . . I don't know."

"It's a complicated, mixed-up world, Corrie. Circumstances don't always fit so neatly into black and white compartments. Sometimes there *is* gray—places where you don't know what's right and what's wrong."

"What are you trying to say, Cal," I asked, getting alarmed by his sarcastic tone. "Mr. Jewks isn't right, is he?" I asked, still not wanting to face the truth.

"Ah, Jewks! What does he know? A low-level incompetent. If he couldn't take care of himself in this game, they should've sent somebody else!"

"Cal . . . it isn't true what he said?"

"We had to win the election. It's a rough game . . . I told you that a long time ago."

"But it's not right."

"Right? What's right? Everything has its twists and ironies. Who's to say what's right in the middle of it all?"

"What twists, Cal?" I asked. "Please . . . tell me what you mean!"

"Don't you see the irony of it? Here I am, out West, on my way up, assistant to one of California's most powerful men, when from out of nowhere my past comes back to haunt me. Suddenly the country is at war, and I am in the *wrong* place."

"What do you mean . . . what about your past?"

"I've made no secret of it, Corrie. I was born in North Carolina. You knew that. I told you about my fondness for the country, and how I admired it in you."

"Yes . . . but, what—?"

"Don't you hear what I am telling you, Corrie—*North Carolina*, I'm a southerner!"

"But . . . you've been a loyal Republican. You've worked for Mr. Stanford and the Union. You left the South years ago, just like my Aunt Katie. Lots of Californians came from the South originally."

"Ah, but there's the bitter irony, Corrie. I'm not just an ordinary Californian with southern roots."

"Why?"

"Because of who I am, because of my position here. Ever since I heard about Edie leaving and returning to Virginia, I realized I had to do the same thing—not for any noble motives, but because if I didn't, everything I had worked for would be lost."

"Cal . . . what are you saying?"

"That I've got to go back too."

"Back . . . back where?"

"To the South. I have no choice."

"But . . . but *why*?" I started to cry.

"Opportunity, Corrie—remember? Suddenly all the opportunities have shifted. My golden goose, Mr. Leland Stanford, has suddenly become a millstone around my neck. My Republican affiliations, all the work I have done for the Union, even my little game with Jewks—don't you see? It will all come back to haunt me when the war's over. Men like Leland Stanford—outspoken Unionists—if they aren't in jail with Abraham Lincoln, they'll be reduced to political impotence. And unless I do something to redeem myself, something to make up for all these years when I put my money on the wrong horse—unless I do something to atone for these transgressions, as it were, I am likely to be right there with them, reduced to a life of mediocrity and meaninglessness."

"You talk as if the war is already over."

"It is . . . virtually. The North has nothing. Washington is about to fall. Lincoln could be behind bars before the year is out. Unless I make my move, and immediately, my opportunity in the new nation will be lost. Opportunity, Corrie . . . I've got to seize it while there's still time. Changing loyalties once Grant surrenders to Lee won't count for much, will it?"

"But what will you do—join the Rebel army?"

Cal laughed. "The stakes for me are just slightly higher than that, my dear naive young friend!"

"You said you always wanted to go to Washington someday."

"I wanted to get to the capital. Once the North surrenders, that will be Richmond. And I don't have to wait until someday . . . the opportunity is before me *now!*"

"I . . . I just don't see—"

"You still don't grasp it, do you, Corrie?" he said, and he sounded as though he were talking to a child. "Does the name Alexander H. Stephens mean anything to you?"

I shook my head.

"Well, he is my uncle, on my mother's side. I know I told you about him. He has been after me for some time, through discreet communications of course, to join his staff—in a very prominent position. I have simply been awaiting the most propitious time for making such a move."

I stared blankly at him.

Cal chuckled. He almost seemed to be enjoying putting me through this, seeing the confused emotions pass through me. I thought he had cared, but I had never felt so small and foolish as I did right now.

"Alexander Stephens," Cal went on, "happens to be Jefferson Davis' vice president. When I arrive in Richmond, I won't have to wait for some distant time . . . my opportunity will have arrived! I'll be working close to the president himself!"

"There's only one president, and his name is Abraham Lincoln."

"I'm sorry, Corrie, but there is the gray again in your world of black and white. Right now there are two presidents, and before long the only one remaining in power will *not* be your friend Abraham Lincoln."

"You have made up your mind?" I said, trying desperately to be brave.

"I'm afraid I have."

"Then why did you wait until now? Why did you keep being so loyal, keep helping us raise funds for the Union, keep working for Mr. Stanford? You gave several speeches, telling people why they had to support Mr. Lincoln and the Federal troops. How could you do that, Cal, when inside you were all along planning to defect to the South?"

"Oh, I haven't been planning to defect all along. I had to keep my options alive on both sides. I have nothing intrinsically against the Union, Corrie. I told you, it's not an ethical or moral issue for me. It's opportunity, and I will go where I can climb the highest. What if I had left, and then suddenly the tide of the war turned, and Davis and my uncle were the ones being arrested for their part in the rebellion? No, Corrie—I couldn't risk that! I've had to bide my time to see how the tide of the war would go. The shifting sands of the political landscape can be treacherous if you don't watch your step. So all year I *have* been watching my step, and now that the sands are about to engulf Mr. Lincoln and General Grant and Mr. Stanford altogether, I perceive it is time for me to be off. My only difficulty will be in explaining to my good uncle, who is not a kindly disposed man, why it took me so long to come to my senses. But I'm sure I will be able to manage that."

I sat stunned. I couldn't believe all I'd heard.

"But I thought," I said at last, fighting a terrible urge to break into tears, "I thought . . . we—that is, Cal . . . you always used to talk about what *we* would do . . . about the future . . . I thought—"

I didn't know what to say. There wasn't much more to say.

"Come now, Corrie, you didn't seriously expect me to marry you, did you?"

His question was so abrupt, so stark, that I felt as if I'd been slapped in the face.

"I didn't say that."

"It's bigger than just you and me. Maybe if things had been different, who knows what might have happened? You're a great kid, Corrie. I like you. There was always something about you I admired. In fact, I always kind of figured you might be on your way up, just like me, and that we might help each other out."

"And now you don't need someone like me anymore, so that's the end of it, is that it?" I said, my hurt turning to anger.

"Please, Corrie," said Cal, laughing slightly, "there's no need to overreact to it. It's just one of those things that happened. My uncle simply happens to have more clout than a young news writer from California, that's all. Look at it practically. But I meant every word I said—I always admired you, and I'll always wish the best for you. But this is not an opportunity I can pass up—for you, or anybody."

I sat silent again. So many thoughts and feelings were raging through me, I felt like screaming and sobbing and running and kicking something—preferably Cal Burton!

"Why don't you come with me, Corrie?" said Cal after a minute. The exuberance in his voice let me know he didn't have any idea what he'd done to me.

"Why should I?"

"Because of the opportunities there would be for you in the new government. Just think—a news writer, right at the center of power. It could put you right at the top, Corrie. You could be one of the best-known writers in the country!"

"Opportunity, is that it?" I said.

"Yes! Why not, Corrie? What's there ever going to be for you here?"

Just my family, people I love, a good home, I thought to my-self. "I don't think so, Cal," I said. "Even if the Union falls, I'm still going to cast my lot with men like Abraham Lincoln."

"Have it your way. But don't ever say Cal Burton didn't give you the chance to hitch yourself to his star on its way up!"

Finally I got up off the grass and started to walk back toward the buggy. "Will you please take me back to the boardinghouse?" I said. "I'm getting cold, and I have to start thinking about getting ready to go home."

Parting of the Ways
CHAPTER FIFTY-EIGHT

If I thought the last night was awful, this one was much worse. Never had I felt so isolated in my life. How desperately I wanted to feel Almeda's loving arms around me, to hear Pa's voice, to retreat to the warmth of our home!

I felt small and foolish. How could I have been so naive? Cal was exactly right—a naive kid, that's what I was, nothing more! All this time I thought I meant something to him, and now I realized it had all existed nowhere but in my own mind!

Lying on my bed at Miss Baxter's, I cried and cried, drenching the pillow with my tears.

Not until late in the evening, after my tears had temporarily dried up, did I begin to think rationally again. Should I tell somebody . . . Mr. King, Mr. Stanford?

I supposed Cal would give the governor some kind of formal resignation. We'd probably not see him again on the fundraising platform! Now that he had decided to throw in with the South, as dreadful as it was to think it, he obviously would be hoping for the Confederacy to win as quickly as possible.

At last I concluded that it was none of my business to tell anyone. Let Cal do his own dirty work! If he was going to betray us all, let *him* tell them face-to-face. I hoped he choked on the words!

I cried some more, but managed to fall asleep around midnight. I woke up several times, suddenly remembering the ache inside my heart and longing so badly for home. Each time, however, I drifted back to sleep again, and the final time slept for several hours. When I woke up, the sunlight was streaming through the window and it was halfway into the morning.

I rose and dressed, wishing I'd gotten up early enough for the morning stage north, but it was too late now. I'd have to wait until tomorrow. The morning edition of the *Bee* had already been delivered. I greeted Miss Baxter, saw the paper lying on her table, and looked down at it. Across the top, in bold black letters, were the words: UNION SUFFERS DEVASTATING DEFEAT AT FREDERICKSBURG, VA. REBEL ARMY 40 MILES FROM CAPITAL.

I sat staring at the headlines, stunned. It was as if Cal had known yesterday.

Suddenly I ran back up the stairs, dashed into my room, and rummaged about until I found the scrap of paper Cal had thrown on the ground. I read the cryptic message again. Of course! He *had* known. The paper said the battle had taken place two days ago, on the thirteenth, the same day he had received the telegram!

But the last words of the message . . . *NO TIME TO LOSE*. What did it mean?

I stood thinking for a minute; then a terrible sense of foreboding swept over me.

Oh no! I thought. *What if . . . ?*

I couldn't even say it! With hardly a word of explanation to Miss Baxter, I ran back down the stairs and was out the door and heading toward the middle of town. I stopped at the first livery stable on the way and hired a horse. The instant it was saddled, I galloped off, and in six or eight minutes I was pulling up in front of the capitol building. I hardly stopped to think whether I was presentable or not. I just ran down the corridor toward the governor's office. It didn't take long to find out what I needed to know: Cal had not yet come in this morning.

I turned around and retraced my steps. How I wished Pa had some business in Sacramento right then! I could have used his help!

I got back on the horse, walked her quietly until I was away from the capitol, then urged her again to a gallop. Three or four minutes later, I arrived at the house where Cal lived. I had never been inside, but we had ridden by several times, and he'd pointed it out. Jumping off the horse, I ran to the porch and knocked on the door.

"No, Mr. Burton isn't home," his landlady said, looking me over from head to toe with a not-so-pleasant inquisitive expression. "I don't know when to expect him, either. I didn't see him come in last night, but then I don't make it a practice to be snooping into other people's affairs."

"Did he come in last night?" I asked.

"I don't know for sure. I thought I heard him, but he might have left again later. I didn't pay too much attention. I don't like to pry, you know."

I had the distinct impression that if she had known anything more than she was saying, she might have thought twice whether to tell me or not.

I ran back and jumped up on the horse's back, wheeled around, and made for downtown.

I hoped Mr. King was still at his hotel and hadn't left for his home in San Francisco! I was at the hotel in five minutes.

I dismounted in front and dashed into the lobby. From all the riding, I was sure I looked a mess.

"Is Mr. King still here?" I asked the desk clerk.

The clerk gave me a look similar to the one Cal's landlady had given me. "He is."

I knew the room. We had several meetings of the committee there. I bolted for the stairs and bounded up them two at a time.

At last I knocked on the door, completely out of breath.

"Corrie!" said Mr. King, answering it, "Come in . . . you look as if you've just ridden one of those Pony Express routes you wrote about last fall!"

"Mr. King," I panted, "have you seen Cal today?"

"Why, no, Corrie, I haven't. As a matter of fact, I was going to get in touch with you to see if *you'd* seen him. I need to talk to him about what I'm sure must simply be a clerical mistake of some kind at the bank."

"What is it?" I asked.

"So, I take it you haven't seen him this morning either?" said Mr. King.

I shook my head.

"Hmmm . . . well, we're going to have to find him sooner or later to clear this up."

"What?" I asked again.

"You and he did make the collections yesterday, did you not?"

I nodded. "Nearly all of them. Several large checks, and a big amount of gold, too. I think the total was fifty-two thousand dollars."

"Yes, it was a marvelous day—sixty-nine thousand dollars in pledged contributions. And you say the two of you collected over forty thousand of it?"

"That's right," I said.

"Hmmm . . . that is peculiar. When I checked with the bank this morning, it seems there wasn't a deposit made to the Sanitary Fund account yesterday. But you and Cal *did* make the deposit?"

My heart began to sink beneath a dreadful weight of doom.

"Uh . . . Cal left me for thirty minutes or so after we were through," I said. "He told me he was going to the bank and asked me to run a message over to the capitol building for him. I met him afterward."

"Hmmm," mumbled Mr. King, pondering it all. "It must be a clerical oversight of some kind. I'll go check with the bank again. In the meantime, when you see Cal, tell him to come see me. Perhaps he can clear it up."

By now I was all but certain in my own mind that Cal could indeed clear it up! Whether Mr. King would ever hear about it from his own lips, however, I was beginning to seriously doubt.

I only had one more stop—the one I hoped I wouldn't have to make. I went from the hotel to the downtown district, where I pulled up in front of the Western Union office and tied up the horse. I walked along the boardwalk and around the corner I had seen Cal disappear around after receiving the telegram. It was a street I knew well from frequent use myself. But it had never occurred to me what he was doing when I'd seen him right here the other day. Three doors down was the stage office!

I walked inside and looked up at the schedule board, then went to the window.

"Morning, Miss Corrie," he said. "You ready for your ticket now?"

"Not yet, Mr. Daws, thank you," I answered. "Only some information."

"Anything I can tell you, Miss Corrie."

"Did you have a passenger on this morning's stage, a Mr. Burton?"

"Well, not exactly," replied the station man, with whom I'd been friendly for several years. "That is, if you're meaning the same young fella I've seen you traveling with a time or two."

"That's him," I said.

"Handsome young man, eh, Miss Corrie?"

"Yes, he is . . . but was he in? Did you sell him a ticket?"

"Yes, he was in. Came in twice, as a matter of fact. But it was yesterday, not this morning."

"He was in *twice*?"

"Yes, ma'am. First time around four, five o'clock in the afternoon—"

That was the exact time when he'd sent me to his office with the message!

"He just wanted to leave his bag right then," he said, "so he wouldn't have to keep lugging it around. Once I lifted it, I knew why! Heavy as the dickens, it was! Heaviest bag I ever recollect. 'What in tarnation you got in here?' I asked him, 'solid gold?' 'That's a good one!' he laughed. 'Taking gold by stagecoach! What kind of fool do you take me for?' he said, still laughing. Nice young man, Miss Hollister."

"And then you say he came back later? But I was sure he would be on the morning stage."

"Yep, he came back later all right—around eight o'clock. Most curious thing I ever saw. Don't know why they never told me about it."

"About what?" I asked.

"Special stage rolled up—all outfitted and ready to go. Driver said it was government business. And your man Burton, why he was the only passenger—other than the two armed guards, that is."

"What stage line was it?"

"The Butterfield."

"Which way did they go?"

"Butterfield only goes south, Miss Corrie. Driver told me they was gonna be driving all night. Said they were heading all the way to Fort Smith, Arkansas."

"That's behind the Confederate lines."

"Yes, ma'am. I . . . I thought you knew all about it, Miss Corrie." For the first time Mr. Daws' voice lost its cheerful tone, and he began to sound concerned.

"Why did you think that?" I asked.

"Well, ma'am, on account of him mentioning you, and saying you'd be along shortly. I just . . . well, I figured you'd be taking the stage out too, one of the regular Butterfield coaches, and that, well . . . that you and he'd be meeting up somewhere, or maybe that you was going all the way back East too. The way they made it sound like government business—I figured it had something to do with you."

Cal knew that sooner or later I'd figure it out.

"He even left a message for me to give you, Miss Corrie," the station man added. "Makes it seem kind of odd now, him doing that, and you not even knowing he'd gone."

Cal had said it himself—the world was full of ironies.

I braced myself. I didn't want to ask, but I couldn't live without knowing. "What was the message?" I asked.

"Don't make much sense now, but he said to thank you for helping him to atone for his transgressions. He said his uncle would be very grateful, and that this would help explain things very nicely. Then he said he hoped to see you when you both got where you were going."

I took a deep breath. If Zack had to learn to be a man by facing Pa with humility, I suppose today was the day when I had to learn to stand up and be a woman by facing Thomas Starr King and Leland Stanford with honesty and humility, too.

I would have to face them both, and tell them what I knew about Cal. And I would have to tell them I had known it yesterday, in time to have stopped him. I would have to apologize. I would have to admit to the two great men of California that they had entrusted too much faith in me, and that I had not been worthy of it. And I would have to beg their forgiveness for allowing over forty thousand dollars of Union contributions to be speeding along its way south toward the government of the Confederate States of America.

"So I take it you won't be wanting a ticket, after all, Miss Corrie?" said Mr. Daws.

I sighed. "I might as well buy it now," I said. "Yes, I do want one, Mr. Daws. Give me a ticket north for Miracle Springs, on tomorrow's stage."

"Round trip, Miss Corrie?"

"No, Mr. Daws. One way will be sufficient. I don't know that I will be coming back to Sacramento anytime soon."

"Your business here all done?"

Again I sighed. "Not quite. I have some very unpleasant business to attend to this afternoon," I said. "But by tomorrow, yes, my business will be done."

Home Again
CHAPTER FIFTY-NINE

*I*t was a lonely, tearful stagecoach ride back to Miracle Springs the next day. I kept thinking I had cried all the tears it was possible to cry, and then more would come. How many tears could a girl have, anyway? There must be an end to them somewhere!

I didn't find out where the tears ended that day. By the time I reached home I had vowed never to have anything to do with politics, writing, or men again!

The minute I walked into the house I fell into Almeda's arms. I was so glad no one else was there right at that moment. She knew from one look at my face that something was dreadfully wrong, but she just let me cry and held me tight. Gradually, through my tears, I told her everything,

"Oh, Almeda," I finally tried to say, still blubbering like a five-year-old, "how could I have been such a downright fool as to think he loved me?"

She probably had seen the whole thing coming long before I had. But if she did, she didn't say so. She just kept comforting me.

"He never cared about anything but himself. He was completely self-absorbed. How could I not have seen it?"

I had done a lot of thinking all day riding on the stage. I had wanted to talk to Almeda so badly back in Sacramento.

Now that I finally had her all to myself, I gushed out with everything I'd been thinking and feeling.

"Hearts can get in the way and cloud how you see nearly everything sometimes, Corrie. It's part of life, part of growing up. I wouldn't feel too badly if I were you."

"How can I not? I was so blinded by everything that was going on. Cal had no real depth—it's all so clear now! All he cared about was his own ambition. We never talked about spiritual things or what really matters in life. Oh, Almeda, I just feel so foolish!"

"Time will help you understand it more clearly. I liked Cal too, Corrie. We all did. Whether he changed after the war started or was out for what you and your father could do for him from the beginning—we may never know for sure. He seemed sincere enough. I was taken in, too."

"Besides everything else, he took the Sanitary Fund money! How can I not feel responsible? I feel as if I've betrayed both the Union and God!"

"They will both forgive you."

"But it's too late about the money—he's gone."

"You said Mr. King and Mr. Stanford immediately sent some fast horsemen after the stage."

"They did, but they didn't have much hope of catching it. They had probably over a two-hundred-mile head start and would be close to the Arizona border by the time they could reach them. Even if they did catch them, it would likely have taken bloodshed to retrieve the money, and neither Mr. King nor Mr. Stanford wanted that."

"I see. I suppose in that case it wasn't worth it."

"They were a lot more worried about information Cal had to give to the South than just the money. Working so close to an important governor like Mr. Stanford, Cal knew a lot of things about the northern war effort."

A lump formed in my throat. "Almeda, how can I not blame myself? All my writing and talk about truth and being a true person, and I can't even recognize someone who isn't true when he's standing right in front of me! How could I not have seen him for what he was?"

"*Was* he untrue right from the beginning?"

"Oh, I don't know! After the way it turned out, how can I possibly know what was there inside him to begin with?"

"I don't know either, Corrie," said Almeda. "I do know we have to learn truth in stages. It doesn't come all at once. We have to learn about truth by encountering some things along the way that aren't true. Otherwise we never learn to tell the false from the real."

"Do those things that come along always have to hurt so badly, and make me feel like such a nincompoop?"

She laughed, and I halfheartedly joined in.

"A lot of times they do," replied Almeda. "Pain is one of the world's best teachers."

"The worst of it is forgetting about God all this time. I was so absorbed in Cal and what I was doing that I thought about him only once in a while, and I hardly prayed at all. I can't believe I didn't realize it!"

"It's all part of the growing and maturing process. Perhaps this will help you remember him more in the future. You've heard the expression about being older and wiser?"

I nodded.

"Well, just consider yourself an older and wiser and more truthful young woman now, after all this. If you grow and mature from it, won't it have been worth it in the end?"

I had to stop and think about that. In my present state of mind I wasn't at all sure.

"Almeda," I said at last, "when I was waiting for God to give me a sign about his will, Cal Burton was the person who finally convinced me to get involved in this election."

"Yes?" Almeda prodded when I paused.

"Well, it's just . . . maybe . . . do you think I heard wrong from the beginning? I mean, how could it have been *right* for me to be involved when Cal was so . . . so *wrong?*"

"Corrie," Almeda said gently, taking my hand, "the Lord uses many methods to open his will to us. Apart from what's happened with Cal Burton, do you think what you've done for the election—and for the Union—has been wrong?"

I thought about it for a minute. "No, I don't. I think it was the right thing to do, but—"

"Then maybe God *did* use Cal to help you make your decision, even though Cal himself wasn't aware of being an instrument in God's hands."

"I hope you're right," I said. "Right now, that doesn't seem to help me feel much better about it."

"It will in time."

"But what about my forgetting the Lord," I went on, "and not making him part of what was happening with Cal?"

"One thing about God, Corrie, that I've learned to take comfort from, is that he never forgets us—he always keeps doing his work in us, never stops working away in our hearts and minds. We may forget him, but he never forgets us. His work down inside us doesn't depend on something so unreliable as whether we happen to be thinking of him or not. His work of maturing us goes on even when we're not conscious of it. And he won't let us remain forgetful of him—not for long, anyway. He makes sure he gets our attention again eventually when he needs to, one way or another."

"Even with an incident like I've just been through?"

"The Lord will use anything or anyone. He uses all kinds of people and all kinds of situations. He will even use people who don't know him to open doors in *our* growth, like he used Cal Burton. He will use them for us, and attempt to use us in their lives at the same time."

"I doubt if I had much impact in Cal's life."

"Oh, I disagree, Corrie! I imagine God was using you to knock on some doors in Cal's heart and mind, just like he will use Cal, even in retrospect, to accomplish some older and wiser maturing things down inside you. Nothing in life ever goes to waste when we belong to the Lord—even the times when we might think we haven't been faithful to him. He takes it all and uses it for the best and deepest purposes."

"Hmm . . . If that's true, I wonder if God was knocking at Cal's heart."

"Who knows how differently it might have turned out if he'd paid attention to the small voice of God inside him speaking through you?"

"But I wasn't saying much of anything to him about the Lord."

"Your life was speaking important things to him, Corrie. I could see that the two times he was here. Your character, your bearing, your truthfulness. You may think you were nothing but a starry-eyed young lady. But your deepest self shone through like a clear-sounding bell. Cal noticed. Yes, God was knocking at his heart through you. But he chose to ignore the voice and to go his own way. So he will have to suffer the consequences, and you will have to go on with your life and learn from it all."

Suddenly the door burst open and Pa came in.

"I thought I heard the sound of someone riding up," he said, striding toward me and scooping me nearly off the ground in his arms. "Merry Christmas, Corrie!"

I'd nearly forgotten. Christmas was only nine days away!

"Merry Christmas, Pa," I said. If only I could keep from crying again!

"You show her the letter, Almeda?"

"No!" exclaimed Almeda. "I forgot, we got so involved in talking. Corrie, you have a letter!" she cried, turning and running across the room.

"What can it be that's worth all *that* commotion?"

"Wait till you see, Corrie!" said Pa, with nearly as much excitement in his voice as Almeda's.

Almeda ran back toward me, carrying an envelope, then thrust it into my hand.

"It came five days ago, Corrie! We've all been dying of curiosity waiting for you to get home!"

I took the envelope. The return address said only: THE WHITE HOUSE, WASHINGTON, D.C.

With trembling fingers I tore open one end of it and pulled out the letter. I couldn't keep my heart from pounding as I read.

MISS CORNELIA BELLE HOLLISTER,

I have been made aware of all your work for the Republican party on behalf of my election, as well as your efforts to raise money for our Union forces in this present conflict. I want to express my deepest appreciation on behalf of the nation, and to tell you that your patriotism has not gone unnoticed. It would be my pleasure to meet you here at the White House in Washington, if circumstances would permit you to make the journey. I would very much like to give you my personal hand of gratitude, as well as ask you to help me in the war effort with a new project here in Washington.

Yours sincerely,
A. LINCOLN
President

The single sheet fell from my hand, and I staggered to sit down in a chair. I sat there stunned.

"What *is* it, Corrie?" asked Almeda. "Is something wrong?"

Pa picked up the paper and read it. "Nothing wrong, Almeda," he said after a moment. "It's an invitation to visit the president!"

"The president!" she exclaimed.

"Signed right here by Abraham Lincoln himself," said Pa, handing the paper to Almeda.

"Corrie . . . that's—that's wonderful!" cried Almeda.

How could it be . . . how could I possibly accept? But how could I *not* accept? Thoughts of the war and the danger and the time and expense involved—none of that entered my mind in the first seconds that I sat there. I thought only of the face of Lincoln from a picture I had seen. The president had written to *me*!

How much time passed as I sat there in a daze, I don't know. When I first became aware of voices around me again, Becky and Tad were there too, and I vaguely heard Zack and Alkali Jones outside approaching the house. Mr. Jones was laughing and cackling over something.

In the blur of my racing brain, there was Mr. Jones on the other side of the house with Zack, both of them laughing and talking. My ears weren't working right any more than my brain. They must have been playing tricks on me from the last time when I'd heard him making jokes about the Hollister clan running for office. Because of what I *thought* I heard Mr. Jones saying was, *Corrie fer President, hee, hee, hee!*

My mind was spinning with thoughts of the war and Mr. Lincoln and stagecoaches and trains and money, and when my eyes and ears finally cleared, the room was quiet.

The whole family surrounded me, staring straight at me as if waiting for me to say something. Not a one of them said a word. They were all just gazing expectantly at me.

"Well?" said Pa finally.

"Well, what?" I asked.

"Are you gonna answer the question we've all been asking you, or are you gonna just keep sitting there staring off like you can't see or hear anything?"

"What question?"

"Are you gonna do it, Corrie?" they all shouted. "Are you gonna go?"

At last my mind seemed to start working again. I took in a deep breath.

"Of course I'm going to do it," I said. "He's the president of our country, isn't he? I can't very well turn *him* down, now can I?"

Epilogue

*M*ost of the Pony Express incidents recorded—including the breakfast incident—are true, as are all the names of the riders mentioned. Nearly all California personalities, politicians, and issues are likewise factual, and the positions, facts, and details represented, as far as can be determined, are historically accurate. Along with other sources, the following books were very helpful in researching early California history, the Pony Express, the election of 1860, and the early Civil War period:

Bartlett, Ruhl, *John C. Fremont and the Republican Party*

Hittell, Theodore, *History of California*

Lewis, Oscar, *San Francisco: Mission to Metropolis*

McAfee, Ward, *California's Railroad Era 1850–1911*

Nichols, Roy, *The Stakes of Power 1845–1977*

Reinfeld, Fred, *Pony Express*

Rolle, Andrew, *California, A History*

Roske, Ralph, *Everyman's Eden, A History of California*

Williams, Harry, *The Union Sundered*

Williams, Harry, *The Union Restored*

In addition: "The Mexican War and the Facts Behind It" by Patrick Phillips, and issue #33 of *Christian History* magazine on "The Untold Story of Christianity and the Civil War."

For all of these, as well as to Sandy Bean for the creation of Edie, the author expresses his deepest gratitude.

About the Author

MICHAEL PHILLIPS is perhaps best known for reawakening interest in the writings of George MacDonald. In the 1980s Phillips embarked on a campaign to reacquaint the reading public with the works of the forgotten Victorian novelist and Scotsman. Phillips edited and published more than fifty of MacDonald's works in twenty years, including his own acclaimed biography of the man. Combined sales total two million copies, inaugurating a renaissance of interest in MacDonald's work. Phillips also began writing fiction of his own, and now is primarily known as a novelist. He has authored and coauthored (with Judith Pella) more than seventy titles in addition to his volumes of MacDonald. His best-known novels include those of the Phillips-Pella writing team, THE STONEWYCKE SERIES, THE JOURNALS OF CORRIE BELLE HOLLISTER, and THE RUSSIANS, as well as his solo THE SECRET OF THE ROSE, AMERICAN DREAMS, and SHENANDOAH SISTERS. Michael Phillips and his wife, Judy, alternate their time between the U.S. and Scotland, where they are attempting to increase awareness of George MacDonald and his work.